2016

2016

James Force

LONE STAR BOOKS

Lone Star Books

Published by Lone Star Books, Austin, Texas.

ISBN-13: 9780615629766
ISBN-10: 0615629768

Dedication

This book is dedicated to freedom.
Free societies support authors and protect them to express
any view without fear of retribution.

Chapter 1

I got off the L at Diversey and walked toward my apartment two blocks east, same as every day. After turning up Newport, a quiet residential street, I noticed a black Lincoln Navigator crawling toward me. The driver was looking at a piece of paper. An address or directions, I figured. Thinking I could help—that's my nature—I started walking toward the car instead of crossing over to the sidewalk. I made eye contact and saw the driver's window start to open, as he realized I was offering to help.

As the SUV was almost even with me, the driver raised a large gun with his right hand. *WTF!* I surprised myself by the speed with which I dropped to the ground and rolled toward the curb. Instinct, I suppose—can't take much credit. It all happened so fast. Bullets flew, exploding the windows of a pickup truck that was parallel parked alongside the curb—bullets that should have hit me! I heard the explosion of bursting car windows followed by the tinkling of glass raining down on the asphalt beside me. But it was strangely quiet too. Rather than the sharp crack of gunshots, I heard the soft *thwap, thwap, thwap* of compressed air. I grew up hunting and shooting, and I know the sound of a gun with a suppressor when I hear it.

As I scrambled away from the gun, I dove under the pickup truck. It must have been a big Ford F250, which was lucky; a regular car would have trapped me. I would have been a sitting duck. I rolled all the way under the truck and smacked the curb. I heard the Navigator's door open and saw a pair of shiny snakeskin boots hit the pavement. The boots crunched on the broken bits of glass.

By the time he bent down and pointed his gun under the pickup, I was leaping over the rusted wrought-iron fence between two three flats. As I made the turn between the buildings, I glanced over my shoulder and caught a glimpse of the shooter. He had run around the pickup, but instead of chasing me, he had stopped and was holding his handgun with both hands, aiming it in my direction.

I made a hard cut right and then back left, thinking that running in a straight line made me an easier target. My last turn was hard and fast, and I rounded the front corner of the three flat. As I disappeared around the corner, I heard bullets ricochet near my head and felt vinyl siding splinter and crack, just inches from my head! I did a quick onceover of my body as I kept running. I was pretty sure I wasn't hit, but then, I didn't know what it felt like to be shot.

I remembered stories of people not even realizing they had been shot, like President Reagan—amazing how much the human mind can process in a millisecond of terror. I was running for my life and at the same time contemplating the decision by the secret service agent who shoved President

Reagan into the presidential limo outside the Washington Hilton Hotel.

At the first sound of gunshots, Special Agent in Charge Jerry Parr shoved Reagan into the limo where the president landed on the floor. Agent Parr landed on top of Reagan, hoping to shield him from bullets. Neither Parr nor the president knew that a bullet had pierced Reagan's ribs and settled in his left lung, an inch from his heart. President Reagan thought his impact on the floor of the limo, along with the agent landing on top of him, had knocked the wind out of him. Parr's decision to reroute the presidential limo to George Washington University Hospital instead of the White House had saved Reagan's life.

My point is, Reagan was shot and did not know it. That bothered me. As I ran, I moved both hands over my neck and torso, feeling for any wetness.

Once I rounded the front corner of the building, I felt safe for a moment. I knew the shooter did not have a line on me unless he ran at least ten yards laterally. And he had to cover more than that distance if he ran on a diagonal straight toward me, following the path I had taken. If he chose the lateral move to his right, he would get a line on me quicker, but it would be a longer shot. I knew handguns weren't very accurate except at close range, and I must have been twenty-five yards from the shooter by then. The flats on my left were—at least for now—protecting me.

So the shooter had at least ten yards to run before he could get a bead on me. But then I realized I had about twenty yards between me and the next corner—the back corner of the flat by the alley. I wondered what kind of shot he was. Most people couldn't hit a human form past that distance with a handgun. But some could.

As a kid, I used to go shooting with my friend Eric and his dad, who was a lieutenant at the Chicago Police Department. We would put an empty Tide gallon jug on a slope a hundred to a hundred and fifty yards away. Eric and I would fire away with a .30–06 rifle. We were pretty accurate, but so were most people with a rifle like that. Then, Eric's dad would take out his .44 Magnum, the gun Dirty Harry called "the most powerful handgun in the world." Even from that huge distance, Eric's dad would nail the Tide jug!

I dug deep, like I did in the fourth quarter of many lacrosse games in college. Leave it all on the field. Do or die. I knew I was faster than most, and the guy was wearing cowboy boots—not the best for running in. I was wearing running shoes. And even if he beat me by a second, it would be a lot harder for him to hit me because he would be panting and out of breath. Not as easy as the relaxed and controlled environment of a shooting range.

I rounded the back corner of the building and started a full out sprint down the alley. I didn't hear any more shots and didn't know if he was still chasing me, but I ran like he was! In fact, I ran all the way back to the Diversey L stop, jumped the turnstile, and ran up the stairs toward the train platform. I blew by a few commuters exiting the station. Don't know if they thought I was crazy or just running to catch a train. I reached the platform just in time to board a train as its doors were closing. I looked back to see if he had followed. I couldn't see him.

At that moment, I wished I owned a cell phone. Sure, it would have been easy enough to borrow a cell phone, but as I looked around the train car, I discovered I was alone. It was already 8:45 p.m., later than I usually got home from work because I had gone out for pizza and a few beers with friends. This late, northbound trains still contained commuters heading home, but no one else was in this train car, heading south into the business district, on a beautiful summer night in Chicago. It gets dark late in the summer, and as I looked out the window, the Chicago skyline was just beginning to light up, contrasting against the darkening sky.

I thought about walking up to one of the next train cars to find other passengers. The entire train would probably not be empty, no matter what time it was. But I was so out of breath, I couldn't talk right then anyway, so I took a moment to catch my breath. My heart was pounding—felt like it was going to jump out of my chest. As I stopped to rest, I held a pole in the train and bent over. I thought I might puke. I could feel my whole body breaking out into a sweat. I sat down in the nearest seat, but breathing was too difficult after my full-out sprint. I stood back up and raised my hands over my head to catch my breath.

It felt good knowing that the train was moving south faster than the guy in the Navigator could drive through traffic on city streets. At the next stop, I thought I could get off and call the police.

My girlfriend, Laura, and a lot of my friends teased me for being the only person left on the planet without a cell phone. I would always tell them, in a self-deprecating manner, that I wasn't important enough to have one. Besides, commuters talking on their cell phones were a nuisance. As I decompressed on my usual commute home, nothing annoyed me more than the useless conversations of loud passengers talking on their cell phones. Metra trains had quiet cars, but no decorum rules seemed to exist on subway trains.

By the way, my name is Christian Roberts. I am a phone clerk on the edge of the raucous T-Bond futures pit on the floor of the Chicago Board of Trade, which is part of the Chicago Mercantile Exchange, or CME, Group. The oldest and largest commodities exchange in the world. If you saw the movie, *Trading Places*, with Eddie Murphy and Dan Aykroyd, you have a good idea of the crazy place I work.

Back to being the only person on the planet without a cell phone: Nothing, I would tell my friends, was so important that it could not wait for my twenty-minute commute to end. After all, I justified, my roommates and I had a phone in our apartment. At work, I juggled four phones simultaneously, two in each hand. I balanced the earpieces so that two phones shared each one of my ears. As I quoted the bond market prices in real time, I spoke into all four phones at once. If I needed to confirm a trade with one of the four institutional desks on one of the lines, I rotated the phones in both hands, up or down, and spoke into just the right one. I know it sounds awkward, but it was second nature to me.

So I joked with my friends about not having a cell phone by choice. *Ahhh, the freedom I enjoy while you all are addicted to the evil little devices!* The truth was a little more pathetic: I could not afford a cell phone.

I was twenty-eight years old with a college degree and could not afford a cell phone. *I know, I know.* While most of my friends had decent-paying jobs, six years prior I had opted for a low-paying job as a runner on the floor of the exchange in order to learn the fast-paced Chicago commodities futures trading business. A runner carries commodities orders that need to be filled to the pits and orders that have already been filled back to the various clearing firms.

After two years as a runner, I jumped at the chance to be a phone clerk. My pay went from minimum wage to barely above minimum wage. But like most clerks, after putting in a few years and doing a great job, I hoped to be offered a plum job as a broker in one of the pits.

I even had some genetic advantages to working in the pits. I'm six feet, four inches tall and weigh 230 pounds, almost all of it muscle. My height would help me see and be seen over other traders, and thanks to my size, I knew I would have no problem holding my own physical space in the crowded pit.

In college, I played Division 1 lacrosse at Duke on a full scholarship. Veteran traders often said successful athletes had the key attributes necessary for success in the pits—competitiveness along with both physical and mental toughness.

My two roommates, buddies from college, were climbing corporate ladders in Chicago. With their degrees from Duke, they landed great jobs, one at a management consulting firm and the other at a big hedge fund.

We all moved in together right out of college, and we enjoyed the young urban life and bar scene in Chicago. Lots of coed activities like volleyball leagues at North Beach on Lake Michigan. And the Lincoln Park neighborhood was full of young college grads that still had the energy to go out drinking several nights per week.

My roommates were making enough to get their own apartments. But we had a great time together. Our lives were an extension of our college days, a refusal to grow up completely. Sooner or later, I knew we would all get married and move off in different directions. But for now we were having a blast, and I hoped they appreciated this phase of our lives and didn't go off on their own just yet, because I couldn't afford my own apartment on a phone clerk's salary.

My goal was to get a shot at being a pit broker. I had worked at Maco Commodities for six years and had been a good company man. In fact, the large hedge fund my roommate worked for was now a client of the firm, thanks to me. That should count for something, right?

The pits of Chicago are a crazy place. You may be wondering why I would even want to work in them. Funny thing is that kind of sentiment is a big reason why I do. Chicago trading pits are a high-stress, frenzied, rough-and-tumble atmosphere. This "last bastion of pure capitalism" is where five hundred traders pack themselves into an area slightly bigger than a boxing ring, with tiered steps rising up from the center. All day long, traders wave their hands in the air, shout, push, and shove as they compete for trades.

There are two types of traders in the pits—locals and brokers. Locals are independent traders, trading their own accounts, making or losing their own money on every trade. Brokers execute trades the exact same way, but the trades are not for their own account and risk. Brokers earn a commission for every contract they fill (buy or sell), but the trades are for the accounts of off-floor customers. Brokers can make millions per year. Locals can make tens of millions per year, albeit with a lot more risk.

Broker or local? I know what I want to be—a broker. To me, the extra money isn't worth the increased stress, heartache, and divorce rate of being a local.

You may wonder why phone clerks like me make little more than minimum wage. Why would a clearing firm pay somebody so little when one mistake by that person could cost the firm millions? Just like others before me, I was willing to pay my dues, to work for very little as I waited for a pit broker position to become available.

The perverse, dog-eat-dog culture of Chicago's pits had changed me for the worse. I swore more. And I no longer felt guilty for hoping that a broker blew up due to a trading error. Never mind the broker's wife and kids. With four years of experience as a clerk, I had a decent shot at replacing him.

Then I could afford a cell phone.

As the train approached the next station, I almost got off to find a phone. But as I replayed the situation over in my mind, I came to the puzzling conclusion that this could not have been a random drive-by shooting or a robbery. Not on the north side. Not by a well-dressed man driving a Lincoln Navigator. Not with a gun with a suppressor.

What if the gunman saw me get on the train and was racing to the next stop south? I figured if I rode the train all the way back into the Loop, there was no way he could keep up in a car and no way could he have any idea where I got off.

So I sat down. I had caught my breath at last. I felt like I was thinking clearly.

Why would anyone want to kill me? A phone clerk? Was it a case of mistaken identity? I had no enemies—no possible reason for someone to pay a well-dressed hit man to get rid of me.

It had to somehow be connected to the Board of Trade, I thought. Millions of dollars at stake every day. What good would the police be, at least for now? The hit man was long gone. The more I thought about it, the more I realized my boss could help. So I decided to get off the train at Van Buren.

My boss at Maco Commodities began his career just like me. He worked as a runner for a summer job in high school. Now, Thomas Minter is a billionaire. President and founder of Maco Commodities, the largest commodities brokerage firm in the world. And, like many successful people in the commodities business, Tom never went to college.

I admired Tom's start-from-nothing rise to the top. Unlike some of the pit brokers and locals, money never changed him. He was downright humble, honest, and straightforward, and he gave away most of his money to charity. He had also become a mentor to me—generous enough with his time to mentor a number of young people. Despite his crushing responsibilities and ninety-hour workweeks, Tom always found the time to say a kind word to everyone—from major clients to clerks and secretaries. Tom, more than anyone else in the Maco organization, knew a fair amount about each employee's personal life, just from talking with him or her, over time.

At first, I dismissed Tom's friendliness and compassion as part of the superficial role a good boss has to play. But over the years, I had come to know that he truly cared.

I got off the train at Van Buren, crossed the street, and entered the Board of Trade Building. I walked past the lone, half-asleep security guard in the lobby, swiped my keycard through the automatic turnstile, and hopped on an elevator to the third floor. I knew Tom Minter would still be hard at work. In fact, in all likelihood, he would be the only one still at work.

Chapter 2

I entered the unlocked glass doors of Maco Commodities and took the shortest route to Tom's office—down the first hallway and through the back-office computer room. Visitors and clients were always escorted the long way to Tom's office, because the long way took you through a beautiful lounge with a wall of windows looking out at The Federal Reserve Bank and the classic, stone-pillared building that used to be Continental Bank.

As I walked through the computer room, I paused as I passed the refrigerator-sized telephone recording systems. These machines recorded every customer phone call to buy or sell commodities, in case of a discrepancy. Every so often, an undercapitalized novice trader would lose more than he could afford to lose and protest, "I said *buy* ten contracts, not sell ten contracts!" Roll tape. Case closed. Another novice commodities trader lost it all. An old joke goes: How do you become a millionaire trading commodities? Start with a billion.

The glass doors of the recording machines were left wide open, and the fourteen-inch round tape reels were gone.

I kept moving to Tom's office. As usual, Tom's door was open, and I walked right in. Then the full gravity of the situation began to set in. Thomas A. Minter lay dead in a pool of his own blood. Bullet holes had riddled his torso. I froze. Although I had never seen a dead body before, I knew that Tom was dead. I knew there was no point in CPR. No rush to call 911.

My first thought was *Occupy Wall Street?* Protesters had staged demonstrations outside Mr. Minter's home and office, as well as outside the homes and offices of a number of other CEOs and billionaires. Police, on hand to keep the demonstrations peaceful, had to escort Tom to and from his car. The police had threatened arrests before protesters blocking Tom's driveway moved out of the way.

Although the Occupy agenda wasn't very coherent, the message seemed to be: "We are unemployed. You are a billionaire. That's not fair!" For the life of me, I could not make any sense out of why the Occupy Wall Street crowd had targeted my boss. Thomas Minter represented the quintessential American success story—the American Dream.

Now I thought, *Could they kill him out of anger and resentment?* There was a lot of hostility and divisiveness. In fact, as strange as this may sound, the president of the United States himself at times fanned the Occupy flames.

I began to reconstruct the facts in my mind. Stolen telephone tapes and Thomas Minter's murder? The attempt on my own life could not have been random. Occupy protesters? Why would they steal the tapes? Unless they were trying to throw people off from the real Occupy motive?

No, I decided. Occupy protesters had barely enough ambition to camp out and smoke pot together. I could not see
them orchestrating a murder along with a clever scheme to
deflect blame.

Was someone trying to cover up something at Maco?
But what? Tom was as honest as the day is long. Who would
want to kill me? I would not be targeted by the resentment of
the unemployed Occupy Wall Street protesters?

I was calm for the situation. Everything seemed surreal.
Almost as if events were unfolding in slow motion. I picked
up the phone on Tom's desk and dialed 911. I was careful not
to disturb his body. I gave the facts and was assured police
would arrive soon.

I walked back to the computer room. I felt I had to do
something, something for Tom. *Stay calm. Think.*

I found the cardboard file box containing original paper
copies of every customer order placed that day. The orders
had already been entered into computers. The box, like many
others before it, would be put into storage after all trades
had settled the next morning. As per Commodities Futures
Trading Commission (CFTC) rules, clearing firms had to
maintain trading records for five years. I thought that whatever was stolen off the phone tape reels might be deciphered
out of the box of original order tickets. In fact, the two should
coincide precisely, as orders are written down by phone clerks
during recorded calls with customers placing orders.

I carried the box back to Tom's office to wait for the police. I thought I would tell them about the stolen phone tapes

and give them the box of order tickets to help their investigation. *Anything to help them nail the SOB who did this!*

As I waited it occurred to me that when I called 911, I
had not even mentioned the earlier attempt on my own life.
I had been so stunned at the sight of Tom's bullet-riddled
body. *I'll tell the police that too when they arrive. Anything to
help.*

I gazed out the window of Tom's office. I couldn't help
thinking about his wife and kids. I also thought I should see
police cars any second. They would be a welcome sight! The
Chicago Board of Trade sat at the foot of LaSalle Street.
Tom's office was on the third floor. Right and left below me
was Jackson Street, running east and west. LaSalle Street
heading south dead-ended into the Chicago Board of Trade,
so Tom's window had a view north, up the middle of LaSalle
Street.

As I gazed out at the city lights, I shook my head. What
a waste! What a remarkable man! From bartender to billionaire, president and CEO of Maco Commodities.

Then I saw the black Lincoln Navigator screech to a halt,
just three floors below, at the corner of LaSalle and Jackson.
I gulped. I fled down a back set of stairs, out an emergency
exit, and off into the darkness.

How did he find me?! Could he have monitored the 911
call? The police dispatch radio? I could have run much faster
without the heavy box full of order tickets. But instinct and
obligation to Tom Minter kicked in: the box might contain
the answer to who killed him.

Where to go? Laura's apartment? It was clear I couldn't go home.

For reasons I did not yet understand, I was being targeted. I couldn't even fathom getting Laura involved. I loved her. I knew she was the one. Seeing Tom Minter dead, it began to sink in just how close I had come to death.

Once I was a safe distance from the Board of Trade, I processed the fact that I had just escaped death twice. I became very angry with myself for having not yet asked Laura to marry me. What an asshole I had been! My pathetic excuse was that, on a phone clerk's salary, I couldn't afford the kind of wedding ring that Laura "deserved." All I needed was one month as a broker, and I would buy her the biggest ring in the world...*one month!*

Laura loved me. She did not care about the size of the engagement ring. Whenever the subject of marriage came up, she was gentle, kind, and patient. And I was defensive. All at once I hated myself. I had been so shallow and stupid. I could die today, and she would never know how much she meant to me! I needed her.

My guilt made me feel nauseated. How foolish and selfish I had been, pretending that Laura deserved a bigger engagement ring! I closed my eyes. The truth was the size of her ring was a statement about me. Amid all the wealth and materialism, I was afraid I would feel ashamed at the size of my fiancée's ring. My damned competitiveness got in the way again.

If you ever hear women say that size doesn't matter, they're not talking about diamonds. Too many times I have seen women gawk at their girlfriends' large engagement rings. They'd muse, "Must be nice," or smile and say, "I'd marry him!" When the ring was small, they'd whisper to everyone but the bride-to-be about how difficult life might be with so-and-so, because he was "only" a mechanic, a plumber...or a phone clerk.

Now Laura didn't know how much I loved her. And all for the damn size of the ring! All because of my stupid insecurities. How unimportant the ring was. I vowed to myself that instant: if I survived and saw Laura again, I would let her know how much I loved her.

I know this may sound like bragging, but if you saw Laura, you would say she is stunningly attractive. She is five feet, ten inches tall—very athletic but still very feminine. She has shoulder-length blond hair, amazing blue eyes, high cheekbones, a slight dimple on her soft chin, and a very natural, beautiful smile. She looks like she could be a pro beach volleyball player—or a swimsuit model. Really.

Laura and I met my first summer of college at a strength and conditioning camp. She was an athlete too, played volleyball at UNC Chapel Hill. We hit it off right away and busted each other about our school rivalry.

We dated for three years, and then she followed me to Chicago because of my dream to work in the commodities business. She found a decent job in sales for a pharmaceutical company, but her heart was always in North Carolina, where she grew up.

Then it hit me even harder how stupid I had been! She loved North Carolina—had family there—and her clock was ticking. I knew I would marry her someday. But did she know? What was I waiting for?!

As I boarded the subway going south, I decided the safest place for now was a motel. Again, I thought about going to the police. But I was rattled by the hit man's arrival at the CBOT. Some instinct seemed to be telling me that going to the police might lead the killer to me. *Had the 911 call somehow tipped the bad guys off?*

And who was behind this? This person did not hesitate to murder a billionaire. He or she must have known what kind of media attention and intense investigation that would bring. I was sure whoever was behind it would not hesitate to hunt down a phone clerk like me.

I emerged from the subway at LaMont, not a friendly neighborhood. I was still carrying the heavy box of commodity orders and began looking for a motel. Within two blocks I saw a half-burned-out neon light that read, "Emerald Hotel." Not much, but I couldn't afford much. The lobby was old, the carpet in some spots worn all the way down to bare concrete. The walls were covered in filth. It looked like the place had not been painted in decades or even cleaned in many months. But at least it had an ATM.

I withdrew eighty dollars, walked past the porn-video vending machine, and approached the front desk where an old lady sat behind bulletproof glass reading the Bible. *Emerald* Motel *would be a little more apt,* I thought.

I had a sick feeling in my stomach—maybe the kind of sudden, unexplainable feeling successful commodity traders learned to trust. If these people were not afraid to gun down a well-known billionaire and were able to beat the Chicago Police Department to my 911 call, what else might they be capable of? How many were there? Could they have the ability to monitor my ATM or credit card activity?

Am I paranoid? Have I watched too many movies?

An image of Tom's dead body popped into my head, and that cinched it. I wasn't taking any chances. I exited the Emerald Hotel and saw a yellow cab waiting half a block away outside a bar.

I beelined it to the cab, opened the door, and hopped into the backseat, startling the driver.

The driver regained his composure. "What's a pretty white boy like you doing around here?" said the seventyish-year-old black man behind the wheel.

"Nothing."

"I've been driving a cab for forty years, and every time a white boy in these parts says 'noth'n,' he's lie'n. Sometimes drugs…sometimes ladies of the night…but never noth'n."

"Look, sir, I just want to wait here a few minutes. Okay?" Then it dawned on me. Rather than flee, I might safely watch from right here. See if my ATM usage was tracked or if I was just paranoid. It would not take too long to find out, based on how fast the assassin had made it to the Board of Trade.

"I don't get paid noth'n for sit'n."

"I have money, sir. You can start the meter."

And so began my time with the old cab driver. I kept looking up and down the street, and back at the Emerald Hotel for any sign of the black Lincoln Navigator.

After five minutes, the cab driver broke the silence. "Got a name? Mine's John."

"Steve," I lied.

"Okay, *Steve*," he said, "but my name really is John. You don't look like the white trash I'm used to see'n round here. Mostly look'n to score some drugs…White Sox fans…" The old man smirked as he said this and looked at me in the rear-view mirror. I cracked a half smile. The old man had correctly pegged me for a Cubs fan.

The old man smiled and nodded as if I had verified his hunch. "What you run'n from, boy?"

"Nothing."

"Lie."

He said this so matter-of-factly it unnerved me. As if I had "liar" tattooed in bold letters across my forehead. Was I that bad at lying?

Realizing there was no way this old man could be connected to Thomas Minter's murder or my own attempted murder, I said, "Okay. I don't know what I'm running from. Or where I'm running to. And my name is Christian."

"Well, ain't that nice?" He bobbed his head up and down as if he knew all this all along. "A white boy in this neighborhood who tells the truth. How can I help you, son? How about I drive you up north, someplace safer?" As he said this, he pointed straight ahead, over the steering wheel.

He actually pointed right at the black Lincoln Navigator coming from the other direction! I ducked into the backseat, but that wasn't necessary. No one could see in the cab at night while driving the other way. The Navigator passed us, continued half a block south, and stopped right in front of the Emerald Hotel.

John, the cab driver, noticed my reaction. "Friends of yours?" He raised his eyebrows.

"Not exactly," I replied, feeling safe for the moment—as if I was now one step ahead of the assassin. I watched the killer, with his slicked back hair and snakeskin boots, walk into the Emerald Hotel. "North please."

"Yessir," chirped the old man.

After a few blocks of silence, the old man spoke again. "Son, those people want to hurt you? What if I take you to a police station?"

"Ever hear of Thomas Minter?"

"Nope."

I felt comfortable with the, thus far, prescient old man. I also felt an urge to unload some of what had just happened to me. I needed to tell somebody, maybe needed to vent.

"The man in that Navigator tried to shoot me. Thomas Minter is a billionaire. And my boss. He was murdered tonight—I assume by that guy," I said, as I motioned behind us. "I found the body, called 911, and moments later the hit man in that Navigator showed up. Before CPD! I ran. And that's how I ended up here."

"Hmmm." The old man thought in silence for a few moments. "I think my son can help you. May I call him?"

I sat in silence. I didn't know what to say or what to do. I didn't even know where I would spend the night.

"My son is a retired police officer. Now he owns his own consulting company."

Great, I thought. *Nobody retires anymore. They all pretend to be "consultants," so they can hand out business cards and deduct some of their personal expenses on their tax returns. How is a retired cop going to be any better than the real police?*

Seeing the doubt on my face in his rearview mirror, the old man said, "My son is a K and R specialist. That stands for kidnapping and ransom. He goes to a lot of foreign countries to bring back American businessmen. Been to more than twenty countries in the last seven years. Very good at what he does and very much in demand."

I had heard of these quasi mercenaries. "Very expensive too?" I asked. I had read that these highly trained pros were paid big money by the insurance companies who underwrote the multimillion-dollar life insurance and kidnapping policies on the executives. It was worth a lot of money to the insurance companies to keep them alive. They sometimes paid a sizeable ransom, which was cheaper than paying out on a big-league life insurance claim.

The US government does not negotiate with terrorists. But insurance companies do. Such negotiations are mutually profitable. Only problem, they haven't figured out that paying off kidnappers begets more kidnappings.

The old man persuaded me with: "Yeah, he's expensive. But let me call him. Won't cost you noth'n. When he hears a billionaire has been murdered…well, he's no dummy. If he can help, he will. Bound to be some reward somewhere…"

Chapter 3

About forty minutes later, the cab pulled up to John's son's house.

This was not a typical house for a retired police officer. We were in Hinsdale, an affluent western suburb. I knew homes in this neighborhood were worth upward of two million dollars. John's son probably had commodities traders and professional athletes for neighbors.

Noticing the look on my face as we drove past a gate into a large, U-shaped driveway, John offered, "I told you my son is very good at what he does. And in high demand." He smiled the confident, but not cocky, smile of a proud papa.

The old man parked the cab, and we both got out. As we approached the very large front door, it opened, before we had a chance to ring the bell. I saw who must have been John's son—a handsome, well-built, fiftyish black man. He welcomed us through the door into a large two-story foyer with marble floors and an immense curved staircase.

The man who opened the door greeted his cab driver dad with a bear hug. Then he gave me crushing handshake. "John Strong Jr. Pleasure to meet you." He spoke with a clear, authoritative voice.

"Christian," I replied, as I shook his hand.

John Sr. asked his son, "When did you get back from Sao Paulo?"

"Six a.m."

"With an executive or a body bag?"

"Executive."

"That's my boy!" John Sr. beamed. Then the old man winked at me. I could tell he had a lot of pride in his son.

"But what about you," John Jr. said, changing the subject. "It appears we may be able to help keep you alive." He said this more as a statement than a question. The tone of his voice was confident and reassuring.

I stood in silence—perhaps a bit overwhelmed, unsure what to say. Too many questions raced through my mind about the assassin and Tom Minter. These mixed with images and curiosity about what John Jr. did for a living. *Sao Paulo?*

Our silence was broken by headlights in the driveway.

We've been followed, I thought.

John Jr. read my mind. He looked me squarely in the eyes, placed both hands on my shoulders, and calmly said, "My associates."

A large white van came into view. Three people poured out and walked in the front door. Two more associates entered the foyer from the kitchen.

"Good. Everyone is here. Let's get down to business," said John Jr., motioning us to the kitchen.

While everyone else headed for the kitchen, John Sr. moved toward the front door. "Past my bedtime. Love you."

"Love you too, Pops," shot back John Jr.

I wondered why John Sr. still drove a cab when his son was doing so well for himself. The house was immaculate, and as I looked around and entered the kitchen, I figured it had to be at least a three-million-dollar house.

Later, I learned John Jr. had asked his father to quit working, as he had enough money for both of them. But John Sr. took pride in taking care of himself, even though he was seventy-six years old, perhaps too old to be driving a cab in the roughest parts of Chicago.

John Strong Sr. could never retire. He was the product of an African-American heritage that had an old school work ethic. John Jr. told me that when his dad was a teenager, he woke up at 3:00 a.m. to put in a shift at the meat packing plant before school started.

Despite the fact that John Sr. earned straight *A*s, he never graduated from high school. When he was in high school, John Sr.'s father was killed in a factory accident, and John Sr. had no choice but to quit school and start working full time to support his mother and two younger sisters. For most of his adult life, he continued to rise before 5:00 a.m., and he worked as many as three jobs at once.

He prided himself on the fact that while he did not finish high school, both of his younger sisters graduated from college, which he paid for. And John Sr. took care of his mother until she passed away at the age of ninety-two.

So, over his son's objections, John Sr. continued to drive a cab on the south side of Chicago. He simply did not know

Seeing his point, Bob nodded his head in agreement. "They'll know our boy is getting help…they'll probably assume from the Feds."

"What else you got?" John Jr. continued. "We want the bad guys to believe our boy is still on his own. They must know for a fact he has not gone to CPD—CPD leaks like a sieve. These guys must have connections in the department. Maybe they think they just missed him at the Emerald." John Jr. paced the kitchen, rubbing his chin as he thought. Then he continued his narrative. "Maybe the kid just got scared by some of the seedy characters hanging around the Emerald Hotel. Maybe a place that is a little nicer will be plausible to the bad guys."

Bob thought a few moments and then said, "Days Inn on Clark."

"Perfect," John Jr. said. "The hunter is about to become the hunted. You all know your jobs. Let's roll."

Everyone sprang up from the table except for me.

John Jr. sat back down next to me with a solemn look on his face. "Christian, I did not want to upset you before getting the details out of you, but when Louie spoke to CPD, we learned that the prime suspect in Minter's murder…is you."

"What! That's crazy! I found him and called 911! Do murderers call 911 to report their own crimes?!"

"Actually, yes." John Jr. deadpanned. "Quite often in fact. In an attempt to deflect suspicion from themselves."

"Well the hit man in the Navigator tried to kill me too!"

"That would help your case, but you failed to mention it when you called 911." John Jr. said this with an air of certainty, not as if he were basing it on the last three hours of his team questioning my recollection.

I replayed the 911 call in my mind one last time. I realized why his team had focused so many repetitive questions around this. But the fact was, in my shock at seeing Tom Minter's dead body, I had failed to say anything to the 911 operator about the attempt on my own life. My face dropped.

John Jr. grasped my recognition of this fact. He offered, "To mention the attempt now would seem a little contrived. And as far as the police are concerned, you fled the scene of the crime. They don't know this assassin in the Lincoln Navigator exists. To them, it fits the pattern."

"The pattern?" I pressed. But I feared I already knew the answer.

"Louie has been in touch with his former colleagues. They already have a theory: Murderer calls 911 to report the crime and say he just discovered the body. These amateur killers think it would make a great defense to say, 'Hey, if I did it, why would I call the police to report it?' But this time, CPD thinks, the killer has second thoughts, gets nervous, and flees the scene before police arrive. As far as the police know, there is no black Navigator and no hit man. Just you, the prime suspect, who fled the scene and is on the run."

I soaked all this in and could not speak. My stomach began to turn.

"What do you think?" I couldn't help asking. He seemed to be the kind of guy that would shoot straight, tell me the truth, even though I might not like it.

"At first, we did suspect you. Nothing personal. Just going with the percentages. But after hours of interviewing you, we all agree: my associates and I are one hundred percent certain you have been truthful with us."

I nodded. He did not state this as if it were an opinion they had come to, but rather a fact they had established and verified. That was the kind of confidence he exuded.

John Jr. added, "This conclusion is not something we came to easily. Louie and I are both experienced detectives and have conducted many witness interviews over the years. We both have developed a knack for telling when someone is lying."

This perked up my spirits a bit. He wasn't just trying to make me feel better. John Jr. must have sensed my inner doubts. I wanted them to believe me. And I was telling the truth after all!

"Then there is Bob, former special agent of the FBI. He is a human lie-detector machine. His experience with the FBI included extensive training regarding how to tell when someone was telling the truth or lying. Or even when someone was telling the partial truth but omitting key details." John Jr. stood once again as he continued. He thought better on his feet. "The FBI has made a real science out of the gut instinct that many detectives like Louie and I have developed. A quick, involuntary glance of the eyes up and left before answering a question indicates that the witness is imagining, or thinking up, a fabrication. Bob can tell from watching a suspect if his or her pulse goes up or if their respiration changes. By the time they fidget, move their feet or move their hands in certain patterns that the FBI has researched and identified over tens of thousands of interviews, Bob already knows."

I didn't say anything, but I was beginning to feel more comfortable. I had told the truth.

"Look," John Jr. offered. "We believe you. And we can help you. But you should understand the motivation of your pursuers. They believe that if they kill you, you will posthumously be identified as Minter's killer. Case closed. They get off free. Because Minter was a billionaire, the pressure on CPD to solve this crime is enormous. They may not care if they get the right guy—as long as it is buttoned up quickly. The media and politicians are already demanding that CPD solve the case yesterday."

Chapter 4

Jorge Moreno was asked to go to a meeting in the Berkshires. A two-and-a-half-hour drive from New York City and Boston, the Berkshires is a beautiful mountainous recreation and tourist area rich in arts and culture. As a lawyer for a big firm in New York, Mr. Moreno scarcely had time to go out of his way like this, but the request came from Simon Tremblay, an investigator with the Ontario Securities Commission, the Canadian province's equivalent of the US Securities and Exchange Commission (SEC). The regulator had assured him that the law firm was not under any scrutiny. Nor were any of the firm's clients. Due to the nature of Mr. Moreno's international legal work, the regulator was seeking some general help, background information. Because the government employee could not justify a business trip to New York to meet with Mr. Moreno, he offered to take time away from his summer vacation in the Berkshires if Mr. Moreno would meet him there.

Tremblay offered two consecutive possible dates to meet for lunch, during his Berkshires vacation, which was coming up in three weeks. Mr. Moreno felt a sense of obligation, but it was also beneficial for his firm to cultivate relationships with bureaucrats from different agencies. Lawyers communicated informally with regulators all the time.

Tremblay was staying at a quaint bed and breakfast in a beautiful secluded area of the Berkshires, accessible by a narrow, winding road. As the lunch meeting was scheduled for a Thursday and Mr. Moreno had not taken a single vacation day all year, he decided to take his wife and kids. This was the perfect excuse for a much-needed vacation. After the lunch meeting, his family would enjoy a four-day weekend of hiking, fishing, and relaxing. When the time came, they piled into their Ford Explorer, excited for their first real getaway of the summer.

Jorge had invited his family inside for lunch, but his wife declined. After being cooped up in the car, she knew the kids would be difficult to keep quiet in a small restaurant. And the last thing the boys wanted to do was sit in a dining room for an hour, so she had packed sandwiches for the boys and herself.

A man with camouflage face paint and a ghillie suit resembling the heavy foliage of the area trained his binoculars on the Moreno family from four hundred meters away. The spotter watched as Jorge kissed his wife in the parking lot of the bed and breakfast and promised to be back in one hour. The inn was in a beautiful location with hiking trails, and she set off with the two young boys, ages six and ten, laughing and running.

Mr. Moreno found Mr. Tremblay in the lobby. After shaking hands, Tremblay led the way to the dining room. They exchanged small talk for a few minutes before

Tremblay made a couple general inquiries about the vagaries of overlapping—and sometimes conflicting—securities regulations of different countries.

Outside the inn, the spotter placed a call on his cell phone. "He has his wife and kids with him!"

"What? Why would he do that?" He paused.

The spotter asked, "Abort?"

"Hold on." Another long pause. "We are still a go."

"But the kids?"

Anger rose in the man's voice. "We are still a go. You got a problem with that?"

"No sir."

Chapter 5

After being shown to a comfortable guest room, I managed to sleep a bit off and on. I was summoned from my half sleep at 4:30 a.m. by a knock on the door.

"John Jr. here. Good morning, Mr. Roberts. Can you join us in the kitchen for some breakfast?"

"Sure. Be there in a minute." 4:30 a.m.! I had barely slept.

I got dressed and went to the kitchen where John Jr., Emily, and Louie had already gathered. They had reams of papers and binders on the table and had already eaten breakfast.

John Jr. took control by saying, "Hope you got some sleep. We had a busy night. Louie found a bullet that missed you on Newport, imbedded in the vinyl siding, right where you said."

I was startled, almost offended. *What—you didn't believe me?* I stared at him in disbelief.

John Jr. paused and looked straight at me. "Like I said last night, we trust you. Still, it is our job to verify. Keep in mind—it is in your best interest that we gather corroborating evidence. What if we believe you but CPD doesn't?"

That hit home. I nodded my understanding and dropped my offended look. I was exhausted and perhaps not thinking as clearly as I should be.

John Jr. replied, "Yes. He is there right now. Nate, how far away is Bob?"

Nate answered, "Already on it. Bob has a visual. He's in a car thirty yards away from Christian's front door."

John Jr. pointed to the largest screen in the center of the wall and said, "Can you move that camera to the big screen?"

Nate clicked a few buttons, and the real-time video of the intruder in my kitchen moved from a small, twenty-inch flat panel mounted on the wall over to the big screen in the center of the wall.

I jumped. "That's him! That's the guy who tried to shoot me! Same guy I saw get to the Board of Trade before the police!"

John Jr. got on the radio and spoke very calmly. "Bob, suspect is our shooter. Look for a black Navigator. You have time. He is in Mr. Roberts's apartment now. We will alert you as he leaves."

Wow! How can he stay so calm and methodically on task? I thought. The guy who tried to kill me is in my apartment!

The big screen showed the hit man just as I had described him—minus the snakeskin boots. Boots were no good for sneaking around my apartment. He had neatly combed but greasy-looking, slicked-back hair. We all sat in silence, watching as he walked through my front room and then toward the kitchen.

John Jr. and his associates were very experienced at this sort of surveillance operation. While I couldn't contain myself, they looked as normal and relaxed as if they were watching a commercial during the Super Bowl.

I was very agitated. "What about my roommates?!" *This guy is an assassin!*

Nate said, "Nah, why bother?" He spoke like someone who had already seen this movie and knew what would happen next.

John Jr. explained, "It's not even five a.m. They will be in REM sleep, very deep. Remember…" He was cut off by the hit man's movements.

The assassin took out a gun, wiped it with a handkerchief, and placed it in a cabinet above the microwave.

As I watched the plasma screen in amazement, John Jr. said, "Well, well, Mr. Slick is planting a gun in Mr. Roberts's apartment." I didn't know if the nickname Slick had to do with his hair or the fact that he was doing sneaky things in the middle of the night.

Nate chimed in. "One hundred dollars says that is the gun used to kill Thomas Minter."

John Jr. turned to Louie. "Louie, I assume CPD is close to getting a search warrant for Mr. Roberts's apartment?"

Louie replied, "Yes, it has been prepared. They are waiting for a judge to sign it. Could have it as early as eight a.m."

Bob's voice crackled through the radio: "Got it. Tracking device installed underneath the Navigator. Listening device within."

John Jr. spoke into the radio back to Bob. "Great. Make sure our Mr. Slick gets into that Navigator. Once that is confirmed, drop back; Nate will assume coverage of Mr. Slick. Stay back a good distance—with the tracking device on the vehicle, we can lose visual contact. We cannot risk him seeing us. We need you to go back inside Mr. Roberts's apartment and retrieve a gun Mr. Slick just planted. Before the police find it. CPD will be there with a warrant in a few hours."

"Roger that!" declared Bob.

Without exchanging words, Nate rose from his chair at the center of the conference table, and Isaac took his place. Now Isaac sat in front of the PC that controlled the wall of video screens. Nate held a rectangular block-shaped GPS device with a four-inch screen and mapping software. Speaking into his radio, he said, "Tracking device activation confirmed. Mr. Slick's vehicle location is transmitting through. I've got him from here."

Isaac meanwhile was watching every move Mr. Slick made on the large flat screen. Isaac transmitted over the radio: "Mr. Slick is on his way out."

Bob's voice returned. "Copy that."

I was amazed how they were all so calm and clinical. *A murderer just planted a gun in my kitchen! How can you be so relaxed about this?* But they all spoke as casually as if they were saying, "Please pass the salt."

I wondered aloud, "So, the whole world is coming and going freely from my locked apartment, right before the police arrive to search it?"

John Jr.'s eyes warmed, and he smiled at my wry crack. He deadpanned with: "Locked doors don't matter much to us or to guys like Mr. Slick. CPD, on the other hand, will break your front door down to execute the search warrant."

John Jr. paced the war room with his arms crossed and one hand rubbing his chin again. "Put me on speaker." Isaac pushed a button on a star-shaped speakerphone in the center of the conference table. John Jr. continued, "Time to get a better handle on who we are dealing with. Does Mr. Slick have friends? Let's flush them out with some activity."

He stopped pacing, leaned in to the speakerphone and said, "At seven fifteen a.m., Louie is going to be at the Chicago Board of Trade. I want you to try to get the attention of Mr. Slick and his associates. One: use Mr. Roberts's credit card near the CBOT. Two: swipe Mr. Roberts's CBOT keycard through the security turnstile in the CBOT lobby. Three: see who turns up."

Turning to me he asked, "May we have your credit cards, ATM card, and CBOT keycard?"

I handed them over to John Jr., but I must have looked worried because he said, "Don't worry. You'll get it all back." He passed the items to Louie. "That will draw them to the CBOT. Then, we'll draw them to the Days Inn with a phone call to Laura. Let's see; Days Inn is a ten-minute cab ride from the CBOT. We want them to think this activity is all generated by Mr. Roberts. We'll spread this activity thirty minutes apart. Far enough apart to be all done by Christian. Close enough, and in two different locations, the flurry of activity might flush out more than just Mr. Slick. So at seven forty-five a.m., Christian will call his girlfriend Laura: 'Hi, honey, I'm innocent. We need to meet; come to the Days Inn on Clark.' You get the idea. Nate, you stay on Mr. Slick. Bob, move on to Laura's apartment. Trail her and anyone trailing her when she leaves. Keep a low profile and be careful! I assume that by now CPD and Mr. Slick's friends may be staking out Laura's apartment in their hunt for Mr. Roberts." John Jr. raised his arms across the war room. "Isaac will mind the store."

Then John Jr. concluded with, "That leaves Mr. Roberts, Emily, and I to see who turns up at the Days Inn. Comments?"

"Roger that," crackled through the radio from Bob. "Wait…damn!"

"Talk to me, Bob; what's wrong?"

"Two unmarked cars just pulled up to Mr. Roberts's apartment. Looks like CPD."

Louie scrunched his lips into a frown and nodded his head, as if to say, "We should have anticipated this." Then he said, "They are staking out Mr. Roberts's apartment. Not surprising, given the high-profile nature of this investigation. Once they decide to get a search warrant, they send a patrol over to keep an eye on the place while they wait for a judge to sign the warrant."

Bob said, "Well, CPD is going to find that gun now. I can't go in."

John Jr. thought this through, paced, crossed his arms, and rubbed his chin. "That's okay. The police will find the weapon, but we have the videotape proving that Mr. Slick planted it. So Mr. Roberts will be fine." He paused as he pondered this further. "The video will tie Mr. Slick to Minter's murder, so this could be good. CPD will follow strict evidence chain protocol."

The others in the room nodded in agreement as they processed this.

Bob replied, "I like it. The whole case against Mr. Roberts is circumstantial. My guess is Mr. Slick's guys are not done framing him. A chunky, untraceable deposit into Mr. Roberts's bank account could seal the case up nicely. But now, they gave us a gift. They just gave us proof positive that Mr. Roberts was set up. Maybe better CPD finds the gun than not."

I nodded my understanding. I had heard of numerous cases where innocent people had gone to jail, even death row, based on far weaker evidence than what was thus far framing me. I felt relieved.

John Jr. looked at me with a bit of sorrow in his eyes and added, "In the short term, things may get a little unpleasant for you." I wasn't sure why, and John Jr. saw that on my face. *Won't the video exonerate me?*

John Jr. said, "The police are about to crack this case wide open—and the smoking gun will have been found in your kitchen."

Of course! I realized. Before this video comes to light, the police would take credit for solving the crime. I was about to go from person of interest to wanted for murder. I began to run through in my mind the lives that I had seen ruined in the news media before this or that individual was proved innocent. *Ugh!*

"Let's roll," said Nate. Enough small talk for him. He was on mission once again. He walked out of the war room.

Louie followed, fishing keys from his pocket as he went.

Chapter 6

A Simon Tremblay did, in fact, work for the Ontario Securities Commission, but the man meeting with Jorge Moreno was not Tremblay. This man was an experienced operator. He had lured Moreno to the secluded location because Moreno had helped a Canadian client negotiate a contract for logging rights to a vast swath of Colombian rain forest. The firm specialized in international transactions, and most of the lawyers knew a second language. Mr. Moreno, fluent in Spanish, had moved to the United States from Colombia as a young boy. He was the logical choice for the contract negotiation involving the Colombian government. While dealings with less developed countries often involved graft, Mr. Moreno and his firm steered clear of such practices. By their reckoning, the Colombian rain forest deal was aboveboard.

After lunch, Mr. Moreno emerged to find his wife and boys sitting in the grass near their car, finishing their sandwiches. He bent over, kissed his wife on the top of her head, and said, "Okay! No more work for three and a half days!" He turned to the boys. "You ready for some fun?"

The boys jumped up and cheered. His wife smiled. Jorge had been working too hard. This was perfect. They piled into the Ford Explorer and began the long, winding road back to the main highway. The drive was beautiful, but a little scary, as the narrow road contained numerous, steep drop-offs with no guardrail.

About two miles into the drive, the couple's older boy giggled and asked his younger brother across the backseat, "What are you going to be when you grow up?"

The happy six-year-old answered as he always did: "A garbage man!" He grinned and pumped his fist in the air.

Jorge and his wife smiled and tried not to laugh. The Moreno's youngest son was mesmerized the first time he saw the claw arm of a garbage truck grab their garbage can, jerk it into the air, dump it, and set the empty bin back down. Since then, he knew what he wanted to do when he grew up. He didn't understand what his older brother found funny about this—it was so cool!

They came to a switchback where the road curved around the outer edge of a plateau. The rugged terrain dropped precipitously on the passenger side of the SUV. They approached a pickup truck on their left, about to pull onto the narrow road from a rutted dirt path on the inside of the turn. Thinking that a local would drive the mountain road faster than he was, Jorge slowed to a stop just before the truck and motioned for him to go first.

The truck driver waved him on, so Jorge took his foot off the brake and continued. A few feet later, when he was in front of the truck, it lurched forward and smacked the driver's side of the Morenos' Explorer. Then Jorge heard the truck engine rev. It was accelerating! The truck's four-wheel drive was chugging, pushing the Ford Explorer to its right, toward the steep cliff! Jorge's right tires went off the right side of the paved road. As they hit the loose gravel, his sideways slide accelerated. His wife screamed as their Explorer began to free-fall.

The crash happened in slow motion for Jorge and his wife. The first feeling of falling, losing their stomach, seemed to last forever. Thinking about the impact their children were about to bear slowed time: *Ten years old! Six years old! Noooo! Why? Oh please, God, just take me!*

The SUV dropped about twenty feet before it struck the side of the steep cliff. The impact spun the vehicle back into the air and into a violent roll down the steep grade. Every twenty feet or so, the Explorer would crash into the cliff, bounce off, and continue rolling—sometimes rolling down the rocks, sometimes flying through the air.

The boys were both intact after the first impact with the side of the steep cliff—a glancing blow that spun the car, but the impact itself was not devastating. The steep slope of the landing softened the blow. But the spinning accelerated. The falling sensation was replaced by the feeling of being in a centrifuge.

The next impact happened on the corner of the driver's side and the roof. It killed Jorge instantly. His wife was badly jolted but still conscious. The boys in the backseat were, at least so far, relatively unscathed. The six-year-old was sitting behind his dad, and while the roof collapsed on that side, he was too short to suffer the fate of his father. Mrs. Moreno had instinctively placed her arms up around her head. The consecutive impacts thrashed her around wildly, breaking bones in her arms and hands, which collided with the car frame, the rearview mirror, and her husband's head.

When the car finally came to a stop, upside down, it was mangled on all sides. Mrs. Moreno was badly injured and in shock but still alive. The two young boys were still breathing but unconscious. They had broken bones, but they had miraculously not sustained any life-threating injuries.

Hikers in this remote area were rare, but a nearby hiker first heard, and then saw, the SUV rolling down the mountain. He ran to the Explorer. As he neared, he heard a woman's voice crying, "Jorge! Jorge?!" Although upside down, she saw the hiker and cried, "Help! Please help!"

The hiker got down on one knee and looked inside. Everyone was unconscious, or perhaps worse, except for Jorge's wife. She was bloody and battered, hanging upside down in her seatbelt, her broken arms hanging toward the crushed roof of the car. As the hiker peered in she yelled, "Help! My babies!"

The hiker looked in the backseat and said, "I see two boys, still in their seatbelts." The woman was relieved. "Just relax," the hiker said. He took his hiking backpack off, set it on the ground, and unzipped it.

He removed a two-gallon plastic jug from his pack and poured it over the undercarriage of the upside down vehicle.

Some dripped on the outside of the car. The woman was confused. She pleaded, "I smell gas! Please hurry!"

The hiker squatted. He looked at the woman but didn't say anything. She saw pure evil in his eyes. Then she saw him hold out a lighter toward the car. He touched the flame of his lighter to the freshly spilled gas and then threw the empty jug on the flames. He knew the fire would melt all evidence of the plastic jug. In fact, it would get so hot it would melt all of the plastic on the car, even the tires.

Then the hiker departed, picking his way along the driest, rockiest parts of the ravine, careful to not leave any footprints. As he walked away, the flames grew. He heard the woman scream. First, screams of anger and exasperation. Then, screams of agony. Then, silence.

They had debated killing Moreno. He had not been involved in any crime. In fact, he had not been aware of any wrongdoing. But he had worked on the Colombian deal. It was possible that, in the future, he might have seen the timing of certain juxtaposed events as suspicious. But that was only if he somehow learned of unrelated events—a series of consecutive and unlikely possibilities. He hadn't even been a loose end. He had just been a person who might, in light of possible future revelations, connect a few dots. Still, he would have had no proof, just a shadowy glimpse of a potentially suspicious pattern of behavior.

Yet they eliminated him. They were not taking any chances this time around.

Chapter 7

I sat in a room at the Days Inn with John Jr. and Emily. John Jr. removed what looked like a smoke detector from a hard, metallic silver briefcase. By now I knew it wasn't a smoke detector at all but a hidden camera. John Jr. stood on a chair in the small room. I heard a *thap* as he pressed the device against the ceiling. Then he let go of the device and examined it for a moment before stepping down from the chair.

I was amazed. It looked like a standard smoke detector, and he had just installed it in a few seconds!

John Jr. spoke into the radio, "Isaac, confirm transmission and catalog video feed from camera 44717, Mr. Roberts's room at the Days Inn. Also confirm and catalog camera 44716, the hallway of the Days Inn outside Mr. Roberts's room."

"Roger, processing," came Isaac's reply.

John Jr. must have noted my amazement at the speed and ease of the smoke detector installation. "We have had a bear of a time with these gadgets over the years. Used to use adhesive tape. Sometimes the adhesive would give way, and the device would fall…talk about a blown cover. Well, not anymore. Nate remodeled these babies to include preloaded wall anchors that shoot out in much the same way as a nail from a nail gun. Just press against the ceiling, and *pop*, the wall anchors shoot in and then expand out, gripping anything from plaster to drywall."

Isaac radioed this message: "Confirming cameras 44716 and 44717. Both feeds streaming and archiving."

John Jr. must have sensed my unease because he said, "Don't worry; we'll be long gone if this camera catches anyone entering. But the room is registered in your name, so maybe we'll gain some info on whoever is looking for you." John Jr. then began to tell me all about tracking devices. He was usually all business and very efficient. I noticed that when he spoke to his team, he never used five words when three would suffice. So his rambling small talk, with no apparent purpose except to fill time was, I figured, catered to me. Designed to distract me and prevent me from worrying too much. Although I saw through this tactic, I didn't mind it. In fact, I appreciated it.

John Jr. said, "Strong and Associates, under Nate's direction, upgraded our surreptitious listening devices to include a remote on/off switch." He pulled a small device out of the silver briefcase and handed it to me.

I turned it over in my hands. It was about the size of a smartphone with a large magnet on one side, similar to the magnets on hide-a-key containers.

Nodding at it he said, "That is identical to the device planted on the Navigator. The on/off toggle enables us to turn the bugs and tracking devices on when we need to and then turn them off at other times. Organizations like Mr.

Slick's will likely have bug-detection equipment and conduct periodic sweeps. The on/off toggle ensures nothing will trip bug-detection devices as long as we turn it off."

He reached into the briefcase and handed me another device. It was smaller and looked like a garage door remote.

"We can turn them on and off anytime with this little baby, as long as we are within a range of about fifty yards. The on/off toggle operates on a simple garage-door-opener frequency. In fact that piece in your hand is a standard garage door opener, adapted for this device."

The relative quiet of the Days Inn hotel room was disrupted as both John Jr.'s and Emily's radios came to life. It was 7:15 a.m. Louie gave the play-by-play of his activities to bait the bad guys. First, a swipe of my credit card at the Starbucks next to the Board of Trade and then, about ten minutes later, a swipe of my employee keycard through the Board of Trade automatic turnstile.

I had confirmed during questioning the previous night that, in order to gain access past the lobby of the exchange, employees had to swipe a keycard through a strip on the right side of the automatic turnstiles. So employees were tracked as they entered the exchange but not as they left. Like most Chicago office buildings, people used to come and go freely from the CBOT. But, after 9/11, all that changed. Employees needed ID cards to enter automatic turnstiles, and all visitors' names had to be submitted to building security. Every visitor was required to show a photo ID and get his or her picture taken before given a sticker with his or her name, photo, and the floor authorized to visit on it. For the first six months, it was a real hassle. After that, it was pretty efficient. I had gotten so used to the security procedures in other buildings that I could barely remember what it used to be like before all of these precautions.

I sat quietly in the modestly decorated room at the Days Inn with intense anticipation. I was trying to keep my mind busy with mundane things, but I was terrified for Laura. At that point, I didn't care about myself. I couldn't even think about Laura getting hurt, or worse, by the thugs who killed Mr. Minter. John Jr. sat with his legs crossed and stirred his coffee with a thin wooden stir stick, while Emily worked on her laptop.

After a brief lull, Nate's voice came over the radio: "Damn—who is Mr. Slick working for? I'm tailing him, and the bug in his Navigator is activated. He just received two phone calls. One, about five minutes after the credit card swipe and the second, within seconds after the turnstile swipe! I assume he is on his way to the Board of Trade now. I am following him at a safe distance, headed south on Lake Shore Drive."

John Jr. replied over the radio, "Roger that." Then he clicked off the radio and looked at me. "Last night, you swiped your keycard when you entered the Board of Trade. That is how Mr. Slick did it. That is how he beat CPD to the building. Mr. Slick's buddies probably have access to police scanners, but there is no way they have access to 911 dispatch—at least not in real time. Besides, any intercepted police radio communications would have been vague. They would not have mentioned your name."

Speaking back into the radio, John Jr. said, "Good work, Nate. Stay with him. We are going to see what kind of support he has by calling Laura at seven forty-five. I want them to be split by drawing them to Board of Trade, tailing his girlfriend, and then getting their asses over to the Days Inn. Everyone we flush out gets bugged and tracked, just like Mr. Slick. Tag 'em and release 'em." John Jr. smiled and spoke as if all this were just another casual day on a hunting or fishing expedition.

I was still feeling tense and nervous and, most of all, worried sick about Laura. We are dealing with professional killers. I looked at John Jr.—the picture of calm—to help quiet my nerves.

John Jr. handed me the phone, saying, "Relax. Remember, Laura's phone is bugged by the bad guys. Now just like we rehearsed." He glanced down at the paper in front of me. "You have a script in case you get nervous and forget your lines."

I nervously crumpled the edges of the paper outlining what I was supposed to say to Laura.

John Jr. pleaded, "But please, don't *read* from it. If Mr. Slick's associates hear what sounds like you reading instead of just talking, the bad guys will think you are receiving help from the Feds. Then we lose the huge advantage we have right now because they underestimate you. They think you are on your own—running—no help and no police."

"What if her phone is not bugged?" I asked.

"It is. While you were still in bed, before Mr. Slick planted that gun in your kitchen, we watched him plant a telephone-listening device at Laura's."

I was exasperated. "What? She is in danger. The bastard who tried to kill me was in Laura's apartment! Can't you do anything?! Bring her in?"

I was shaken.

John Jr. looked at me. "We are doing everything we can to get both you and Laura to a safe place while not jeopardizing anyone in the interim. Remember, unless you want a witness-protection-where-you-can't-so-much-as-call-your-mother-on-the-phone-ever-again life, we need to find out who is behind this and why. We rush in and grab Laura," he paused and wrinkled his face. "You both spend the rest of your lives looking over your shoulder. Neither you nor Laura will ever be safe."

Although this was difficult to absorb, I knew he was right. I spoke in a quiet, defeated tone. "Please, just tell me what to do. I can't...if anything happens to Laura..." I shook my head, and my voice trailed off.

John Jr. checked his watch and said, "Christian, after your stop by Starbucks and the Board of Trade, you just took a cab here." He lifted the phone toward me and said, "You can do this; you have to do this for Laura. Let us know when you are ready.

"You are going to call her and follow the script. Without reading the script. And in advance of your first recorded telephone performance, bear in mind: they will not harm Laura as long as they think they can follow her to you." His tone dropped a bit. "However, once they catch on to us, say because of a bad telephone performance by you, then all hell breaks loose. They will either kidnap her as a bargaining chip or just kill her in anger and revenge."

Emily jolted up from her laptop and glared at John Jr. She tilted her head, pursed her lips, and squinted her eyes as if to say, "That was a bit harsh."

John Jr. looked at Emily and extended both palms up. "I know, I know, but we promised Mr. Roberts we'd be straight with him. He's a big boy. He can handle it. When the stakes are high, we tell him."

Later, I learned that John Jr. had said that to intentionally rattle me. And Emily played along perfectly. After all, I had been feeling comfortable and safe in the custody of Strong and Associates, same as if I had gone to the FBI or the police. John Jr. knew that. If I were in fact on my own, I would be very stressed and nervous. The bad guys would sense this—or not—in my voice. Given the level of sophistication demonstrated so far by the bad guys, they might even digitally measure the stress level in my voice. So what may have seemed harsh words by John Jr., had in fact just put me in a very realistic, Academy Award-winning zone. And I am forever grateful to John Jr. for messing with my head like that.

Emily's fake frown was a great example of how well the Strong and Associates team worked together. Without discussion or rehearsal, John Jr. and Emily played off each other to put me in the right frame of mind for the call.

Of course, at the time, I was very nervous. I breathed deeply a few times. "Okay, I'm ready."

John Jr. dialed Laura's number.

Laura picked up on the third ring. "Hello?"

My voice rose a bit. "Laura, it's me."

"Christian! Oh my gosh! Are you okay? Where are you? What happened?!" She was excited and worried and speaking very fast.

"I'm okay. I'm okay."

"But the police—they questioned me and are looking for you. I thought they wanted to arrest you! And of course I saw on the news what happened to your boss. Oh my gosh!" She was very upset and very emotional.

"Did they say they were going to arrest me?"

"Nooo." She hesitated as she thought about this and then definitively said, "No. They said you were just a possible witness and they just wanted to ask you some questions. But they were intense. This is freaking me out, Christian! I called you at least twenty times, and you never called back!"

I surmised that the police did want to arrest me. But stating that outright was no way to get a girl to give up her guy. So the police tried to trick Laura by saying I was not a suspect, just a witness. Bummer was, as I figured this, I realized that Laura had probably also reached the same conclusion.

I became a little defensive and veered off script. John Jr. and Emily had instructed me that it was okay to go off script to keep the conversation natural sounding. "Laura, I didn't do anything. And I don't know what is going on, but we need to talk." I paused and then blurted out, "I love you!" There, I said it and off script too.

Laura did not say anything, but I could hear her trying to hold her crying in.

I tried to explain and got back on script. "I was so scared last night; I didn't go home. Didn't get your messages. I am sorry. But I need to talk to you. I'm staying at the Days Inn on Clark. Can you jump in a cab and meet me here? In the breakfast lounge area by the lobby?"

"I'm so worried, Christian. I have never been so worried! I don't understand any of this. I don't want to get in any trouble..."

"You are not in trouble. And you won't be. Nothing wrong with catching a cab. You said yourself the cops don't want to arrest me, just want to talk to me as a witness. So you are not doing anything wrong. Please just come meet me. Look, here's the deal: I found Thomas Minter's body last night. He was shot. I am freaking out too, and I need you. Please come right away, and I will tell you everything that happened last night."

Laura began crying, almost hysterical. She said, "I love you, Christian. I'm so sorry."

Wow, that felt good to hear! She was feeling guilty for doubting me, which she had, due to the police questioning. But after hearing my voice, she knew that I was not involved with killing Mr. Minter.

She continued, "I know how much Mr. Minter meant to you. But the police and everything…"

"Laura." I stopped her. "I love you."

Silence.

"And I just need you now. Everything will be all right. Will you meet me? In the lobby, in five minutes?"

After a brief pause due to crying and sniffling, she said, "I'll be there right away."

"Thank you."

"Good-bye."

"Bye."

Click.

John Jr. stood up and clapped his hands together one time. "That was a damn fine performance, son!" He slapped me on the back.

Emily nodded her agreement and smiled. She appeared somewhat relieved.

"Now what?" I asked. "Isn't that whacko going to put a bullet in my head as soon as he follows Laura here?"

"Mr. Roberts, gunning you down in the hotel lobby in front of a bunch of witnesses does not fit their agenda. Why would they plant the gun in your apartment? The story they are weaving goes like this: You acted alone in killing Mr. Minter. Now you are on the run. Who knows? Maybe you embezzled a bunch of money? Minter is dead, and you have disappeared." He paused and shook his head. "No…you being gunned down in a public place would blow that theory out of the water. Then the police would begin investigating to find out who killed Mr. Minter and you. So these guys need you to disappear. Dead or alive, they don't care. But gunning you down in a public place does not work for them. First, you disappear. Then the police pin the murder on you, and the bad guys sail off into the sunset. Or perhaps crawl under a rock. Wherever guys like Mr. Slick go."

I processed this, and it gave me some comfort. It made sense.

John Jr. added, "But to your point, we still don't know what we have stumbled onto here. And therefore we cannot be certain of anything." He waved his hand in a dismissive way. "That was just speculation. Maybe they do just want to put a bullet in your head."

I felt my breakfast rising in my esophagus. Emily shot John Jr. the same "that was harsh" look as before.

John Jr. looked at Emily with both palms up again. "Sorry! I want the kid to be reassured. Not complacent. These are dangerous people."

"You don't have to worry about that," I muttered.

Chapter 8

Once again, John Jr. and Emily had put me into the sober frame of mind required to stay alive. John Jr. said, "We need to get to the lobby to wait for Laura. But we are prepared for every contingency. Emily, please…" He motioned to Emily and tapped his ear.

Emily pulled out a very tiny earpiece. "Please hold still," she said. "This will allow you to hear us. I need to plant it deep enough in your ear so that no one will see it." And she did just that. I cringed a little as she gave it one final twist and push. "Does that feel okay?"

"Yeah."

"Nice," John Jr. opined. "I can't even see that sucker, and I am sitting right in front of you." Then he pulled up his polo shirt and flipped a switch on a beeper-like device clipped to his belt. He gave me an identical device. "Battery pack and bluetooth. Just keep it in your pocket to power your earpiece." Then he flipped a switch and said, "Test. Test. You copy?"

I held my hand to my ear and nodded.

"But don't ever raise your hand to your ear like that. It makes it obvious what we are doing. Bad guys see you raise your hand to you ear, all hell breaks loose. Understand?"

I nodded. "Yes, sir."

"Excellent."

As we took the elevator to the lobby, John Jr. rehearsed the plan once again with me. We had already gone over it more times than I could count. The basic plan was to get Laura and me safely away from the bad guys without the bad guys knowing I had sophisticated help in the form of law enforcement—or Strong and Associates.

I sat alone at a table in the lobby, a short distance from the complimentary breakfast buffet. A man in work coveralls and a baseball cap pushed a large bin of towels and sheets through the lobby. He smiled and nodded at me. I figured he must be the friend of Strong and Associates that John Jr. told me about. An outside consultant hired by John Jr. to help out when the core team of six was spread thin—as they had been since they met me last night.

John Jr. saw me eye the laundry man and said, "That's our friendly neighborhood helper. Consider him one of my team. He's solid. We have used him when we needed extra manpower many times. He is very good." He spoke in a reassuring voice through my tiny, hidden earpiece.

I nodded as I looked far across the lobby to John Jr. who was eating breakfast and pretending to read a newspaper.

"Don't nod. Don't look at me. You are doing great, but remember, do not acknowledge me or anything I say. If you copy this, rub your eyes."

I rubbed one of my eyes with the palm of my hand.

"Perfect. I'm just that voice in your head; don't acknowledge me. Remain calm. Follow the plan. If someone throws a wrench in things, focus on my voice. I will tell you what to do." John Jr.'s voice was calm and in control, soothing to hear.

Just then Laura came through the revolving glass door at the front of the hotel lobby. I saw her before she saw me. I stood, and Laura ran over to hug me. Just as instructed, I wasted no time in hugging or greeting her. Instead, I gently but firmly grabbed her arm and began to guide her toward the elevator.

Laura was a bit puzzled by this.

I asked, "Do you trust me?"

She looked at me in astonishment as I continued to whisk her toward the elevator.

I said, "This one time, I need you to trust me." And with that, I guided her into the elevator—the elevator that I was assured would be open and waiting for us because Emily had hacked into the elevator system. She was controlling all the elevators from her laptop.

I caught Laura by surprise—threw her off balance on purpose, just enough to allow herself to be guided into the elevator before she stopped and demanded some answers.

John Jr. had made it very clear that we could not loiter in the lobby. We had to get to the elevator, which would carry us to safety and hiding. I understood how dangerous our adversaries were. Laura did not. If necessary, I would have carried Laura to the elevator.

But that wasn't necessary. I was so in love with Laura at that moment and so relieved to see her that I was focused on her as soon as she entered the hotel. I did not notice the man enter the revolving door behind her. But as I entered the elevator and turned back toward the lobby, I saw him. The instant we entered the elevator, I heard John Jr.'s voice: "They're in. They're in. Close. Bring it up." He was giving the play-by-play to Emily.

The man stared right at me as he walked briskly toward the elevator. It wasn't the hit man with slicked back hair and snakeskin boots, but it was obvious by the intense stare that he was one of them. *Why aren't the doors closing?* I repeatedly pressed the button for floor nine.

The instant before the staring man reached the elevator, he was cut off by the sudden appearance of the laundry guy. The laundry guy, and his big bin full of towels and sheets, rolled in front of the elevator and blocked the entrance just in time.

Close doors, close, I willed at this welcomed extra few seconds.

But the man with the cold stare reached over the laundry cart and caught the elevator door open with one hand. Turning to the laundry guy, the man smiled and said, "After you."

Shit. I rehashed Plan B in my mind. I had been counting on Plan A, which was to take the elevator up with Laura to the safety of the room where Emily was waiting.

Plan B, which was decidedly less appealing, was to have Laura and I attempt an exit out the back elevator doors. The elevator had doors on both the front and the back. The front doors opened out to the lobby; the rear doors, which were now closed, opened to the backside, which included the parking garage and loading dock areas of the hotel.

John Jr.'s voice came through my earpiece: "Stay calm. Listen to me." Although his voice was calm and reassuring, I was terrified, more for Laura than for myself. I stood frozen in the elevator. It felt like everything was happening in slow motion.

John Jr.'s voice in my earpiece said, "Move to the back of the elevator with Laura. Wait for my cue. Exit the back elevator doors. Go right. Get on the freight elevator."

John Jr. was speaking as much to Emily as he was to me. Emily sat poised over her laptop keyboard ready to trigger the rear elevator doors. With any luck, she already had the freight elevator waiting for us.

The laundry guy made eye contact with me and said, "Excuse me." Laura and I slid to the far back of the elevator, against the back doors, to make room for his laundry cart. The laundry guy pulled his cart onto the elevator lengthwise, almost pinning us against the back doors. He stood on the side of his cart and made room for Mr. Slick's buddy to come in next to him, also on the side of the cart.

As I stood with Laura, pinned between the laundry cart and the back elevator doors, the only remaining space was to the left side of the cart, where the laundry guy now stood as a barrier between this new bad guy and Laura and me. The fact that Mr. Slick's buddy had to step to the side of the cart so the front doors could close made me wonder if this laundry cart was chosen by Strong and Associates for this particular elevator and this particular scenario. Either way, it was comforting to have an ally standing between Mr. Slick's partner, Laura, and me.

This comforting feeling was short lived, as the bad guy looked directly at me. He did not speak, but his eyes did not waiver, almost as if he wanted me to know that he was not a random guy just trying to catch the elevator. He was communicating: "That's right—I'm here for you!"

I stood frozen—four people in the elevator: Laura, laundry guy, myself, and this apparent associate of Mr. Slick, who might just blow us all away right there.

Laundry guy, who was separated from the elevator buttons by the bad guy, nonchalantly pointed to the buttons and said, "Three, please." This caused the man to turn his stare away from me and look at the front elevator panel, long enough to find the "3" button.

"Now!" came John Jr.'s voice through the earpiece. On cue, the rear elevator doors opened.

I grabbed Laura's arm and pulled her out. She must have been freaked out by the guy staring at us because she cooperated with me.

At the same time Laura and I exited out the back, the laundry guy, our guardian angel, slid in and took our place at the back of the elevator. I knew that, according to this Plan B, he would stand there nonchalantly, blocking the rear of the elevator and preventing Mr. Slick's associate from following us. Of course he couldn't hold the bad guy off in this manner for very long. Not to mention we still wanted Mr. Slick's associates to think I was alone, not getting help from the police or the Feds.

I ran with Laura twenty feet to the right where, as Emily had promised, the freight elevator was waiting with open doors. We ran inside, and I hit the button for any floor I could, repeatedly hitting the "close door" button. I watched intently as the elevator doors slowly began to swallow us up, hoping that an arm—or a gun—would not squeeze in before the doors were closed.

At last the doors slowly closed all the way. Would they reopen? I didn't breathe a sigh of relief until I felt the elevator begin moving. Then I took a deep breath. Laura and I emerged on floor nine where we were ushered into our hotel room by Emily.

Laura could not contain herself anymore. "What is going on? Who was that freaky guy in the elevator?"

I held Laura's hand and replied, "I know this seems crazy, but I can explain everything. Thank you for coming."

Laura moved closer to me. She wrapped her arms around me and placed her head on my shoulder. She was trying hard to hold back a bunch of confused and raw emotions.

John Jr.'s voice came through my hidden earpiece: "Time for Phase Two, ladies and gentleman. Our pissed off elevator man just walked back outside through the revolving doors in the lobby."

"Louie and I have a visual," replied Nate's voice.

John Jr. continued, "Mr. Roberts, the coast is clear. In the laundry bin. Down the freight elevator. Into the van. Mr. Slick and his buddies will be swarming the place soon, and they may already know which room you are in."

We heard a crisp knock on the door. My heart stopped. Emily peeped through the eyehole and then opened it. The laundry guy from the elevator wheeled his cart into the room.

"Hop in," said the laundry guy, motioning to Laura and me. He lifted up some sheets and towels for us to get in.

Laura was puzzled and overwhelmed. She froze. "No. Wait a minute. What is going on?" I realized that she had no earpiece and hadn't heard John Jr.'s last transmission.

Emily looked at me with a sense of urgency—almost fear—and shook her head no. She tapped her wristwatch with her right pointer finger. *The assassins could be here any second!*

Chapter 9

held Laura's hands, looked her in the eyes, and said, "I know this is difficult. I found Thomas Minter's body, and someone also tried to shoot me. I don't know why. But we are not safe here." I motioned to Emily and then to the laundry guy, "These are the good guys; they're here to help us." I looked at Laura with pleading, almost desperate eyes. "Please, hop in," I said, as I pointed to the laundry bin. "It's not safe here. Let us get away from the people who killed Mr. Minter. That guy in the elevator was one of them. Then we will all slow down and figure this thing out."

Laura looked petrified, and tears were welling up in her eyes. Without a word she raised a leg over the bin, and I helped her in. I always admired her strength. I knew this was a lot to expect of her. Then I lay down right next to her and held her close.

Man, it felt better than ever just to hold her, despite the circumstances. I still needed to tell her how much I loved her.

Cramped in the laundry bin, Laura started to sob on my chest. As Emily and laundry guy covered us up with towels and sheets, I held her tight and said, "Please, you have to be quiet. You can let it all out in a few minutes." Laura squeezed me even tighter and grew still.

We felt the cart rolling down the hall and then into what must have been the same freight elevator we had just taken up. Then we felt the vertical movement as the elevator descended.

We heard the elevator doors open, and then we were rolling again. Instead of rolling on carpet, this was louder, like concrete. The loading dock. We felt a sizable bump as the cart rolled into the van and heard the metallic clunk and tang of the rear van doors closing. The van began moving.

As someone pulled the sheets and towels off of us, John Jr.'s voice came from the driver's seat: "Mr. Roberts, Ms. Baldwin, please say hello to our friend Todd."

Laura and I sat up in the laundry cart and looked around. We were in a cargo van with no windows and a curtain partition between the driver's area and the cargo area. John Jr. was driving us away from the loading dock at the back of the Days Inn. Safe. For now.

Chapter 10

Six Years Earlier...

Jimmy Hughes was escorted into the Oval Office by presidential staff, and the doors were closed. He shook hands with the president and his chief of staff and exchanged pleasantries about his trip and the weather.

The president was warm and friendly to Jimmy, as if seeing an old friend. Jimmy was the president of the International Brotherhood of Teamsters. In fact, the president owed his presidency and his previous seat in the US Senate to support from Jimmy's friends in organized labor.

"Well, Jimmy," started the president, "it's nice to see you. What brings you to town?"

"Thank you, Mr. President. Karl said this would be a private meeting." Right down to business. Karl was the most respected political strategist the Democrats have ever had. The president also owed his presidency to the strategy and calculations of Karl.

The president raised an eyebrow, tilted his head, and, with an alarmed look, glanced at his chief of staff. He realized he had showed too much concern.

That was smooth, thought Jimmy Hughes. *Hell, I've been active in politics decades longer than this yokel.* The president was somewhat famous for his inability to speak without his teleprompter. Every time he tried flying solo, his words were peppered with "uhhhs" and long, awkward pauses. It was sometimes painful to watch. It didn't surprise Jimmy that the president looked to his chief of staff.

To deescalate the situation, Jimmy decided to downplay the actual nature of the meeting. He said, "Early campaign strategy ideas." He looked at the president's chief of staff, held out his palms, and shrugged. "You know Karl. He's crazy about leaks. Nothing personal, but Karl insists, at least for now, that campaign strategy ideas be vetted by the president." He rolled his eyes as if he could care less if the president's chief of staff sat in on the meeting.

The president knew full well what "Karl said this would be a private meeting" meant. And he didn't like it. But he took the cue. He smiled and shook his head as if Karl's paranoia was silly. Then he turned to his chief of staff and said, "You have a crazy day today, don't you?"

The chief of staff did not like being excluded from anything. Especially from meetings the president had from time to time with high-level lobbyists for the unions. But he was no fool at taking a hint, which was a sugarcoated order from the president of the United States of America.

He agreed. "I'll be here until two a.m. again tonight, so I'll let you two catch up while I get back to work." He nodded to Jimmy and was out the door. He was suspicious of Jimmy and his associates, and he hated being out of the loop—and rarely was.

After the last such private meeting, the president vetoed a popular bipartisan bill to build an oil pipeline from Canada to Texas. The project would have created more than thirty thousand jobs at a time when the economy was sputtering. It would have also reduced America's energy dependence on extreme radicals in the Middle East in favor of friendly neighbors in Canada. The reduction in transportation costs alone was projected to shave twenty cents per gallon off the price American consumers paid at the pump.

A pipeline was the cheapest, safest, and most efficient way to ship petroleum products. Oil from the Middle East had to be shipped in oil tankers, halfway around the world. Even most environmentalists favored the safety of pipelines over the risks of oil spills from tanker ships and train cars. But other environmentalists invariably tried to block every new pipeline from being built.

The president showed Jimmy to a couch in the Oval Office and sat down in a large armchair to Jimmy's right.

"Mr. President, do I need to remind you on whose behalf I speak?"

"No," the president muttered, less upbeat than before. Jimmy was here on behalf of Karl. This was no longer a social call. The president took off his glasses and began to rub the bridge of his nose. Karl had a history of calling in favors, like the pipeline veto. The president thought, *What does Karl want this time?*

Karl was known, not just as someone who could get meetings with the highest-level officials but as a person who could turn in bona fide chits at those meetings. Using Jimmy as the messenger, Karl and his vast alliance of businessmen and lobbyists were about to cash in the biggest chit ever.

But the president did not know that, so he decided to draw a line in the sand. "Tell Karl I will always consider him a friend, but there are limits to friendship. My veto of the Keystone oil pipeline cost me a lot of votes. And the damage was far worse than Karl predicted." Jimmy didn't know which the president was concerned about—economic damage or political damage.

But lines in the sand were temporary and illusive, easily brushed over and filled in, to the point of disappearing. Jimmy nodded. No more calling in favors, attempting to influence. As expected, it was time to raise the stakes. It was time to cross the president's red line.

Karl was one of those rare people that came to be known by just his first name. Like Bono, Cher, or Madonna, everyone in politics knew Karl by one name. He was the most successful political strategist ever. He was loved by his allies on the left and feared by his opponents on the right. He had managed numerous successful campaigns for Congress and various governorships, culminating in three successful presidential campaigns. No other strategist, Democrat or Republican, had ever come close to this astounding track record.

It had been almost ten years since Karl had managed a political campaign. But he was still a kingmaker. He worked as a lobbyist for specific issues and specific candidates. He was a political consultant who was paid big bucks for offering his insights on how to win a campaign, how to spin a bill to get it passed, or in some cases, how to ensure a bill did not get passed. These days, he did not have to tire himself with the day to day operations of a long, arduous campaign. He gave his Solomon-like advice and then left the details to others. Karl had become a very rich man in the last ten years.

He worked for a wealthy alliance of billionaires. Some were US citizens, but most were not. These billionaires manipulated the policies of the US government to the benefit of their global business interests. Karl now worked exclusively for this elite group of wealthy businessmen, known as B6. The name came from the fact that the group initially consisted of six billionaires. Now, the alliance had grown to include more than forty wealthy businessmen. Karl himself did not even know everyone in the alliance, only that they paid him well. While B6 funded everything and dictated policy, they relied on Karl for wisdom and guidance in the execution of their plans. Of course, money was no object.

Many years ago, B6 began lobbying for individual bills in Congress as well as for specific rules from various government agencies. In time, B6 grew frustrated with the difficulty and uncertainty of America's democratic process. Thus they started a "farm team" of young politicians in the hope that some of their candidates (in their view, they owned these candidates) would win small, local elections. With luck, they hoped a few might make it to the US Congress or to various governors' mansions. Due to some good planning and more than a bit of luck, one of their protégés now sat in the White House.

The Keystone oil pipeline would have decimated one of the founding B6 members most profitable businesses, the largest fleet of mega oil tanker ships. The oil tankers, owned by a French billionaire, were overbooked for the next ten years, and it took almost that long to bring a new ship online. The tankers took about two years to actually build, but every step in the process was overregulated and tangled up in red tape. Designs and the actual construction were subject to inspections and required approvals by multiple jurisdictions at every step.

Years ago, after acquiring several of the largest tanker fleets through mergers and acquisitions, the French billionaire himself had lobbied for the red tape, anonymously, through various environmental groups. Now, his fleet of oil tankers had a virtual monopoly that was guaranteed for at least ten years. Naturally, the pipeline had to be stopped at all costs. This was a very tall order, because the pipeline had bipartisan support and was beneficial to America in multiple ways.

Jimmy delivered the message to the president. "I will be brief. Two things. One, the UAW is getting killed in this auto bankruptcy. We need some preferential treatment." Jimmy was referring to the imminent bankruptcy of one of the big three US automakers. At ninety billion dollars, it was about to become the largest bankruptcy in US history.

"I sympathize with you. And with the UAW. But I am not in a position to help you. You and Karl should know that this country has well established laws governing bankruptcy proceedings. The UAW is an unsecured creditor. Period. Even if I wanted to help you, what could I do?"

Jimmy was ready for this and did not hesitate to say, "Bully pulpit. You persuade the other stakeholders to vote to approve a reorganization that recognizes the rights of the UAW."

"Rights? What rights?" The president scoffed. "The UAW is an unsecured creditor that, according to the rule of law, needs to get in line with all the other unsecured creditors."

Jimmy, sensing that he was not going to convince the president said, "Do you know why you are president right now? If you didn't agree with us and the UAW, Karl told me to remind you that he made you!"

The president knew this was true. Karl and his people had flexed their muscles, back in 2006, to get him appointed to a US Senate seat in Illinois. The seat was vacated by a bribery scandal that resulted in resignations and jail terms for both the previous senator and the Illinois governor. Four of the past seven Illinois governors had been sentenced to prison. This was the political cesspool from which the president was drafted. The president knew how to play ball, and he also knew that Karl and his associates in organized labor were influential in the decision to appoint him to the vacated Senate seat. They had lobbied for him. However, the president did not know that B6 had purchased his senate seat for him.

After B6 bought the senate seat, Karl was the only democratic strategist to advocate the relatively unknown senator from Illinois as a Democratic presidential candidate. Other Democrats scoffed at the idea of putting the Illinois senator at the top of their ticket. Not a recognizable name...no prior political experience...no real world business experience...a part-time college professor for heaven's sake!

But old Karl got his way. And he turned out to be right! A no-name candidate was just what the electorate was looking for versus all the career politicians. Voters had grown weary and cynical of the Washington establishment. The young president was an outsider, if nothing else.

But he was also the president of the United States of America, and it was hard not to let that go to your head. He brimmed with self-confidence, stood straight with perfect posture, and spoke in a tone that, although bordering on arrogance, implied strong leader during a time of economic difficulties.

Since his inauguration, nobody had ever spoken to him as Jimmy Hughes just had.

"Do you realize who you are talking to?" the president demanded. And in the Oval Office no less! The president had grown accustomed to being treated with awed respect. Not like this. Not from this piece of crap! After his inauguration, he had gone on a world tour where he was met with large standing ovations multiple times per day. He was getting angry with Jimmy.

Sensing that he was about to get kicked out of the Oval Office before presenting his case, Jimmy said, "Mr. President, before we continue I think you should see something very important." He pulled out a small tablet computer, clicked "play," and handed it to the president.

The president took the tablet and began watching a video. It was a gay sex orgy, featuring himself.

He knew it was from about ten years ago, long before he had even entered politics. He hoped that maybe it would have poor definition. Maybe it would be difficult to identify any of the participants. Maybe it could be dismissed as a fake.

Unfortunately, the video was all too clear, and the president was all too identifiable. Still carrying the tablet and watching the video, he got up and walked around his desk. Never taking his eyes off the tablet, he slunk down in his chair. He was speechless. He had not known this video existed.

In truth, the president owed his career to this video. B6 had selected him to be appointed to the vacated Senate seat in Illinois because of this tape. They had almost selected another more experienced candidate. But successful politicians sometimes forgot about the folks who helped them get there. In fact, it appeared Karl was already losing his sway with the president after just a few favors. Years earlier, B6 gave the Illinois Senate seat to someone they could bank on controlling.

Jimmy decided to adopt a softer, more subdued tone. That was the funny thing about true power: you could be quiet and soft spoken. Men of true power did not need to raise their voices.

"What the hell is this?" the president asked, more defeated and upset than angry. The color and energy had already drained from his face and his voice. He pushed the tablet computer back across his desk to Jimmy, who had followed him to the desk and took a seat opposite him. The president didn't need to see more. In fact he couldn't bear to watch anymore.

"It is not just a gay orgy," Jimmy said, "It's a meth-fueled gay orgy. You can be clearly seen smoking meth."

The president just sat in depressed silence and despair. That was all no longer a part of his life, hadn't been for some time. The president had thought, and hoped, that those days were long since forgotten. He never imagined it had been captured on video! He was now married and had two young daughters. Tens of millions idolized him. He was mortified. Drug use or a heterosexual sex scandal could sink him. Drugs and gay sex were unthinkable to Americans when it came to their president. He was already imagining the nightmare this could create in the news media. Hypocrite. Coward. Druggie. Irresponsible. Bad role model.

Jimmy continued, "My clients always thought that if you got this far, there was a risk you might start believing too much in yourself. So I am here to remind you. You were nobody. A community organizer. An unemployed lawyer. My clients took you from a nobody community organizer and got you appointed to the US Senate! The US freak'n Senate! Hell, you never even ran for any political office until you ran for president!"

Jimmy paused as he pondered this truth. He spoke softly and shook his head in disbelief. "Unbelievable, when you think about it. None of the other Democrats dared enter the race against a popular Republican incumbent with a sky-high wartime approval rating. And so they put you up—a sacrificial one-term senator from Illinois. And of course, even that was only because Karl backed you."

Leading up to the 2008 presidential election, nobody thought the Republican incumbent could be beaten. So the usual democrat suspects sat out, knowing that a drubbing in the presidential election would mark the last run of their careers. Most politicians got one shot at president. Out of the blue, the Federal Reserve came to the Democrats' rescue by raising interest rates too far, too fast.

Right now, as the president pondered the improbable chain of events that catapulted him into the White House, he could not shake the idea that much of it was due to luck. It was universally accepted that the Fed's tightening was a colossal economic mistake.

The rest was now history. The overly tight monetary policy caused an unexpected recession. With the economy in trouble and unemployment rising, the unbeatable Republican president had become vulnerable. At the same time, Americans were growing tired of the once popular war. But it was too late for the strongest and most likely Democratic presidential contenders to enter the race. Their party had already picked a no-name senator from Illinois.

Jimmy was enjoying this a bit too much. "To be honest, we never thought you would win, but my clients like to have call options with unlimited upside in their portfolio. You were just one of those call options. Granted, you sounded so damn good on the stump: Hope! Change!" he mocked the president. "Who cares that you never ran a campaign before? Hell, you never ran anything before! You got elected without even articulating a single policy—unless you call "Hope and Change" a policy. The election was a referendum on the economy; voters never knew you. But I'll be damned—you exude a helluva lot of confidence for someone with no experience. And voters like confidence!"

A thousand thoughts raced through the president's head. But all he could do was weakly interject, "Do you realize you are breaking at least a dozen laws here?"

Jimmy rose to his feet and spoke through clenched teeth, "Laws! Gimme a break!" He jabbed his finger when he spoke. "You better understand where I stand on this. I don't give a rat's ass about bribery, extortion, or the fact that this video," he said, shaking his finger at the tablet computer, "would never be admissible in a court of law." Pointing at the president, he continued, "You live and die in the court of public opinion!"

Sitting back down and regaining full composure, Jimmy said, "I assume you are recording this conversation."

This was true, as so many presidents had since Nixon. In fact, the president was recording everything in the Oval Office on both video and audio. At this moment, the president doubted the wisdom of this policy. He thought he was making a bunch of cool clips of the "president in action" for his future presidential library. He was known for enunciating everything so clearly. Wouldn't it look great to have videos of him in his arrogant, professorial tone lecturing people: "Let me be perfectly clear…"

He imagined how this episode would play and began to feel nauseated.

Jimmy continued, "I don't care about breaking the law. I will go to jail for our cause. And this will stop with me. Trust me—we have evaluated and prepared for this possibility. I will go down alone. No bigger fish with me. You see, we are in a war, and I am a proud foot soldier. Union membership has been declining for fifty years, but we are taking a stand, and we will fight this war with everything we have."

Jimmy's passion rose as he continued. He was now pacing back and forth. "It's time for some of those Tea Party sons of bitches to be taken out! This is just the first of many battles. Besides, in this war I don't die. Worst case, I go to jail and become a celebrity. When I get out, I will be a hero to the labor movement, and I will be rich! So forget about me. Focus on you."

Jimmy paused for effect and glanced at the tablet between them. "This will define you."

The president swallowed hard. He knew Jimmy was right about that.

Jimmy said, "You can go down admirably as the first African-American president of the United States of America. Or you can go down in such flaming disgrace that previous presidential scandals won't even seem like scandals. Think about what your fall from grace would do to the black community. Think about the ammunition it would give to low-life racists!"

He paused again for effect. "Or return a few small favors to the folks who put you here, and preserve your good place in history." He smiled. "If you leave here of your own accord, you will make five hundred grand a pop for repeating the same speech over and over again. And history will remember you as the first black president. History books won't delve into the nitty-gritty policy issues of the day, like this auto bankruptcy. That will be forgotten about."

The president sat in silence. But Jimmy could see he was weighing the options. The president felt like he had aged about twenty years in the last few minutes.

Jimmy reassured him, "Nobody of course has to know about this video. Ever. That is our assurance to you. As for the bankruptcy plan, worst case, cynics say you pulled a favor for organized labor, a big political donor. So what? Show me a president in the last two hundred years that didn't help the folks who got him elected!" He paused to stress the next point. "And you can say you did it on principle, not because of campaign contributions." Jimmy smiled.

Relative to the sex tape, the president began to think how nice it would be to be accused of stealing from old lady bondholders to give to political donors. As president, he had grown accustomed to a cacophony of criticism and cynical motive guessing. It came with the office.

In fact everything was starting to sound a whole lot better to the president. Just a political payoff to the unions. Not a gay sex tape cover-up.

The president straightened some papers on his desk and said flatly, "You said you were here for two things."

Jimmy smiled to himself and relaxed a bit. He correctly surmised that he had won the president's intervention in the auto bankruptcy.

"Yes, Mr. President," he said, adopting a far more respectful tone to the commander-in-chief, who was about to catapult the UAW up in the capital structure. "We also have an issue with Aerowing's plans to manufacture their new jetliner in South Carolina."

"Are you kidding me?" Nothing could have surprised the president at this moment, but Jimmy just did.

"No, Mr. President. We are very serious. Up until now, Aerowing has built its planes in Washington State, which offers workers the benefit of compulsory union membership and the mandatory payments of union dues. As you know, those mandatory union dues were critical in getting you elected. And, as you know, South Carolina is a right-to-work state, which gives workers a choice to join the union—and pay union dues—or not. Aerowing is obviously relocating to cripple the unions."

The president tried hard to hide his shock and disbelief and simply understand what was being asked of him. "Okay. A private, respected American company that has created hundreds of thousands of jobs in this country has decided to open up a new manufacturing facility in South Carolina instead of Washington State." His tone was rife with, "What the hell do you expect me to do about it?"

"Yes, sir, I understand what you are getting at. But we can't let these bastards kill the unions by putting these jobs in South Carolina. We can't let them hire nonunion workers."

The president was now exhausted and exasperated. "So what, damn it? What the hell do you expect me to do?"

"Beauty is, you do nothing. You remain silent, at least publicly. But, on your orders, the National Labor Relations Board files a suit against Aerowing alleging unfair labor practices. We have a bunch of smart lawyers that have already drawn up the complaint. In short they say that, by relocating from a union state to a right-to-work state, Aerowing has, prima facie, adopted an unfair labor practice and thus violated the National Labor Relations Act of 1935."

He let the president soak this in before continuing. "We have a detailed plan for how to implement both the auto bankruptcy and the NLRB complaint. The arguments are very elegant, and they complement each other. To advance the unions over other creditors in the auto bankruptcy, you say with a straight face, 'No reorganization will be successful if the company does not recognize the needs of its valuable American workers.' Karl says that sound bite alone ought to carry Michigan and Ohio in the next election."

Now he had the president's attention.

"Our plan has you bashing what are likely to be the largest bond owner holdouts—hedge funds and banks—for being greedy and for not sacrificing along with everyone else. Of course the UAW will very publicly make some token concessions."

Under the established rule of law, the UAW would have lost everything in the bankruptcy. The automaker could have started anew with a clean slate—no more burdensome union contracts. If this plan worked, the UAW would remain intact, save for a few concessions similar to what were routinely given up in the course of collective bargaining agreements. The UAW was about to emerge unscathed on the other side of a bankruptcy designed to shed it.

Jimmy gave the president some time to ponder this and then continued the sales pitch. "Politically, we think you can be seen as a helpful mediator in the bankruptcy. Helping all parties work out a compromise, saving a big American auto company and a hundred thousand union jobs in the process. As for the holdouts to the bankruptcy reorganization, we will orchestrate simultaneous declarations from the SEC, the Fed, and FINRA stating that they are reevaluating their oversight of hedge funds and banks. It will all be done with a plausible fig leaf of legitimate basis. But with both presidential and regulatory pressures mounting, we are confident enough constituents in the bankruptcy will cave to our demands."

The president was shocked by the audacity of the plan. He shook his head slowly, almost imperceptibly, from side to side as he thought about it. But the more he thought about it, the more he began to feel it might work.

Jimmy said, "Meanwhile, Aerowing will receive an unscheduled visit from FAA inspectors to help them appreciate the government bullying of hedge funds and banks for what it is. They will get the message: if you ever want to sell another plane to the US government or get FAA approval for a new passenger jet, don't fuck with the unions!"

The president nodded.

"This is just a broad overview. We have the details and will work with your staff on making this work. You can rest assured that Karl himself says this is a brilliant and doable plan."

The president stood, signaling an end to the meeting. All White House visitors were logged by the secret service, including the time they arrived and the time they left. These records were available via Freedom of Information requests, and the media always scrutinized White House comings and goings. The president thought it wise to keep this particular White House visit as short as possible. Later, it could be explained as a simple hello.

Jimmy, taking the president's cue, stood and said, "I should let you get back to work. But Karl wanted me to give you a heads up on the theme and tone of your reelection campaign."

And, the president now remembered, his chief of staff might expect to get filled in on this aspect of the meeting. The president was at least no longer afraid of what bomb Jimmy might drop next. Karl was a wizard at crafting campaign messages. He had two unique gifts: understanding what would play with the electorate and what would not, as well as a detailed knowledge of which sectors of the electorate would be the deciding factors in the next election. Other political consultants had one or the other of these gifts, but not both. Karl had often predicted the eventual outcome of a candidate's pandering to a special block of voters. Many times, candidates connected with a target block of voters, only to learn later that the particular block they pandered to couldn't deliver the win.

Seeing that he had the president's full attention, Jimmy said, "Democrat or Republican makes no difference. History shows that when the economy is struggling the incumbent loses. Period. As you know, we have a big problem here because the economy has not responded to your policies, and you can't blame your predecessor forever. Historically, you have no chance of getting reelected."

The president nodded his understanding of this reality.

"Karl says this leaves one possible winning strategy. A Hail Mary of sorts. You are going to divide the country. The rich versus the poor, the haves versus the have-nots. We are talking class warfare the likes of which this country has never seen."

The president grimaced. He was elected to unite, not divide. He had promised to reach across party lines. As a relative outsider, he had vowed to change the partisan atmosphere in Washington.

Jimmy anticipated the president's discomfort with this strategy. Or, more accurately, Karl had. "We know this strategy sounds ugly, but please hear it out, and think it over. That's all Karl asks you to do for now—think about it."

The president nodded, but he was skeptical.

Jimmy argued the case further. "Unemployment is ten percent. More if you count all the people who are underemployed or just gave up looking for a job. Karl wants me to stress: no president has ever been reelected with unemployment at ten percent. Look, we want you to win more than anyone. But your supporters are dreaming if they think you can buck this reality without a radical new strategy."

Jimmy paused to gauge the president's reaction. He thought he was beginning to convince him, at least a little. He concluded by saying, "You have no choice but to divide the country. The evil millionaires and billionaires versus the working class."

The president interrupted sarcastically, "You mean the evil job creators versus the middle class Americans in need of those very jobs?"

"I get your point. And Karl knew you would have valid counterpoints. But desperate times call for desperate measures. If we execute this successfully, the voters will blame the wealthy elite for their problems instead of you and your failed policies. It's that simple."

"Karl believes this is the only viable strategy?"

"Yes. It even worked for Hitler. Blame somebody else. Harness the people's anger."

The president winced and shook his head at the Hitler comparison. But he also knew there was some truth to it.

Jimmy added, "Do the math. You will alienate one percent of the voters—one percent! Inflammatory class warfare rhetoric wins you countless votes, and it only upsets one percent! You have to ask yourself how much of that wealthiest one percent would have voted for a Democrat anyway?"

The president nodded. It was ugly, but it made a lot of sense. A helluva lot more sense than the oil pipeline veto, he mused to himself.

The president began ushering Jimmy to the door. *A new campaign strategy*, he thought. This gave him something real to tell his chief of staff when he inevitably asked what the meeting with Jimmy was about. The president couldn't tell him the truth—sex tape and blackmail! Even his own chief of staff would have to believe that the decisions to intervene in the auto bankruptcy and the airplane manufacturer's new plant were the president's own.

"Thank you," said the president, thinking about the new campaign strategy that he would share with his chief of staff.

A split second later, he felt stupid for thanking a man who had just threatened and blackmailed him.

"Karl thinks you should start thinking about the class warfare rhetoric now. The auto bankruptcy and Aerowing's new nonunion factory are ideal opportunities to open up this dialogue with the voters. But go slow, Karl advises. Plant the seeds of division now. Then dial up the rhetoric later. We can't let voters' anger peak too soon. We want to time the crescendo of class warfare resentment for next November."

The president nodded in silence.

Jimmy departed, and the president stood motionless in the Oval Office for a full minute. He was contemplating the merit of Karl's new campaign strategy. He shook his head in disbelief as he realized that, in order to get reelected, the president of the United States was about to bash something that had stood for centuries as one of the greatest symbols of America—hard-working, successful Americans, the American Dream.

Jimmy Hughes was a blue-blooded American, current Teamsters president, and son of a past Teamsters president. He believed in, and fought for, unions in America. He was a patriotic American. But politics always made for strange bedfellows.

The true goal of B6 and its foreign billionaire members was to support unions in America as a means of crippling the US businesses that their collective empire competed against. Billionaire members of B6 owned everything from French airplane manufacturers to Chinese automakers.

The small amount of money these foreigners had invested in affecting US policies had already been earned back many times over through a few, simple red tape edicts from Washington bureaucrats.

Now, they owned the White House.

Chapter 11

In the van on the way to John Jr.'s house in Hinsdale, I spilled my guts to Laura. I told her I loved her and wanted to marry her. I didn't hold anything back. I admitted my insecurities over the size of her engagement ring. I told her what a fool I had been. She started crying, tears of joy, and we held each other tightly until we arrived at John Jr.'s house. She must have known I meant it, because I never open up about my feelings. I thought being emotionless, or at least concealing my emotions, was strong. Boys don't cry, man up—call it what you will. Hanging out with a bunch of tough lacrosse players in college did not lend itself to warm, touchy-feely moments. And my current work environment? Forget about it—no room for emotion there. Yet here I was, saying these things in the van, in the presence of other people. It was cathartic, even liberating. Laura and I held each other in blissful silence.

John Jr. said, "Laura, may I please see your phone?" He must have been waiting to ask Laura that the whole time I was spilling my guts to her.

Laura handed her phone to him, a bit puzzled. John Jr. powered Laura's cell phone off as he spoke. "Sorry, but we have to power it off. Otherwise it can be used to locate you."

Laura and I nodded. I thought she might protest, but she didn't.

Todd said, "You may remember seeing in the news: this capability did come in handy by locating that kidnapped girl in California a few months ago. We use cell phones but only temporary, prepaid, burner phones."

About thirty minutes later, we arrived at John Jr.'s house. He ushered Laura and me into the war room and made introductions. Then he asked his crew, "How many did we tag and release?"

He was speaking both to those in the room and over the speakerphone to his crew in the field, because Nate's voice replied through the speakerphone: "Three. Mr. Slick, an older gentleman who came with Mr. Slick to the Board of Trade, plus the guy in the elevator at the Days Inn."

"Tell me about the gentleman with Mr. Slick."

"Older gentleman, maybe sixty years old, well dressed. Appears Mr. Slick and Mr. Elevator take orders from Mr. Gentleman."

John Strong Jr.'s team was not very creative at coming up with names for suspects. Just as John Jr. had dubbed the first assassin Mr. Slick, now Nate had dubbed the other two. Although not exactly creative, their system was simple and effective. From then on, Strong and Associates pursued Mr. Slick, Mr. Elevator, and Mr. Gentleman. In fact, Strong and Associates would continue to use these code names even after they learned a suspect's true identity. Better to avoid the use of actual names when you never knew who might overhear, which was a huge risk with most forms of communication these days.

John Jr. nodded in approval, processing what he had just been told.

"One more thing," said Nate. "Mr. Gentleman uses an EPhone." Although I didn't have one, the EPhone was the world's most popular smartphone.

John Jr. enthused, "Great news! Think you can get it? How long do you need?"

Nate replied, "I'm on him right now. All I need is one chance, or one mistake by him. I can download the history on a high-speed compact flash in less than a minute."

"Good luck, Nate. I want that EPhone." John Jr. signed off.

Laura and I looked at each other and shrugged. Laura asked John Jr., "Mind if I ask what the EPhone is all about?"

"There is a hidden app on EPhones. It tracks every phone call and text message and also synchs with the EPhone's built in GPS navigation software. If we can download that data, we will have every number this Mr. Gentleman called or texted along with a detailed history of where he has been."

Laura said, "The EPhone can do all that? I have an EPhone! Most of my friends have EPhones!"

John Jr. continued, "Most EPhone users don't realize their phones secretly track so much activity. The techies who stumbled on this hidden app have two schools of thought. First, the cynics say Big Brother has arrived. Only he is not the government. He is for-profit businesses looking to sell your personal information to marketers." He shook his head in wonder. "Think of the targeted marketing they can do with that kind of detailed info on you, tracking everywhere you go, every call you make, and every text message you send or receive."

"Kind of creepy," I said. For the first time in a while, I was glad that I couldn't afford a cell phone. Who knows? If I had an EPhone, I might be dead already.

Nodding in agreement, Isaac mused, "Creepy, yeah. But think about it: How much would a retail store or a restaurant pay to target advertisements and coupons to those people known to drive by their location? Or how about you receive hotel offers just because you mentioned "Cancun" in a text message? Customized, targeted advertising is the new wave; it is changing the world."

I asked, "How can this be legal? Where are the privacy advocates?"

John Jr. nodded. "The fans of EPhone are a little more fanatical about their beloved E-Corp than fans of the Green Bay Packers. They dismiss all this controversy about invasion of privacy and tracking software. They say it is simply the smart technology built into the GPS navigation software. It enhances the navigation capabilities by recognizing a traffic jam, say because other EPhone users are traveling slowly on the Kennedy Expressway. It is the best source of real-time traffic data because the EPhone is so popular. The EPhone fanatics claim E-Corp innocently built this feature for real-time traffic data and did not even realize this navigation history was being archived, along with all the calls and texts."

Laura asked, "Can't you delete calls and texts?"

John Jr. replied, "Good point, and no. You can delete them from the display. It will look like they have been deleted. But it is not very difficult to get into the storage on the phone and that mini hard drive stores everything."

Isaac held up a pair of tweezers in which he was holding a thin wafer the size of a fingernail. He said, "This is a SIM card. Every cell phone has a built in SIM card with an encrypted key. The only way a cell phone can work on a cellular network is with one of these. Every time you make a call or send a text, the network authenticates your phone based on this. Once this digital handshake between the phone and the cellular tower confirms your phone, the communication is permitted to proceed over the network. This unique identification process is what makes it possible to track a cell phone's complete history—calls, texts, even location. Simpler, unencrypted communications, such as walkie-talkies, are impossible to trace or track."

John Jr. said, "Bottom line, Mr. Gentleman's EPhone is more valuable to us right now than it is to some targeted marketing firm."

Turning to me, John Jr. said, "As you know, you are safe here. We want you and Laura to be comfortable. Just let us know what you want to eat or anything else. We are in a bit of a waiting mode here as we track and eavesdrop on Mr.

Slick, Mr. Elevator, and Mr. Gentleman. But our team is doing all that."

Laura and I nodded.

"You still have an important role here. We need you to reconstruct yesterday's trading day based on the box of order tickets. We know the telephone audiotapes were stolen. Maybe you can figure out why."

A realization hit me. "Wait! There is a backup tape. I don't think Maco Commodities ever envisioned someone stealing the trading line audiotape reels. But there is another independent tape, just in case there was a power failure or a glitch in the recording machine."

John Jr. said, "We need that tape. Where is it? How do we get it? And do you think Mr. Slick and company know about it?"

I thought for a few moments. "I doubt Mr. Slick's friends know about it. Very few employees know about this backup tape system. As far as I know, it has never been needed. It is located under the Maco Commodities Trading Desk that I sit at every day, mixed in with all the other computer towers, network cables, phone lines, and electric cords."

John Jr., "So it is on the trading floor?"

"Yeah. Under the Maco counter just outside the T-Bond pit."

"Sounds like a job for Nate."

Another thought entered my mind. "The original tapes are saved and placed in storage, all organized by date. The backup tape on the floor was intended for temporary emergencies. It runs on a continuous loop."

"How long is the loop?" asked Isaac.

"When it was installed, we were told forty-eight hours. But so far, we've never had to use it."

John Jr. spoke to Nate over the speakerphone. "Nate, you getting all this?"

"Yes, sir," Nate replied. "Under normal circumstances, I could blend in during the day and go on the floor dressed as a tech or electrician. Crowded place like that, people wouldn't even notice me, and no one would care to check my credentials. But since Minter's high-profile murder, and Mr. Roberts's disappearance, I don't think I can go snooping around the Maco trading desk without attracting attention."

I said, "I still think during the day is the best time. And like you said, the exchange floor is so crowded no one takes notice. After hours, the floor is empty except for security guards. You will stick out like a sore thumb and have to deal with security guards asking you questions."

Bob handed me a pad of paper and a pencil and said, "Show us the layout."

I explained the layout as I sketched a picture of the pit along with the outer walls of the exchange floor to show them where the bond pit was located. Then I drew the trading desks. Although they were called desks, they were actually long counters. Each clearing firm had a designated spot where an employee like me could man the phones. Other phone clerks from other clearing firms sat on my right and left. There were four rows of trading desks wrapping around the bond pit in a series of steps rising up from the pit so that all phone clerks would have a direct line of sight into the pit.

John Jr. said, "So underneath these counters is a big mess of phone cords, computer towers, power strips, electric cords, Ethernet cables, other miscellaneous equipment—and this continuous-loop tape recorder?"

I nodded.

Bob pointed to my diagram and said, "Show me exactly where you sit, where the clerks near you sit, and where this tape recorder is."

I think I saw where he was going with this. I said, "The next clerk, about six feet to my right, is with Dreyfus Corp. The tape recorder is right in the middle of us, under the counter."

Bob smiled and nodded. Before he could ask anything further, I said, "Dreyfus employees wear distinct trading jackets—white with blue trim and a big patch with their logo, the head of a lion, on the shoulders."

Bob and John Jr. exchanged a knowing glance. Bob smiled and said, "And how hard is it to borrow one of these jackets?"

"Most employees check their trading jackets at the coat check on the ground floor. There will be tons of Dreyfus Corp. jackets in there." I paused as I had another realization. "Most employees leave a lot of junk in their trading jackets— including their employee keycards to swipe the turnstile to get access. The keycards are identical to mine. The same keycard works for both the ground floor lobby turnstiles and the turnstiles leading to the exchange floor. Dreyfus is one of the biggest firms on the exchange. The floor is crawling with employees wearing those white-and-blue jackets. No one would notice another new employee, happens all the time."

John Jr. patted me on the back and said, "I like the way this kid thinks."

Bob nodded, "I can do this. Nate has his hands full. Isaac, can you help Christian pinpoint the exact type and size of tape reel I'll need to swap out?"

Isaac nodded and started Googling images of continuous-loop tape recorders. It didn't take long to find what I thought was the model of tape recorder. Bob asked me a few more questions about the floor layout, and then he left to purchase an identical tape reel and go to the CBOT.

Chapter 12

Laura and I sat at John Jr.'s kitchen table. The box of trading tickets from the day before was strewn across the table, and Laura was helping me put them in chronological order, based on the fact that every order ticket was time and date stamped. It was hard to believe the trading tickets were just from yesterday. So much had happened since then, it felt like yesterday's trading session was eons ago.

As we reviewed the trading tickets, I began to recall the actual session. It was one of those choppy days where a lot of locals lost money. Most locals and brokers became very inhospitable when they were losing money. Yelling more. Pushing more. Swearing more. I felt sorry for their wives on their losing days. If I ever got a shot in the pit, I knew that I would be like the Iceman. Calm, cool, and collected, taking it all in a stride. Win some, lose some, all just part of the game.

Iceman was the nickname given to the biggest local in the T-Bond pit. He made or lost hundreds of thousands of dollars every day. On some days, he made or lost seven digits. Yesterday was memorable because it was one of those days—Iceman made at least a million dollars. But by his stone face and calm demeanor, no one could ever tell if Iceman was winning or losing. Most couldn't even figure out if he was long or short. If they did know, it was by watching the Iceman trade and keeping track of his position, not by looking at his expressionless countenance.

I had learned from watching traders that composure was essential to long-term success in this stressful business. Now, watching John Jr. and his crew, I was learning that remaining cool under pressure was helpful in a different line of work. Worrying never produced anything. I was determined that, if and when I became a pit broker, I would have the ability to understand that occasionally losing large amounts of money simply came with the territory. No reason to get depressed about the bad days or euphoric about the good days. Stay on an even keel. Iceman.

After several hours of painstakingly reconstructing the order tickets on the large kitchen table, Laura and I took a break. Emily joined us. Over a snack, I shared with them the story of Iceman's Christmas bonus to his clerk last year.

Every year in December, locals and brokers gave their clerks or assistants bonuses. Last December, Iceman decided to make things a little more interesting. He gave his clerk a choice: "Your Christmas bonus is thirty thousand dollars, or whatever I make or lose today. If I lose money today, you get no bonus. If I make money today, you get whatever I make."

Soon the whole pit was abuzz with talk of Iceman's offer to his assistant. *What would you choose?* Most trader assistants made about thirty thousand dollars per year. So a thirty-thousand-dollar bonus was very important to him. In fact he was counting on it: Take the thirty thousand dollars… or risk getting no bonus at all…or perhaps much more…or perhaps something in between?

Iceman's clerk made a gutsy choice. He needed the thirty thousand, but he decided to go for more and opted for the Iceman's trading day. It was the talk of the trading floor as the Iceman started off the morning with a two-hundred-thousand-dollar loss.

It was an interesting experiment. All the clerks and assistants were now rooting for the Iceman. Seeing their friend stare a thirty-thousand-dollar loss in the eye, I think they all gained a little more respect for the pressure of being a pit trader. For once, the assistant's money was at stake!

By noon, Iceman was up four hundred thousand dollars on the day. You could see the clerk's face: "Let's call it a day—go home!" But that is not how traders operate. Take the good and the bad—never leave when you are up or when you are down. The clerk had seen his boss lose hundreds of thousands in the last couple hours of a day many times. The clerk was sweating. I saw him popping Tums for the first time ever. As a joke, other traders began offering Tums to him.

The last two hours of the day, Iceman made and lost fifty thousand here and there. At the end of the day, he was up three hundred and fifty thousand dollars. Hundreds of locals and brokers congratulated Iceman's very relieved, but stressed out and exhausted, assistant. They patted him on the back, gave him a bear hug, put him in a headlock, and rubbed his head. What a day!

With yesterday's order tickets laid out before us, nothing seemed unusual, except for two order tickets with no account numbers. This happened on rare occasions due to a simple clerical error. But it was intriguing that the only two orders without account numbers were both very large and they were identical but opposite. One was an order to buy ten thousand bonds, the other an order to sell ten thousand bonds.

I explained to Emily that a clerk might sometimes forget to time stamp an order. But it would be very rare for a clerk to not be extra diligent on such a large trade. Adding to the suspicion, both trades were executed at the exact same price, 135-27. Large market orders were unlikely to all be filled entirely at one price. Here, that happened twice. And they were both filled at the same price.

Regulations required that every order have an account number and a time-and-date stamp before it was executed. These rules were designed to ensure that brokerage firms did not show favoritism to their best clients. In the old days, before everything was computerized, when multiple customers bought the same commodity but at different prices, brokerage firms had discretion in how they allocated different trades to different customers at the end of each day. It became such a lopsided game, with preferred customers getting the best fills (lowest prices for buy orders and highest prices for sell orders) and small customers getting screwed, that the CFTC finally stepped in.

In fact, due to the rigged system, more than a few politicians, or in some cases their wives, demonstrated an incredible knack for trading obscure things like cattle futures with spectacular profits. These outrageously and consistently lucky amateur traders attracted scrutiny because politicians often felt obligated to publicly release their tax returns. Although the trading profits seemed to defy all probability, investigators never found proof of wrongdoing, and the investigations were inevitably dropped. The old system was not capable of detecting, let alone proving, such trading abuses. But such abuses were rampant.

Since the implementation of the new rules, along with computerized systems to track and record all trades, every trade was already allocated to a specific customer's account before it was executed. Further, due to the time stamps, it would be impossible to allocate a trade to a 10:03:57 a.m. (to the second), time-stamped order ticket unless that was the price the market was trading at that time. The exchange developed a computerized system to red flag any orders if the time stamp and price did not reconcile with official exchange time and sales data, which was a detailed, second by second price history for each futures contract.

The new rules and computerized systems marked the end of the era of politician's wives/trader/savants. Investor confidence in commodities exchanges increased as these outrageous examples faded. Market participants began to see a level playing field, and trading volumes skyrocketed. Turns out, there were a lot more would-be market participants if the game hadn't been rigged. Exchange volume was still exploding due to these changes six years ago when I got my first job as a runner on the floor.

Chapter 13

Louie entered the war room distracted on his Blackberry. He had just received a message: "Ballistics came in at CPD. The gun they found in Christian's apartment is the gun that killed Thomas Minter."

I swallowed. Laura reached her hand over and patted my leg. I grabbed her hand and held it tight.

John Jr. said, "That was fast."

Louie explained, "Ballistics test only takes an hour or so. Problem is a backlog at CPD. High-profile murder like this, goes to the top of the list." Louie tried to console me, "Not a problem, Christian. We have Mr. Slick on video, planting that gun in your kitchen. Of course none of your fingerprints are on the gun either."

John Jr. said, "We expected this. In fact, this is good. Now, we can connect Mr. Slick to the murder of Minter."

I deadpanned with: "Yeah this is great."

John Jr. smiled. He appreciated my ability to maintain a sense of humor at a time like this. He asked Louie, "Are we going to be seeing Mr. Roberts's picture in the news—wanted for murder?"

"Not for now. But CPD is putting the word out big time with Christian's picture, his license plate, and his vehicle's make and model. All law enforcement agencies have been alerted to help find him."

I asked, "So does that mean my parents aren't going to see my photo on the ten o'clock news with a 'wanted for murder' caption?"

Louie said, "Eventually, I'm afraid they probably will. Right now, CPD would like to draw you in on the pretense that it is simply for questioning. In their mind, you don't know they found the gun or matched the ballistics with the weapon that killed Minter. So they keep the murder charge quiet while they aggressively try to find you. They figure once you see your picture on the news, it will become even harder to find you. I give it a few days. If they can't find you, then they will turn to the public for help. We probably have a few days before your face is on the evening news."

John Jr. said to me, "Well, wanted for murder or not, you still have work to do." He motioned to the box of order tickets.

While we were busy reconstructing the trading session from the box of order tickets, Bob was attempting to get the Maco backup tape, and Nate was pursuing Mr. Gentleman, waiting for an opportunity to access his EPhone.

Mr. Gentleman was staying at the Ritz Carlton Chicago. Located on Michigan Avenue's Magnificent Mile, the Ritz Carlton was in the same building as Water Tower Place, the famous upscale shopping mall. Nate had already installed a smoke detector camera in Mr. Gentleman's room at the Ritz. That was the easy part, because he did it while Mr.

Gentleman was not at the hotel. Now, Nate had to enter his room and copy his EPhone—while the target was still in the room. There are two basic ways to do this—when the target is sleeping or taking a shower.

Back in the war room, Isaac was monitoring the live stream from the smoke-detector camera, while Nate strolled through Water Tower Place. The camera was located in the entryway of the hotel room, near both the hotel room door and the bathroom door. The fisheye lens had a wide view, encompassing both the bathroom door and also in toward the rest of the room.

Isaac radioed Nate. "EPhone is on the desk, charging. Looks like he is about to take a shower."

"Roger."

Nate hustled over to the elevators and went up to the room. He slowed as he approached the door to Mr. Gentleman's room, waiting for confirmation from Isaac. Isaac radioed Nate. "He just started a shower, but he left the bathroom door open. Crack the door, then wait for my signal."

Nate swiped a key card and unlocked the door. It was amazing to me how unsecure even high-end hotels were. Rooms at the Ritz ran about eight hundred dollars per night, yet it was easy—at least for Nate—to find a maid's or a bell-man's key card that worked on all rooms in the hotel.

The door beeped and clicked as Nate swiped the key and unlatched the handle. He opened the door a fraction of an inch and waited.

We needed to make sure Mr. Gentleman did not hear the beep or the door latch. At this point, Nate could abort with no harm done. Isaac had a good view through the open bathroom door. It was interesting to watch this unfold on a TV screen in the war room. We could hear the shower running and see the clear glass beginning to fog over.

Isaac radioed Nate. "No sign he heard the door. You are clear. He won't have a direct view of you, but there will be a reflection in the bathroom mirror visible from the shower. Stay low and get past the bathroom."

Nate slipped in the room, crept low past the open bathroom door, and then stood up and walked over to the desk. We watched from the war room as Nate connected a small notebook computer to Mr. Gentleman's EPhone with a USB cord.

Isaac explained, "Funny thing, he probably has a passcode on his phone, so Nate could not access the phone itself. But plug the smartphone into a computer through a USB port—no passcodes, no security. Download five gigs of data in a minute or two."

It was interesting how casual and clinical Nate and Isaac were. They were breaking and entering while someone was in the room, yet they both seemed calm, even bored. Less than two minutes later, Nate unplugged the smartphone from his notebook and plugged it back into its charger, just as he found it. He walked over to the bathroom door, ducked, and left. He closed the door quietly behind him.

Isaac waited, and then radioed this message: "No reaction. He didn't hear the door close. You are clear."

"Roger."

Mr. Gentleman would have no idea that the entire contents of his smartphone had just been copied.

Chapter 14

Laura and I were sitting around the big conference table in the war room with John Jr., Emily, and Isaac when Bob arrived in an upbeat mood. He pulled out the tape reel.

I asked, "Is that the Maco tape?"

He nodded. "Thanks for your help. It was just like you said. I casually walked up in my borrowed white-and-blue trading jacket, went straight to the machine, and swapped out the tapes. The Maco clerk and the Dreyfus clerk both barely noticed me or didn't seem to care. I had an air about me like I belonged and had a job to do." Bob handed the tape reel to Isaac. "No worries—I replaced this tape with another, so I don't think anyone will ever notice it missing."

About thirty minutes later, Nate arrived. He handed the notebook computer to Isaac and said, with a bit of mock flourish, "Voilà! I give you the entire contents of Mr. Gentleman's EPhone. Let's see what you can pull off the history. We already know who Mr. Gentleman is though—Vince Fleming." He paused and looked around the room, gauging reactions as he continued. No one recognized the name. "Vince Fleming is the special assistant to the deputy chief of staff."

Everybody was silent as the seriousness of this sank in.

John Jr. exclaimed, "A White House staffer?!"

Laura said, "Are you saying the president of the United States is behind this?! The president of the United States is trying to kill Christian!"

John Jr. said, "No, no, that would be a giant leap at this point. We have no connection to the president."

"Not yet," Emily said, narrowing her eyes and smiling.

John Jr. was thinking out loud. "The special assistant to the deputy chief of staff..." He crossed his arms, paced, and rubbed his chin with one hand. "He is an assistant to an assistant to an assistant to the president. No one would recognize him walking down the street—unlike the chief of staff. Hell, most folks wouldn't recognize the deputy chief of staff, this Fleming character's boss. If memory serves, the chief of staff might have two or three deputy chiefs, and they in turn might each have three or four special assistants. So let's not get ahead of ourselves. A lot of these staff positions are patronage. No real responsibility. Just fancy titles and gold-plated, lifetime benefits. Presidents dole them out to their campaign supporters."

Emily focused on what we did have. "Okay, so we have a special assistant to the deputy chief of staff giving orders, trying to kill Mr. Roberts here. A White House employee!"

Bob said,, "And they killed Mr. Minter. Why would anyone in the White House want Minter dead?"

John Jr. said, "Ballistics proved the gun found in Mr. Roberts's apartment killed Mr. Minter. We have a direct link of Mr. Slick to Minter's murder and, perhaps, an indirect link to the White House." John Jr. seemed to have mixed feelings about this new development.

I pondered the fact that a gun found in my apartment killed my boss and mentor. Although John Jr. had already alluded to this being "unpleasant" for me, I was beginning to realize how ugly this might be. I couldn't contain myself and blurted out, "Excuse me, but when do we tell CPD that I didn't shoot Mr. Minter and show them the tape to prove it?"

John Jr. tried to calm me by saying, "Patience, my boy. We can't bust this open too soon without sending all the cockroaches running. It would be nice to link higher-ups before all trails go cold."

Nate added, "It would be easy to disavow a special assistant to a deputy chief of staff—off the reservation, acting on his own. Hell, at this point, we can't even prove the chief of staff is involved, and he is several layers removed from the president."

"I am about to be accused of murder! It will be on the news, with my picture!" I began to imagine what my friends would think—and my parents.

John Jr. softened his tone. "I understand. Look, do you want to nail the lowlife who pulled the trigger? Or do you want to nail the people he works for? The people who really killed Mr. Minter? You may have to endure a little heat to get justice here. Remember, getting to the root of this will make you and Laura much safer."

I processed this and realized he was right. I looked down and shook my head.

John Jr. said, "You can speed things up right now by reviewing this tape." He handed the Maco forty-eight-hour backup tape to Emily. "Emily is assigned to help you. See what you can figure out. What is on the backup tape? Why did someone steal the primary tape? Why did someone kill Thomas Minter?"

With that, Emily left the war room, and Laura and I followed. As we were leaving, John Jr. said to Isaac, "Let's start connecting the dots. What can we learn from Fleming's EPhone?"

Emily, Laura, and I gathered around the large granite kitchen table and examined the stacks of order tickets. Emily placed the backup tape in a playback machine. I was still bothered by the offsetting buy and sell orders, each for ten thousand T-bond contracts, both executed at the exact same price of 135-27. Maybe the trading-line phone tape could shed some light on these orders.

I shared my concern with Emily and Laura as we began listening to the tape. When we had finished listening to the whole tape, no telephone orders were placed that day to either buy or sell the ten thousand bonds in question. Those two orders were the only two orders that lacked account numbers. We listened to the tapes twice to make sure.

There were a handful of ten-thousand-lot orders, but they all reconciled between the backup tape and the orders themselves. We even cross-referenced those valid ten-thousand-lot orders to ensure they meshed with the official CBOT exchange time and sales data. They did.

I could tell that Emily's suspicion was growing, and she seemed to become even more focused. At the same time, we were all exhausted after combing through the tapes, twice. We were tired and perhaps needed a break. I asked her about her career with the secret service.

She explained, "Most people associate the secret service with protecting the president. Agents with squiggly corded earpieces willing to take a bullet." She put one hand to her ear, raised the other one up as if holding a gun, and squinted her eyes. She relaxed and continued, "While this is true, the secret service does much more, including investigations on counterfeiting American currency, money laundering, and financial fraud crimes."

Emily never protected the president; she was one of an elite team of forensic accountants. She performed countless detailed investigations of money laundering and financial frauds. It was a tedious—sometimes frustrating—job, but she pursued it with remarkable tenacity and also demonstrated tremendous insight at unraveling complex financial schemes designed to obfuscate criminal activities. I thought she was the perfect person to unravel these Maco commodities order tickets.

The three of us now had a working theory. The evidence wasn't on the tape, as I had hoped. *It wasn't on the tape!* The two suspicious orders could not be found on the tape recording, and the written orders lacked the proper time-and-date stamp as well as proper account numbers.

We speculated that the orders were never routed to the trading floor or executed in the pit. Rather, it appeared that somebody crossed the two orders with each other and entered them into the clearing system computers, making it appear as if they had both been executed properly in the pit. But it would be impossible to prove the orders never got routed to the pit if the telephone tapes were missing.

You could explain away a missing account number or time-and-date stamp here or there due to clerical error. But there was no reasonable way to explain why neither order showed up on the recorded phone line. The trades were bogus.

Emily asked, "How many telephone clerks like you work the bond pit for Maco?"

"Just me. Maco has other clerks for other pits, but the bond pit is just me."

Emily said, "I think we just figured out why they tried to kill you."

"You mean because I might know these trades never went through my desk?"

"Yes. Besides the phone tapes, which were stolen, you are the only person who could know these trades never went through proper channels. I think this is why you were targeted."

"But so many orders get communicated through me every day. There is a good chance I wouldn't remember any particular order."

"Maybe. But you might. Ten-thousand-lot orders are more likely to be remembered, right?"

"Yeah, orders that big are rare."

Emily said, "I think you are a loose end, and they are not taking any chances."

Under the supervision of Emily, we decided that I would call one of my friends and coworkers at Maco. We timed the call for 11:45 a.m. because that was when many Maco employees would be getting lunch or taking a break. Eleven forty-five in Chicago was 12:45 p.m. in New York City. Most sizable market participants had already placed their trades for the day and were at lunch. In the absence of market-moving news, the markets were likely to remain calm until later in the afternoon.

I assured Emily that the direct line we were dialing was not a recorded line, because only the trading lines were recorded. This was the direct line of an employee who never took customer orders.

A voice answered midway through the first ring, an efficiency of the telephone headsets worn by Maco back office staff. "Maco, Kurt here." We had Kurt on speakerphone so Emily could hear what he said.

"Hey, Kurt, how's it hangin'?"

"Christian! What the hell! Where are you?!" This reaction was why we timed the call for now. Hopefully, no one else had overheard Kurt say my name.

"I guess I'm taking a sick day."

"Come on, dude. What's up? People were all over here asking questions about you."

"So, you think I killed Mr. Minter?"

"Of course not. But some of the dumbasses coming through here seem to think so." Kurt settled down a bit.

"We've known each other a long time, man; gimme a break. But what gives?"

"I found Minter's body and called 911. But someone began chasing me—maybe the same guy who killed him. I don't know. But I don't like getting shot at and figured I'd better lay low until this is sorted out."

John Jr. and his associates calculated that, due to Minter's murder and ongoing investigation, Mr. Slick's buddies would not have the audacity to bug Maco's phone lines right now. Still, just in case, what I disclosed to Kurt was cautious. In the event that Mr. Slick's associates heard the call, they would still think I was on my own.

"Kurt, I need you to help me with something, and best if you keep this conversation between us. Remember someone killed Tom already, and tried to kill me."

"Sure. I understand. What do ya need?"

"The day Minter was killed two strange trades took place. One to buy ten thousand bonds. One to sell ten thousand bonds. Both executed at 135-27. Can you tell me what customer accounts they were for?"

Kurt oversaw margin requirements at Maco, both for individual customers as well as Maco's firm-wide obligations to the various exchanges. I knew that any order as large as ten thousand bonds would already be on his radar screen.

"Yeah…I remember those," Kurt replied. "Both accounts remained adequately funded and in good standing. But now that you mention it, I didn't notice that both orders were filled at the same exact price. That is a huge coincidence!"

"Or maybe the trades were crossed, matched with each other—never executed competitively in the open market," I set the hook. I knew that Kurt would see the situation for what it was: two highly unusual trades, both occurring on the same day Minter was murdered.

Kurt would also know that because I worked on the trading floor and not in Maco's back office, I would not have had the ability to cross trades in the system. I thought this realization would remove any suspicion Kurt may have had of me. But I don't think he had any doubts about me, nor I him. We had worked together for a number of years and were good friends.

I cut to the chase. "Can you tell me what accounts those trades were allocated to?"

"Christian, a lot of investigators have combed through here asking questions. I want to help you, but I'm not sure I can."

I tried to sway him. "Kurt, the trades are suspicious, and Tom was murdered. You and I both want them to catch whoever killed him, right?"

Kurt hesitated. I could tell he was thinking. I wanted to argue my case, but I waited for him to speak first. After a long silence, he said, "Nobody has told me not to share information with you." I liked the way he was rationalizing. "So I can't be doing anything wrong. You are, officially, still an employee in good standing, until someone tells me otherwise." Now he was on a roll! "In the normal course of business, it is routine to share this information with other Maco employees, including you."

"Thank you, Kurt!"

"No problem. Give me a second, looking it up now. Want me to e-mail it to you?"

I looked at Emily who shook her head no and made a motion as if she were writing with a pen. Then she made a throat-slicing motion with her hand.

Ahh, I realized, *best to avoid e-mail trails, particularly ones that could get Kurt killed.*

"No," I replied, "just give it to me now. I'll write it all down."

Kurt rattled off the relevant information for both accounts: names, addresses, phone numbers, and e-mail addresses. One of the accounts belonged to Byson Foods, a large corporation. The other account was a hedge fund I had never heard of, based in Bermuda. Then Kurt added, "Hang on a sec."

Emily was already springing to action on her laptop.

Kurt continued, "You may want to know this. Both of these customers closed out the positions later that same day. Byson Foods, the buyer of the ten thousand bonds, sold their bonds at a loss of fifteen million dollars. About that same time, Serenity Fund, the Bermuda-based hedge fund, covered their short at a profit of fifteen million. Looks like those two trades were executed separately, but both properly—nothing crossed or matched with another order."

I said, "Thanks, man!" thinking that was it. But Emily slid a paper to me with a question on it. I read the question into the phone: "Kurt, when did Byson and Serenity each open these accounts?"

"Hold on. I'm getting to that screen. Byson, I'm sure you know, is a large commercial food company—chickens, cattle, grains, lots of stuff. They're qualified as a bona fide hedger, allowing them to exceed the normal position limits, and they have had an active hedging account with us for, let's see, more than fifteen years." I could hear pecking on Kurt's keyboard. "Here, looks like Serenity is a brand-new hedge fund client of Maco. In fact, that was their first and only trade thus far. Wait! I remember helping set up this account, not long ago. This new hedge fund client was brought in by Mr. Minter himself."

Emily nodded her head indicating to me that was all she needed to know. I said, "Thanks, Kurt. I owe you one."

"Just take care of yourself and get back here soon, okay?"

I was feeling guilty for potentially putting Kurt at risk. I said, "Look, Kurt, a guy tried to kill me, almost got me. And they got Tom. Please be careful! I think you should pretend we never spoke, and I think you should not poke around asking questions about these two accounts. Just for now."

Silence.

I implored, "Promise me, Kurt, just for now. It is being investigated. But you should keep a safe distance. Trust me, they shot at me!"

"Okay."

"Thanks. See you soon. Bye,"

"Bye," he said, and we both hung up.

Emily raised her eyebrows and asked, "Well, what do you make of this?"

I had the sense that Emily already knew what to make of it but wanted to test me. I was game. "The first two buy/sell trades were illegal, offsetting crossed trades that were arranged after bonds broke a point and a half. After the fact, the winning side of the trade was allocated to this Serenity hedge fund, and the losing side of the trade was allocated to Byson Foods. Then both customers exited their positions the normal, legal way. In effect, Byson Foods just gave fifteen million dollars to this Serenity hedge fund."

"Nice. I agree," said Emily, "Now let's find out who runs this Serenity hedge fund!"

Laura said, "Although they transferred or gave this money to the hedge fund illegally, they will still be able to deduct it on their taxes as a trading loss."

"Good point," Emily said, already knowing this, but impressed with the insight. She added, "And the hedge fund does not have to launder this dirty money. It looks like a normal, profitable commodities trade."

Isaac walked in with lunch—tuna salad sandwiches and iced tea. Small portions, but very good. Even the nutrition at Strong and Associates was controlled to keep people productive through the afternoon. After the short break for lunch, Laura and I found Emily with notes sprawled out in front of her, preparing to make a phone call.

She said, "The address and phone number for Serenity Fund is not for the actual hedge fund. It is the address and contact details for the hedge fund's offshore administrator, based in Bermuda."

Laura raised an eyebrow and gave a suspicious look.

Emily continued, "Nothing wrong with this; it is industry standard, in fact. Despite common misconceptions, there is nothing illegal at all about most 'offshore' accounts. And the hedge fund managers themselves do not avoid US taxes. The offshore jurisdiction for their funds avoids US taxes for some of their tax-exempt clients such as pension plans and foundations. All routine and legal. The hedge funds, in order to be deemed operating in these offshore jurisdictions, are required to have certain functions performed within those jurisdictions. The functions include basic record keeping, maintaining the shareholder registry, calculating monthly performance, issuing client statements, and so forth. Administrators popped up and have grown in all these tax havens to capitalize on the growth in the hedge fund industry, which is now more than three trillion dollars. Your typical hedge fund administrator has hundreds of hedge fund clients, all of whom remain in New York City, or Jackson Hole, or wherever they want."

Emily dialed the number and put it on speakerphone, so we could hear.

"City Fund Services, Ingrid speaking."

"Hi, Ingrid, Kathy here. Not sure if you remember me. I am with Ernst & Young, and we have a number of mutual clients." Emily was smooth, I thought.

"Oh hello," replied Ingrid, trying to place the name.

"We have just been engaged by one of your hedge fund clients to perform their annual audits. Name of the fund is Serenity Fund. The investment manager said I should call you and have you e-mail me the fund's Private Placement Offering Memorandum and shareholder registry so that we can get the ball rolling." It was a confident statement anticipating quick action rather than a request. Hedge fund service providers including banks, prime brokers, accounting firms and administrators frequently had to share information with each other.

"Hmmm, let me see…" We heard her pecking on the keyboard. "I have the PPM. But I will need to confirm our client has authorized us to release it to you."

Emily had timed this call for 2:30 p.m. Chicago time, which was 4:30 p.m. Bermuda time. Ingrid was about to leave for the day. "Ingrid, my goodness, do you know who the investment manager is? He is on a private jet right now! He is on his way to Singapore to make a presentation to their sovereign wealth fund. We assured him that he would have a signed engagement letter from our firm by the time he landed. As you know, we cannot do that without this most basic information from you. You see, he can't very well tell a prospective investor of the size and stature of Singapore's sovereign wealth fund that his firm has not yet even named an auditor. Of course a prospective institutional client like this will gain a lot of comfort in the fact that Serenity is utilizing the biggest and best service providers—us as auditor and you as administrator."

Ingrid was contemplating this. It was a brand-new hedge fund. The request was routine. And in this business, people were always scrambling around with start-up details like this. It was a pain for all of them, and they were just paper pushers, not some demanding Type-A, hedge fund guru on a private jet.

"Ingrid, I hate to put you in the middle like this. But if he doesn't have his engagement letter by the time his jet lands, he is going to demand somebody's head." Softening her tone she added, "You know how arrogant and obnoxious these guys can be. I'd hate for him to make a stink about you. You know, we can follow up and make sure you have all the authorizations in place first thing tomorrow."

"I guess that should be okay…"

Before Ingrid had time to reconsider, Emily said, "That is Kathy Perez. *K P E R E Z* at *E* underscore *Y* dot com."

"Okay."

"Thank you so much, Ingrid!"

"I will send you the PPM right away. Looks like we have not yet finalized the shareholder registry, brand-new fund you know."

"Yes, of course, the PPM should be adequate for now. Thank you so much. Have a great evening."

"Good-bye." Click.

"Nice," I said. "But what about the e-mail address you gave her?"

"That is a real e-mail address at the actual Ernst & Young domain name. So if she compares it with another e-mail address for someone else at the company, it will look legit."

"And how do you have this?" I asked.

"Standard trick of the investigative trade. E-mail address is real, but of course Ernst & Young does not know it exists, so their e-mail servers are not set up to capture any e-mails sent to it."

Laura asked, "So no Kathy Perez works at *E* and *Y*?"

"Goodness no. Using a real employee name for something like this could get that employee killed."

Laura and I snapped back a bit in our chairs. We had not considered this. It seemed Emily, and all of Strong and Associates, routinely dealt with deadly people. Emily seemed casual about it. Laura and I weren't quite used to it.

"Problem is," Emily stated, "the Private Placement Memorandum won't tell us much. We need the shareholder registry. That will tell us who the beneficial owners are, who benefited from that fifteen-million-dollar illegal trade." She walked over to the war room to speak with John Jr. Laura and I followed.

Emily summed up our findings regarding Byson Foods, the Bermuda-based hedge fund, and the suspicious trades. In conclusion she stated, "Unless Isaac can hack into City Fund Services's servers from here, I think Nate is going to have to catch a plane to Bermuda."

John Jr. looked at Emily, Laura, and me and said, "Great work, everyone." He turned to Isaac. "Well, Isaac, what do you think?"

"Offshore hedge fund administrator?" Isaac wrinkled his face and shook his head back and forth. "Firewall will be very tough. It could take me weeks, and I may not be able to get in at all."

"All right. Somebody get Nate a ticket on the next flight. I'll call him and reroute him to O'Hare."

Emily said, "I've already checked flights. If he hurries, he can catch one that departs O'Hare at four ten p.m.—arrives in Bermuda just after ten p.m."

Living in Chicago has one advantage: O'Hare is one of the busiest airports in the world. You can fly almost anywhere in the world direct, and on short notice. Laura and I retreated to the guest bedroom of John Jr.'s house. There wasn't much else we could do at the moment, except sit and wait. I let out a sigh and rubbed my eyes. I was exhausted. Laura walked over to the door, closed it, and locked it. She turned and gave me sly smile. Walking over to me, she said, "You were worried about the size of my engagement ring? That was the only reason? Or are you not sure? Not sure about us?" She smiled coyly and moved in closer to me. She is so beautiful.

She wrapped her arms around my neck and pulled herself against me. She unbuttoned the top two buttons of my shirt, slid her hand inside, and moved her fingers across my chest. She put her free hand in the small of my back and pulled me in tight against her body. I cupped both my hands on her chin and cheek and kissed her. I wasn't exhausted anymore.

She took off my shirt and embraced me. Then she gently released me from a hug and took a step back. She slipped her shoulder straps down over her shoulders, and then let the straps go. Her light, summery dress slipped all the way to the floor. Her beach volleyball body was so perfect. She eased her feet up and out of the loop of a dress that now sat wrinkled around her feet and stepped back into my arms. We kissed as her hands found my belt buckle.

Then we heard a commotion: Isaac was urgently calling everyone to the war room. *Ugh.*

I put my shirt back on and tried to regain my composure while Laura quickly slipped on her dress. She was gorgeous, even putting on clothes! We walked hand in hand to the war room. John Jr., Emily, and Isaac were already there. Louie and Bob were in the field, and Nate was en route to O'Hare.

Isaac said, "I called you as soon as I heard this. I'll play the tape and let you hear it for yourself, but it is pretty clear. Mr. Slick and Mr. Elevator were just given a new assignment: 'Take out Jack Thompson!'"

John Jr. shook his head and said, "Damn. These jerks have orders to take out a presidential candidate!"

I asked, "The former governor of Ohio?"

"Yep," replied Isaac. "Of course it is a somewhat common name, but who else can they mean?"

Jack Thompson was the former governor of Ohio and the Republican frontrunner for the 2016 presidential election.

John Jr. asked, "Did the order come from Vince Fleming?"

"I'd say yes, but not certain yet. Have to run a voiceprint analyzer, but it sure as hell sounds like him."

"Thoughts, people?" John Jr. invited.

"We need tighter surveillance on these thugs," said Bob over the radio.

John Jr. looked to Emily for confirmation of something—I didn't know what.

Emily answered his unspoken question: "We have to report this. We can't sit on something this big while we continue our investigation regarding Mr. Minter. Imagine if Jack Thompson is murdered, and it is discovered that we had this information and sat on it?"

John Jr. nodded. "Agreed, but who do we report it to? Thompson's campaign? CPD? The FBI? Hell we could report it to the secret service, but they are not in the business of protecting candidates."

Emily thought for a few seconds before answering. "I think we have to tell the FBI. If we tell them, we do not have to tell CPD, and CPD is full of leaks. As for Thompson, I think we have to tell him too, but maybe we can ask the FBI to inform him of the threat. We keep a low profile."

"I like it. Anyone else?" John Jr. sounded like an auctioneer going three times. "Done deal. Bob, who is the best contact at the FBI Chicago office for something of this magnitude? Can you set up a meeting ASAP?"

"Yes, sir," came Bob's voice over the speakerphone.

Chapter 15

Just one hour later, Bob and John Jr. were sitting down with Special Agent Dan Bruner at a Starbucks across the street from the FBI's Chicago headquarters. Bob still had some pull at the FBI.

"Thank you for meeting us on short notice like this, Dan," said Bob. Most people could not get a meeting with the FBI like this. Bob had called Dan on his personal cell phone. As a former agent and colleague of Dan's, Bob had promised Dan that this was big enough to drop whatever he was doing. Special Agent Dan Bruner also knew quite a bit about Strong and Associates.

"My pleasure," said Dan, shaking hands with Bob and John Jr. "Good to see you both. I know you wouldn't ask if this wasn't going to be worth my time—so let's get to it. I have to be back for a debriefing in twenty minutes."

John Jr. let Bob tell the story, but they had planned what would be disclosed to the FBI.

Bob kicked it off, "We overheard some guys receive orders to 'take out Jack Thompson.'"

"Some guys?" inquired Special Agent Bruner. He left a lot of suspicion hanging in the air, as if they were holding back.

"We don't know who the guys are. Don't even know their names," Bob said, although Strong and Associates were working to learn the true identities of Mr. Slick and Mr. Elevator. "Two men. Here are detailed descriptions." He slid a manila envelope over to Dan.

Dan glanced at the contents, brief physical descriptions and a photo of the two men together taken at a distance by Bob the day before. The agent tucked the photos away and looked back at Bob.

"They appear to be field operatives, hit men. For whom, we don't know." This was technically true, even though they suspected links to the White House.

Fifteen minutes before this meeting with agent Bruner, Isaac had called John Jr. to share the results of the voiceprint analysis. John Jr. cut him off, "Isaac, no time now, we are about to meet with the FBI, to share all known facts. Sorry have to go…" Click.

Isaac understood. Later, John Jr. and Bob could testify that at the time they met with special Agent Bruner, they did not know who called the thugs and ordered them to take out Jack Thompson.

Special Agent Bruner picked his next question carefully, "Overheard them?" Again, his question was dripping with suspicion and innuendo.

Bob, a former FBI agent himself, knew Dan's tone implied illegal wiretaps of private citizens. He answered by repeating, verbatim, what he had already said, "Correct. We overheard some guys receive orders to 'take out Jack Thompson.'"

Bob's answer was technically true. It wasn't good to tell the FBI about their illegal eavesdropping. It also wasn't good to lie to the FBI. This artful wording did neither.

Dan nodded his head. He knew that John Jr. and Bob had most likely bugged somebody, without the proper authority and warrants. He knew that when a smart person answers your further inquiry with a repeat of the exact same answer, you were not going to get anything more.

The more he thought about it, Agent Bruner didn't care how they got this information. In fact, if it was obtained illegally, he was better off not knowing that, at least for now. He trusted Bob and John Jr., and he was glad they shared this information with him. Bob used to be a great agent, and he was very credible. The case they just handed him would enhance his standing in the bureau.

"Anything else?" asked Dan.

Bob knew they were walking a fine line with the FBI. They had an obligation to report everything regarding the threat to candidate Thompson. However, they did not want to hand over their investigation of Minter's murder.

"That's about it," responded Bob. "About" created a hole that a first-year law student could drive a truck through. "Will you tell the Thompson camp? As I'm sure you know, we feel a real obligation to get this information into the right hands." Dan took that as a compliment to both himself and the FBI.

"We'll see to it."

The three men rose, shook hands, and left.

The FBI acted on credible threats to public figures. But it would still take more than twelve hours to commence an inconspicuous protection detail for Jack Thompson. They would keep a low profile, not wanting to alert any bad guys that the FBI had gotten wind of their plot. This would suit candidate Thompson just fine, as he preferred to go about his life without the oppressive presence of a swarm of bodyguards.

Chapter 16

1:30 pm. The FBI protection detail for Jack Thompson was not yet in place. It had been just a few hours since they learned of the plot, and they were evaluating how seriously to take it. Politicians received threats every day, most of them harmless.

Strong and Associates were busy keeping close tabs on Mr. Slick, Mr. Elevator, and Vince Fleming, all of whom were nowhere near candidate Thompson.

Mr. Thompson and his top aide exited the elevator on the nineteenth floor of the Peninsula Hotel, a five-star hotel located on Chicago's Magnificent Mile. They had just left another fundraiser, a dinner gala, one of three this week. They proceeded down the hall to their hotel rooms, which were across the hall and two rooms apart from each other.

The couple in the hallway had just exited a room, or so Mr. Thompson and his aide thought. The man and woman were now walking together toward the elevators, but also toward Mr. Thompson and his aide. In fact, these two professionals did not have a room at the Peninsula. They had just stood in the hall and waited for Mr. Thompson to get off the elevator. An accomplice had radioed them when Mr. Thompson was on his way.

The woman was somewhat attractive, about fifty years old. The man she was with appeared to be about the same age. Both were fit and athletic looking. He was wearing a suit and the woman a cocktail dress. The well-dressed couple in a nice hotel would not draw any suspicion.

The couple walked toward Mr. Thompson and his aide. They slowed their pace to allow for Mr. Thompson and his aide to split off as they approached their respective rooms. As Mr. Thompson approached his hotel room door, his aide had already swiped the room key to his door a short distance away. The aide was opening his door when the commotion began.

The woman brought her left hand up and cupped it over her mouth, in some state of shock. With her right hand, she pointed at Mr. Thompson and walked toward him saying, "You…you are that politician! You…You voted for the Iraq War!"

She slapped Thompson hard with her right hand on the left side of his face and neck. He put his own hand up to the left side of his face. It was stinging from the slap and also burning.

The man escorting the woman restrained her and guided her back away from Mr. Thompson. "I am sorry, sir. Please forgive this. She lost her son in Iraq. She doesn't know what to do. Very distraught."

Thompson's aide was still standing at his hotel room about twenty feet away. His hand was on his door, and the door was open. He had almost started toward Mr. Thompson after he heard the slap, but the situation had defused. The matter appeared to be over. The man seemed to have the woman under control, and the woman, now sobbing with her head on the man's shoulder, did not seem to be a threat. The man was already escorting her toward the elevators.

Mr. Thompson was shocked and caught off guard. He did not feel pain in his neck and face right away. Rather, he felt empathy—intense pain for a woman who had lost her son.

Thompson said, "Very...very sorry about your son, ma'am." He thought about explaining that he never voted for the Iraq War, or any war for that matter. He wasn't in Congress. He was, thus far, a former governor and a current candidate for president. But what was the point of trying to explain all that to a woman grieving the loss of her son? To her, all politicians were the same. Maybe, he thought, she recognized him from the news coverage of his campaign.

He just added, "Very sorry, ma'am—sorry about your son, ma'am," as the man and woman walked off.

With the couple now almost to the elevator, Mr. Thompson and his aide looked at each other from in front of their hotel room doors. Mr. Thompson shrugged his shoulders, raised his eyebrows, and tilted his head to the side as if to say, "Oh well."

His aide took this as a sign that everything was okay and shook his head in return. Both Mr. Thompson and his aide nodded good night to each other and entered their rooms.

Before the couple got to the elevator, the man brought a zip lock sandwich bag out of his pocket, and the woman placed her right hand in it. She then placed her hand, with the plastic zip lock bag over it, down into her purse and held her purse close to her chest. She would keep her fingers in the bag and in the purse until they were in the car.

The couple looked down as they entered the elevator, concealing their faces from the security camera that was mounted in the top corner. The woman appeared to be crying, with her head down in the man's chest. He had his head down over her, comforting her. They stood at the front of the elevator, facing the doors, keeping their heads down and their backs to the camera.

Very professional. No one would get a good ID from the security cameras. And if they did, so what? The man and woman both had elaborate disguises on—the woman a curly wig and the man thick plastic eyeglasses and a hairpiece.

Inside his room, Mr. Thompson removed his jacket and tie and started to unbutton his shirt. He looked in the bathroom mirror because he could still feel where the woman had slapped him. He was surprised to see three deep fingernail gouges running along his neck, from just in front of his left ear to the corner of his jawbone. The scratches weren't dripping blood down his neck, but they were red and pooling blood. He rinsed the scratches with cold water to clean them and to stop the blood from oozing. He thought about asking his aide for some Band-Aids or ointment but decided against it. They all needed to get some sleep. His neck would be fine.

As soon as the couple got into their car, the woman held out her hand, with the bag still on it. He pulled out a small, sterile metal nail file. While leaving her fingers in the zip lock bag, he reached inside the plastic bag and scraped the nail file under each of her fingernails, scraping out some material and capturing it all in the bag.

"Nice," he said. "I think you got some real good ones here."

Chapter 17

At 2:00 a.m. Bermuda time, which was midnight in Chicago, Nate picked a lock and broke into the darkened offices of City Fund Services, administrator to the Serenity hedge fund. He found a secretary's desk at which the computer had been left on and sat down. He took out a flash drive and plugged it into a USB port. He thought how nice it was since computer makers began putting USB ports on the front of computer towers. No more fishing around under desks behind dusty computers amid a tangle of cords. After inserting the flash drive in the USB port, prompts popped up on the screen. He hit "run" and "continue." In less than thirty seconds, he had installed remote control software designed to give Isaac, back in Chicago, control over this computer. Nate called Isaac from his cell phone. "I've opened the door for you. Test it out; see if you can drive this baby."

It was difficult to break through most company's external firewalls from the outside. However, if you were already on the inside and had access to a computer connected to the company's internal network, even a low-level computer hack could access everything on the company's servers.

Within seconds, Nate saw the mouse moving on the secretary's screen in front of him, and he knew Isaac had remote access. Isaac was seeing the secretary's screen back in Chicago and controlling the cursor remotely.

"Bingo!" said Isaac, "It used to be a lot harder than this when I had to be there. Glad I'm here at home and able to leave the breaking and entering to you." While Isaac was remotely operating the secretary's computer, there was a slight delay in what he saw due the connection speed. But it was almost as if he were sitting at the secretary's desk.

"Alert me when you're done. I'm going to look around." Nate got up and walked around the office. He was calm for someone who had illegally entered an office in a foreign country in the middle of the night. In fact, this was one of the least stressful assignments of his illustrious career.

After five years as a Navy SEAL, Nate was recruited to join the CIA. He worked as a field operative for fifteen years before "retiring" to what he considered a low-stress, low-risk job with Strong and Associates. Strong and Associates rescued kidnapped businessmen and tourists from gangs in foreign countries and was also one of the select firms that provided independent contractors to the US government.

Nate surveyed the office as he waited for Isaac to access City's computer servers, locate the right files, and commence the download. On a counter in the middle of a group of desks sat several rows of manila folders in metal stands. He scanned the labels on the folders.

The administration firm processed a lot of paperwork for their hedge fund clients, and this counter served as the in-box. Secretaries occupied the desks around the counter and had the job of scanning and electronically filing every incoming shareholder subscription. The manila folders contained signed subscription agreements from the individual hedge fund investors who had subscribed to the various funds at the beginning of the current month. Every month, a whole new batch of subscriptions would come in for the hundreds of funds City administered, and this process would begin again.

Nate scanned the folders, each labeled with the names of the various hedge funds. For this month, some funds had a mountain of incoming subscriptions, while others had very few. As he moved along alphabetically he came to a file labeled "Serenity." It was thinner than most, and as he opened it, he saw it contained just one investor subscription agreement. He located the name of the investor, and his heart skipped a beat: Abigail Mason Trust. Abigail Mason was the secretary of state. She was also almost certain to be the Democratic candidate for president in 2016.

He placed the agreement in the automatic document feeder of a nearby copy machine and pressed "start." After his copy was printed, he placed the original back just as he had found it and sat back down in front of the computer Isaac was remotely operating.

Nate's mobile phone vibrated due to an incoming text message. He opened his phone to see a message from Isaac,

"Download commenced. Will take time. Okay to remove flash and leave."

"*K*," replied Nate.

Nate removed the flash drive, checked to make sure he was leaving everything just as he found it and exited City's offices. The small flash drive held a whopping sixty gigabytes of data. When Nate arrived, all it had contained was the remote operating software.

It was much faster to transfer files to a flash drive inserted in the computer than to download them over the Internet from Bermuda to Chicago. But there was the risk of getting caught, and there was no need to keep Nate there any longer than necessary. Although the remaining download might take a few hours, they had at least that long before City employees arrived for work in the morning.

The download would continue for four more hours, so inconspicuous that even a janitor or security guard walking past the secretary's desk would not be aware of it. Once the download was complete, Isaac would remotely delete the remote control software. When the secretary arrived at work, she would have no reason to suspect anything was amiss.

Chapter 18

A few minutes later, the phone in the war room rang. Recognizing Nate's burner cell on the caller ID, Isaac said, "That's him," as he answered the call on speakerphone. In addition to Isaac and me, Laura, John Jr., and Emily were all gathered around the conference table.

Isaac said, "Nate, you're on speakerphone."

"I'm out. No trace I was there. Just taking a stroll now on a beautiful night in Bermuda."

"Atta boy." John Jr. congratulated Nate.

Nate continued, "I found a subscription agreement for Serenity Fund for the first of this month. It is in the amount of one million dollars, and it is for the account of..." He paused for effect and then said, "Abigail Mason Trust."

John Jr., the master of understatement, calmly said, "Wow. Anything else?"

"Not on my end. Let's see what else we find. I'm on a nine a.m. flight, should be back there by one p.m."

"Roger." Click.

This was sobering news back in the war room. Not only was a special assistant to the deputy chief of staff giving orders to professional hit men like Mr. Slick, but the secretary of state was connected to the whole mess. She was one of the investors in a hedge fund involved in an illegal trade, which was related to the murder of Thomas Minter. A lot of very important dots, but they still needed to be connected. Emily and Isaac began sifting through the massive download. Laura and I, at the suggestion of John Jr., decided to get some much-needed sleep.

We went to the guest bedroom. I was exhausted physically and emotionally. I was also worried that, at any minute, TV news would start broadcasting my name and photo: wanted for the murder of Thomas Minter.

Laura locked the door and then turned, gave me a sly smile, and said, "Now, where were we?"

I forgot all my troubles. I was no longer tired. She walked over to me, and we hugged. We held each other tight, standing there next to the bed, for almost a minute without saying anything. I said, "I almost died last night."

She swallowed, nodded, and put her head into my neck. I could tell she was on the verge of crying. I said, "Last night I realized how lucky I am to have you. I realized that I have taken you for granted." I got down on one knee and held her hand. "I'm soooo sorry."

Sniffling, she said, "You don't have to be sorry for anything." I looked in her eyes, they were tearing up. She added, "Well, maybe a little." We both laughed.

I said, "I don't even have a ring. Don't worry; I'll get one. But after being such a fool, and almost ending up dead, I don't want to wait one second longer."

As I held her left hand, she placed her right hand on my cheek. She smiled at me, and her eyes sparkled as they welled up with tears.

I looked up at her and said, "Laura, will you marry me?"

She pulled me up off my one knee so that I was standing and then pushed me back on the bed where I landed on my back. She jumped on me, smiling.

"Is that a yes?" I asked.

She bit her lip. "Yes."

We both smiled. I held her tight and kissed her. Then I sat up, and she helped me off with my shirt.

She felt so good. No one interrupted us this time. Eventually, I lay on my back. She was next to me with her head on my chest and her right leg over me. We held each other more meaningfully than ever before and fell asleep all tangled up.

Laura and I slept in until eight the next morning and then showered, together. We walked out to the kitchen holding hands. I felt a sense of calm and complacency. As long as I had Laura, nothing else seemed to matter.

Emily walked into the kitchen to refill her coffee. I wondered if she had gotten any sleep at all. I realized that most of this team hadn't slept at all since two nights before, the night of Minter's murder. Laura and I followed Emily back to the war room.

John Jr. nodded good morning. He said, "We've found some interesting things." He motioned to chairs. "Please have a seat."

Emily began, "It's worse, or better, I guess, depending on your perspective, than we thought. You already know that Madam Secretary, Abigail Mason, made a million-dollar investment in this Serenity hedge fund, effective at the beginning of this month. We found a wire transfer receipt confirming this. It came from a bank account in the trust's name."

As a result of the 9/11 terrorist attacks, banks, brokerage firms, and investment managers had to comply with very strict anti-money laundering regulations. No firm could credit money to a hedge fund capital account in the name of Abigail Mason Trust unless it had originated from a bank account that was also in the name of Abigail Mason Trust. It was the responsibility of City Fund Services, as administrator for numerous hedge funds, to process incoming subscriptions and ensure these rules were complied with. They also had to check every investor name against a list of known terrorists and terror-related names in a government database known as OFAC, which stands for Office of Foreign Asset Control. This was the investors' equivalent of a no-fly list.

The rules were designed to cut off the flow of laundered money intended to support terrorist organizations. It was effective because, under pressure from the United States, all but a few small dictator-run countries had adopted the same international anti-money laundering laws. The few countries that did not adopt the new rules were isolated and marginalized because one of the new rules prohibited transfers to or from any country that had not adopted the same rules. In other words, certain countries were named on the OFAC no-fly list. In effect, the United States and its allies were able to say, "Adopt these rules, or we will cut you off from the rest of the civilized world." In the wake of 9/11, no reasonable country could say no. The new rules also proved to be a boon to the IRS because it became more difficult for wealthy families to pass large amounts of money among themselves, or to their heirs, in order to avoid estate taxes.

Emily continued, "So Abigail Mason holds an interest in Serenity Fund Limited, which, as with any hedge fund or mutual fund, entitles her to her pro rata share of the fund's investment gains and losses based on the size of her individual investment relative to the size of the whole fund. Now, for the good part: Abigail Mason is the *sole* beneficial owner of Serenity Fund Limited."

Isaac said, "We have the accounting records of Serenity from the administrator's server along with the client capital account statements. It all looks legit, and it all agrees. Abigail Mason owns one hundred percent of the Serenity fund. She is the only investor in the fund."

I summed it up. "So, the secretary of state invests one million dollars on Monday, and by Wednesday, her hedge fund investment is worth sixteen million—a profit of fifteen million dollars. In two days. All from one illegal commodities trade."

"Yes," said Emily, adding, "and the beauty is, on the surface it all looks legal. She could cash this money out at any time. The Serenity fund offers unusually generous redemption terms for a hedge fund—daily liquidity. Most hedge funds require a one-year lockup of your money, and after that, they often only allow annual or quarterly redemptions. Here, you ask for your money back at any time and get it the next day."

John Jr. shook his head and said, "Brilliant. Most high-level politicians and cabinet members place their assets in a blind trust. And she wants to be president. Abigail Mason Trust has gotta be a blind trust. Blind in the sense that the politician has no idea what investments are held on his or her behalf. Outside money managers make all those decisions. This way, the politicians can never be accused of making policy decisions in order to benefit their investments."

Isaac said, "Damn, talk about layers and layers of plausible deniability."

John Jr. said, "But I'll bet my right arm Abigail Mason knows about this investment."

We all shook our heads in disbelief.

Emily added, "And, the way they set it up, she'll receive all the appropriate year-end statements, showing a gain of fifteen million dollars. No alarm bells would be triggered at the IRS or the banks. Everything is perfect."

John Jr. was pacing and rubbing his chin again. He concluded, "In effect, Byson Foods just gave Abigail Mason, the secretary of state and a presidential candidate, fifteen million dollars. Let's call it a campaign contribution. But Byson

Foods doesn't have to worry about those pesky campaign finance laws, limits on contributions, or reporting requirements. They even get to deduct the political contribution as a business expense, a trading loss."

I asked, "Have you looked into why? Payback, or investment in the future?"

John Jr. answered, "Maybe both. It could be as simple as she plans to run for president. But we're working on all angles. So far, we have two connections between Abigail Mason and Byson Foods. First, Byson donated five million dollars to the Bill and Abigail Mason Foundation. Byson can deduct it as a charitable donation, and it was disclosed. The nuance is, filings show the Mason Foundation spends more than ninety percent of its budget on salaries, overhead and travel expenses. While technically legal, in essence, the so-called non-profit foundation is a giant slush fund the Masons use to reward donors allies and political operatives."

I said, "Try proving that though?"

John Jr. nodded. "That's the problem. Very difficult to prove any sort of quid pro quo. And Abigail Mason isn't dumb enough to leave e-mail trails about it. Which brings us to the second angle we are working: Back when Abigail Mason was a senator from Illinois, she spear-headed the mandate that all gasoline contain ten percent of the fuel additive ethanol. Ethanol is derived from corn. Pundits at the time thought it was a giveaway to Midwest farmers—Illinois has a lot of them. Mason played it off as one of her pioneering green initiatives. Of course the environmentalists loved it, and the green aspect of it is politically popular."

I said, "It's no secret Abigail Mason has strong presidential ambitions. In addition to playing to farmers in her home state, support for ethanol subsidies has become a litmus test for presidential candidates in the Iowa caucuses—one of the earliest and most important events in presidential campaigns."

Isaac shook his head and said, "Damn, she is one calculating bitch."

John Jr. said, "Hold on. Back to this trade. Guess who is both the largest grower of corn in the United States and the biggest processor of ethanol?"

We all said in unison, "Byson Foods."

"Yep." John Jr. shook his head.

At Maco, I followed a lot of commodities besides bonds, including corn, wheat, soybeans, pork bellies, oil, and gas. Compared to gasoline, it costs five times more to grow corn, harvest it, and then distill it down to usable ethanol. In fact it requires more energy to produce ethanol than the ethanol in turn produces. One reason is that it burns faster and delivers lower fuel efficiency than unleaded gasoline. It is grain alcohol in your gas tank. In fact, they add a bit of real gasoline to ethanol for the express purpose of preventing people from bootlegging it.

Ethanol is also very costly to deliver. I know spread traders who arbitrage price differentials in different parts of the country based on this. Ethanol adheres to water and carries sediment with it, which is why it gums up carburetors. This adherent property also means it would muck up pipelines. So, it is not allowed to be shipped through pipelines like other petroleum products. It would contaminate the pipelines, the same way it does small engines. So, ethanol has to be delivered by individual tanker trucks, which is much more expensive.

My oil and gas trader friends just shake their heads in disbelief about ethanol subsidies. It is much simpler and cheaper to pump oil out of the ground, especially since the fracking boom. Add the overall cost to the US economy of engine repairs and failures, and the true cost of ethanol is growing at a staggering rate. Ethanol subsidies are aided by the common misconception that legislation intended to help farmers helps small family owned farms. All kinds of farm subsidies have cropped up over the years, including things as nonsensical as paying farmers not to farm their land. Imagine getting paid not to work! Why not do the same for plumbers or auto workers? But this is how the US Congress doles out pork to constituents. While most Americans think farm subsidies benefit small family farms, the truth is, small family farms do not have that kind of lobbying clout. Large corporations, like Byson Foods, do.

Large corporations grow 95 percent of US crops and rear almost 98 percent of the country's cattle and poultry. The stereotypical family farm is an anomaly in America, has been for decades. Crony capitalism from politicians, like the president and Abigail Mason, has replaced traditional welfare for the poor with corporate welfare for the wealthiest companies, like Byson Foods.

Illinois, the home state to both the president and the secretary of state, raised the Illinois state income tax while handing out hundreds of millions of dollars in tax breaks to large corporations who had threatened to leave the state, including Byson. In effect, the politicians took hundreds of millions of dollars from the hard-working people of Illinois and gave it to a handful of large corporations.

I said, "I guess a fifteen-million-dollar payback to Abigail Mason is chump change compared to how much the Byson Corporation is profiting from ethanol subsidies. And now she is, maybe, the next president of the United States."

Chapter 19

Mr. Slick's real name was Anthony Silvasconi, but his friends called him Tony. He came to a career in crime almost by accident five years ago. After serving in the army, he was hired as a private contractor with Stonewater Incorporated, the largest private contractor to the US military during the Iraq War. The government outsourced to Stonewater many activities that the US military normally conducted itself. This included providing security and handling logistics for equipment and supplies. These private soldiers did the same thing as, and in many cases worked alongside, US soldiers. The only real difference was that they did not wear the US uniform. And they got paid about ten times more.

This enabled the US government to lower the troop count in Iraq and Afghanistan. This metric was important to the powers that be in Washington, irrespective of the astronomical cost of contracting out to private mercenaries provided by companies like Stonewater. It seemed the presence of ten thousand more American troops in Iraq ruffled people's feathers and cost congressmen votes. However, another billion dollars here or there, as part of the cost of the war, was just a footnote. Nobody cared. In fact, by 2011, private contractors represented more than 50 percent of the total force in Iraq and Afghanistan.

As the Iraq war wound down, Stonewater contractors like Tony Silvasconi were no longer needed, and Silvasconi returned home to California without any job prospects that interested him. He longed for adventure and adrenaline and knew he could not tolerate the boredom of a normal forty-hour work grind.

Joey Carapocci, a fellow Stonewater alum, hooked Tony up with a security firm in Los Angeles that provided security guards for concerts and other events. They needed muscly guys in yellow T-shirts to stand in front of the stage and face the crowd. The security firm also provided bodyguards for celebrities, a role Tony applied for.

Tony was saleable as a celebrity bodyguard due to his military background. His lean, dark, rugged looks, square jaw, and serious-looking demeanor fit the role. The head of the security firm, who knew more about marketing and promotion than bodyguard services, touted his "senior officers," of which Tony was instantly one. He even embellished their military backgrounds to the firm's celebrity clients and agents. Clients who hired Tony as a bodyguard were told he formerly was responsible for escorting and protecting such high-level people as the secretary of state and the chairman of the joint chiefs of staff. All lies, but the Hollywood folks ate it up and never questioned it.

He dressed like a secret service agent—suit, sunglasses, even a squiggly cord connected to an earpiece. Although the earpiece appeared high tech, it was just a standard cell phone earpiece, another Hollywood embellishment of the security firm's founder.

As exciting as the idea had sounded to Tony, he quickly bored of this work. He endured long hours doing nothing. No danger, no excitement, rarely even an overly enthusiastic fan to push back. Tony found himself protecting self-important B-list actors who, for public appearances, hired a bodyguard to create an aura of stardom that they would never achieve. In effect, Tony had become a prop, an accessory for the shallow people of Hollywood.

And then one day, Tony got the call. A former security guard with Stonewater, Mark Hansen, called Tony to tell him that he had finally found it. An exciting job that offered the adrenaline rush and excitement with very limited real danger, at least as compared to working as a Stonewater contractor in Iraq. Hansen was working for a very wealthy Italian businessman—one with rumored ties to organized crime. Not the knock-off organized crime found in the United States, but the real Sicily-based mafia. Tony didn't know what that meant, but the way Mark spoke about it piqued his interest. Mark explained that he was shorthanded, and, while he could not guarantee the length of employment, the pay was five thousand per week. Tony just about fell out of his chair when he heard that.

Tony's first assignment with Mark was simple. They broke into a house in which the security system was not even activated and planted a gun in a dresser drawer. It was uneventful, even easy. This first assignment almost seemed boring. Then Tony saw the house they had entered on the news. Yellow crime-scene tape surrounded the house, and news cameras and their vans clogged the quiet suburban street. Police had to push back a throng of reporters.

The house belonged to Brian Olsen, a successful California businessman who had launched a bid for the US Congress. Brian's business partner had been gunned down in a parking lot, after eating dinner with Brian. Witnesses placed both men in the restaurant together. No eyewitnesses saw the shooting, but the time of death was estimated to have been shortly after they left the restaurant.

The media had a field day with the investigation, and ballistics tests confirmed that the unregistered gun found in Brian Olsen's home was the gun that killed his partner. The media frenzy peaked, and the case was closed. Brian Olsen, of course, dropped out of the race for Congress. A few months later, he was convicted of murder and sentenced to life in prison.

Wow! As boring as the initial job had seemed, that was exciting! Tony felt powerful. Sometimes he asked Mark, "Who killed Brian's business partner?" or "Who are we working for?"

But Mark always played coy. He liked to say, "Come on, Tony! You know how it works, 'need to know.'"

Mark did not tell Tony that he himself did not need to know. All their operations were run very professionally.— compartmentalized so that whoever killed Brian Olsen's partner did not know who planted the gun and vice versa. And neither team knew who they were working for. They just received their assignments from a middleman and got paid in cash. Their anonymous employer was insulated from any potential prosecution. So while Mark loved pretending to be more connected than Tony, in reality, he had no idea who they worked for. Mark was just happy to be making two grand per day.

Mark and Tony did many assignments together; so varied were their victims that the two eventually gave up trying to guess who they were working for. Some of their set-up victims were businessmen, others were politicians, and one was a university professor. They lived in various places across the United States, and although Tony and Mark discussed it, there was no apparent common thread between them.

Early assignments involved stealing and planting evidence. In time, they moved up to more serious crimes, including assault and murder. The pay went up as well.

An interesting assignment involved making a murder look like a suicide. Wealthy European businessmen had been swindled out of hundreds of millions of dollars in what was the most infamous Ponzi scheme ever. The mastermind of the fraud, Gerard Randolph, was serving a one-hundred-fifty-year prison sentence. But the Europeans, members of B6, wanted more than that in revenge.

Rather than have Gerard killed in prison, something that was within their capabilities, they settled on a plan to murder Gerard's forty-one-year-old son, Michael Randolph. To send a not-so-subtle message to the convicted con man, they decided to exact their revenge on the anniversary of Gerard's conviction.

Silvasconi and Hansen staked out the son's house for weeks in preparation for timing the crime on the anniversary date. By a stroke of luck, Michael's wife left town to visit an out-of-state friend two nights before. Had she not, they would have had no choice but to kill her too, and make it look like a murder-suicide. As it turned out, the only people remaining in the house were Michael Randolph and the couple's three-year-old son, Ryan.

At 3:00 a.m., Silvasconi and Hansen entered the house. At gunpoint, they roused Michael from his sleep. They were careful to not inflict any injuries that would indicate a struggle. He was blindfolded, and his hands were placed into thick work gloves that came up almost to his elbows. His wrists were bound behind his back with a zip tie. The zip tie was placed over the thick work gloves in order to not leave any marks on his wrists. As long as he cooperated, they promised not to harm his son. If the boy woke up, they warned, they would have no choice but to kill him. Michael was very quiet and compliant.

Silvasconi and Hansen led Michael to the basement. They took Michael's EPhone, which had been on the nightstand next to his bed. After attempting to access the phone, Hansen saw it had a screen-lock passcode.

Hansen said in a quiet, threatening voice, "All I want is the passcode to your EPhone."

Michael gave it to him.

"Tell me your wife's cell phone number."

Michael did, and Hansen confirmed he had the right contact. His wife was about to receive a text message from Michael's phone—a phone that was passcode protected, leading investigators to believe that the text was in fact from Michael.

Hansen and Silvasconi eased Michael over to a chair and helped him stand up on it. They had already tied a rope to an overhead beam. To aid the suicide story, they used a rope they found in Michael's own garage.

To prevent any wounds caused by Michael resisting, Hansen leaned in to Michael's ear and said, "We just have a few questions. Give us some answers, and nobody gets hurt. Especially your little boy."

Michael was terrified, and he complied. Silvasconi slipped the noose over his head and snugged it up around his neck. Before Michael had any idea what was happening, they kicked the chair away. After he was dead, they removed the blindfold, zip ties, and gloves.

Hansen picked up Michael Randolph's cell phone and sent a text message to Michael's wife: "Can't live in my dad's disgraceful shadow any longer. Please send someone to get Ryan." The death was ruled a suicide, which earned Silvasconi and Hansen a twenty-five-thousand-dollar bonus.

Murder was rare though. Most of their assignments involved obtaining or planting evidence. Frequently the evidence was biological. Although the results of their efforts were pretty exciting, and often newsworthy, the work was tedious.

Their most recent target was a guy they had never heard of from Ohio named Jack Thompson. They soon learned that he was a successful businessman, former governor, and Republican candidate for president. Their assignment: collect both blood and semen samples. By now, this type of assignment was routine to both men. They had been following Jack Thompson for almost three weeks before they got pulled away from that assignment for work related to Maco Commodities, its billionaire founder, and a phone clerk.

Years earlier, the first time Tony was tasked with obtaining blood and semen DNA evidence, he thought it was a joke. "Semen!" Tony laughed. "Do they expect us to extract it ourselves?"

"You'll see, smart ass," said Mark as they began Tony's first DNA stake out.

During that first DNA stakeout, Mark explained to Tony that getting a specific individual's DNA for use as evidence was much easier than you might think. No, they were not going to grab the target, hold him down, and stick a needle in him.

They were going to wait patiently, until their target gave them the DNA they needed. Mark had been doing this for a long time. Sometimes blood evidence could be retrieved from bathroom wastebaskets. Bloody nose. Menstrual period for women. Semen could be obtained from bedding and towels, although that required an extraction process performed in a lab. Mark would just collect the bedding or towel, place it in an airtight bag, and then wait to hear whether they had obtained what they needed or not.

"When you're lucky," explained Mark, "you find a condom full of the stuff right in the garbage can."

"Oh yeah, my lucky day," quipped Tony with a disgusted look on his face.

But these days, they were both experienced in DNA collection. In the case of Jack Thompson, they checked every hotel room after he left, but before the maids came through. Mark had a special black light, the kind used by investigators at a crime scene to find minute traces of blood or other biological material. With the room darkened, Mark and Tony would spread out the bedding and towels and scan the black light over them. Any organic material would glow distinctly.

Mark told Tony about a disaster several years earlier in a similar assignment. Mark's supervisor had obtained a used condom belonging to the target, and the semen was planted at a crime scene. Only problem was, the DNA did not belong to the target! It belonged to the target's daughter's boyfriend.

The DNA intended to convict the target exonerated him! Mark never saw that supervisor again and was told he had been "reassigned," but Mark suspected much worse. He emphasized to Tony, "No screw-ups." He did not want to get reassigned.

In the case of the botched DNA sample, the boyfriend's semen was collected from the target's home. Mark learned an important lesson. With a house full of people, you could never be certain which resident or visitor left the DNA behind.

When a businessman entered a hotel room, they had a clean source for only his DNA. This was the key benefit of hotels. They were lucky that their current target, Jack Thompson, traveled and stayed in hotels four to five nights per week. For this reason, Mark and Tony ruled out any attempt to get DNA evidence from his home. Hotels were much easier to access than most expensive homes, and they knew that any fresh DNA they found in a hotel room would in fact belong to Mr. Thompson.

On the current assignment they thought they hit pay dirt in a crusty towel that lit up under the black light. They packed it in an airtight bag and delivered it. The next day they received the lab results. The sample was semen, but they wanted a better sample to replant as evidence. They still needed a blood sample. After four weeks on the assignment, they still had no blood and a weak semen sample. A weak biological sample could be used for identification. But they needed more to be confident that police investigators would both find it and have enough to run their own DNA test.

They were disappointed that Jack Thompson never brought a woman back to the hotel with him. On earlier stakeouts of other victims, encounters with strange women frequently produced a used condom, even when encounters with the wife had not.

On the Thompson case, something changed, and things began to move ahead. Their unknown employer had grown impatient. It was decided that the weak semen sample was going to be used after all. The new orders: A fifty-thousand-dollar job. They both knew what that meant. Soon they would be given genetic material in a usable form. From that moment, they had twelve hours to execute their fifty-thousand-dollar orders. The DNA they were about to plant had a short shelf life.

Chapter 20

Laura and I sat alone in John Jr.'s kitchen. She asked, "How well do you know these people?" She pointed her finger around in a circle, meaning how well did I know Strong and Associates.

"What do you mean?" I asked defensively.

"Well, you said this Slick guy tracked you to the Board of Trade and also to some motel on the south side of Chicago? How do you know John Jr. didn't do the same? How do you know John Jr. isn't working with this Mr. Slick?"

"They've been helping us!"

"Are you sure? Look, I'm just saying—don't you find it a bit of a coincidence that you happened to find them?"

"If that's true, why would they string me along like this?"

"Look how helpful you are being at helping them cover their tracks. They didn't know about the backup tape. Now, thanks to you, they have it."

I was unsettled. I never questioned John Jr. and his team. "So what do you think? You really think Emily is going to kill us once we are no longer useful?"

"I'm not saying that. I don't know. I don't know who to trust. But look at it this way: They don't have to kill you. They have the only evidence proving your innocence—the tape of Slick planting the gun in your apartment. The gun used to kill Mr. Minter. What if they destroy that tape? They can turn you in to the police for a huge reward. You'd be convicted for sure. What's the reward? You're worth that much to them."

Although uncomfortable, I had to admit she had a point. I didn't think Strong and Associates was mixed up with Mr. Slick. But a huge reward was a pretty big incentive to lose the only exonerating evidence.

We heard a commotion, and then Isaac entered the kitchen. "What's going on?" I asked.

"Breaking news. A hotel maid was found raped and murdered—in Jack Thompson's hotel room! The police are pretty tight lipped, but the media is already starting the feeding frenzy. Someone reported that Mr. Thompson has what may be defensive wounds. I don't know if the police believe this, but according to the news media, he is already the prime suspect."

"Oh my gosh! I had no idea!" Emily gasped.

The surveillance efforts of Strong and Associates were stretched thin. Multiple video feeds were monitoring The Days Inn, CBOT, my apartment, Laura's apartment, the list went on.

After learning of the threat to Thompson, they installed one of their smoke detector/hidden cameras in Thompson's hotel room. But Isaac could not watch all the video feeds at once, let alone for twenty-four hours per day. And there was no point monitoring Thompson's hotel room when he wasn't even there. The focus was on protecting him, thinking an attempt would be made on his life. Just like Thomas Minter and myself. We all followed Isaac from the kitchen back to the war room.

John Jr. asked Isaac: "Have you checked the feed from Thompson's hotel room?"

"Not yet. Just heard the news." He sat down at a computer in the war room and had it cued up in a less than a minute, by which time the rest of us had settled in to the plush leather chairs around the conference table.

"Here we go," said Isaac. "I think I found it. Eight forty-eight a.m. Here is the maid entering Mr. Thompson's hotel room. Mr. Thompson is long gone, already at a breakfast meeting."

We sat in silence staring at the big screen on the wall. It was risky to put a hidden camera in Candidate Thompson's hotel room. Strong and Associates had debated whether or not they should. Placing surveillance on Mr. Slick and Mr. Elevator was an easy choice, but a presidential candidate? It reeked of Watergate, but Nate pushed for it. They didn't care what the Thompson team was strategizing about, and they would never release the tapes. Their motive was to protect Mr. Thompson. Eventually they agreed to plant the hidden camera. Now they were glad they did.

Strong and Associates had identified Mr. Slick and Mr. Elevator through fingerprints obtained in the course of their surveillance. Bob called in another favor to a contact at the bureau. The prints identified Mr. Slick as one Tony Silvasconi and Mr. Elevator as Mark Hansen.

As we watched the videotape, Mark Hansen could be seen entering Mr. Thompson's hotel room, which the maid had propped open with her cart. He was walking toward the maid, waving a hotel key card with his hand.

John Jr. showed some alarm. "Stop! Pause the tape!"

Isaac did so with a click of his mouse. John Jr. turned to Emily and glanced at Laura. "Emily, please take Laura to the kitchen." He did not need to explain why.

Emily stood and so did Laura. Laura did not argue. She did not want to see this. She followed Emily out of the war room, shaken. Emily stayed with Laura to keep her company, but also to keep tabs on her. Strong and Associates did not need any scared girlfriends running to the police. Laura had been through a lot, and they knew from experience that, in her state of shock, Laura might panic or react in unpredictable ways.

After the door was closed John Jr., looked at me and asked, "What about you, Mr. Roberts? You don't have to watch this. In fact I recommend you don't. We will tell you what happened, which is a whole lot better than having some images burned into your memory." He seemed to say this based on experience.

I considered this for a moment before replying, "No. I am in the middle of this thing. These guys tried to kill me. No sense sitting out. I'll be okay."

"Okay. Suit yourself."

Isaac was about to resume the tape when John Jr. motioned for him to stop. "Son of a gun, we missed it. *Take out Jack Thompson.* We assumed this meant kill him, after Minter and the attempts on Mr. Roberts. But this isn't the movies where people talk like that—take out this person or that person. Why not just say, 'Kill him'? No. They meant take him out, as a candidate, not kill him."

The rest of us absorbed this and nodded. He added, "Bob, can you call Agent Bruner, before we watch this tape." It was an order, not a question.

Bob understood right away. "Good idea. We need to tell him that we think we were wrong on the meaning of 'take out.' It wouldn't be right to let them continue the protection detail with this new information. He will understand. Hell, he may have already come to the same conclusion himself."

John Jr. raised his eyebrow. "Anything else we have to tell him?" He gave Bob a suspicious "Are we on the same page?" look.

"At this moment, we don't know who killed that maid. Granted, we have our suspicions." He pointed to the frozen image on the screen of Mark Hansen approaching the maid. "But I don't need to share my suspicions with the FBI." They were on the same page.

Bob motioned to the paused TV screen. "After I speak with Dan, we may come across new information."

Bob dialed Special Agent Dan Bruner on his cell phone and got voicemail. This was good in that Dan couldn't press him for more information. Bob thought about how he would word the recorded and archived voicemail.

"Dan, Bob here. Look, I am sorry about this, but I think we jumped to the wrong conclusion. We now think 'Take out Jack Thomson' did not mean kill him. We are watching the news and we think that maybe they meant set him up, frame him, not kill him. Maybe you already came to the same conclusion yourself. Sorry if we gave you a false alarm." He hung up. Less was more.

They sat back down, and Isaac continued the tape. Mark approached the maid, pretending to have an issue with his room key as he was holding one out. Without warning, he reached over her head with a cord, brought his hands forward so the cord went around her neck. In one fluid and fast motion, he then crossed his hands with a thrust in front of her. The maid was unable to scream and unable to breathe. She raised her hands helplessly to her throat.

Tony Silvasconi—Mr. Slick—could then be seen entering the room. He pushed the maid's cart into the room and closed the door. By the time Tony approached Mark, the maid was lifeless, being lowered to the ground by Mark, who was still holding the cord tightly.

We all sat motionless, staring at the screen. It was unbelievable to me that this was captured on tape like this. After the maid was dead, Mark slipped on gloves. Tony was already wearing gloves. They tore off some of the maid's clothes and used some type of an object to simulate a sexual assault. It was disturbing.

John Jr. said, "Disgusting. They know investigators will conclude that the sexual assault occurred after the maid was dead. Tissue damages and bruises differently depending on whether or not blood is moving through the victim's blood vessels at the time of the assault."

I shook my head, aghast, as I realized what John Jr. was getting at. The maid being dead made the crime easier for the two thugs, because she didn't put up a fight. Deviously, these guys must have also known how much more it would embarrass the suspect. Sexually assaulting a dead body! Talk about taking him out of politics forever.

As we watched the screen on the edges of our seats, Mark took out a small plastic syringe with a dull plastic point, similar to the syringes used to give children liquid antibiotics. He injected the syringe where medical examiners were sure to find it.

Then he took out a very tiny glass jar and removed the lid. Tony held the dead maid's right hand up. Mark separated her fingers and, holding the fingers one at a time, carefully scooped something out of the tiny glass jar with tweezers. Using the tweezers and his latex glove covered fingers, he pressed the contents of the glass jar under the maid's fingernails.

"I'll be," was all John Jr. could say. It was all anyone in the war room could say. We sat in solemn silence, thinking about the innocent maid that was just murdered, for several quiet minutes.

"Turn on channel five," said Emily from the kitchen. "Mr. Thompson is coming up to the podium in front of a bunch of reporters who smell blood."

Before Jack Thompson even got to the podium, a swarm of reporters were already shouting questions at him. It was chaotic; no one could hear anything. Mr. Thompson held his hands up toward the throng of pushing and shoving reporters and motioned his hands in a "calm down" gesture.

That quieted the reporters just long enough for the most aggressive reporter to repeat his question: "How do you explain the scratch marks on your neck!" It wasn't stated as a question but as an accusation.

This had not occurred to Mr. Thompson. He was so innocent that, up until that instant, he hadn't even thought about being a suspect. He paused for a moment. Then he regained his composure and began to speak. "Look, look, if you all calm down, I will address..." and he gestured with his hands once again for them to stop shouting.

Mr. Thompson continued, "I will make a brief statement, and then if you all would please settle down and take turns, I will take your questions." The throng quieted a bit, surprised. They were expecting "no comment" or nothing at all. But now they would have their feeding frenzy. Their prey had just consented to it. So they settled down.

Thompson opened with: "Tragically, an innocent life was callously brought to an end earlier today. First, I want to express my sincere condolences and deepest sympathies to the family of Maria Gonzalez. I support the police, always have, and now I support them in catching this ruthless killer. We cannot bring Ms. Gonzalez back. But we can and should

provide some closure for her family and justice for this heinous crime."

Reporters could no longer contain themselves. They began shouting over each other. "Are you a suspect? Is it true she was murdered in *your* hotel room? What about the scratches on your neck? Do you deny any involvement?"

Jack Thompson raised both palms again and gestured for the crowd of hungry reporters to settle down. When they did, he continued. "Let me be as clear as I can on these ridiculous questions. Yes, she was found in what *was* my hotel room. I had already left. I say this unequivocally: I had absolutely nothing to do with this. These rumors and innuendos are ridiculous and irresponsible. Please let the police conduct their investigation. They will get to the bottom of this." Although the reporters continued to shout questions, one of his staffers escorted him away.

The television cut back to the studio where a newscaster said, "Well folks, there you have it. Republican Jack Thompson denies any involvement in the brutal murder. Emphatically denies any involvement." Turning to the other newscaster, he added, "But, Alicia, we all saw that. He was given the chance to explain the scratches on his neck, and he *refused* to answer! What are we to make of that? If there is an innocent explanation for the scratches, why not get it out there, clear the air now?"

The news cast cut to an enlarged close up picture of the scratches on Mr. Thompson's neck.

The newscaster's sidekick, Alicia, nodded conspiratorially. "That is certainly a question a lot of people are asking right now. That is a question I am sure the family of Maria Gonzalez would like to hear an answer to."

"And now if you look at the screen, we have a second close-up of Jack Thompson's neck. This one from a picture taken last night at a fundraising dinner. Note there were no scratches. No scratches last night—late last night!"

The night-before picture of Thompson was added back to the screen to the left of the newer photo. The pictures were labeled "Before Murder" and "After Murder."

The newscaster continued, "And as you can see here, this picture on the right was taken at that news conference moments ago, scratches! So sometime between late last night and today, those scratches occurred on Jack Thompson's neck. Sometime between late last night and today, an innocent woman was brutally murdered, in— by his own admission—his hotel room!" The tone of the newscasters was unmistakable. They thought Thompson was guilty as hell.

The photos faded away, and the camera cut back to the newscaster. "Coming up, we are going to have an expert witness on the program. An expert in analyzing crime scenes, an expert in forensic evidence. Crimes just like this brutal murder. He is going to discuss 'defensive wounds' and whether or not the scratches on Jack Thompson's neck…would they… could they possibly be a dead woman's last message to us, identifying her killer? Stay tuned. We'll be right back with that and more on this developing story."

Chapter 21

Nicolas de Gaulle, was sipping a glass of chardonnay aboard his four-hundred-forty-foot yacht, named *Cui Bono*, in the Mediterranean when the news of Jack Thompson and the maid came across CNN. He laughed out loud and held his glass toward the TV in a toast.

Nicolas hated all US politicians, but he had a particular disdain for Republicans, like Thompson. He blamed them for reduced red tape and lower taxes, all of which made American companies more difficult for his numerous enterprises to compete with. He preferred to compete against businesses burdened by excessive regulations and onerous tax rates. He lobbied hard for protectionist trade policies, both at home and abroad. The Thompson news was cause for celebration aboard *Cui Bono*.

Nicolas de Gaulle was one of six founding members of B6, a secretive alliance of wealthy businessmen. All six founding members were billionaires. None of the original six were American citizens, but over the years, the group had grown to include a few. Nicolas cinched his spot as one of their strongest voices several years ago during the global credit crises.

Nicolas and several other B6 members owned Societé Paribas, the largest French bank, and the largest privately owned bank in the world. Although each B6 member owned a variety of other unrelated businesses, for most of the founding members, their stake in the French bank was their largest holding.

Like most Wall Street powerhouses, Societé Paribas had lucrative lines of business across investment banking, research and trading, and asset management. One of their most lucrative divisions had been generating consistent profits selling securitized mortgages, which were individual home mortgages bundled up in a group and then sold as a single security. Selling the securitized mortgages earned fat fees for the bank without giving the bank itself any exposure to the mortgages.

The problem was, unbeknownst to Nicolas, Societé Paribas was not just bundling and selling the securitized mortgages. They were also investing in them. Nicolas was of the view that the bank should sell anything they had a demand for, while taking a nice cut of course. Let the buyer beware. But buying toxic securities? Not on his watch.

Nicolas scoffed at US banks' foolishness in granting mortgages to Americans who put no money down and, in some cases, did not even have a job. A Ponzi scheme propelled by Congress. It did not matter how much you paid for a house as long as some sucker came along willing to pay even more. The US Congress had even mandated, through various programs, that banks make loans to those most likely to default. What folly! Under his direction, Societé Paribas maintained strict underwriting standards.

In the short term, the bank's profits were less than some other banks, but he reassured the bank's directors that the Americans were playing Russian roulette. Under his leadership, the bank would broker securitized mortgages, but they would not own them.

When Nicolas found out that the treasury department at Societé Paribas had loaded up on US-based, mortgage-backed securities, or MBS, he became enraged. He summarily fired the five top lieutenants in that department and then called an urgent meeting of B6. He had been very clear that the underwriting department was not to invest in their own deals. He was blindsided by the realization that the bank's own treasury department had.

In that B6 meeting, he explained the hazards of loose lending standards and how devastating the losses would be if the economy slowed or home prices flattened out. He boasted how diligent the underwriting department had been in avoiding this exposure in the first place. But now, their own treasury department had loaded up on mortgages in the secondary market, in an effort to make a few extra basis points in yield on the bank's fixed income portfolio.

The treasury department had bought into the idea that a diversified pool of mortgages would always be safe. To Nicolas, that was like saying if you bundle of bunch of individual pieces of crap together, somehow the aggregate bundle is no longer crap. To him, it was clear—it was all crap, and it threatened to bring the bank down. When the tally was complete, the numbers were staggering. Societé Paribas, through leveraged investments of their treasury department, owned $120 billion of MBS.

Nicolas, an effective executive, would never identify a problem without offering a solution. And his solution was bold—in fact, too bold for some of the more squeamish members of B6. The plan was both illegal and immoral. While the B6 members agreed that the mortgage exposure was toxic, and that it could ruin the bank, they wrestled with the ethical questions associated with his proposed solution. Nicolas reminded them that most of their net worth was tied up in the bank. Soon, the members voted unanimously to implement Nicolas's plan.

One hundred twenty billion dollars' worth of MBS was way more than they could unload due to the illiquidity of the MBS market. Worse, if word got out that Societé Paribas was liquidating its MBS, the market would panic and implode. As a fixed income instrument, most holders of MBS intended to hold the securities until maturity. As such, the size of the MBS market was gargantuan relative to the daily liquidity.

Nicolas's plan was simple. If the MBS market could not absorb the bank's holdings as quickly as they wanted to sell them, then the bank would create its own outlet—and demand—for the securities. The plan began with Pierre Voisard, who headed up Societé's asset management division.

Pierre began by hiring two new hedge fund managers, Jacques Constantineau and Samuel Evans. Both were re-garded as experts in the mortgage industry. Unbeknownst to these two mortgage experts, they were patsies. In a few years they would be infamous. As authorities searched for scape-goats to the credit crisis, the two hedge fund managers would even face overblown criminal charges in the United States, charges that they would ultimately be acquitted of.

A new hedge fund, under the direction of the new-ly hired mortgage all-stars, Jacques and Samuel, was launched with one hundred million in seed capital from Societé. The fund was to invest in a diversified pool of "safe" Residential Mortgage Backed Securities (RMBS) and Commercial Mortgage Backed Securities (CMBS). The fund's goal was to enhance the returns of the safe underlying RMBS and CMBS through the use of leverage. The fund's offering documents were clear: no limit was placed on the amount of leverage that could be utilized. Let the buyer beware.

B6 members initially balked. How do you reduce your MBS exposure by investing a fresh one hundred million dol-lars in the crap?

An aggressive marketing road show commenced to raise money from investors for the new fund. Pierre, the head of asset management, directed his institutional marketing team to focus their efforts on raising as much money as quickly as possible, and he offered them significant bonuses for success.

Soon the marketing team had created an aura, a buzz in the industry, about Societé's two new hedge fund manag-ers. Jacques Constantineau and Samuel Evans were being quoted in the Wall Street Journal and appearing as guests on CNBC.

Inflows into the "hot new fund" were attributed to investor appetite, not to the heretofore unprecedented marketing efforts to which they were actually due. The fund became the new institutional investor must-have.

In the first six months, marketers raised three billion dollars from investors. By the fund's first anniversary, assets had risen to nine billion. Meanwhile, the bank quietly withdrew its seed investment of a hundred million, by then valued at $130 million, due to the positive 30 percent return the first year. The fund levered itself five times, giving the nine-billion-dollar fund total buying power of forty-five billion. This did enhance the returns in good times. But at five times leverage, a simple 20 percent decline would wipe out all investor money.

Societé had taken great care in the negotiation of the wording of the fund's agreements with prime brokers and counterparties. If the fund defaulted, the losses would remain confined to the assets of the fund. The fund's structure and the counterparty agreements created a liability barrier protecting Societé Paribas. While investors and counterparties stood to lose tens of billions, the bank itself was insulated.

During the first year, numerous large block trades occurred in which the hedge fund purchased MBS from the bank's treasury department. MBS market participants and Societé's hedge fund investors did not realize that Societé Paribas had dumped more than fifty billion dollars of toxic assets off of the bank's balance sheet and into the hedge fund.

Another unexpected development made Nicolas de Gaulle giddy with laughter. The initial success of Societé's MBS hedge fund spawned a bunch of copycat funds. Other Wall Street firms decided that they too could capitalize on investor demand for leveraged hedge funds dedicated to MBS. As competing hedge funds marketed and grew their leveraged MBS hedge funds, Nicolas had yet another bunch of unsuspecting rubes to dump his toxic inventory on. It just didn't get any better than that, laughed Nicolas with the other members of B6. They created a hedge fund designed to fail, and soon others jumped in to catch a piece of the action.

In the end, under the Nicolas plan, Societé Paribas unloaded their entire $120 billion of MBS in just eighteen months. This was many years ahead of initial estimates. According to internal initial estimates, the plan required at least five years to implement—time through which the bank would be remain vulnerable to a collapse in the toxic mortgages.

During the implementation of this grand scheme, the economy marched along without a hiccup, and the housing bubble in the United States rose ever higher. By the time the bubble finally burst, Societé Paribas was the strongest and best-positioned major bank in the world with zero exposure to the toxic crap that brought down other major players.

Societé had even acquired a large short position in MBS via CDS (credit default swaps) on RMBS. The CDS positions were the equivalent of buying homeowners insurance on a house you did not own, when the house next door was already on fire. Like home insurance, CDS coverage was very cheap to buy, and if there was a catastrophe, you got paid in full.

Just three months after Societé had finished unloading its toxic assets, the MBS market experienced a decline coupled with a bout of illiquidity. The bank's then twelve-billion-dollar MBS hedge fund imploded in just one month. Hedge fund investors lost 100 percent. The hedge fund's banks, prime-brokers and other counter-parties lost much more.

Soon, the hedge fund made history as the catalyst for the worst ever global economic crisis since the Great Depression. It was seen as the canary in the coal mine. The high-profile hedge fund collapse sparked a rush to the exits, first from MBS. When investors could not fit through the MBS door all at once, panicked investors began to sell their high yield bonds. The contagion infected investment grade bonds and, ultimately, equity markets worldwide. The rout was on.

It took unprecedented and coordinated intervention by the world's Central Banks, along with a huge fiscal stimulus package in the United States to stabilize the world economy. When the smoke cleared, in typical kneejerk reaction, US prosecutors began the hunt for a scapegoat. They narrowed their sites on Societé's two "all-star" hedge fund managers, Jacques Constantineau and Samuel Evans, and filed criminal charges on forty-two counts of fraud.

Although the two men were French citizens and employees of a French bank, the US claimed jurisdiction because

Societé had offices in New York City and the hedge fund had numerous US clients. Prosecutors wanted to hold them accountable for a global credit contagion whose true blame lay at the feet of the entire banking and mortgage-lending industry, including US legislation that encouraged giving loans to unqualified borrowers. In Jacques and Samuel, prosecutors found the perfect targets. Rich, French, "Hedgies." Three strikes. Go get 'em!

Jacques and Samuel were guilty of believing that a levered portfolio of MBS instruments would never face this type of hundred-year flood scenario. But they were innocent of fraud, and they were unaware of Nicolas's and Pierre's master plan to get MBS securities off the bank's balance sheet.

Their risk models, which of course were backward looking, predicted that such an event could never happen because, so far, it hadn't. The stress tests they ran, anticipated that they could unwind enough of the fund's positions to weather any storm. That of course assumed that liquidity would remain constant, even in a crisis. They did not anticipate the extent to which liquidity could evaporate overnight, leaving them unable to exit any positions at any price.

Jacques and Samuel took a very public fall in the news media. Prosecutors made a stink over internal e-mails in which the two men discussed concerns about the portfolio: "I think this may be overvalued…What if the market corrects?" In the end, the jury found the e-mails to be what they in fact were: routine discussions everyone managing money would be expected to have. Jacques and Samuel were found innocent on all counts.

As planned, Societé Paribas itself was insulated and unscathed. Of course they had a minor black eye from the hedge fund's collapse, but the bad press would pass. The bank itself did not lose any money. In fact, within a few months, the press was full of stories about Societé's financial strength, how the venerable French bank did not go off the mortgage cliff with all the other lemmings.

The success of Nicolas's bold plan to save the bank made him think he was invincible. Fresh off the victory, his forays around the globe grew ever bolder.

Chapter 22

Over his lawyer's objections, Jack Thompson submitted to blood/DNA tests so that the police could see he had nothing to hide. He was confident the tests would clear him. He was anxious to put this episode behind him and get on with the campaign. All campaign events had to be cancelled. He couldn't talk about the issues. Everywhere he went, there was a mob of hostile reporters shouting accusations dressed up as questions.

But his nightmare had not yet even begun. Police officers arrived at a friend's house where he was staying in Winnetka, a north suburb of Chicago. Although he couldn't campaign until this firestorm passed, he decided it would look bad if he fled back to his home state of Ohio. He did not expect that police would arrive at this house with a warrant for his arrest. Prosecutors tipped off the media in advance of the arrest, to ensure there were cameras present to capture the spectacle. The politician doing the perp walk, humiliating to Thompson and his family, would no doubt be the lead story for the next few days.

Mr. Thompson's lawyer, Alan Fink, protested to the arriving officers: "Come on, gentlemen! You know my client would have voluntarily come in. Why go through this media circus when we don't have to?" But this was to no avail. The office of the US attorney for the Northern District of Illinois wanted the media spectacle. Three officers entered the front door, ignored Mr. Fink, and walked straight to Jack Thompson.

"Mr. Thompson, you are under arrest for the murder of Maria Gonzalez." One of the officers held up papers, which Alan Fink grabbed and examined. The second officer read Mr. Thompson his Miranda rights straight from a cheat sheet, while a third officer videotaped the Mirandizing. They were taking no chances with procedure on this arrest.

Jack was in shock. Alan protested again. "Gentlemen, please. Mr. Thompson has cooperated and will continue to do so. You see the army of reporters out there," he said, as he pointed to the crowd. He pleaded, "Please, let him walk to the car with a shred of dignity; there is no need for handcuffs."

But as Alan said this, the cuffs were already coming out, and one of the officers placed them on Mr. Thompson. Alan saw he couldn't stop it. He looked desperately to his friend and client as Jack was escorted out of the house. "Jack, don't say anything. I mean it. Not. One. Word." He wagged his finger to emphasize his point.

The news footage of Mr. Thompson's arrest, handcuffs and all, was played constantly for the rest of the day by multiple local and cable TV channels. Because he was the Republican frontrunner, the media frenzy was over the top. Rumors, innuendos, and even false accusations about his past history, all from unnamed sources.

The news talk shows, in their quest for ratings, disregarded normal journalistic standards. Hell, if they were going to have their show cancelled, just because they were more worried than a competing talk/news show about a lawsuit. It became a race for the jugular. Most news talk shows had by now dispensed with the custom of qualifying the allegations as "allegations," or noting that Mr. Thompson denied all the charges. "Innocent until proven guilty" was history. The evidence, they were told, was that strong. Why sound weak by hedging and qualifying every word they spoke?

All local stations and national news channels anxiously awaited the upcoming news conference to be hosted by the US attorney for the Northern District of Illinois along with Chicago's chief of police. Multiple channels interrupted normal programming at the start of the news conference.

The US attorney was a shrewd and handsome man. He was on the fast track to the governor's mansion himself. He was happy and upbeat today, but not because justice was being served. He was satisfied that he was in line to get credit for convicting a famous and well-known politician. He was basking in the adoring TV reporters.

The news conference began with a statement by the chief of police, who was not enthralled with all the media attention. He came off, in his thick south side of Chicago accent ("Pass da kielbasa; da Bears game is on!"), as a no-nonsense guy, just another day at work. He had no career aspirations higher than Chicago police chief. He outlined the investigation very matter-of-factly and then introduced the US attorney. His comments lasted twenty seconds.

The US attorney stepped up to the podium as if he were about to give his inaugural address. He commended the police chief and all of CPD and then rambled on about how the Chicago Police Department and the US attorney's office had cooperated so splendidly together on this case. Two minutes into his speech, he had yet to say anything. If it was the Academy Awards, they would have long since cued the music and cut to a commercial. Then he dropped the bomb:

"Semen recovered from the deceased victim was identified as belonging to Jack Thompson. Tissue, also identified as Jack Thompson's, was recovered from under the victim's fingernails."

The US attorney had rehearsed those two lines, knowing that they would be replayed on multiple news and talk shows. As he spoke, one of his staffers placed a poster-size picture of the scratches on Jack Thompson's neck on an easel next to the podium.

The US attorney then cleared his throat, as if he were getting a bit emotional, which he wasn't, but he was a good actor and an even better politician. He had an instinct for what played well. He then lowered his voice to a quieter tone, and the roomful of reporters hushed. In a somber voice, he said, "The medical examiner has confirmed that the victim was raped. The medical examiner's office has also confirmed that the rape occurred postmortem." He looked down and shook his head as the crowd gasped. Inside he was ecstatic.

He wished he had a press conference of this magnitude to deliver every day!

The media went nuts. OJ Simpson and Michael Jackson all combined on steroids nuts. None of those cases were as clear cut as this one. The evidence was overwhelming! The US attorney reveled in the twenty-four-hour news coverage, most of it repeating, over and over, the same few sound bites and showing the poster of Mr. Thompson's scratched neck. By the next day, the US attorney was thrilled to see himself on the front page of the *Chicago Tribune* and the *Chicago Sun Times*, as well as a few national papers including *USA Today*.

Back at John Jr.'s house, a serious discussion was taking place regarding if and when and how to inform the police that Jack Thompson was innocent, that in fact, the murder was caught on tape.

On the one hand, we felt an obligation to come forward with the video exonerating Mr. Thompson. He was going through hell. On the other hand, once we came forward, the people who Silvasconi and Hansen worked for would compartmentalize. The real perpetrators would do everything to cover their tracks and our investigation would likely hit a dead end. No bigger fish. Set Jack Thompson free? Or delay that while we pursued leads?

We kicked around another issue: What would happen to Strong and Associates if they came forward with the video? The video was obtained illegally.

I asked, "Maybe prosecutors would go easy on the illegal wiretapping because Strong and Associates did the right thing? Strong and Associates ensured justice was served?"

Bob said, "If we come forward, the US attorney will be very upset. We'll be pulling the rug out from under him on the biggest case of his career—the murder trial of a presidential candidate. You see how much he is enjoying these news conferences? No, I think he will hate us and throw the book at us."

Finally John Jr. stood and said, "We all know what we have to do, right? We can't let an innocent man rot in jail—whatever the damage or consequences may be."

We nodded. Bob said, "You're right. We don't have a choice. We do the right thing. We have to give the video to police."

John Jr. said, "We do the right thing—agreed. But our obligation is to Jack Thompson, not CPD. Let's show him what we have. He may want to continue the investigation, figure out who set him up? He may agree with us that, if the video comes out now, he may never learn who set him up?"

We all nodded and had formulated a plan. After discussing the details a bit more, John Jr. contacted Alan Fink, Jack Thompson's attorney. At least for now, he was still Mr. Thompson's attorney. Alan handled countless business matters for Mr. Thompson, but he was not a criminal defense lawyer. Jack Thompson was now in need of one of the best specialists in criminal defense.

John Jr. told Alan that he had information that would exonerate his client and friend. But John Jr. refused to give it to Alan, or even tell him anything specific. He said he had to meet with Jack Thompson personally, and he would, of course, allow Alan to sit in on the meeting.

Alan hesitated because he was deluged with all types of people trying to get in touch with himself and Mr. Thompson. A lot of crazies, some threats, and more than a few investigative reporters who outright lied and posed as something they were not in order to worm their way into the very juicy unfolding news drama that was now captivating America.

John Jr. finally said, "Look, you check me out, and you check on my firm, Strong and Associates. You will find out that we are for real. I will, at some point, meet with Jack Thompson, with or without your cooperation. I hope I don't have to tell him you stood in the way of his release."

Chapter 23

Abigail Mason was a tough, smart, no-nonsense lady—a Yale-educated lawyer, former senator, and now secretary of state. Her husband was a politician too, having served as governor of Illinois years before. The ultimate power couple. While Bill Mason faded into retirement, Abigail Mason worked seventy hours a week.

Bob and Nate sat around the war room digesting Abigail Mason's commodities trading windfall. They had researched Abigail Mason, her husband Bill, as well as Vince Fleming, the special assistant to the deputy chief of staff. Fleming was a political appointee. Also from Illinois, he had been a political operative for years, part of Chicago's infamous Democratic machine. Illinois politicians in general and Chicago politicians in particular had a long history of seedy behavior. Patronage, graft, corruption, and ties to organized crime were intertwined with politics in Illinois more so than any other state. How many states can claim four of their last seven governors went to prison?

After long hours cross-referencing the histories and ties between the president, the secretary of state, and Vince Fleming, Bob and Nate grew tired. They needed a break.

Bob began by saying, "In the bureau we were pretty big on facial recognition. We learned to focus on those features people can't change with a wig or different clothes. You did a lot of that too, right?"

Nate agreed. "Yeah. You can't change certain features, and, we also emphasized that you can't hide certain mannerisms. A particular gait, or hand-gesture habits. Take Abigail Mason—sometimes her mouth smiles while her eyes seem angry, stare a hole right through you. Strange dichotomy."

"I hear you. A person can force a smile with his or her mouth, but the eyes are the windows to the soul."

"I wonder if she has a soul. Pretty calculating bitch I hear."

"And very ambitious. About her eyes staring a hole though you—did you see the case studies on Botox?"

"Yep."

"So, Ms. Mason may not be as disingenuous and calculating as she appears."

"Yeah, she had Botox. It messes with your facial muscles and expressions big time. Maybe her eyes are smiling, or at least trying to, but those muscles just don't work."

"The Botox sometimes makes them look…almost crazy. You ever notice what happens when somebody with a Botox-filled forehead laughs? Crazy eyebrows, man, like the Joker from Batman comics!" They both laughed.

"Abigail Mason is a little tough on the eyes, ain't she?"

Emily approached the war room and stopped in the doorway. Bob and Nate didn't notice she was there.

Bob chuckled. "No wonder her husband is rumored to have a thing for interns. A guy needs an outlet, right?"

Now they were both snickering. They still didn't see Emily standing in the doorway.

Bob said, "Naked political ambition might explain why she sticks with a husband who has a bimbo eruption every six months. But maybe she doesn't care. I hear she likes to wear the pants, if you know what I mean." He raised his eyebrows a couple times.

Emily cleared her throat.

"Emily!" Nate blushed. "Bob and I were just discussing the pathological profiles of Vince Fleming, the president, and Abigail Mason. You know, textbook stuff, comparing notes, trying to solve the case."

Emily shook her head and smiled. "What textbook? *Middle School Boys and Their Clever Banter*?"

Bob smirked. "Okay, okay, you busted us. But you have to admit, Abigail Mason…"

Emily crossed her arms and frowned at him, but she was fighting back a smile, and Bob and Nate knew that. They all enjoyed a very comfortable relationship with one another.

Bob changed course, raised his arms in surrender. "Okay, sorry. But we do have to tie the secretary of state to what we already know. Or maybe even the president."

Nate said, "Vince Fleming, a White House staffer, gave orders to professional hit men. The same hit men who killed billionaire Thomas Minter. This points straight to the president."

Emily interrupted. "That's conjecture at this point." She sat down with them.

Bob conceded. "Right now, we can barely tie this Mr. Slick character to Vince Fleming. So we can't tie him to anyone else."

Nate replied, "Yes, but this isn't a court of law, just our opinions. Opinions lead to theories, which lead to evidence, which ultimately leads to the proof that convicts." Turning to Emily, he asked, "We can't prove much right now. So forget proof. For the moment, what's your gut?"

Emily didn't take long to answer. "At first, I thought the Masons were dirty as hell. Thought they had Minter killed to cover up Abigail Mason's illegal commodities trading windfall. Thought they were trying to kill Jack Thompson because he is a political rival. They are both frontrunners in the primaries. Soon, they'll be running against each other for president. Crazy stuff! All of it." She shook her head almost in disbelief.

Bob and Nate nodded.

Emily said, "But the Thompson situation changes everything for me. If Thompson was set up, maybe someone is also trying to set up Abigail Mason. It would be kind of foolish for her to take these risks now. She is the next Democratic presidential candidate. She doesn't need the money. Her husband cashed in big time since he left politics. She'll make millions whenever she leaves politics for the private sector."

Nate jumped in, saying, "She already made millions from her recent book."

Bob nodded. "I read about that. Fourteen-million-dollar advance for a book that barely sold any copies. I guess it's nice to be known as a presidential contender. So if she doesn't need the money, and she doesn't want a potential scandal to end her presidential aspirations, why? Why risk it?"

Emily said, "That's my point. She has too much to lose. It would seem irrational to be involved in any of this. She would have to be so arrogant to be this brazen, thinking the rules apply to everyone else but not to her. So I wonder if maybe someone is trying to set her up, just like Thompson was set up."

Bob said, "Thompson and Mason are the clear frontrunners. Who would benefit if one or both imploded?"

Emily said, "That's hard to say. A lot of other potential candidates, but none as strong and likely as these two."

Nate continued this line of reasoning. "Why kill Thomas Minter unless you wanted the illegal commodity trades to be traced back to Abigail Mason?"

Bob agreed. "That's been bugging me. We found the illegal trades quickly. But after Minter's murder, Maco Commodities is being turned upside down. I have no doubt investigators would have found these trades."

Emily said, "And it's a great setup: the hedge fund under a different name, Abigail Mason the sole beneficial owner. It's all mysterious enough to look like Mason was trying to get away with it, yet at the same time, because of Minter's murder, it was certain to be discovered."

Bob theorized, "Maybe Mason did intend to get away with it, but Minter's murder messed the whole scheme up."

Nate replied, "So killing Minter wasn't part of their original plan?"

Emily shook her head. "Or maybe one person on the inside saw an opportunity to turn on Mason—mess up the whole scheme and ensure she gets caught."

Nate shook his head. "So Thompson and the secretary of state are both innocent, both being set up?"

Bob looked uneasy. "Maybe some other potential candidate is behind all this. Who would advance by both Thompson and Mason going down in scandals?"

Nate said, "Let's not forget Vince Fleming. He works for the president, not the secretary of state."

Emily said, "I know. But I just can't see the president stooping this low. He's already president. Second term, can't run again. Mason, on the other hand, is full of political ambition and still has everything to gain. She can take risks the president would not."

Bob said, "Feels like we are back to square one. Hell, Mason, Fleming, and the president are all a product of sleazy Illinois politics—it could be any of them. Or all of them? Or someone else?" He sounded exasperated at the circles they were going in.

Emily nodded. "The Masons are on the take from big corporations like Byson Foods, whether we can prove it or not. Since Bill Mason left office, public disclosures show their net worth jumped to more than two hundred million!

Who knows, maybe that is how they finance these illicit activities, with hit men and such?" She paused for a moment. "Whoever is behind it, it's hard to believe. This is America, not some backward banana republic or Putin's Russia. Politicians aren't supposed to eliminate their adversaries here. We are supposed to have evolved past that."

Bob nodded. "So how do we nail them? Maybe nail Fleming and get him to turn on the president or whoever in exchange for leniency? To do that, we need more on him than we now have."

Nate said, "Fleming could be acting on his own. I don't believe that. But that's what the president would say if Fleming is caught."

Bob added, "Turn him on Abigail Mason. She is no stay-home-and-bake-cookies gal. She is smart, tough, and full of ambition, motive, and opportunity. And enough arrogance to think she could get away with it. We've seen this before from her—scandal, after scandal, after scandal. Basic rules, like using your official e-mail for official business apply to others, not to her."

Emily summed up their thoughts. "Either way, Fleming is the key, for now. Focus on him, and see where it leads."

Chapter 24

John Jr. persuaded Jack Thompson's attorney, Alan Fink, to arrange a meeting with Thompson. The meeting would be in jail, where Thompson was being held. I wanted to go to the meeting, wanted to be involved every step of the way. But I was wanted for murder, even though they were not yet plastering my picture on the news. We knew numerous law enforcement agencies were circulating my picture in connection with Minter's murder. John Jr. thought I might be recognized, especially at a jail full of law enforcement personnel. I turned the argument around and said the last place they would be looking for me was in jail.

John Jr. thought it too risky. Unnecessarily risky was the word he used. I insisted. This was my life hanging in the balance through all this. I pleaded, "Even if I am caught, I'm okay with that. Just like Jack Thompson, I will be exonerated as soon as police see the video of that scumbag planting the gun in my kitchen."

John Jr. said, "Yes, but Thompson is in jail right now! Proven innocent doesn't happen instantly. Criminal procedures can move at a glacial pace. You might still spend time in police custody being questioned. Maybe even jail for several nights."

"I'm okay with that."

John Jr. frowned. "You don't know what that's like. Besides—these thugs want you dead. Think they can't get to you in police custody?"

I hadn't thought about that. They probably could, based on everything we had seen thus far. But I wasn't going to be passive. This was my life. I looked straight at John Jr. and said, "I understand. But after what these bastards have done, I'm not sitting these events out. What about a disguise like we discussed earlier?"

John Jr. nodded and then said, "Okay. Okay." He looked at me. "I'm trying to protect you, but I understand. Truth is, if I were in your shoes, I'd be involved every step of the way too."

Emily clipped my hair into a flattop, and I tried on at least a dozen pairs of glasses. We settled on a pair of thick, dark-rimmed glasses with nonprescription lenses. They were tinted so slightly that you could wear them indoors without attracting too much attention. I wasn't crazy about the glasses, but everyone assured me they did a great job of disguising my natural look. CPD had distributed pictures of the old me.

Isaac also brought out an assortment of men's suits and dress shirts in a variety of sizes. I found a crisp white shirt in my size and blanched at the $275 price tag that was still on it. Laura and Emily selected a silk tie—dark toned, a conservative business look, according to Emily. We also found a gray suit that fit well. Gieves and Hawkes, a brand I had never heard of—Emily told me it cost $2,800!

Next she handed me a pair of Salvatore Ferragamo wing-tips. They fit well enough. I could almost see my reflection in the tops of the shoes. I read the price tag on the shoe box and jerked my head back as if I had been electrocuted.

Emily smiled and said, "You look like a very successful young lawyer."

Although the short-cropped hair, glasses, and expensive suit seemed simple as far as disguises go, I did feel unrecognizable. Laura smiled and nodded approvingly. But I couldn't believe the prices. In fact, I felt guilty about the costs and told Emily and John Jr. I would never pay this much for clothes or shoes.

John Jr. said, "That, Mr. Roberts, is exactly why you are dressed so expensively! CPD is not looking for you." As he said this, he held his hands out toward me in a sweeping motion from my head to my toes.

Laura looked me over, smiled, and said, "Pretty schnazzy."

Emily loaned Laura a white blouse, conservative skirt, and matching blazer. No time was spent disguising her; she wasn't wanted for murder.

Alan Fink led the way to our jail house attorney-client meeting with Jack Thompson. John Jr., Laura, and I accompanied him. The jail staff initially balked at allowing all four of us into the interview room, which was normally reserved only for suspects and their attorneys.

Alan Fink, in a very lawyerly, threatening way reasoned with the main guard. "You obviously have not read the relevant statutes. My client is constitutionally guaranteed access to his legal representatives. That means team, not lawyer.

Just because your garden variety car thieves and drug dealers only have one lawyer doesn't change the law. All four of us are critical parts of Mr. Thompson's legal team. If you do not let us in to see our client this instant, I will march straight outside to all those reporters and announce to the world that you," he said, jabbing a finger at the guard, "refused to grant Mr. Thompson access to his legal team. I will scream from the rooftops that I suspect you won't let us see him due to the harsh treatment that I fear he has received here." He looked at the head guard nose to nose. "We both know what the news media will do with that."

I added, "The US attorney prosecuting our client has an army of people on his side." I looked at the guard. "That seem fair to you?"

The guard looked at me. He held his gaze for an uncomfortably long time without replying. Then he squinted his eyes and turned his head slightly to the right, while his eyes remained locked on me—like he knew me from somewhere and was trying to remember from where.

Oh shit, I thought. *He recognizes me.*

Alan interrupted the guard's thought process. He stared a hole right through the guard and wagged his finger at him. "The person who denies Mr. Thompson his constitutional right to legal representation will lose his job over this fiasco!"

The guard looked uncomfortable. He was used to being in charge at the jail. I could almost see the mental calculus of the guard as well as his conclusion: this wasn't a battle he wanted to fight.

Salvaging a little dignity, the guard said, "Fine, but we will have to check you and your briefcases before you enter."

After a cursory frisking and a quick check of our bags, which contained the usual papers and laptops of lawyers, we were shown into a concrete-walled room with a small metal table flanked by two metal chairs. Both the table and the chairs were fastened to the concrete floor. It took about five minutes before Jack Thompson was escorted, shackled in handcuffs, to the interview room.

As he was led inside, the main guard said, "Thirty minutes." This was out of habit. Most criminal lawyers didn't even take that long with their clients. Alan Fink again stared a hole through the guard and said, "There is a gaggle of hungry reporters waiting to speak with me outside. I will let you know when we are finished. And if you even think of interrupting us or in any way trampling on my client's constitutional rights, I will go nuclear." He pointed in the direction of the hungry reporters.

The guard nodded. "Uh, I guess just knock on this door when you are finished. Heavy door, may have to knock pretty hard." Standing in the open doorway, he glanced around the tiny room, and his eyes stopped on me again.

Why was he fixated on me? Most guys' eyes would be drawn to Laura. Did he look at me with jealousy (younger and apparently richer) or resentment (hates all lawyers)? *Did he recognize me?* The guard stared right at me as he slowly closed the door. *Is he going to confirm his suspicion while we are in the interview room? Am I not leaving the jail with John Jr.?*

"Well done, Alan," admired John Jr. after the door was closed.

Alan ignored John Jr.'s comment and took control. He approached Jack, placed both of his hands on Jack's shoulders, and said, "Jack, sorry for the surprise here, but I think you will want to hear this." He motioned to John Jr. and then to myself and Laura as he said, "John Strong Jr., Christian Roberts, and Laura Baldwin."

We shook hands, which was a little awkward due to Jack Thompson's handcuffs. His hands were bound in standard handcuffs in front of him, but those were connected to a chain around his waist. Another chain ran straight down from his waist and connected to his ankles, which were also chained to one another so that he had to walk in half-size shuffle steps.

Alan asserted, "Just to be clear, everything here is subject to attorney-client privilege. We can speak freely, and they," he said, motioning to the guards, "cannot and will not eavesdrop on us. This room is designed for confidential attorney-client meetings."

John Jr. opened politely with: "Mr. Thompson, please have a seat." He motioned to a chair and then sat down opposite Mr. Thompson. The rest of us had no choice but to remain standing.

After they were seated John Jr. said, "Thank you to your attorney Alan here, for setting this meeting up. You have been through hell, so I will get straight to the point. We have proof that you did not harm that maid."

John Jr. was opening up a laptop as he continued, "I know a lot of whackos are trying to get your attention now, and I wouldn't put it past some scummy reporter to lie to you about having information that could exonerate you." Looking sympathetically at Mr. Thompson, he said, "I don't want you to have any doubt that we are for real. It would be disgusting to lie to you about something like this."

By now the laptop was open and ready to play a video. "For reasons that I will explain later, we have video footage of your hotel room." He pressed play and pushed the laptop over to Jack. Alan stood behind him and peered over his shoulder.

"We spliced together a few bits here, so that you would know we are not staging this in some other hotel room. They're all identical, right? See, here you are, getting ready that morning."

Alan and Jack stared open-mouthed at the video. Alan demanded, "How the hell did you get this, and what right did you have to invade Jack's privacy?!"

John Jr. remained very calm and said, "I will explain that later. But right now, irrespective of how we got this video, I think Mr. Thompson will just be very glad that we did."

Alan and Jack thought about this. Jack looked to Alan and nodded. Alan's indignation subsided.

John Jr. narrated further: "There was a camera in the ceiling, disguised as a smoke detector. We want to show you here that this is in fact you, and this is your hotel room. If you have any questions about the authenticity of this tape, I assure you we will work with Alan right after we leave here, show him the whole continuous tape, and let him, or his experts, examine it. But for now, we are going to skip ahead, in the interest of time."

Jack and Alan huddled together, speechless, watching the computer screen.

"You have long since left the room. Here is the maid. The door to your room is blocked open by her cart. You now see a man we have identified as Mark Hansen enter your room. I apologize in advance; this is very graphic. You may not want to watch. But it clearly exonerates you." He paused the video.

John Jr. looked to Jack and Alan.

Jack nodded. "It's okay; I guess we have to see this."

John Jr. pressed play.

Laura was glad she was standing opposite the laptop and could not see the screen. She squeezed my hand. Jack and Alan jumped when Hansen jerked the cord around the maid's neck. They each looked away several times, but their eyes were drawn back. Despite the graphic nature of the horrendous crime, they both had to see it. They had to know for sure if this video would exonerate Jack.

When the worst and most violent part was over John Jr. said, "The second man has been identified as Anthony Silvasconi. I assume this is obvious to you, but to be clear, you can see them plant DNA evidence. Semen first. Then the tissue planted under her fingernails."

Alan was bewildered. "Is it Jack's semen? How the hell do they have that?"

"It's easier than you might think. They have probably been following Mr. Thompson for some time, going through his linens and his garbage." John Jr. pointed to Mr. Thompson's neck. "I have a pretty good guess, but who scratched you and when?"

John Jr. held his left hand up to the deep scratches on his neck. "The night before, as I was entering my hotel room. Some lady blamed me for her son's death in Iraq. I thought she mistook me for a congressman who voted for the war."

"Any witnesses?"

"One of my aides."

"Did he or she see the scratches?"

Jack thought for a moment. "He. And no, we were both going to bed. He was already entering his room when it happened. I didn't realize myself how bad she got me until I was in my room." Jack looked worried. *Nobody saw the scratches!*

Alan recognized the worry in his client's eyes. "Don't worry about that, Jack. This tape is enough all by itself. With this tape, people will believe you got scratched as part of the setup."

Alan started walking to the door of the small interview room. "Well, let's get you out of this godforsaken nightmare!" He raised his arms up and motioned around the dreary concrete block room. He was ready to rush out of the room to secure Jack's immediate release. He couldn't wait to put a stop to the continuous inflammatory news coverage. Jack wasn't just his client; he was a friend.

This was why we had insisted on meeting with Jack Thompson, even though the tape could have been given to his attorney.

John Jr. looked at Jack Thompson. "Do you want to know who set you up?"

Jack looked up, tilted his head at John Jr., and narrowed his eyes. Alan, who was about to pound on the thick metal door, froze.

"We have proof. I will share all the details with Alan after we leave here. Those two killers," he said, pointing to the laptop, "were taking orders from the White House."

"What!" Jack screeched in disbelief.

"Let me clarify. We do not yet have direct evidence connecting this to the president or other high-level officials. But we do have proof that these men took orders from Vince Fleming."

Thompson blurted out, "Fleming is a Democratic political hack in Chicago!"

John Jr. added, "Did you know he is now a special assistant to the deputy chief of staff?"

"No…wow." Thompson shook his head in disgust.

John Jr. said, "We also have evidence that Secretary of State Abigail Mason benefitted from related events."

Thompson was in shock. He muttered, "The president and the secretary of state?" He and Alan shook their heads in stunned silence.

John Jr. added, "The president and the person you will be running against next year. We have no direct evidence linking the president or the secretary of state. Circumstantial stuff, and Vince Fleming."

Thompson fired back: "Easy for them to disavow."

"Exactly. If we go public with this now, we nail Hansen and Silvasconi. Two thugs who deserve to rot in jail. And they will, no doubt. But, two low-level thugs. The link to the president and/or to Abigail Mason right now is circumstantial at best."

Alan opined, "I don't think I like where you are going with this."

John Jr. said, "I see two choices. One: get out of jail right now, and two low-level thugs go down. Maybe we can link Fleming beyond a reasonable doubt, maybe not. But the Masons and the president will deny everything. Even if Fleming goes down, they won't."

Jack nodded. "Bastards. I can see it now: 'We are shocked and embarrassed by Vince Fleming…'"

"Option two," John Jr. continued. "We keep quiet. You remain a suspect. We continue the investigation until we nail the real powers that be."

Alan and Jack both cringed. Jack looked down at the handcuffs on his wrists.

John Jr. said, "I know, I know—it's not ideal. But we have a chance to nail these bastards. If this evidence comes out now, the trail goes cold. We may never establish a link to anyone higher."

Jack sighed as both Alan and Jack pondered all this.

John Jr. explained to Alan and Jack the balance of what we knew. That Hansen and Silvasconi, who were tied to Fleming, were also connected to the murder of Thomas Minter, the billionaire founder of Maco Commodities. He went on to explain the possible motive for killing Minter: Abigail Mason's fifteen-million-dollar commodities trading windfall through illegal, prearranged trades. Last, he explained why they had placed the hidden camera in Mr. Thompson's hotel room.

"We just need a little time," John Jr. pleaded.

"How long?" asked Jack.

"Hard to say. We are working around the clock. The FBI is involved." That much was true. John Jr. knew they would have to share the evidence exonerating Mr. Thompson with Special Agent Bruner very soon.

Jack Thompson sat in silence for a full minute. John Jr. and Alan did not interrupt the silence, as it was clear Jack was deep in thought.

Finally Jack sat up indicating he had made his decision. He asked Alan, "The bail hearing is tomorrow morning, right?"

"Yes. Eight a.m."

Jack Thompson looked at John Jr. and said, "Okay, one more night you have, minimum. I'll stay here tonight. If they release me on bail tomorrow morning, you have all the time you need. I can endure the media firestorm from my home. But not here. If they don't grant me bail," he said and looked down and shook his head, "I just can't stay here." He glanced around the tiny, dreary room.

John Jr. nodded. "Fair enough. I understand." But we all knew the chance of bail being granted was very low. The crime was horrific. The evidence was scientific and conclusive. Without the exonerating video, it was almost impossible that any judge would grant bail in such circumstances.

Jack explained, "Look, I want to nail the bastards. But you don't know what it's like in here. The guards think I'm guilty. They act like they are ready to impose justice, vigilante style on me. And I need to be with my family. They are being harassed and even threatened over this. I can handle the shellacking I'm taking in the news media. But not the threats to my family."

Jack turned to Alan and smiled. "I want you to issue a very strong and decisive statement from me. Something like, 'I am innocent. I was framed. But I still have faith in the American justice system that I will be completely exonerated."

Alan said, "The evidence they think they have is overwhelming. The media will jump all over such a statement. They will crucify you if you issue a statement like that!"

Jack smiled even bigger. "That is the point. I want to give them some rope to hang themselves with. Bait the jackals out there to be even more irresponsible in their news coverage of me. Then, when the truth comes out, it will be fun to watch them run for cover."

Chapter 25

Within two hours of leaving the jail, John Jr. and Bob were having an emergency meeting with Special Agent Dan Bruner. I wanted to go to this meeting, of course, but couldn't. Pictures of me had been shared with all local police and sheriff's departments as well as the FBI and TSA. While it was one thing to get past a guard at the Cook County Jail, John Jr. and Bob explained that they could not bring me to a meeting with an FBI agent without serious ramifications.

In their meeting, John Jr. and Bob brought Dan up to speed on Minter's murder and the connection to the White House via Vince Fleming. They also documented Abigail Mason's fifteen-million-dollar "gift" from Byson Foods via the offshore hedge fund. Dan was impressed.

All three men knew that investigative leads like this would enhance Dan's standing in the FBI. They were doing Dan a favor. John Jr. and Bob made a proposal: They would turn over everything to Agent Bruner. All they wanted in return was proper credit, when credit was due, for the five-million-dollar reward now being offered by the family of Thomas Minter.

Laura reminded me that Strong and Associates now had five million reasons to destroy the video of Silvasconi planting the gun in my kitchen and simply turn me over to CPD.

Back to the meeting John Jr. and Bob were having with Agent Bruner, it was a good deal for everyone present. Strong and Associates got credit for information leading to the arrest of Minter's killer. Special Agent Dan Bruner could take all the credit for everything else: unraveling the maid's murder, Jack Thompson's setup, and most important to Dan's FBI career, the possible resulting case against a sitting president or the secretary of state.

This was shaping up to be an historic case: White House officials involved in the murder-for-hire plot to kill an innocent maid, all to frame and destroy a political rival. Then Dan would still get to pursue an investigation of Abigail Mason's illegal commodities trading profits. And that could lead to a prosecution of Byson Foods. All in all, this was shaping up to be a very productive day for Special Agent Bruner.

They warmed up Agent Bruner with all these career-making cases before they showed him the video of the maid's murder. Dan understood why they did not lead with this, the most dramatic piece of evidence. Strong and Associates had violated the law in obtaining it. But it was hard to be mad at folks who just handed you several ground-breaking cases.

After watching the tape, even Dan, a veteran FBI agent, was stunned. "Unbelievable," was all he could say as he shook his head. Then he began to process things. "We have the issue of how you got this tape." He looked straight at his former colleague Bob when he said this. "But that is at the bottom of my priority list right now. You did the right thing coming forward."

Bob nodded. There would be hell to pay on the issue of illegal wiretapping. But Strong and Associates was not withholding key evidence from the FBI.

This would be a big victory, in fact multiple victories, for the FBI. While on the surface, the FBI and other police departments cooperated with each other, there still existed a lot of rivalry and competition—competing over jurisdiction or competing over credit for successful investigations. The Chicago Police Department had thus far owned the investigation of the maid's murder and the prosecution of Jack Thompson. CPD was ready to hang Jack Thompson on the spot. CPD also owned the investigation of Minter's murder, for which they were preparing to hang me. Now the FBI had a chance to ride in on a white horse and, not only exonerate two innocent people but convict the real killers. This would be a big day for the bureau and a real coup for Bruner. And a real embarrassment to the CPD. They had the wrong guy—twice.

John Jr. redirected the conversation. Time was critical, and running out. "Do we agree that this investigation is better pursued and will more likely result in the conviction of higher-ups, if this evidence stays under wraps?" He pointed to the laptop computer with the video of the maid's murder.

Dan became alarmed. This was going to be a career-making case for him. But on the surface he was cool. He thought before answering. "Absolutely. If this gets out, the real investigation might as well be over. Everyone connected to these crimes will crawl under their rocks and never come out. We will be left with trying to tie higher-ups to all this through the testimony of these two thugs," he said, as he motioned to the video of Hansen and Silvasconi.

John Jr. finished Dan's thought for him. "The testimony of convicted killers seeking leniency for cooperating, by naming a bigger fish. It would be easy for higher-ups to deny any involvement. Claim the convicted thugs will say anything the prosecution tells them to, in the hopes of a lighter sentence."

Bob summed it up: "Their testimony won't stand up beyond a reasonable doubt. Period. We all know that. We need direct evidence."

John Jr. and Bob had Dan's attention. John Jr. said, "The problem is you can't let an innocent man rot in jail while you pursue your investigations. Jack Thompson is a very decent human being. If he is released on bail tomorrow morning, this stays under wraps, and you," he said, looking at Dan, "get to continue these investigations."

Dan nodded. He was practically salivating at the thought of busting White House officials.

John Jr. said, "But if Mr. Thompson is denied bail, the video comes out. Tomorrow morning. One way or the other, tonight is Mr. Thompson's last night in jail."

Dan nodded his understanding of this, and they could see him trying to think up a solution, which is just what John Jr. and Bob had hoped for.

Dan said, "I understand. That's fair, I guess. Thompson must be going through hell. Leave it with me."

"Okay," was all John Jr. could say. He wasn't assured. Neither was Bob, and Dan sensed this. Tomorrow morning was not enough time to link the bigger fish to these crimes. It was all but certain that the judge would not release Thompson pending the trial.

Dan said, "Will you be at the bail hearing?"

"I don't know."

"You should be." Agent Bruner winked.

John Jr. raised his eyebrows, and Bob tilted his head and cracked a smile. They did not know what Dan had in mind, but they were reassured, maybe even optimistic. Dan Bruner seemed to have something up his sleeve.

Chapter 26

The handler was a high-level position within the organization. Highly trusted, he served as a firewall between thugs like Silvasconi and the real powers that be. Because of handlers like him, the higher-ups never got their hands dirty. In fact, Silvasconi did not even know the identity of his handler. Silvasconi and the handler—indeed the entire organization—were completely compartmentalized. Layers and layers of compartmentalization separated thugs like Silvasconi from the top powers.

The handler had a great deal of autonomy and authority. Because of the compartmentalization, he had to make decisions when the true powers that be were unavailable. The handler received an urgent call on a secure line from one of his hackers. It was the same hacker who had tapped in to the employee turnstile ID system at the Board of Trade and called Anthony Silvasconi when Christian had entered the building.

"Looks like we have a problem, sir."

"What?"

"I've been trolling the Maco network, as directed. One employee, Kurt Devitt, has logged in to the accounts of Byson Foods and our Serenity hedge fund."

"Who is this guy?"

"Margin department."

"So it could be nothing; isn't that his job?"

"Yes, but his computer activity is suspicious. Both accounts are in good standing as far as margin goes, so why check on them repeatedly? He also looked at the trading history of both accounts—not much to do with current margin requirements there. Lastly, at least three times he pulled up the accounts of Byson and Serenity back to back. Seemed like too strong of a coincidence to ignore, sir. He also hit the print-screen button for both accounts."

The handler processed this new information.

After a long pause, the hacker said, "Sir, are you there?"

The handler said, "Nice catch. You were right to call me. When did he hit 'print screen'?"

"Less than a minute ago. It's why I decided to call you."

"Get a picture of this Kurt to our boys. I want him dead yesterday."

"Yes, sir."

Click.

Kurt left the Maco offices a short time later to grab lunch. Anthony Silvasconi and Mark Hansen were waiting in the lobby of the Board of Trade. They recognized Kurt and began following on foot as soon as Kurt exited the revolving door to LaSalle Street.

The sidewalk was crowded with pedestrians, but orders were orders. Sometimes they could wait and be discreet. Other times the powers that be wanted someone dead immediately, no matter the cost, collateral damage, or difficulty. And these orders were clear: They wanted Kurt dead ASAP. No waiting to get him alone. Kill him on sight! Silvasconi knew this would create a scene, but he and Mark would be long gone before anyone knew what happened.

Kurt walked north up LaSalle on the east side of the street. Silvasconi and Hansen had gained on Kurt, through the crowded lunchtime sea of people. They could now see him less than twenty feet ahead. They picked up the pace and began to close the gap. When they were directly behind him, Silvasconi looked to Hansen, and Hansen nodded.

At that instant, Kurt turned right and entered a Subway.

Damn, Silvasconi thought. *Follow him or wait outside?*

Hansen knew what Silvasconi was thinking. He put his hand up to stop him. "We have to wait." He didn't need to explain that restaurants like Subway were sure to have video cameras rolling. It was safer to wait until he came out. Get him on the sidewalk. The two men stood outside, glancing in the Subway every few seconds, not wanting to lose their target.

Looking at Kurt through the window, Hansen tapped Silvacsoni and said, "Shiiiiiit!"

Kurt shook hands and then sat down with two men in suits. One of them flashed a badge.

Tony asked, "What the hell do we do now?!"

Mark pulled out his cell phone and called the handler, thinking how he would explain their screw-up. They could have been more aggressive and nailed him already. In fact, that's what their orders were. Now he knew why.

"I hope you have good news."

"We came straight here, as directed, sir. We never had a chance. He met with lawmen immediately. Meeting with them right now in fact. He must have arranged it from Maco by phone." Mark spoke nervously and defensively. "Our orders were that Maco offices were off limits, sir."

Silence. Hansen squirmed inside. He knew what happened when his predecessor screwed up. Hopefully the handler wouldn't view this as the screw-up it was. Hopefully he would think they never had a chance to get Kurt.

Hansen broke the long silence. "He came out of Maco and met straight up with these guys." Just a small fabrication to stay alive.

"Who is he meeting?"

"Plainclothes, sir. Could be CPD detectives, could be FBI. But they flashed a badge. And this Kurt guy handed them some paperwork."

The printouts! Linking Byson and Mason. Silence again. Hansen was uncomfortable with silence from the handler.

"What would you like us to do, sir?"

"Stand down. Abort. Can't go killing in present company. And they already have the information now. You saw Kurt hand them papers?"

"Yes, sir."

"Hmmmm. This is Kurt's lucky day. He will live."

Hansen wondered if the same would be true of him.

The handler thought to himself, *Maybe this is not a bad thing. Abigail Mason will endure some heat, but she is a big boy. She can handle it. She'll catch hell for her commodities trading profits, but it is not our problem she got greedy. And nothing illegal about profits in a blind trust she doesn't control. Investigators will never prove anything. Like other scandals, this will fade.* Of course he could not say any of this to Hansen. And the handler did not know if Abigail Mason knew anything about this account and the fifteen-million-dollar, ill-gotten gain. He was a middleman several layers from the top.

More silence.

The handler said, "It is time to compartmentalize."

Hansen knew what this meant. Just like cutting off a leg that was gangrene or closing a bulkhead taking on water. They killed to cut off the further spread of investigation. Hansen was thankful that he was already compartmentalized—he did not even know the identity of his handler.

Hansen stammered, "Uh, you mean Fleming, sir?" Hansen was astounded. Vince Fleming was a White House official!

The handler was half thinking out loud as he spoke to Mark. "I think the investigators learning about these commodity trades could be good for us. Attention will focus on that. Away from more important things. Ultimately, this will prove a dead end."

"What would you like us to do, sir?"

More silence. Then he said, "Nothing. Don't you boys worry about this anymore, understood?"

"Yes, sir."

Hansen was uneasy. He reassured himself that he was already compartmentalized. He had no idea who he and Tony worked for.

Chapter 27

Over a late dinner of deep-dish pizza in John Jr.'s kitchen, I said that I wanted to attend Thompson's bail hearing the next morning. After some discussion, John Jr. and his associates reluctantly agreed. Much like the jailhouse attorney-client meeting with Thompson, the last place CPD would be looking for me was in a public courthouse swarming with police officers. I was more confident in my new look too. The short, cropped hair had created a dramatic transformation.

After dinner John Jr. said to Laura and me, "That's it for tonight. Why don't you both get a good night's sleep? We leave for the courthouse tomorrow morning at six thirty sharp."

Laura and I retired to the guest bedroom. Once the door was closed, she made a bit of a display over locking it. She turned to me with one of those devilish grins that only meant one thing.

As she approached, she looked me over once more from head to toe in my new very expensive suit. She grabbed my tie and pulled me in close to her. In her most seductive voice, she said, "I like you in a suit."

I wrapped my arms around her, and we kissed. She loosened my tie and undid the top two buttons on my shirt. She said, "I like the suit, but I like you more without it." She smiled her devilish grin again and raised her eyebrows.

Laura was naked and in bed in about two seconds. I was always impressed with how quickly she could drop her clothes. After a brief delay to drape my expensive new garments over a chair, I joined her. It was amazing how much had changed between us in such a short time. A few days ago, I was in no rush to get married—my career had come first. Now, I just wanted to hold Laura all night. After being careful to not make too much noise, we drifted off to a good night of sleep, all tangled up again.

At 5:45 a.m. our alarm went off. It felt so good to wake up next to Laura! Our relationship was so deep now. Regrettably, it took almost losing her to reach this level of intimacy and closeness.

We showered, ate breakfast, and at six thirty we left John Jr.'s house in his Cadillac Escalade. We stopped at a Starbucks, and by seven thirty, John Jr., Bob, Laura, and I were waiting outside the courthouse for Jack Thompson's 8:00 a.m. bail hearing.

"Well, time to meet Alan Fink," said John Jr. The courthouse was going to be packed. In fact most of the hopeful spectators and reporters would not be allowed in. However, the defendant and his lawyers always had some front row seats set aside for them, and Alan Fink ensured that we would be among them.

I thought about waiting in the Escalade. According to Louie, the police were intensifying their hunt for me. He figured CPD was close to giving up on finding me or hoping that I might still come in voluntarily for questioning. Soon, CPD would turn to the public for help. Soon, my picture would be on the news, wanted for murder.

After getting out of the Escalade, I checked my reflection in the dark tinted windows. Wow! Simple, but effective. I looked like a young lawyer or a paralegal, a different person. I began to feel more confident as we walked to the courthouse. CPD was not looking for the new me.

The courtroom was packed with reporters, relatives of the deceased maid, and Jack Thompson's family. Hundreds more people waited outside. Jack Thompson was brought in through a side door and ushered to the defense table. He had handcuffs and leg chains as well as a single vertical chain connecting both of those. He was wearing an orange jumpsuit.

For the actual trial, he would be allowed to wear a nice suit and tie. Courts had ruled long ago that a man wearing an orange prison-issue jumpsuit, handcuffs, and chains would predispose jurors to the defendant's guilt. But this was just a bail hearing. No jurors. The judge was deemed capable of seeing past the defendant's appearance.

Jack looked tired but strong. Stoic, not defeated.

The state went first. Lawyers described in great detail the violent nature of the murder and sexual assault. Then they detailed the overwhelming physical evidence. They concluded with a plea for the judge to keep the defendant locked up, pending trial. Due to the overwhelming DNA evidence, they argued Mr. Thompson was a serious flight risk. In addition, they said that, as a wealthy businessman, he had the means to disappear. It was a compelling argument.

Alan Fink first emphatically asserted his client's innocence. He alleged that his client was framed for political reasons. This drew more than a few guffaws from the audience. Twice, the judge had to restore order. Alan ignored the snickers and continued.

There was no motive. Why would Thompson kill a maid? He had no history of violence and he had a long track record as an honest, law-abiding, contributing member of society. Even if he were to commit such a crime, he would not be so stupid as to perpetrate it in his own hotel room. And leave behind physical evidence! No, this crime fit the profile of being framed. It too was a compelling argument.

"Your honor, just moments ago I received this sworn affidavit from the FBI crime lab that ran the DNA tests in this case." Alan held up the papers.

Bob nudged me and nodded his head. *Interesting,* I thought. *Could this be how Special Agent Dan Bruner was going to help Mr. Thompson get out on bail while keeping the real reason a secret? Thus allowing the FBI to continue the investigation and connect the dots to bigger fish? The FBI crime lab!* I smiled.

"Bailiff," the judge said and motioned for the bailiff to get the documents from Mr. Fink and hand them to the judge.

As the bailiff walked the papers over to the judge, Alan said, "Your honor, I just learned of this myself a few minutes ago. Seems there was a mix-up. Correct that, a potential mix-up, at the FBI lab. The FBI had two sets of DNA in this case. One recovered from the crime scene and one that my client voluntarily provided."

Alan was talking as much for the reporters in the court room as he was to the judge. "The FBI lab technicians initially concluded a match. However, after double-checking the lab protocols, they discovered the potential mix-up. In short, they may have matched up the defendant's voluntary blood, saliva, and hair samples with the very same voluntary blood, saliva, and hair samples. Of course, this would yield a positive match, but not to the DNA collected at the crime scene!"

The courtroom erupted in commotion.

"Objection, your honor," said the state's attorney. "This is an outrageous and desperate surprise maneuver."

The judge just looked over his glasses at Alan for his response to the prosecutor.

"Your honor, the FBI brought this to our attention, and they proactively gave us that sworn affidavit. This is much more credible than if defendant's counsel were to stand before you and question this evidence." He paused. "Your honor, this is a surprise to me too. But it is clearly relevant to the issue of bail."

Alan paused. He spoke to the packed courtroom as he continued, "The state has no witnesses. We have two dozen witnesses that will testify Mr. Thompson was at a breakfast meeting at the time of death estimated by the coroner. This time of death is further corroborated by the hotel's house-keeping schedule on the morning in question."

Alan turned to the crowded courtroom and spoke even louder. "Your honor, without the DNA match, they have no case whatsoever. An FBI technician is here, voluntarily, to right this wrong." Alan motioned to the first row of people behind the defendant's table.

The FBI technician rose and stepped forward.

The judge said, "State your name and affiliation for the record please."

"Ronald Sacowitz, Forensic Specialist, FBI Crime Lab, Chicago." He held out an identification card on a lanyard. Lab workers did not carry badges.

"Do you understand that statements made in this court-room constitute perjury if proved false?"

"Yes, sir, your honor."

"And you state that you may have mixed up these tests?"

"Yes, sir."

"Can the tests be rerun? Or is the sample evidence now gone or in any way tainted?"

"The evidence gathered from the crime scene is still intact, and has been subject to, and still is subject to, a rigorous chain of evidence protocol. We can rerun the tests with new additional samples from the defendant."

"How long?"

"Conclusive results will take three days."

The courtroom erupted again, and the judge had to silence the crowd.

"Three days?"

"Yes, your honor. The initial, potentially flawed results were preliminary, not conclusive. Full conclusive testing requires three days."

The judge turned to Alan. "Well, what would your client say to providing additional samples? Does the state need a court order?"

Alan spoke more to the courtroom and the media present than to the judge. "Your honor, my client voluntarily provided blood, saliva, and hair samples for the express purpose of proving his innocence."

Translation: *Hell, yes they'll need a court order! My client is done cooperating with these assholes.*

Alan did not answer the judge's question. But the judge respected that and nodded his understanding. Back when the judge himself was a lawyer, he would not have answered such a question. That was what good lawyers sometimes did—give a very strong answer, even if it does not address the question.

The simple truth was that obtaining additional DNA samples was beyond the scope of this morning's bail hearing. That was something the prosecutors would have to worry about. In fact, both sides would have months to build their cases.

Today, the judge's job was simple: make a ruling on bail based on the evidence before him right now.

"Your honor," the state's attorney pleaded, "this was a vicious crime. The defendant has significant means. We believe there is a high risk of flight."

The judge scowled and cut him off with a wave of his hand. "Does anyone have anything new to add?" The judge peered condescendingly over his reading glasses at the state's attorney.

The state's attorney stood silently and looked down. He knew repeating himself, although a good show for the reporters, would anger the judge.

Alan Fink stood. "Your honor, we of course request full release. However, as a middle ground, if you deem it necessary, the defendant is willing to remain under house arrest. My client agrees to pay all costs associated with any court-appointed security that this court deems appropriate. We are confident that, once the correct DNA results come back, Mr. Thompson will be completely exonerated. So he is willing to bear this cost for what we anticipate will be only three days."

This was something new to add, a goodwill gesture. Or a compromise, just in case one was needed. It probably did not need to be said. Although it sounded good, and perhaps bolstered the case being tried in the news media.

None of the lawyers were surprised when, after a few moments of thoughtful silence, the judge cleared his throat and the courtroom fell dead silent.

The judge spoke decisively: "The state has relied entirely on a flawed DNA test. To date, they have not gathered any corroborating evidence." The judge removed his glasses before delivering the final blow. "Defendant is hereby released on twenty-five thousand dollars bail." The gavel slammed down, and the crowded courtroom exploded with noisy conversation and frantic reporters calling in the ruling.

Jack Thompson sat motionless, with his head bowed down, resting on his folded hands. An officer gingerly approached to unshackle him.

Chapter 28

As we rode back to John Jr.'s house in the Escalade, Isaac's voice came over the radios to the Strong and Associates team. "Story just came across the newswire. I quote: 'Vince W. Fleming, special assistant to the deputy chief of staff in the White House was found dead in Millennium Park early this morning by a jogger. Police are at the scene now. No official police statement has been released. However, an unnamed police source said that Mr. Fleming's death appears to be a suicide.'"

It took a few moments of stunned silence as we digested this news.

"Damn," said Bob, not angry but disappointed. The primary lead was dead.

I shook my head in disbelief. "I assume you don't think he killed himself."

John Jr. said, "I'd bet my life on it. But these folks are professionals; maybe the police will rule it a suicide."

Bob added, "I'll call Dan and get the FBI's take. He is probably already investigating this with a bias that it is a phony suicide. Problem is, the police will approach it with a bias of suicide. Less paperwork. And a lot less subsequent legwork. Rule it a suicide, close the case file, and be home in time for dinner."

John Jr. interjected, "If these guys are pros, they know how to make it look like a real suicide."

"True," Bob nodded and looked down. I got the sense that he had overstepped a boundary. Had he insulted John Jr.? I reminded myself that John Jr. used to be a Chicago police officer.

I shook my head and said, "Last week, if I heard this news, I wouldn't have thought twice about it. Suicide." In a tired, almost defeated voice, I said, "Now I am a cynic. No way he committed suicide. And I am not some freaky conspiracy theorist." I paused and sighed. "The world is much different than I thought it was…" My voice trailed off.

Chapter 29

Strong and Associates sat in the comfortable living room of John Jr.'s home. Everyone was present this time including John Jr., Nate, Emily, Bob, Louie, Isaac, Laura, and me. We faced a serious dilemma. The one link higher, Vince Fleming, was dead.

Bob began. "I spoke with Dan. He was more open than usual. I guess he feels he owes us. At any rate, the preliminary information on Fleming's death is highly suspicious. First, the gun was found in his hand. Allegedly, he put the gun in his mouth and pulled the trigger. Problem is, in decades of experience, the FBI is not aware of one instance in which the gun of a suicide victim was found in their hand. Nearby, of course. But in their hand, never. The kickback of the gun combined with the collapse of the body has, up until last night, knocked the gun out of the hand of the victim."

I noticed Nate and John Jr. nod their heads in agreement.

Bob continued. "Second, there was very little blood on Mr. Fleming. As you may know, and Agent Bruner reminded me, a gunshot to the head typically causes immediate brain death. But the heart can keep beating for some time. This is why such victims are good candidates for organ donation. But it also means that after brain death, the beating heart forces a lot of blood out of the trauma site: out of entry wounds and exit wounds. In other words, there is usually a lot of blood when someone is shot in the head or face. Suicide or murder is irrelevant. The victim is covered in blood."

John Jr. and Nate nodded again in agreement. Nate said, "Bullet to the head, bleeds like crazy. Unless the victim also took a bullet to the chest, stopping the heart too."

"Well, according to Dan," Bob continued, "Vince Fleming had only one shot—in the head. And he had just a trickle of blood."

Nate jumped in. "Then he was already dead when he was shot!"

Bob nodded. "That is what the FBI is focusing on. Mr. Fleming appeared to have some sort of carpet imprint on one side of his face. It was faint, but the FBI thinks it may be significant. They are pursuing the possibility that, rather than driving himself to Millennium Park, as the killers would have us believe, maybe he was brought to the park in the trunk of a car. Lastly, his EPhone was wiped clean; everything was deleted. Why would a man committing suicide bother to do that? Dan will keep me posted, but that is all I have for now."

Nate said, "Covering their tracks, already. We should have seen this coming. These people are careful. I underestimated the people we are dealing with. There is more to this than Hansen and Silvasconi. Frankly, I am not very impressed with them."

John Jr. stood. "Agreed. But suicide or murder is somewhat irrelevant to us right now. Dead is dead. We know Hansen and Silvasconi killed the maid. We suspect they killed Thomas Minter. Problem is, we had them covered pretty tight, and they could not have killed Fleming last night. They were nowhere near Millennium Park last night."

Nate said, "There are others. The man and woman who scratched Jack Thompson's neck at The Peninsula Hotel, just to name two. Real pros, better than Hansen and Silvasconi. And they are connected to Hansen and Silvasconi because they gave them the DNA from Mr. Thompson."

John Jr. said, "If these people felt it necessary to erase all the data off Vince Fleming's EPhone, then there is information on that phone they don't want anyone to find. Isaac, find it. You need to focus on the contents Nate retrieved from it before Fleming's death."

Isaac nodded.

Maybe I was just being vindictive, but I had an idea. "Why don't we turn up the heat on the White House? They are trying to cover their tracks with the murder of Fleming, but we have enough to make them squirm right now. Remember they are politicians. Their battles are fought in the news media, not in a courtroom, where the burden of proof is higher. Let's bring it to 'em, their style, in the news."

John Jr. nodded. "I'm with you so far."

"Well, we know the secretary of state just turned one million dollars into sixteen million in one day. Let's leak that to the media. We have the actual account statements!

The account statements are real; they will be difficult to dis-avow. Remember, on the surface the investment is legitimate. Because the statements originated in the fund administra-tor's offices, nobody will ever figure out how they leaked out of that office. We also know that Silvasconi was taking orders from Vince Fleming, an aid to the president! And Silvasconi killed the maid and probably killed Minter. I am thinking news headlines, not proof beyond a reasonable doubt. Take the president and his administration down by their own game—in the media."

Emily said, "I like it. We handicap ourselves if our game plan is limited to court admissible evidence and procedural standards."

Bob smiled and said, "We also have our own surveillance photos: Vince Fleming meeting with Hansen and Silvasconi. I like this. First, the media receives a leaked account state-ment showing the fifteen-million-dollar profit in a Maco ac-count, the same day Maco's founder is murdered. Second, they receive pictures of Fleming, a White House official, meeting with the hit men that will soon be known by every-one to have killed the maid. I don't think we need to explain it to them. The news media will have a field day."

John Jr. said, "I don't disagree. But if we go this route, the lid is blown off of this whole thing. The FBI would prefer if the video that exonerates Jack Thompson stays under wraps a while longer, so they can pursue bigger fish."

Bob said, "Yes, but Fleming's death changes everything. The trail to the White House is now at a dead end. Let me talk to Agent Bruner. I think he may agree with our plan. In fact, the bureau is not in the business of leaking this type of stuff to reporters. So we may be doing them a favor if we leak it for them." He smiled.

John Jr. stated, "The cockroaches are going to start running for cover. With Fleming dead, this could be the best option for all of us to nab some bigger fish."

Strong and Associates put the plan in place with remarkable speed and efficiency. With off-the-record help from the Strong tracking devices and surveillance, the FBI located and arrested Tony Silvasconi and Mark Hansen for the murder of Maria Gonzalez.

Then the real fun began. With the FBI's tacit approval, we leaked the damning evidence to the media.

Chapter 30

Jack Thompson appeared in a dramatic news conference with the US attorney who had been prosecuting him. For several hours, news channels had been running the incredible breaking story of Jack Thompson's innocence, along with the arrests of the real killers, Silvasconi and Hansen.

The US attorney stepped up to the podium first. He looked tired, almost depressed. He had been looking forward to the media spectacle that would be his trial of Jack Thompson, a notable public figure. He would bask in the attention. He would have taken full credit for a conviction, which had nothing to do with his efforts, but rather the DNA evidence. Then, with a little luck, he would have ridden a tough-on-crime persona all the way to the governor's mansion. The Equalizer, fighting for the common folk against the powerful elites!

Alas, none of that was to be. Jack Thompson was, unfortunately, innocent. The US attorney took a deep breath and mustered up the courage to backtrack from his previous statements.

"Ladies and gentleman, I want to apologize to all of you, but, first and most importantly, I want to apologize," he said and turned to Jack, "to you, Mr. Thompson."

Jack Thompson stood with his hands folded together in front of him. He looked down and nodded.

The US attorney continued, "I know you have been through hell. And I am sorry. I sincerely apologize. I jumped to a premature, and completely wrong, conclusion. It was based in part on a mistake made by the FBI crime lab. But I still made a mistake, a rush to judgment. I want to take responsibility for my actions. I am truly sorry. After what you have been through this week, I understand if these words are not enough, but they are all I have. I am sorry."

Jack was impressed with the sincerity. And he knew this hurt the prosecutor's political ambitions. That sound bite would also get replayed and could haunt him for a long time. He could have tried to blame the whole thing on the FBI crime lab. But here he was, accepting responsibility.

The US attorney turned to the crowd of reporters and continued, "All charges against the honorable Mr. Jack Thompson are dropped. He is an innocent man." With that, he bowed his head and backed away from the podium, allowing Mr. Thompson to step up.

Jack approached the podium. He had intended to get a few digs in at the US attorney. He was angry. He was bitter at the media spectacle that had engulfed his family, the spectacle that the US attorney had poured gasoline on.

But as he approached the podium, he reminded himself that his anger and bitterness would not hurt the US attorney, nor would they have any effect on the irresponsible journalists. No, his anger and resentment would only hurt himself. It would consume him from the inside, if he let it. He remembered what his pastor said about not forgiving: "Holding on to bitterness was like drinking poison—hoping that it would kill someone else."

Jack realized forgiving those who wronged him would, paradoxically, be the most selfish thing he could do. Forgiving would be healthy for his family: truly let it go, put the incident behind them.

He looked at the US attorney, who was looking down. "My friend," he began, and the US attorney made eye contact with him. "Your gracious apology is accepted, and I wish you all the best in the future. Truth is, I may have done the same thing based on the evidence at the time." He may have laid that on a little too thick, but he wanted the prosecutor to know he was forgiven.

The US attorney had braced himself to take a few licks. He managed a small smile and relaxed.

And that was it. Jack let it go, as simple as that. He let out a breath, a cathartic sigh. He felt a heavy weight lifted from his shoulders. He turned to the crowd of reporters a new man, a man who would not let his legacy be defined by the recent events. He had moved on. "I want to express my deepest and sincerest condolences to the Gonzalez family. Maria Gonzalez was a hard-working wife and mother. She was a well-respected member of this community. It is tragic that the perpetrators of this political setup, to which Mrs. Gonzalez was an innocent bystander, could have so little respect for human life. My prayers go out for the Gonzalez family, in your time of grief. I hope you feel some small measure of closure that the real killers have now been caught, and there is no question, this time, that they did in fact commit this terrible crime."

He paused for a long while before shifting gears. "I know many of you anticipate my return to the campaign trail, now that the accusations against me have been proven false. To my supporters, thank you. With no regrets, I announce, effective immediately, I am withdrawing from politics. I will never run for any public office again."

The mob of reporters broke into a commotion among themselves.

"This past week has been difficult for me, and for my family. But it has also served a higher purpose. It served the good purpose of reminding me what is truly important—my family."

More audible gasps could be heard from the mob or reporters. Was he really quitting?! After this incident, and the grace he had exhibited throughout, he was a shoo-in!

"I had hoped to serve you as your president, to give back to the system that has allowed me to prosper. But now, I will find other ways to give back." He stared straight at the cameras as if to clarify the decisiveness and finality of his decision. "I will never again run for public office. Ever."

The mob of reporters began shouting questions, but Jack just put his hands up and shook his head. No questions. He waved and walked off.

Chapter 31

One hour later, Jack Thompson arrived at John Jr.'s house in Hinsdale. We all shook hands and congratulated him. He handed John Jr. a check for $250,000.

"Wow," said John Jr. "You don't have to do this."

"Two hundred fifty thousand, officially, is for security services. Unofficially, it is a thank-you gift because you saved me from a lethal injection. I figure I owe you a lot more than that, but some debts will never be repaid. Please accept this token of my gratitude."

"Sir, you don't have to…"

Jack Thompson waved his hand dismissively and interrupted John Jr. "After everything I just went through, money no longer seems important." He looked around the foyer at all of us. "And I am grateful to you for that too."

John Jr. showed Jack in to the living room, and we all sat down.

Jack relaxed and took a deep breath. "More important than the money: This check is dated two weeks ago, and I have a contract, also dated two weeks ago. This payment is from me to Strong and Associates for security consulting and surveillance system setup. Without this contract," he said, holding it up in the air and handing it to John Jr., "prosecutors have no murder case on behalf of Mrs. Gonzalez's family. The video evidence of the brutal murder is the fruit of a poisoned tree. It came from what was, in fact, an illegal wiretap put in my hotel room by your crew. The judge will throw it out."

"Ahhhh." *Good point*, thought John Jr. I don't think any of us had considered this.

"You show this contract to the police or the prosecutors. If asked, I'll show them my copy. I hired you because we received threats. Politicians and candidates are always receiving threats, so my hiring of Strong and Associates can be explained. Anyhow, it's a damn lucky thing I hired you for security because you caught this terrible crime on tape." He lifted his eyebrows and smiled, waiting for a reaction from John Jr.

I was impressed. Jack Thompson had just been through hell, yet he had the presence of mind to think through the legal ramifications and ensure justice for the slain maid and her family.

John Jr. nodded in agreement.

Sitting back, Jack said, "Now, the video of the murder will be admissible in court. It was my hotel room. And I authorized the security cameras. I had not yet, at least formally, checked out of the hotel. Of course, your crew would have removed the hidden camera before I checked out." He winked. "That makes it just like a crime caught on a home, or store, security camera. The evidence is now admissible. Period. My lawyers have researched it. We have been through the facts a thousand times. There is no evidence against these scumbags, except for this tape. No tape, no case, and these killers walk! Imagine that. You commit murder on video, and the state cannot convict you!" He shook his head in disgust.

John Jr. nodded and said, "Brilliant. Without a proper wiretap warrant, which of course could never be backdated, it should all boil down to a legal—indeed routine—security camera tape."

"Yes. The defense will have no way to get the video thrown out."

We sat in silence for a few moments as we absorbed this. I think we all struggled a little with the moral concern over fabricating a small lie, even if it was to nail two cold-blooded killers.

Jack said, "Look, I have never been an ends-justifies-the-means guy. But that maid deserves justice. Without your tape, the police and prosecutors have nothing." He paused. "Do you have a problem with this?"

John Jr. said, "No, sir. I agree. And thank you."

Bob nodded too and said, "Yes. Thank you."

And then something else hit me. With this contract, there would be no hell to pay with the FBI for illegally bugging Mr. Thompson's hotel room. It was now done with permission. John Jr. and Bob were relieved. No unpleasant follow-ups from Special Agent Dan Bruner.

We all nodded and looked at Jack Thompson.

Jack smiled. He had probably already thought this through from Strong's angle, and from the FBI's too.

Jack stood up. Winking again he said, "You folks should deposit that check. What kind of idiot sits on a two-hundred-and-fifty-thousand-dollar check for two weeks?" He smiled as he got up to leave.

We shook hands with Thompson and said polite good-byes. As soon as the door closed, I turned to John Jr. and said, "We need to add a clause to my contract with you. I authorized Strong and Associates to install surveillance equipment in my apartment."

John Jr. raised both eyebrows in understanding. He smiled.

I said, "The conviction of Mr. Slick for killing Thomas Minter could hinge on the admissibility of the video showing Mr. Slick planting the murder weapon in my kitchen. I want that bastard to fry."

John Jr. smiled in the direction of his associates while gesturing toward me. "I told you this kid is sharp!" He looked back at me, nodded, and said, "Good point, and done."

Thus far, I had contemplated that the video would prove I did not kill Minter. Strict rules of court admissibility do not apply to evidence used to exonerate. But if that same evidence were to be used in the murder trial of Silvasconi, the barriers to admissibility would be much higher. And in favor of the scumbag.

John Jr. waved the check from Thompson in the air and smiled at me. "Speaking of that contract between us, you just earned fifty thousand dollars. Twenty percent of two hundred fifty thousand."

I had not considered that angle! After some discussion, we agreed there was no rush to pay me. Thomas Minter was murdered. I had fled the scene and disappeared. Police found the gun in my kitchen but had not yet seen the tape of Mr. Slick planting it. We shared a laugh over the conniption investigators would have if they saw a fifty-thousand-dollar check land in my bank account right now. That was more than I made in a year.

John Jr. added, "Don't get your hopes up yet, but we know Mrs. Minter and her children are offering a five-million-dollar reward for information leading to a conviction." He paused and then winced. Maybe he had sounded a little too opportunistic, given the tragedy.

I said, "I don't want a penny from Tom's family. I want justice for Tom."

Chapter 32

John Jr. convened a meeting of Strong and Associates. Laura and I joined them around the big conference table in the war room.

John Jr. refocused us. "Okay, people, with Fleming dead, he is not going to lead us to the Promised Land—White House officials. We need a new strategy. I am going to assume, for now, that following Abigail Mason will lead nowhere. And following her or the president is impossible anyway. They have other people do their dirty work."

Bob and Louie nodded. "Agreed."

"Emily, you keep digging on Byson Foods. Maybe we can link Minter's murder to them. Nailing the president would be a big deal, but let's not get myopic."

Emily nodded. "Will do."

John Jr. turned to Isaac. "Isaac, of course we need you here." He spread his arms out referring to the war room. Then he turned to Nate. "Nate, Isaac's analysis of Mr. Fleming's EPhone has turned up some curious travel in the last few months."

Isaac tapped a few keys on his computer, and a detailed map popped up on the largest TV screen in the center of the war room wall.

John Jr. pointed to the map. "Vince Fleming travelled to Europe three times in the last two months."

Isaac pointed to the map and said, "I've labeled everything as usual. He has made multiple calls both to and from various locations in France and Italy. The EPhone GPS tracking info shows us this timeline for his whereabouts." Isaac pointed out a part of the map, and Nate nodded in understanding.

Isaac explained the map for the benefit of Laura and me. It had a series of dots connected by lines showing the exact path Vince Fleming had travelled. It even showed the dates and times, mapping precisely when Mr. Fleming had arrived and departed each dot.

Isaac continued, "He stopped in several major cities, and one most curious spot—the middle of the Mediterranean! He spent the night right here." Isaac pointed to a tiny dot in the middle of the sea. "From there he moved slowly, at twelve knots to be precise, to right here." He pointed to another dot.

Nate cracked a smile and nodded. He understood where this was going.

Isaac said, "Monaco. Mr. Fleming was onboard a luxury yacht. We saw from his text messages that the yacht is named *Cui Bono*. We tracked down ownership of the yacht to French billionaire Nicolas de Gaulle. At one hundred thirty-four meters—that's four hundred forty feet—she is one of the largest private yachts in the world. Due to *Cui Bono*'s size and flamboyance, we have already confirmed that she arrived at, and was docked in, Monaco on the night coinciding with Mr.

Fleming's EPhone's GPS tracking. It seems yachts of this size draw a lot of attention. They even have websites and blogs where yacht aficionados post sightings of these megayachts, owned by folks like Larry Ellison, Paul Allen, and Nicolas de Gaulle."

John Jr. said, "Mr. Fleming met with this de Gaulle character, or at least we know he met on de Gaulle's yacht. He departed Europe after that meeting, flew nonstop to Chicago, and gave the two goons, Silvasconi and Hansen, the order to take out Thompson."

Nate nodded in understanding. I could almost see the wheels turning inside Nate's head.

John Jr. continued, "Circumstantial, I know. But the best lead we have for now. Nate, I think you need to go to Monaco, or wherever de Gaulle's yacht may be by the time you get there."

Isaac said, "We'll keep you posted on the yacht's whereabouts as you are en route. We booked a direct flight to Paris. It departs O'Hare this evening at five after six. Arrives eight hours later, breakfast time in France, nine twenty-five a.m. From Paris, if the yacht hasn't moved, we will book you on a connecting flight to the Nice Côte-d'Azur Airport, about forty kilometers from Monte Carlo. If the yacht has moved, we'll get you on the next flight to the nearest city, most likely Naples, based on what we have learned of *Cui Bono*'s past itineraries."

"The yacht won't move," Nate stated with certainty.

John Jr. and the rest of us looked at Nate, inquiring how Nate could be so sure.

"Formula One Grand Prix race is in Monaco this weekend."

John Jr. exclaimed, "I should have known that!"

Nate said, "This is the premier Formula One race of the year. It is also the premier European social event of the year. Formula One race cars ripping through the downtown city streets of Monte Carlo as partiers watch from apartment terraces and yachts."

I had heard of this race and could recall seeing it on TV.

Nate said, "The best seats for the race are aboard luxury yachts docked in Port Hercule. Partiers on the yachts with the closest berths are just a few yards away from the race track. Nicolas de Gaulle sounds like a classic French narcissist. He will want his beautiful *Cui Bono* to be seen at the Grand Prix. I hear it costs more than a hundred thousand Euros—about one hundred twenty thousand US dollars—per day to dock trackside for the Grand Prix. And de Gaulle probably loves it that other people know he can pay that much just to park his boat. Arrogant and flashy." Nate paused. "Boat ain't moving 'til after the race. Look up the history; I bet his beloved *Cui Bono* was parked there for previous races."

The rest of us nodded in agreement. I said, "I want to go too."

Before anyone could respond, Laura surprised me by blurting out, "Me too!"

The room went silent. I think each person was waiting for someone else to say why this wasn't a good idea.

John Jr. went first. "Too risky, these are dangerous people, and Nate is an experienced pro."

I said, "We'll tag along on the nondangerous parts. We'll sit tight at the hotel or wherever, when he does his breaking-and-entering thing."

Emily said, "It will look like you are fleeing the country after murdering your boss."

I remained very calm but unwavering. "This is my case. My life. My boss was murdered. I have already been instrumental in piecing key bits together." I looked at Emily and raised my eyebrows, pleading silently, *I pieced the Byson Foods and Serenity hedge fund trades together.*

Emily said, "You have been very helpful…"

"Look, these guys tried to kill me. You have this case because of me. I think I earned the right to remain involved. I understand the risks." I looked straight at John Jr. "I want to go. I want to help."

I think John Jr. and Nate were impressed with my conviction and seriousness. I had learned in the investment business that analysts did not just present bull or bear cases with facts alone. Portfolio managers and CEOs also judged the level of passion and conviction the analyst showed in deciding whether to go with a trade recommendation or not.

John Jr. said, "You were pretty smart at piecing together the illegal bond trades. And you did, after all, escape an ambush assassination attempt." John Jr. looked at Nate.

Nate raised his eyebrows, pulled his lips up together in a thoughtful curve, tilted his head, and nodded as if to say, "I like this kid."

John Jr. looked at Nate and said, "Your mission, your call."

Nate smiled and said, "The kid does have good instincts. Without those, he'd already be dead."

Knowing that the decision had already been made, Bob said, "But what about Laura?"

Laura walked over to me and put her arm around my lower back. She said, "From now on, we stay together." She smiled lovingly at me, and I never felt better.

I added, "No matter what." Laura squeezed me tighter.

John Jr. wrinkled his forehead and sighed but said, "All right then. We have to get you three out of the country with the glitch that Christian is wanted for the murder of Mr. Minter. We have to assume he has already been red flagged if he tries to leave the country."

Emily said, "Laura, do you have a passport?"

Laura replied, "Yes. At my apartment."

"We will get it for you," Emily said. "We have a new identity ready for Christian—based on the new look that worked for him at Thompson's bail hearing. Cropped hair a nice suit and glasses. A new man."

I chuckled. "My own mom wouldn't recognize me in a suit and tie." The trading floor was a casual place, and we typically wore golf shirts under smock-like trading jackets.

John Jr. looked at Laura. "Let's keep it simple. We already have a good look for Christian. He looks like a young lawyer or banker. Let's get similar business attire for Laura. They will blend together well. Of course this is just for getting out of the country. Once you are in Europe and no one is looking for you, dress as you please, or as required for the mission."

Emily said, "I'll get her sizes and run over to Nordstrom. I can be back in less than an hour." She smiled at Laura. "Don't worry, I'll grab a variety in several sizes and just return anything that doesn't work."

Laura and I shrugged. We didn't care how we had to dress as long as we were together. But I needed a passport to get out of the country. Later that same day. Strong and Associates knew this, yet they agreed to let me go. I asked, "You can get me a fake passport?"

Isaac waved his hand in the air as if to say, "piece of cake." He handed me a perfect-looking passport that included a picture they had taken of me before Thompson's bail hearing.

I was stunned as I examined the passport and noted my new name.

Isaac declared, "A fake passport for getting out of the US: yes, no problem. Getting back in is more difficult. I figure by the time you come home, you will no longer be a suspect in Minter's murder."

Laura and I were both a bit flabbergasted by the fake passport. They were thorough and planned for every contingency.

I wondered if it was a real passport with my picture substituted in it or just a fake. I couldn't tell the difference.

John Jr. spoke to me. "Think of this as a game of chess. We were already prepared for you to leave the country under a false identity because we logically thought ahead several moves, through several different scenarios." He grinned. "Not you jetting off to the Monaco Grand Prix, by the way. We feared we might have to move you out of the country to a safe house." He paused and looked from me to Laura and then back to me, making sure we were listening. He said, "You would do well to start thinking ahead several moves yourself."

I nodded.

"One more thing. These operations function with a proper chain of command. If we let you go with Nate, you listen to him. You follow his orders. Agreed?"

"Yes, sir," I said without hesitation.

John Jr. and Nate both smiled.

Chapter 33

Reporters received the damning bits of leaked information—my idea, courtesy of Strong and Associates. First, Abigail Mason's hedge fund account statements, along with the fact that Byson Foods was on the losing side of her winning trade. Second, a photograph of the deceased White House official Vince Fleming, meeting with Silvasconi and Hansen, the men now in custody for the maid's murder.

Reporters speculated that Vince Fleming had given the orders to murder both the maid and Thomas Minter. They also lampooned the secretary of state for her fifteen million dollar profit and noted that Maco's founder and CEO was murdered on the same day as the improbable trade. All of this happened in Chicago, the president's hometown. Fleming was a political appointee from Chicago. Reporters were giddy over the prospect of another Watergate.

News reporters noted that, as the Republican frontrunner, if Jack Thompson went down in a scandal, such as the attempt to frame him, Abigail Mason would likely waltz into the White House after the current president's second term. I speculated to myself, *Was this an orchestrated handoff of the*

American presidency to Mason—the president picking his successor? Preserving his legacy?

I am not very political, but from what I could see, except for Jack Thompson, there was a surprising lack of viable Republican candidates. Meanwhile, Abigail Mason and her camp had been carefully grooming her for the presidency for more than thirty years. The secretary of state appointment was the capstone to her career. It would solidify the last piece of her credentials, her bona fides in international affairs.

National news mentioned that the scandal reached all the way to the Oval Office. But such comments were hedged with the characterization that Fleming was a low-level political appointee. There was, across the board, a subdued tone to the reports. Every potential accusation was prefaced with the word alleged, and every news account was balanced with, "The president and his administration deny any involvement..."

When the Jack Thompson story broke, the news and talk shows went straight for the jugular. Now, those same news organizations were huddled with their lawyers, reviewing their coverage of Jack Thompson. When they did, they cringed. They had behaved irresponsibly. They had assumed Thompson was guilty. In hindsight, it was clear that their coverage had been unfair and biased. Shoot first and ask questions later. In the fight for sensationalism and ratings, they had ignored Thompson's verifiable alibi that he was at a breakfast meeting, with more than thirty witnesses, when the maid was murdered.

If Thompson had been guilty, the news organizations had no liability. You can't be sued for defamation if what you wrote or said was in fact true. But they never imagined Thompson was innocent based on the preliminary DNA reports. Now, they sat waiting, fearful that Jack Thompson would sue them. The national media had learned a lesson in discretion from the Thompson affair. They went old school—back to simply reporting the facts.

Meanwhile, the White House and the Masons demonstrated their media savvy once again. First, the president and Abigail Mason never addressed the questions surrounding the White House staffer. They left that to spokesmen. They knew that any words uttered by the president or the secretary of state on the subject would make the nightly news. Statements by their spokesmen usually did not. So they could avoid some of the extra news coverage by remaining quiet. If the president denied it, that would become a sound bite. He would give the controversy legitimacy. Their strategy implied, "This is silly, it will blow over."

They coordinated their talking points and would begin prepared remarks with comments like, "I have a jobs plan to discuss. And I know the working people of this great state deserve to hear that. And they deserve the legislature to take action on this…"

Abigail Mason in particular had a history of deftly deflecting scandals. First, she'd say nothing, and weeks would go by. Second, she'd say, "Let's wait until all the facts are in."

Then months would go by. Finally, after questions remain unanswered due to her own stonewalling, her spokespeople would address the issue with a dismissive: "Gimme a break; that's old news."

Chapter 34

Strong and Associates picked up Laura's passport from her apartment while we packed for our trip to Monaco. I studied my passport and memorized my new name and birth date. Laura and I listened as Nate and John Jr. explained the behavior profile that would cause police officers and security guards to take a second look at us in the security lines and departure lounges of O'Hare. Police would be looking for people keeping their head down, acting nervous. Not confident people in expensive business attire with their heads held high.

To help Laura not appear nervous, they reassured her that she had nothing at all to worry about. The police were not looking for her, and she was using her real passport, not breaking any laws. This helped her to relax. When it was time to leave for the airport, we stood in the foyer of John Jr.'s home to go over final logistics and say good-bye. Emily gave Laura a reassuring hug. Laura squeezed her tight, like saying good-bye to a big sister.

Laura put a spring in my whole mood too. While I wore the same suit and tie from the bail hearing, she looked striking in her attire: a tight navy skirt with a slit half way up one side, a white blouse, and a matching blazer. She looked professional and businesslike—and hot as hell. It felt good to be so madly, and confidently, in love with her. My near-death experience was, I decided, very good for me. I was still mad at myself for having taken Laura for granted, but I was enthusiastic about my second chance and my newfound commitment to her.

Laura and I climbed into the backseat of the Escalade. Nate sat in the passenger seat, and Louie drove us to O'Hare. Going through O'Hare was easier and less stressful than I had feared. Nate reminded us to relax, walk tall, and be aware of our surroundings. Laura and I were just young professionals on our way to Paris.

I walked with my head up. It helped that the woman I was in love with was on my left arm. And looking hot. Although I was used to other guys noticing Laura, I smiled when I saw a police officer checking her out. What a great disguise for me! With Laura at my side, the cop did not even notice me.

We knew the airline ticket agent would request our passports at check-in, followed by the TSA agent at security. It was that simple. Getting back into the country could be much trickier, as we faced an immigration officer in uniform at a computer screen with a passport scanner. But we would worry about that later.

We made it past the ticket agents and TSA agents without incident and sat together in the first-class departure lounge. I told Nate that I was a simple guy—maybe the first-class seats were a bit of an unnecessary extravagance. He explained that we were "on mission," and you could not put a price on being well rested and prepared for whatever we were about to face. With his former military and CIA experience, he was accustomed to going long periods without sleep.

"You never know how long it may be before you get your next chance to sleep. I suggest you use this flight well."

I nodded. "I guess you haven't slept much since meeting me."

Nate smiled. "I'm used to it."

So Laura and I sucked it up and accepted that flying first class was a practical necessity. We boarded the plane, ate a good dinner, and attempted to catch some sleep. Nate offered us each a melatonin tablet, and we took it. After I settled in with a pillow and a blanket in the first-class lie-flat seat, I decided Nate was right. My six-foot-four, two-hundred-thirty-pound frame would have been quite uncomfortable in a coach seat. After an eight-hour flight with cramped legs and sitting upright, I would have been a wreck. As it was, I slept for the better part of six hours.

The three of us landed in Paris refreshed. Flights into the Nice Côte-d'Azur Airport were sold out due to the Formula One race. Because of this, while we were over the Atlantic, Isaac booked a small, private turboprop to take us to Nice. The short charter flight from Paris to Nice cost $12,500. I have to admit, traveling first class was beginning to grow on me.

Laura and I had never flown on a small, private plane. It was clear to us that Nate had, and he fell asleep before the plane even took off. Laura and I tried to do the same, but we could not relax on this last leg of our journey. We had already slept well from Chicago to Paris, and we were both a bit nervous and apprehensive about the entire situation we found ourselves in.

The small plane landed in Nice, France, at 11:00 a.m. local time. Monaco, our final destination, was located about twenty-five miles east of the airport.

The principality of Monaco is a sovereign city state on the French Riviera. Although independent, it is bordered by France on three sides and by the Mediterranean Sea on the other. Famous destinations, including Cannes and Antibes, lie a short distance to the west. Italy is ten miles to the east.

The entire country is less than one square mile in total area, with a population of thirty-five thousand. Monaco is home to Monte Carlo, famous for its casinos. With its beautiful location on the French Riviera, along with its lavish resorts and casinos, Monaco is a popular hotspot for the rich and famous. Actors and athletes are among the few who can afford the sky-high property prices of Monaco. Most of France's top tennis players left France for Monaco to escape France's confiscatory 75 percent personal income tax rates. Imagine busting your butt to get to the top of your sport, knowing that you will only have a few years at that level of competition and income. Then, if you live in France, for every four grueling tennis matches you play, you get paid for one match, and the French government gets paid for the other three. So they move to Monaco, and with that kind of tax savings, who cares what homes cost?

Monaco also grew to be one of the world's largest banking centers and a popular tax haven. The combination of beautiful tourist destination coupled with tax haven, resulted in Monaco having the world's lowest poverty rate and the highest per capita number of millionaires and billionaires in the world. Monaco boasts an unemployment rate of zero. In fact, about forty thousand French and Italian citizens (more than the entire population of Monaco) make the daily commute to work in the city state.

Nate told us that, because it was a tax haven, and also accessible via private yacht from anywhere in the world, it had long been popular with criminals including arms dealers and international organized crime. Consequently, Nate had traveled to Monaco numerous times during his tenure with the CIA.

A rental car was waiting for us at the private jet terminal. Within minutes of landing, we were in the car with Nate driving for the thirty-five minute trip to Monaco. We checked in to our hotel room, a two-bedroom suite, and had a small snack. Nate suggested what Laura and I should wear for touring around Monte Carlo. Laura wore gray Lululemon yoga pants with white tennis shoes and a blue-and-white-striped shirt that evoked a nautical theme. As usual, she looked hot.

I grinned at Laura and said, "Nate, I'm not sure if I should thank you or Emily for Laura's yoga pants...but thank you!"

Nate smiled but replied, "Keep your head in the game—no distractions."

I stood in the sitting area of the suite, naked from the waist up, in a pair of pressed chino pants and boat shoes. Although the shirt I had been given was a very expensive polo style, I held it up and winced. It just wasn't me. It was bright red, almost shiny, with a wide, vertical white stripe running the length of one side in front. Large Ferrari emblems were emblazoned on the sleeves and back. I wrinkled my nose at the shirt. It was too loud for my taste.

"Trust me: you will fit right in around here with that shirt," consoled Nate.

I slipped the shirt over my head and looked at the bright side—I was happy to dispense with the thick, black-rimmed, bogus glasses in favor of a pair of Oakleys. No one was looking for me in Monaco. Laura topped off her look with a pair of Wayfarers that, at first glance, seemed too big for her face. But as I gazed at her, I again realized that she could be a professional model. At the risk of repeating myself, she looked awesome. The expensive, oversized glasses added a sophisticated touch. Nate also pointed out that our mirrored sunglasses were great for basic surveillance: you could scan crowds and focus on individual subjects while appearing to look at your menu, for example. Nate had a similar, but more conservative look. His shirt was white and had a tasteful Renault logo on the left side of the chest. We looked like three ordinary race fans.

By the time we left our hotel and set out for the F1 race, it was one o'clock in the afternoon on Saturday. Although the main Grand Prix race took place on Sunday, the city streets surrounding the race track were crowded as the Formula One cars took turns doing their qualifying laps, the drivers getting used to the track and the pit crews making small adjustments to the cars based on temperature and humidity.

Laura and I were astounded at the magnitude of the crowds for practice laps the day before the actual race. Every terrace overlooking the track was packed with people enjoying cocktails and socializing in between the deafening passes of the Formula One cars.

"So this is a pretty big deal here? I was half expecting a bunch of Eurotrash rednecks."

Nate said, "This is nothing; wait 'til tomorrow. And this is not NASCAR. Residents lucky enough to be right on the track," he said and pointed to a private terrace, "rent out their apartments for as much as fifty thousand dollars per day. It is the European equivalent of a Super Bowl skybox. And no rednecks. This is a champagne, caviar, and private jet crowd."

As we meandered our way through the crowds and along the track, I saw what he meant. Instead of beer trucks with taps coming out the sides, well-dressed bartenders were serving up martinis and mojitos. I noticed a number of European men take second, and even third, glances at Laura. They seemed to gawk a lot more than would be acceptable back home.

In the cross streets that the race ran along, elaborate two- and three-story temporary structures had been erected. With comfortable awnings and catered food, they too looked like high-end skyboxes. We arrived at Port Hercule, a calm marina so dense with yachts I marveled at how they had been packed in to such a tight space. Looking around, it was easy to understand why this was the most famous racing venue in the world. Two sides of the harbor sat directly on the race circuit. F1 cars raced along Avenue d'Ostende until they made a hard, ninety-degree left turn down Boulevard Albert 1er. Yachts moored along the sea wall had front row seats for that stretch of track. A reinforced metal fence barricade protected the yachts from the potential debris of crashing cars. The path of the race circuit separated the yachts from the other side of the track, where more race fans packed the private balconies and terraces. The only access to the harbor, and all the yachts, was farther up Boulevard Albert 1er, from a street named Avenue de la Quarantaine. Nate led us to a vantage point on Avenue de la Quarantaine. It was the perfect setup for surveillance. We could stand out in the open, taking pictures of *Cui Bono* all day long without being noticed. We were surrounded by tourists and race fans, all pointing telephoto lenses in the same general direction.

Cui Bono stood out from the large number of expensive private yachts docked along the race circuit. In fact, *Cui Bono* dwarfed most of the yachts. The yachts were backed in to their moorings with their bows facing away from the racetrack. Most yachts were designed for this. The bows were narrow and often full of mooring lines, anchors, and dinghies. The sterns of the yachts were wide and spacious, designed for entertaining. They had comfortable couches, chairs, and tables along with bars and sometimes hot tubs.

Unlike some of the smaller yachts, *Cui Bono* had multiple decks overlooking the track. She was a gorgeous three-story skybox on water.

Although we could have found a surveillance point much closer, our vantage point offered a diagonal view of *Cui Bono*, which gave us a clear view of the entire ship from tip to stern. The powerful zoom lens on Nate's camera was honed in on the stern of *Cui Bono*, scanning the crowd of guests.

The megayacht had a prime spot to watch the race. Revelers on her stern looked right to see the F1 cars emerge from the famous tunnel and accelerate up to 180 mph. Right in front of her, the cars dramatically slowed to navigate an *S* turn, known as a chicane. Then, the cars delivered a deafening roar as they emerged from the chicane and accelerated up the straight away to the left of *Cui Bono's* guests.

Nate was scanning the guests through his zoom lens, when he snapped his head back from the lens and straightened up. He looked surprised. Laura and I both noticed his reaction and couldn't help but become a bit alarmed ourselves. He rarely reacted to anything. Calm and cool always.

Nate put his eye back to the camera and snapped off about a dozen digital images. He paused, pulled his head back to look at the digital display on the back of the camera, and scanned through the photos he had just taken. He settled on one. He transferred the photo to his smartphone using bluetooth and e-mailed it to somebody. Then he crossed his arms and rested his chin on one of his hands.

Laura and I could almost see the wheels turning in Nate's head. "A friend of yours?" Laura asked, nodding to the smartphone picture he had just sent.

"An enemy of the state." Nate deadpanned before adding, "Maybe."

Before we could ask anything more, Nate began packing his camera equipment and said, "Let's go." And he was off. Laura and I hurried to keep up. Moments later Nate's cell phone chirped, and he stopped in an opening, away from other tourists and race fans. He read the reply to his e-mail and shook his head.

"I thought I recognized one of the guests on de Gaulle's yacht." Motioning to his cell phone, he added, "I was right. Identity just confirmed."

"So who is it?" I asked.

"Dr. Fuhrmann. A former military doctor. Psychiatrist to be precise. I knew him from my days with the United States government." That was Nate-speak for CIA. "He was always pushing the envelope with the latest cutting-edge interrogation techniques."

"You mean torture?" inquired Laura.

"Yes, if you ask me. But Dr. Fuhrmann would be insulted at the notion. He considered himself much more sophisticated than your garden variety torturer. He mixed up various drug and chemical concoctions. Always trying to invent a truth serum. I witnessed a few of his failed formulas injected into prisoners in the war on terror. In one, the prisoner convulsed violently for ten minutes before his heart gave out. In another, within seconds of receiving Dr. Fuhrmann's injection, the prisoner nodded off unconscious and began bleeding from the mouth and nose."

I saw Laura close her eyes for a second as she absorbed this.

Nate continued, "He is viewed by many, myself included, as a dangerous nutcase who is a major liability to the United States. Others view him as a bold pioneer of safer and better intelligence-gathering techniques. An important weapon in the war on terror. When I retired from my service to Uncle Sam, he stayed, but he remained as controversial as ever."

Nate received another text message, read it, and said, "We have to meet an old friend a few blocks from here." And he started walking. Laura and I caught up again. Nate said, "Dr. Fuhrmann disappeared several weeks ago. I know this because I still have friends in government. Heard it over a beer. The United States is very concerned about his disappearance. He knows a lot. They fear that maybe someone made him a better offer."

"You mean another country? He's a traitor?" I asked.

"Possibly. He had become renowned in military circles. Maybe he got fed up with the limits his superiors had placed on his experimental interrogation techniques. Maybe they said, 'No more human guinea pigs for your truth serum concoctions.' Who knows, maybe he got greedy for money? None of that speculation matters. The key point is, he is AWOL, and the government wants very badly to find him."

"Who would hire him?" I asked.

"The list of possibilities is almost endless. And it is scary to think what he might attempt without supervision, or with the backing of significant resources." He gestured in the direction of the harbor as he said this. "Most of the countries or organizations that would hire him don't think too much of concepts like human rights and the Geneva Conventions. Problem is, seeing him on de Gaulle's yacht all but confirms he has turned."

Laura and I absorbed this in silence.

Nate looked at us with a serious expression. "Look—I'm about to bring you 'over the wall,' into the realm of classified material that you can never disclose to anyone. Ever. If you can abide by that, come with me. If you can't, wait for me at the hotel."

Laura and I pondered this. But we already knew the answer. Maybe our thoughtful pause would assure Nate that we understood the seriousness. I grabbed Laura's hand and said, "They killed my boss and tried to kill me. We're in."

"Okay, let's roll."

Chapter 35

Laura, Nate, and I strolled down a quaint, narrow street of Monte Carlo that was dense with people. We followed Nate into a crowded coffee shop and sat down in a corner. Soon we were joined by a man Nate introduced as Matt. No last name. Matt had a large camera equipment bag that he placed on the floor as he sat down.

Nate said, "You got here pretty quick?" I sensed a question behind his innocuous comment: "You were already here. Is there an operation in progress right here, right now?"

Matt smiled. "Right now I'm just glad I happened to be in the area, because you just handed us the big break we've been looking for."

Nate glanced at the oversized camera bag. "Standard gear?"

Matt replied, "Yeah, I don't think it has changed much since you left. What about them?" Matt asked distrustfully, looking at Laura and me. In a normal social setting, such a question in that tone would have been considered rude. Apparently in spy circles, it passed.

Nate assured Matt by saying, "They're over the wall."

"Says who?"

"Says me." Nate gave Matt a stern look.

"Okay, all right." He put his hands up. "If they're okay with you, I'm sure they'll be okay."

"So what's the story?" Nate got right down to business.

Matt explained, "Dr. Fuhrmann is extremely wanted by the Pentagon, but they can't post him on INTERPOL, given his background and the nature of his dropping out of sight. And, to our knowledge, he hasn't done anything illegal. But the folks back home get very uneasy when assets like him disappear."

"I could understand that," concurred Nate.

Matt said, "No, I mean more than that. I can't put my finger on it, but the Pentagon's interest in Fuhrmann is disproportionate."

Nate nodded.

Matt continued, "Fuhrmann had access to classified intelligence well above my pay grade. So while I don't know what secrets he knows, the top brass is very worried. Otherwise, a military doctor goes AWOL, who cares?"

Nate glanced at the equipment bag and said, "So, does this mean I'm working for the man again?"

"Officially, no, nothing happens that fast. Unofficially, Webster says 'Welcome back.'"

Nate and Matt both laughed. James Webster was the station chief, and Nate knew him well.

Matt continued, "This is a big one. Webster will give you anything you need. Preprogrammed cell phones are in the bag."

"Any limits?"

"Well, yeah. This is just intelligence gathering."

Nate looked at him sideways with a knowing frown.

"Really." Matt paused. "You can't go around shooting things up. Especially in Monte Carlo during the Grand Prix! They want you to be discreet."

Nate seemed incredulous; he held his hands palms up in the air as if to say, "What do you expect me to do then?"

Matt said, "Look, I know 'discreet' is not something you are known for." Matt tilted his head and cracked a smile. "Results, on the other hand, are. So I suspect orders may change. But please. They don't want an ugly incident in the headlines at a major tourist event."

"Who might I run into here in Monte Carlo?"

Matt said, "No one else, just me. Webster is already on his way here, but other assets are on other assignments, at least thirty-six hours away." He looked at the duffel bag and then back at Nate. "That's why you get the goody bag. I'd say you have about a day and a half before Webster thanks you for your temporary help."

"Thanks. Anything else?"

"I guess not. Good to see you though. And good luck." Matt got up and left without even glancing at Laura or me.

Laura asked Nate, "What did you mean by 'any limits'?"

Nate said, "I need to know the limits of my authority for this operation."

I laughed. "Sounds a bit like asking if you are licensed to kill."

"That is exactly what I was asking." Nate showed no emotion as he said this.

Laura and I glanced at each other in silence.

I changed the subject. "So what's in the bag?"

Nate smiled and said, "Camera equipment." He stood and added, "Let's take it back to the hotel."

Back in the hotel room, Nate placed the equipment bag on the bed and opened it up. Laura and I gawked at the cache of guns and electronic equipment. Nate seemed very decisive, quick, and comfortable as he unpacked the bag, taking inventory as he spread the contents out on the bed. Once the bag was empty and everything was spread out on the bed, Nate surveyed the contents one more time. Then he repacked it.

"Standard equipment. As you know, it's a bit tough to get guns on planes these days. Guess I didn't have to bring mine after all." He smiled as he admired a hand gun from the bag. Then he pulled a suppressor out and screwed it on. He held the gun and aimed it across the suite. I could tell he was gauging the balance of the gun in his hand with the suppressor attached.

"You brought a gun from Chicago! How?"

"Yes. And maybe I'll tell you someday."

I nodded. It almost sounded like a compliment.

Nate looked at Laura and me. "You are going to sneak aboard de Gaulle's yacht."

My heart skipped a beat but I tried not to show it. I felt Laura squeeze my hand.

Nate continued, "I would go aboard. But Fuhrmann will recognize me. You can both go. Or Laura can stay with me. Christian, you can go by yourself."

I could tell Laura was uneasy, so I tried to give her an out. I asked Nate, "What do you think?"

"No incremental benefit to both of you going. Twice the risk."

"So I'll go by myself," I decided.

Nate nodded. Laura was still uneasy. Nate consoled her. "Simpler and safer for all of us if only you go. Laura will be safe with me."

Nate could tell I was nervous and scared. He said, "Look, I know you can do this. You are humble in a good way. Humility is integral to these operations—not bravado. Bravado is what guys have after six beers. But after six beers, your judgment is impaired. Bravado gets good people killed. Fear is your friend. Courage is not the absence of fear. It arises out of understanding the risks, calculating and acting accordingly."

I thought to myself, the same traits that make for a good field operative also make for a good commodities trader. Cool under fire. Deliberate. Don't let your emotions cloud your judgment. Bravado and the absence of fear will lead to bankruptcy in the markets. Be humble enough to admit when you are wrong and change course when necessary. The comparison made me miss the excitement of the exchange floor. I still felt I had the right stuff to succeed in the pits. I was calculating that, if I helped solve Thomas Minter's murder, I might be next in line for a pit broker position. Thomas Minter was an icon in Chicago, much revered by the whole financial community. I was inching closer to getting my shot at the big time back in Chicago. I thought wistfully about moving beyond my current predicament and getting my trading career back on track. If I had to sneak aboard a yacht, fine—as long as I was working toward a pit broker position.

Looking at me, Nate smiled, nodded, and said, "Iceman." Nate pulled out some other items and electronic gadgets from the bag. Then he took out a white Oxford long sleeve button down shirt. "See this button?" He pointed to the second button from the top. It looked like all the rest. "It has a minicamera, with a live wireless feed to me. I will see everything you see. And with this," he said as held up an earpiece much like the one I wore back at the Days Inn so John Jr. could speak to me. "I will guide you every step of the way."

Boarding de Gaulle's yacht alone seemed overwhelming, but with Nate as my eyes and ears, I nodded. I said, "I can do this," almost to myself.

Nate must have sensed my uneasiness. "Christian, I've been in this business a long time. I would not put you in this position unless I knew you could do this. I will have your back. And Matt and the agency will have both of our backs. You will have friends close by."

Chapter 36

Back in Chicago, Jack Thompson took to the podium, once again in front of a large crowd of reporters. His near conviction, for a crime he did not commit, had continued to mesmerize the media and dominate the news and talk shows.

He cleared his throat and began by saying, "As you know, thanks to video footage recovered from the hotel, we know who killed Mrs. Gonzalez. I said all along, it wasn't me. But here is the real kicker that has not yet been reported: DNA recovered from the crime scene did in fact belong to me! I would have been convicted for a crime I did not commit, but for the fact that the real criminals were caught on tape. These heartless and gutless thugs murdered an innocent woman and then, right on tape, planted my DNA!"

He paused for a moment as the crowd absorbed this in astonishment, and reporters scuffled closer, murmuring to each other. When they settled down, Jack continued, "Turns out, they acquired my DNA after an extensive stakeout." He motioned to his neck and said, "And from the now-famous scratches on my neck." The scratches had scabbed over but were still visible. "What I thought was a distraught mother slapping me in the face, was an experienced pro—a field operative—on a mission to get my DNA."

Reporters in the crowd shook their heads in amazement.

"These killers were caught on tape planting my DNA under Mrs. Gonzalez's fingernails!" He pointed again to his neck when he said this. He did not mention that semen, also taken from his hotel room, was planted on Mrs. Gonzalez. Mr. Thompson was not embarrassed by this, but he felt it was a sordid detail the Gonzalez family did not need to dwell on.

The crowd of reporters gasped as they took this in. "Fortunately, both killers have been caught. The two individuals tasked with obtaining my DNA, however, have not yet been identified or apprehended."

A palpable chill swept through the crowd. Jack was a good politician and a good storyteller, good at creating the desired effect. *This could happen to anyone…this could happen to you! They're still out there!*

"We have launched an investigation into our reliance on DNA evidence. Our preliminary findings are devastating."

The reporters once again mumbled to each other and jockeyed for better positions, closer to Mr. Thompson.

"Since DNA testing of crime scenes began, we have come to rely on DNA evidence as the gold standard. The science of DNA seemed irrefutable. Incontrovertible. Well, we were—and we are—wrong. Everything you thought you knew about DNA evidence is wrong."

The crowd of reporters jostled even more. If true, this was a big story. Hell, even if it wasn't true, the controversy would give the twenty-four-hour talking heads something to discuss for the next few weeks. If they could discuss a missing airplane incessantly for five weeks in the absence of even the smallest shred of new information, this story would be a gold mine. The reporters all seemed to sense the bigness of it. But they also wanted proof.

Several of the reporters shouted over one another: "What evidence do you have?" and "Can you substantiate this?"

Mr. Thompson put his hands in the air to calm them down before continuing. "We have uncovered several Internet chat rooms, all rife with chatter about planting DNA. This chatter is not always about framing other people, as happened to me. Much of the chat room dialogue is among criminals, often boasting of how they 'dropped' DNA at the scene of their crimes. DNA that did not belong to them. DNA that they dropped for the express purpose of exonerating themselves!"

The crowd was now getting worked up. True or not, they recognized that this story could occupy a lot of print and news/talk shows.

"We even discovered several online businesses selling DNA. One of them blatantly advertises, and I quote, 'Untraceable DNA—will get you off!' These websites contain testimonials of suspects boasting, 'As soon as the DNA tests came back, my case was dropped. Never even went to trial. Best ninety-nine bucks I ever spent!' The websites state that the DNA is from anonymous donors who, having never been convicted of a crime, will not show up in any criminal DNA databases."

As they absorbed this, the crowd of reporters grew silent. Stunned.

"Some of these businesses started out selling drug-free urine specimens, intended to circumvent employer drug testing. At some point they discovered there was also a market for other forms of bodily fluids, including blood and even semen."

Jack motioned to his staffers who were standing on the edge of the crowd with tall stacks of bound reports. "My team is now handing out copies of a report we put together. It lists the Internet chat rooms and DNA-selling websites that we found. We are certain that, with your resources," he said and motioned to the mob of reporters, "you will find much more."

"Our research demonstrates that we are in a forensic science arms race. DNA was an important weapon in the fight against crime. But not anymore. Now, the criminals are exploiting this against us. They have created simple counter measures, rendering our methods useless, obsolete. It is time for us to advance the technology we use. It is time for us to regain the upper hand in this scientific arms race. Before more innocent people are condemned to death or sentenced to life in prison."

Jack continued by saying, "Everything contained in this report has already been turned over to the FBI." He motioned to Special Agent Bruner who was standing about ten feet off to the left of the podium. "The FBI has already commenced investigations and raided the offices of several DNA-selling companies. At least one of these companies kept meticulous computer records of every transaction. Detailed records of every DNA sample they sold and to whom they sold it. Through these records, the FBI has already identified the alleged real perpetrator of a brutal rape based on the DNA he purchased, online with his credit card. In other words, for the first time in history, a rapist will be conclusively connected to his crime with someone else's DNA—the DNA he dropped."

The reporters erupted again. You could feel the astonishment in the crowd. Jack concluded with, "Welcome to this new frontier in the fight for justice. Ladies and gentlemen, I am asking for your help, your investigative reporting expertise." He did not mind sucking up to reporters when it suited him. "I was lucky. Others like me have been wrongly convicted of crimes they did not commit. And many victims are still waiting for justice. I implore each and every one of you to devote some time and resources to righting these abhorrent wrongs. FBI Special Agent Bruner will now discuss how your organizations can share anything you find that may be of value with the FBI."

Agent Bruner shook hands with Jack Thompson and stepped up to the cluster of microphones. He thanked Jack Thompson for everything he had done to help the FBI. Then he gave a brief statement encouraging and welcoming all the help the reporters and their news organizations could muster. The FBI had already set up a website specific to DNA case reviews, to make it easy for individuals to provide information to the FBI.

For once, the reporters did not have questions to shout. They were still shocked at the totality of what they had just heard. Jack had baited them well, turned it into a challenge for competing news organizations. They were about to work feverishly to one-up one another by investigating harder and finding more outrageous examples. Exonerated innocent people always made for spectacular human interest stories, even won Pulitzers.

Like most politicians, Thompson had a good nose for news. He knew this was a sensational story that would dominate news coverage for several weeks. But, unlike the stories accusing him of murdering Mrs. Gonzalez, he welcomed the competition—the race of reporters to sensationalize this story even more. He smiled, satisfied at what he had just set in motion. The news media was about to do some good. A thorough investigation to help ensure that others would not endure the false accusations he had.

The news media did go bonkers over the DNA story. First, leading stories on the nightly news questioning DNA science. Then incessant news/talk show coverage debating the pros and cons of DNA evidence. You could not channel surf without finding multiple talk shows with various experts, some stating forensic DNA was flawed and obsolete and others stating that it was still valid and necessary.

Thompson knew the talking heads on TV would superficially debate what was already known. He marveled at how long they could discuss, rehash, and speculate on the same few facts.

The second wave was what he was eager to see—the wave in which serious news organizations with intelligent reporters would invest tireless research efforts investigating the DNA issue. Within two to three weeks, the results of the first of these comprehensive reports would show up on magazine covers, with provocative headlines.

Chapter 37

Due to the fact that *Cui Bono* had a front row seat to the Formula One Grand Prix, it was impossible to board the megayacht the usual way, across a walkway connecting the stern of the yacht to the shore. De Gaulle's guests had to meet on a dock across the harbor and shuttle back and forth to *Cui Bono* on the yacht's tenders.

Yacht tenders, sometimes called dinghies, are typically small wooden rowboats or zodiac inflatables with small outboard motors. They are used for getting to and from shore when a yacht was at anchor.

Cui Bono was much larger than most yachts, and her tenders were too. They consisted of two thirty-eight-foot Intrepid center console boats. Each Intrepid was powered by a neat row of four three-hundred-seventy-five horsepower, four-stroke outboard engines. The Intrepid boats could hold more than twenty-five people each and, if needed, reach speeds of eighty-five mph.

I was learning to appreciate the detailed scientific manner in which Nate evaluated the situation. First, we noticed which tenders were shuttling guests to the *Cui Bono*. This was followed by a close examination of the security procedures, which in this case consisted of a clipboard held by the first mate on each tender. Each Intrepid tender was staffed by a crew of three—the captain or boat driver, a first mate with the invitation list on a clipboard, and a bikini-clad cocktail waitress who welcomed guests with a glass of champagne. Before passengers could board the tender, they were asked for their name, but not for any ID. Once the first mate located their name on the list, the guest was welcomed aboard the tender.

Guests were then shuttled across the harbor to the *Cui Bono*. We could see that no additional security procedures existed to board the yacht. De Gaulle's crew had been instructed to make his guests feel welcome and not burdened by excessive security precautions. The cocktail waitresses looked to be in their twenties and were wearing very skimpy bikinis. Given that most tenders were tiny, cramped little boats, the luxurious thirty-eight-foot Intrepids stood out. Having cocktail waitresses on the tenders was over the top, by design—ostentatious even by de Gaulle standards. Guests would talk about this, and de Gaulle would bask in their amazement.

Nate pointed out that although names were checked off the list, the lists were not being compared between the two tenders. "All we need is to find a male guest arriving alone, get his name. Then you board using the same name on the other tender."

It sounded simple enough, but my stomach was still churning.

Nate walked over to the slanted ramp that went down to the floating dock in order to get an elevated vantage point.

He placed an oversized special lens on his digital camera, one that looked like the giant lenses used on the sidelines of football games. Once again, people thought nothing of tourists taking pictures of the race, or of the harbor or any of the yachts. In fact, many of the race fans had very expensive professional-level camera equipment with them. Many of de Gaulle's guests were taking pictures, including selfies with the bikini-clad cocktail waitresses. Their bikini bottoms were black-and-red thongs. The bikini tops were also quite small and had a checkered flag pattern that fit the weekend's race theme.

As a group of passengers boarded the first Intrepid tender, Nate focused on the first mate and shot off a series of continuous photos. As soon as he was confident he had what he needed, he scrolled through the pictures he had just taken on the camera's view screen. He stopped on several pictures long enough to zoom in on the clipboard the first mate was holding. I was amazed at how adept Nate was at scrolling through the photos and then zooming in on certain ones. Then I was stunned when he showed me what he had just zoomed in on: the names on the guest list!

"Here, we have one. That guy doesn't look much older than you and look at his name." William Patterson. Nate looked at me and said, "William, it is time for you to mingle with the next group. Tender number two is on its way. Make sure you get on it—not tender number one, where they already checked your name off the list."

I gulped.

"Relax. Remember what we discussed. If you get caught, they have no reason to suspect you of anything. Your buddies dared you to try to sneak aboard the biggest yacht in the harbor, and so you did. Just a dumb prank. Worst they'll do is escort you back here."

I nodded. This did make sense. They wouldn't kill a party crasher, would they? Of course most party crashers did not attempt to download data off of the computer in de Gaulle's office.

I said, "Sure, just enter de Gaulle's office." I held up a flash drive. "Insert this in his computer. Copy his hard drive." I smiled and tilted my head a bit to the side. "Piece of cake."

I was all set. My name was now William Patterson. Once on board *Cui Bono*, if anyone asked, I would be Ron Mikulecky. William Patterson would satisfy the first mate holding the guest list. However, once on board, Nate explained I could not risk meeting someone on the yacht who happened to know Mr. Patterson. Nobody aboard would know the name Ron Mikulecky.

"Relax, and listen to me, just like you listened to John Jr. at the Days Inn."

Once again I was wearing a tiny earpiece deep inside my right ear, identical to the one Emily and John Jr. had fitted me with at the Days Inn. In addition to the earpiece, the second from the top button of my shirt contained a tiny camera, while the top button had a microphone, all enabling Nate to see and hear everything in real time. The rather stiff but natural-looking collar of the shirt contained an antenna for transmitting. Nate would practically be onboard the yacht, eyes and ears; I was simply his legs.

Under Nate's watchful eye, I boarded the Intrepid tender as William Patterson. *That was easy enough*, I thought.

"Relax," I heard in my tiny earpiece. "You look a little nervous. How many people do you know who get to watch the Monte Carlo Grand Prix from a megayacht?"

I tried to relax as the first mate threw the lines, and the tender began to pull away from the dock. As we moved slowly across the harbor, the bikini-clad cocktail waitress approached and offered me a glass of champagne. As I took it, I noticed something I had never seen before. The bikini on the cocktail waitress was painted on her skin! She was totally naked, casually offering me a glass of champagne. She smiled, enjoying the moment that guests realized she was naked. From a distance I had thought it was an actual bikini, but both the top and bottom were painted on. The cocktail waitress was young and beautiful with a very tight body. I tried not to stare.

It was mesmerizing. Just from an artistic perspective of course. I wondered about the artist who painted it on. *How do you get that job?* As other guests realized the bikini was painted on, they all began laughing and talking about it. A few cracked jokes. It was a welcome diversion that lightened the mood aboard the tender and helped me relax. It also helped take away any undue attention from me. I sat and looked out at the scenery of the harbor, trying to avoid conversation with other guests and trying to avoid any more involuntary gawking at the naked waitress.

The tender docked alongside the megayacht, and I followed the other guests aboard. We were led up one flight of stairs and then along an outer walkway toward the stern. I accepted a glass of chardonnay from another cocktail waitress and placed my untouched glass of champagne on her serving tray.

In case you are wondering, yes, she had a painted-on bikini too. The yacht was full of at least a dozen gorgeous young women who were completely naked except for white boat shoes and painted-on bikinis. I don't know where a guy like de Gaulle hires such waitresses. They looked like they stepped out of a Victoria's Secret catalog, except they were naked.

Just as with the champagne on the tender, I held my wine glass but did not drink it. I did not want my judgment to be impaired. I walked among the guests on the aft deck and settled with my arms rested on the railing overlooking the race track. When the next Formula One car passed by, I winced at the approaching noise and then felt the force of it hit my body. *Wow! That was cool!* It felt similar to standing in front of a large speaker at a concert. Maybe not just for rednecks, I thought. I stood at the railing and enjoyed the sensation of several more cars passing by.

Through the earpiece I heard Nate's voice: "Nice work so far, very natural. Time to mosey on back and find de Gaulle's

office. One deck up, and then about two hundred feet forward, midship. Stay on the starboard side, so I can see you."

I strolled along with my glass of chardonnay, just one
of many guests who couldn't help but wander around this
amazing megayacht. With de Gaulle's narcissistic personal-
ity, I figured he delighted in the fact that his guests walked
around and gawked at the lavishness of his beloved yacht. I
found an outer staircase, took it up one level, and then began
walking toward the ship's bow.

"I see you. Keep going." It was comforting to hear Nate's
voice. "Twenty more feet, then stop to admire the view across
the harbor…Ten more feet…There! Stop and look."

I stopped, rested my forearms on the railing, and bent
my left leg a bit. I was admiring the view out over the harbor,
but I knew de Gaulle's office was directly behind me.

"Casually turn to your left and face the inside of the
yacht."

I turned and rested my left hand on the railing behind
me. I still held the glass of wine in my right hand. I was looking through a glass door, into a richly appointed office. It
looked like a lawyer's office, with a dark mahogany desk and
bookcases and heavy leather furniture—much nicer than any
office I expected to see on a boat.

Nate spoke through my hidden earpiece. "Confirm the
office is empty. Take your time. If it is empty, take a sip of
wine."

I looked back and forth, twice, and then raised the glass
to my lips. I didn't see anyone.

"Excellent, now just walk in; see if the door is unlocked."

I nervously approached the glass door, with a part of me hoping it would be locked. It was open! I entered and closed the door behind me. I walked around behind the large, expensive desk and looked at the computer. I leaned forward to position my body so that the button on my shirt with the camera was facing the computer, giving Nate a good view.

"Lean forward and closer a bit."

I did, making sure the button on my shirt was aimed at the computer.

Nate was sitting nearby with Laura watching my real-time video on a laptop. He directed me. "Now toward the black rectangular attachment on the side of the monitor…" I leaned in even closer. Mounted on the right side of the monitor was a small rectangular device. The top of the device had a small eye that looked like a tiny camera lens. Below that was a small, flat, clear pad similar to the fingerprint scanner on laptop computers. The device said, "Biometrix Inc."

"Got it," Nate said. He recognized the biometric computer security device. "The clear pad scans a fingerprint, and the digital eye scans your retina. Unless you are Nicolas de Gaulle, we're not going to retrieve any data today unless he left his computer on and it has not yet timed out into sleep mode. Tap the spacebar or move the mouse and see if the screen perks up."

I did, and the screen came to life. In the center of the screen was the same User ID box I was used to seeing on my computer. I clicked on it, and it prompted me for a password. No luck, the computer was logged off.

Nate warned, "Two security guards walking toward you. Very briskly, and with purpose. We must have tripped something in the office. Stash the flash drive—now!"

I fumbled through the front pocket of my pants, fished the flash drive out, and stuffed it down my underwear. Figured they might search my pockets, but not the front of my underwear. As I did this I walked over to the bookshelf. By the time the two security guards rushed in, I was casually perusing the titles of the books on the shelf.

The door to the office flew open, startling me, even though I had been expecting it. I turned toward the security guards.

Nate spoke through my earpiece: "Relax. The door was open. You thought it was okay to wander around the yacht…" But he did not need to say that. We had already rehearsed this.

The security guards were big, beefy men. "What are you doing here?" demanded one of them.

I replied, "Just wandering around…appreciating this beautiful boat. Isn't that okay?"

"Not here." He spoke almost angrily, as if he himself might be in trouble for my intrusion. "Off limits." He motioned around the office.

I put my hands up. "Okay…no problem." I started to leave.

The more senior guard raised a hand toward me in a stop motion, and demanded, "Who are you?" I grew very nervous. He was angry and aggressive. I tried to play it cool, hoping they would just let me go back to the party. But then the two security guards and I were startled by a crash outside the office, accompanied by terrible screeching and cracking noises.

The guards instinctively looked toward the noise. They rushed out of the office to the walkway and peered over the railing to the water below. I followed them and couldn't help but look over the railing myself. Someone had accidently rammed a small runabout boat right into the side of de Gaulle's megayacht. Then, rather than back off the throttle, the driver continued to turn the boat to the left and power ahead. In trying to extricate himself from the mess, he was making it far worse. Fiberglass splintered and cracked.

I heard Nate through the earpiece: "Walk to the exit. Go!"

As the two security guards shouted obscenities at the idiot below, I slipped away. As I left I could still hear the cracking and splintering. The tender driver was still trying to power his way through the mess, rather than backing off the throttle and reversing.

The bow of the runabout broke free from the side of the massive yacht. But the driver continued to power ahead and, as he did, with the wheel turned sharply to the left, it was only a second before the back right side of the runabout also smacked the megayacht's hull and scraped along it. As I started down a flight of stairs, the two security guards were still yelling unheeded instructions at the boat driver below.

Once on the staircase and out of sight, I moved quickly down the stairs and at the same time removed my white Oxford shirt and tied it around my waist, revealing a short-sleeve blue V-neck T-shirt. I removed a Formula One baseball cap from my back pants pocket and put it on. Nate watched me as I entered the staircase and left his view. When I emerged one level below, looking like a different person, he smiled to himself, knowing that de Gaulle's security guards might be on the lookout for me. I walked to the side entrance of the yacht where de Gaulle's tenders dropped off and picked up guests. A new batch of guests was arriving and stepping off one of the tenders to board the yacht. I waited for the arriving guests to step off, and then I approached the tender before it left to head back to the main dock.

The first mate must have remembered me from earlier because he said, "Leaving already?" He offered me a hand as I boarded the tender. I wasn't sure if the guards were looking for me or if they had radioed the tenders about me.

"Yes, unfortunately. But I should be back soon," I lied.

The tender eased away from the yacht and started across the harbor. While the tenders arriving at *Cui Bono* were full of passengers, on the ride back to the dock, there were just four of us—the tender driver, the first mate, the naked cocktail waitress, and me. She walked over to me, shrugged, and raised her eyebrows as she offered me a glass of champagne. She pursed her lips in a pouty frown and said, "Leaving so soon?"

I accepted the champagne glass and downed half of it in a single gulp. She smiled. I relaxed a bit once we were halfway across the harbor. The commotion of the small boat ramming *Cui Bono* caused the guards to forget about me, or at least lose interest, long enough for me to escape further questioning.

I sat on the right side of the tender just in front of the boat's center console. The waitress looked me over from head to toe. Twice. She smiled and then turned to set down her serving tray on the bench across from me. The first mate began filling glasses for the next group of guests. It was hard not to stare at the painted-on bikini bottom. I shook my head and glanced back at the tender driver. He was grinning from ear to ear, having busted me looking at the waitress. He grinned even bigger and gave me a thumbs-up. Like an airplane descending, my heart was settling down from the panic of getting caught in de Gaulle's office.

I was flattered that the gorgeous cocktail waitress was flirting with me. She was intentionally seductive in the way she bent over to set her tray down. She stayed bent over longer than necessary and smiled back over her shoulder at me. She gave me the head-to-toe once-over again followed by an approving smile and a raised eyebrow. I was in pretty good shape, but I didn't let her apparent interest in me go to my head. I realized that she was getting paid to do what she did. She had probably been told to flirt with all the male guests—and maybe even the female guests.

We pulled up alongside the dock, and the first mate secured the lines. The cocktail waitress shot me one last seductive smile. I nodded back and set down my empty champagne glass as I stepped up and out of the tender and walked up the dock and into the crowd. Nate was waiting for me.

"Well I guess that was a bust," I said. "I'm sorry."

"No, you were great. That biometric security system on the computer—fingerprint and retina scanners; we never had a chance of bypassing it. Maybe Isaac, but not us. But just knowing that it is there is good. That means there is important info on that computer." Nate smiled and nodded.

I said, "Good thing some idiot crashed into the yacht when he did, eh?"

"That was our friend Matt, from the coffee shop."

It took a moment for this to register with me. Nate smiled. "I told you we got your back."

Chapter 38

Nate, Laura, and I set up once again for surveillance of the megayacht. This time, no cameras or telephoto lenses were needed. We sat down at a small table in a café on the south side of the harbor, about one quarter of the way out on Avenue de la Quarantaine.

Security around de Gaulle and the yacht were tight, so we were focusing on Dr. Fuhrmann. Fuhrmann was on board *Cui Bono*, so we sat and waited, knowing there was one way on and off. He would have to take one of the tenders across the harbor to the main dock, and then he would have to walk past the café where we sat. Of course this assumed he wasn't going to stay overnight aboard the yacht, but we had few other options to pursue. So we would wait.

Nate took the seat at our small table with a perfect view of the harbor and volunteered for the duty of keeping an eye out for Dr. Fuhrmann. Laura and I sat facing Nate, with our backs to the dock where the tenders picked up and dropped off passengers. Nate told us to relax, try to enjoy ourselves. He had this covered; he was watching the dock.

Laura and I sat very close to each other. She held my hand with her far hand and then put her closest hand on my thigh. She rubbed and patted my thigh and then held her hand still. I couldn't believe how in love I was. I placed my right arm around her shoulders, and she crossed her legs toward me, crossing her right leg over mine. I felt so relaxed intertwined with her. Strange, I thought, that a week ago I would have shied away from such a public display of affection. Now, I didn't care. I could snuggle up to her like this all day. And as Nate pointed out, couples being affectionate toward each other were perfect for surveillance operations.

I was beginning to understand that, while I had not physically strained myself, I was exhausted from my confrontation with de Gaulle's security. Perhaps, I thought, I had gained a better understanding of how risking millions in the pits at the Chicago Board of Trade could be exhausting, even though it did not always seem so from my vantage point as a phone clerk—an observer, not a participant. An armchair quarterback versus a real quarterback.

We sat for more than four hours at the waterfront table with no sign of Dr. Furhmann. It turned dark. This was a prime week for a waitress at a waterfront restaurant on Port Hercule. They made a lot of money during the Grand Prix. Knowing this, Nate tipped the waitress fifty Euros in cash every forty-five minutes or so. More than she would have made if the table continually turned over.

Even though we were not ordering much, the service became much more polite, and the waitress stopped more frequently by the table. Nate spoke to the waitress, in fluent French, which surprised me. After she left, he translated: "I just told her we appreciated her allowing us to take up a prime table for so long, but she needn't bother herself with stopping by every few minutes. I said we are simply enjoying the atmosphere and waiting for a friend whose flight has been delayed." That polite comment, coupled with another fifty Euros, kept the waitress from bothering us too often.

At about 11:00 p.m., a slow stream of guests began to leave de Gaulle's Formula One party. Nate sat up straighter. The trickle of departing guests continued, traversing across the beautiful harbor from the yacht to the dock where we sat. Just after midnight, Nate said, "That's him. Get ready."

I turned and looked over my right shoulder at the Intrepid tender heading toward the dock. About a dozen of de Gaulle's guests were calling it a night, Dr. Fuhrmann among them. I was ready. Over the course of our stakeout at the waterfront café, we had discussed and rehashed the plan for following Furhmann. We had gone over every conceivable scenario, more than once. Laura and I left the table and walked to the valet attendant at the beginning of Avenue de la Quarantaine. I gave the valet five Euros and asked him to hail a cab.

Once Laura and I were in the cab, I told the driver to pull ahead a bit to wait for a friend. After our taxi pulled off to the side, I saw Dr. Fuhrmann approach the valet. He too hailed a cab. By the time Furhmann's cab was pulling out, Nate came into view. He was riding a scooter he had parked against the building near the valet, and he began following

Dr. Fuhrmann's taxi. Nate was wearing a full-face motor-cycle helmet to ensure Fuhrmann could not recognize him.

I told our driver to follow Nate on the scooter, but not too close. A taxi cab following Dr. Fuhrmann might raise suspicion. Laura and I knew not to worry if we got separated in traffic, or at a red light. Nate would not lose Furhmann, and we had burner cell phones preprogrammed with each other's numbers.

Although Nate's scooter looked normal, it was an agency-issued scooter. Under the cheap plastic veneer was a powerful four-stroke 350cc engine designed to keep up with anyone, even on a highway. As it turned out, it was not difficult to follow Dr. Fuhrmann. His taxi rolled through Monte Carlo and stopped just a few blocks away in front of a small apartment building. Nate stopped his scooter and silenced the engine about a hundred yards behind Furhmann. The doctor exited his cab and walked a few steps to the entrance of the building. It was hard to tell at first glance, but the small building contained no more than three or four separate apartments.

I instructed our cab driver to continue on past Dr. Fuhrmann's apartment. By the time we passed the apartment, the doctor was already inside. We continued one more block ahead and then two blocks east before Laura and I exited the cab and waited. As promised, Nate called.

"Hello," I answered.

"You ahead two blocks?"

"Yes, sir."

"Good. Walk on back here. I'll meet you at the corner on your side of his apartment."

When we found Nate, he said, "Three units in his building. His door is up half a flight of stairs and on the right. I saw him turn on the lights. I think he is alone."

Laura and I knew what this meant. The plan was quite simple. It would allow Laura to utilize her great looks and charm. This was the best of all possible scenarios we had discussed at the café. We intended to kidnap Furhmann. Finding him alone like this in a private apartment was better than if he was with a group of people or in a crowded hotel with security cameras.

Nate reminded Laura what to do and said, "Just give me five seconds to get up the stairs past his door."

Laura and I waited on the corner while Nate picked the lock of the shared entrance to the building. As soon as we saw Nate enter the building, Laura approached the door and buzzed Furhmann's apartment. I waited back in the shadows, out of sight.

Nate had gone up half a flight of stairs to a landing with the entrance to Dr. Fuhrmann's apartment on his right. Then he U-turned to the left and went up another half a flight of stairs to the next landing. He crouched low, behind the half wall that separated the two zigzag flights of stairs.

Dr. Fuhrmann's voice came over the intercom. "Yes?"

Laura stood back a few feet from the buzzer and held up a small gift-wrapped box. We didn't know if the apartment intercom allowed Dr. Fuhrmann to see her, or only to hear her.

Laura smiled and said, "Dr. Fuhrmann, I am a member of Messier de Gaulle's crew. I'm afraid you and a few of the other guests left without party favors. Messier de Gaulle really outdid himself this year. He insisted that we deliver them." If Furhmann's intercom allowed him to see Laura, she fit the part of one of de Gaulle's female crew. She was hot and young and dressed in a nautical theme.

Dr. Fuhrmann must have smiled to himself, because he said, "Just a sec."

We knew that Laura's story was plausible, based on research of de Gaulle. A grand party aboard a megayacht wasn't enough. Naked cocktail waitresses serving drinks aboard the Intrepid tenders wasn't enough. Nicolas de Gaulle was famous for his over-the-top parties and eccentric party favors. News articles abounded about his lavish fiftieth birthday party, which included a ten-foot ice sculpture replica of Michelangelo's *David*. The *David* ice sculpture was also a fountain, streaming Tito's handmade vodka. And yes, the vodka was streaming out of David's most famous body part. The party favors for his fiftieth included ten-thousand-dollar Rolex watches for the men and Tiffany bracelets for the women.

Laura and I saw the door to his apartment open. It cast a bright light into the dimly lit stairwell. Dr. Fuhrmann came down the half flight of stairs to the front door and saw Laura through the glass, standing there with the gift. Laura held the box toward the glass window built in to the door. Dr. Fuhrmann opened the door and extended a hand.

Laura smiled a flirty smile. "Thank you, Dr. Fuhrmann." She handed him the gift box.

"Yes. Uh, thank you," the doctor replied. Like a lot of guys, he acted a bit awkward around Laura who, in addition to being very beautiful, had put on a very flirtatious smile. He smiled and then turned back to his apartment and started back up the stairs.

Laura blocked the front door from latching shut with her foot. I approached the door but remained to the side, out of Furhmann's view.

When the doctor was halfway up the short flight of stairs, Laura walked into the entryway and said, "Oh and Dr. Fuhrmann…"

She held the door open as she stood in the entryway. Dr. Fuhrmann stopped, a few steps short of his landing, and turned toward her.

She said, "Excuse me, sir—one more thing. I believe you know my friend?"

Dr. Fuhrmann looked confused.

From above on the stairs, Nate slipped silently behind the doctor. He slid his left arm under the doctors left arm and then brought his hand back up behind the doctor's neck, in a half nelson. With his right hand, Nate placed a large knife against the doctor's neck.

Nate spoke in a whispered, but very intense tone: "Don't. Make. A. Sound. If you do, you're dead. Nod if you understand." As Nate said this, he pushed his left hand into the back of the doctor's neck, shoving him forward a bit and pushing his neck against the knife. Furhmann could feel his skin pressing against the cold steel. He was off balance, precariously perched on stairs with a knife biting into his neck. He strained to look down at the knife while nodding.

"Good. Then maybe I won't kill you." Nate was still whispering. "Come." He turned back toward the door to Fuhrmann's apartment. Nate leaned in to the doctor's ear and gritted his teeth. "Is anyone else in the apartment?" Nate said this in a terrifying tone and pressed the knife further into Furhmann's neck.

"No." Dr. Fuhrmann whimpered.

"Alone?" Nate demanded both with his tone and with his knife.

"Yes. Just me," the doctor confirmed.

I slipped in the front door that Laura was holding open, and then we let it close behind us. Nate pushed Fuhrmann inside his apartment. Laura and I walked up the half flight of stairs and entered his apartment. I closed and locked the door. I was impressed. Laura was executing flawlessly.

Nate ordered, "Open your mouth." He jammed a rag into Fuhrmann's mouth and then slapped a piece of duct tape over it from ear to ear. He manhandled the doctor to an armchair in the living room, forced him down, and tied his arms and legs tightly to the chair with large plastic zip ties, the type of restraints police sometimes use in lieu of handcuffs.

Nate walked around in front of Fuhrmann, allowing him to get a good look at Nate's face for the first time.

Dr. Fuhrmann's eyes grew wide, startled with recognition. He struggled to move but was helpless against the restraints. Whatever he muttered was blocked by the rag and duct tape. His excitability caused him to choke on the rag stuffed in his mouth. Nate let him settle down.

"So you recognize me?"

Fuhrmann's eyes got wide again, and he nodded his head vigorously.

"So you know what I am capable of?"

Another vigorous nod.

Nate put his face down close to Fuhrmann's. "I am going to remove the gag. If you scream, you will regret it."

The doctor nodded again, less startled now, but still deathly afraid. Nate removed the duct tape from Furhmann's face with a forceful rip. He threw the tape and rag on the floor. Laura and I stood behind Dr. Fuhrmann's chair, out of his sight, but our presence could be felt. I moved up right behind Furhmann. When Nate made eye contact with me, I shifted to one side or the other or placed a hand on Fuhrmann's shoulder. The first time I touched Furhmann's shoulder, he jumped out of his skin. While discussing this plan earlier, I did not quite understand the purpose of remaining silent behind our captive like this, moving noticeably or touching his shoulder. Nate had assured me it was critical to the interrogation. Now, I understood. How unsettling, to be strapped helplessly to a chair. Every time Nate, who Fuhrmann could see, cast a sharp glance at me; Fuhrmann winced. He never knew what kind of order was intoned by Nate's sharp glance. He never knew when the silent presence behind him was going to hit him, stab him, or shoot him. At least with Nate, he would see it coming. The constant anticipation and uncertainty must have been draining. The pressure was getting to Fuhrmann.

Dr. Fuhrmann weakly said, "I thought you were out, no longer with the agency?"

Nate smiled. "Maybe that's what people like you were supposed to think." While with the agency, Nate had been authorized by the US government to use any and all means necessary, including lethal force, in the course of his missions. If Dr. Fuhrmann thought Nate was still with the agency, then Fuhrmann would believe he was still authorized to kill. Nate's bluff was working. Fuhrmann was terrified.

The United States had a ban on assassinations, dating back to President Ford, when, in the aftermath of Watergate, it was revealed that the CIA had attempted to assassinate Cuban President Fidel Castro. To restore confidence, President Ford had issued Executive Order 11905, banning political assassinations.

In times of war, of course, the ban did not apply. President Reagan dropped bombs on Colonel Moammar Gadhafi's house in response to Libya's terrorist bombing of a night club in Berlin.

Without divulging anything classified, Nate was quite candid with us as we sat for six long hours at the waterfront café. He had told us that most of his operations involved threats, issues, or people that the US government had elevated to, effectively, a state of war. The War on Terror fell in to the "any and all means" category. We had a fleet of drones assassinating terrorists. Anytime a threat was determined to create an imminent danger to the safety and security of the United States of America, lethal force was justified. Extrajudicial action. No courtroom trials or legal proceedings got in the way.

Based on Fuhrmann's own familiarity with Nate's CIA work, Furhmann would believe that Nate was authorized—perhaps even ordered—to kill him. When Nate was with the CIA, detainees, particularly high-value targets, were often brought in by agents like Nate. Fuhrmann's job was to help with the interrogations. Furhmann would get called in as soon as an important suspect was en route.

Nate had developed a reputation within the agency. Often times, the suspects Nate brought into Dr. Furhmann's group for interrogations were already dead or near dead. Furhmann and Nate had clashed at the Agency because Furhmann wanted all of the interrogating left to himself and his sadistic syringes. Nate, on the other hand, always believed his more primitive methods produced better, quicker, actionable intelligence.

"I am going to give you one chance." Nate leaned in and clenched his teeth as he spoke. He held up one finger and said, "One chance. Give me something. Evidence. And then I might decide to let you live. But it had better be good."

Nate shot a sharp glance in my direction. I placed a firm, sudden hand on Fuhrmann's neck. He jumped and let out a whimper. I removed my hand and leaned my head in behind Fuhrmann's. Fuhrmann could feel my presence behind him. He could hear my breathing. A very nice, improvised touch, I thought.

The doctor blurted out in a pleading voice: "They are blackmailing the president."

Chapter 39

"De Gaulle?"

"Yes. And his network."

Nate was surprised, but he did a good job of not showing it. "Proof."

"There," Furhmann said, glancing toward a cabinet. "I have a safe."

Nate walked over and opened the cabinet. A small hotel-room-type safe was mounted inside. It had a numeric keypad. Nate got down on one knee in front of the safe and glared back at Fuhrmann. He did not speak. His cold steely glare said, "The combo!"

Fuhrmann shakily said, "Seven, nine, four, two." No hesitation this time. I did not even get a chance to place another firm hand on his shoulder to rattle him. I guess he was about as rattled as one could be.

Nate entered the code and cautiously opened the safe, aware that it could be booby-trapped. Inside was a sleek tablet computer. He withdrew it from the safe, opened the screen cover, and turned it on.

"This had better be good," Nate said.

"Open the digital video on the desktop—the one named 'Money.'" Dr. Fuhrmann was very eager to please Nate. He believed it might save his life.

The video began playing on the tablet in Nate's hands as he paced back and forth. Nate's eyes widened. He walked behind Furhmann and held the tablet so Laura and I could also see it. I couldn't believe it! The video showed the president of the United States in a gay sex orgy!

Dr. Fuhrmann raised his pleading eyes toward Nate. Maybe this was good enough to let him live, he must have thought.

Nate looked closer at the screen. "How long ago was this? The president looks younger?"

"Ten years ago. He was nobody. After this was recorded, he was appointed to the vacated senate seat in Illinois." He raised his eyebrows as he said this, implying that there was a connection.

Nate demanded, "Is this real or digitally faked?"

"Oh it's real. A digital fraud would easily be proved as such."

The video was spliced together in a few different clips. Some showed the president walking around, socializing, and drinking. In a few shots, he could be seen smoking something from a small glass pipe.

"How long have you been a traitor?" Nate said, considering that the video was ten years old.

"I had nothing to do with that video!" He saw the anger in Nate's eyes and grew more desperate. He looked at Nate as if he were pleading for his life. "I had nothing to do with blackmailing the president. People I work for did that. They obtained this video before I even met them."

"De Gaulle?" Nate demanded.

"Among others. Remember, the president was nobody back then."

"And?" Nate's tone was calm but very intimidating.

"De Gaulle's secretive group likes to dig up any dirt they can on political types. They had this tape because one of the other guys at that party was a Chicago city councilman. They use tapes like this to guarantee the councilman's vote for or against various zoning issues."

Nate paced in front of the doctor with his hands clasped behind his back.

Fuhrmann continued, "Almost by accident, they realized that another guy caught on this tape was a potential political candidate—a college professor and part-time community organizer. Now, our president." He paused as this sank in. Sensing Nate's anger, he said, "I had nothing to do with any of this, but de Gaulle has bragged that he and his wealthy friends purchased the Illinois senate seat for him, bribed the former governor to appoint him—because of this tape."

Nate nodded. An awkward silence. He was waiting for Fuhrmann to continue.

"They never thought he'd be president. That was just dumb luck, according to de Gaulle. The president represented the fastest, meteoric political rise ever—and it all started because they purchased a senate seat for him."

Nate drew his knife and approached Fuhrmann in a rage. "You are scum. You are a disgrace!"

I flinched. I didn't know if Nate was angry or putting on a show to scare Furhmann. I thought Nate might kill him.

Nate was in control, but pretending to be out of control to scare Furhmann into giving truthful answers. Nate clenched his teeth and said, "Who knows about this video, and who has copies?" He held his knife, threateningly.

Furhmann stuttered as he thought, "Very few…"

"Who!"

"The B6 board members…Jimmy Hughes…"

"Saw it, or has a copy?"

"Those people saw it. Nobody has a copy except de Gaulle and myself."

"So if you wanted to destroy all copies of this video, name them!"

"Uh, this copy and de Gaulle's…that's it."

"Why would de Gaulle trust you with this video?" Nate demanded.

"I am the only one he trusts with these videos."

"Why you?"

"Well, I made many of them. I mean some politicians and businessmen are being blackmailed with fabricated stories. Compromising videos and photos we obtained after they were drugged."

"Ahh. And you were the expert who drugged them to set them up?"

The doctor nodded.

Nate thrust the knife in the air toward him. Fuhrmann pleaded, "Wait—there's more! There's more! More politicians owned by them! They are blackmailing at least a dozen major US politicians right now!" Fuhrmann was whimpering, desperate.

Nate paused. He seemed torn between executing this scum, because he deserved it, and letting him live. But part of him wrestled with the potential value to the United States of what Fuhrmann knew. *Should we kill him or take him alive?*

Sensing the mental calculation going on in Nate's head, Furhmann said, "I can give you names, bribes, blackmails. Everything." He was desperate to live. "There are more tapes! United States senators! Cabinet positions!"

Nate seemed to be thinking it over.

Furhmann pleaded, "A terrorist plot! I know about a terrorist plot!"

"Tell me. Now. Impress me, and I'll haul you in. Don't and I'll leave your dead ass right here."

Fuhrmann understood the choice: custody, and probable jail time, versus being killed right there, on the spot. He would much rather take his chances with the US judicial system than with an angry, half-crazed CIA agent.

Nate was very good at breaking people psychologically. I was impressed. The man was terrified, sweating profusely, spilling his guts. Yet Nate had not touched him! Not even a slap. No physical torture of any kind. All the pressure was psychological. I wondered how effective Nate might be at interrogations if he touched the person.

"Osama bin Laden!"

Nate said, "Old news. They found him. He's dead." Nate thrust his knife toward Dr. Fuhrmann.

Furhmann shouted, "No he's not!"

Nate hesitated.

Furhmann said, "Osama bin Laden is alive."

Chapter 40

Furhmann said, "You of all people should not be surprised at this!"

"Prove it. I don't have time for your bullshit."

"I can. It's all right there." He looked at the tablet computer. "See for yourself."

Nate picked up the tablet again.

Dr. Fuhrmann said, "Digital video file, also on the desktop screen. Named 'Osama.'"

Nate double-clicked it and walked behind Furhmann. He held the tablet so that Laura and I could also see the video. We stared in astonishment at the world's most-wanted terrorist—alive and being questioned by American interrogators. Dr. Fuhrmann himself then stepped into the picture frame of the video and crouched down near bin Laden. He smiled for the camera, like a hunter posing with a big game trophy.

Nate, Laura and I nodded at each other, grasping the magnitude of this secret.

Nate asked, "Bin Laden is in US custody?"

Fuhrmann said proudly, "I pulled this off. We fooled the whole world!"

Everyone knew that Navy SEALs, working with the CIA, had stormed a compound in Pakistan and killed bin Laden. To ensure that his grave did not become a shrine used to incite and recruit future jihadists, the US administration decided to give him a quick burial at sea. Officials took photographs of the dead body and also extracted DNA for the purpose of proving to the world that it was bin Laden and he was dead.

Nate smiled to himself and shook his head. "It makes sense," he whispered to us.

Bin Laden was wanted, dead or alive. Despite the largest manhunt in world history, and rewards in excess of fifty million dollars, he had managed to evade capture for more than ten years.

During that time, Saddam Hussein, was caught and put on trial. Hussein used his trial as a public forum to espouse his disgusting justification of violent terrorist acts against innocent civilians. Many of the victims of Hussein's terrorist attacks were women and children—easy, unsporting targets to most. The "soft underbelly of the great Satan" to Hussein.

Hussein's trial lasted three years, during which he was protected and cared for by the very same people he had attacked. Throughout he proselytized more violence and gained more followers.

After a full and fair trial, Hussein was sentenced to death by hanging. No matter what manner of due process he had been given—much more than the victims of his attacks over the years—his followers derided the process as a sham trial with a preordained conclusion.

Some of Hussein's victims' families were invited to attend the execution. As he was led to the gallows, a few of the spectators shouted at him and taunted him. Hussein defiantly argued back, until the floor dropped. One of the spectators recorded everything on a cell phone, and the video found its way to the Internet.

Hussein's followers lambasted the video and renounced the trial once again as a farce. The courts had done everything they could to ensure a fair trial, and the justice meted out should have been cathartic. Unfortunately, the cell phone video of the hanging reduced the whole three-year affair to little more than a sordid snuff film[1], not much different than the Internet videos circulated by terrorists, including beheadings of journalists and civilians.

US Special Forces and CIA agents learned from the disaster of Hussein's public trial and execution. Many Op-ed articles stated the takeaway was clear: "dead or alive" was understood to mean "better off dead." Bin Laden deserved a quick death sentence, not a three-year forum to spew his hatred and gain followers while in safe custody.

Hungry for vengeance after 9/11, the world was not surprised that SEAL team members killed bin Laden, despite reports that he was unarmed and did not put up a fight. Americans weighed the plusses and minuses: Take him alive, and you might gain valuable intelligence about terrorist networks and future attacks. But the cost of the intelligence gained would be high, as bin Laden would be given a stage from which to preach for many years.

This was the ultimate solution: take him into US custody for the high-value information he could provide under interrogation, while making the world think he was dead!

"How did they do it?" asked Nate.

"I bet you could figure out several ways."

That was true. But he repeated, with less patience, "How did they do it?"

"Nonlethal force of course. You've used it many times yourself to haul in suspects. We used a nonlethal knock-out dart."

"I want details," Nate demanded.

"Specially modified Heckler and Koch 416 assault rifles."

This was the weapon of choice for elite soldiers like Navy SEALS. It came in a variety of barrel lengths, the shortest versions better for close quarter, room-to-room searches. It also had an attachable suppressor. Most civilians thought suppressors were used for stealth kills, but they were vital to communicating via radio headsets once the shooting started.

"Modified how?"

"Two triggers, one below the other. The standard, trigger shoots the usual 5.56 by forty-five millimeter cartridges. The additional trigger, below the real trigger, shoots a nonlethal tranquilizer dart. The extra barrel for the darts was connected to the underside of the rifle barrel. The add-on dart gun was done very seamlessly, and in preparation for the mission, the SEALs had plenty of practice time getting used to the modified guns and making the critical split second decision: top lethal trigger or bottom nonlethal trigger. The SEALS were prepared to meet any resistance with standard 5.56 NATOs, and, if they found bin Laden, they had orders to take him alive. If possible, they were to leave survivors behind who saw him get shot."

Nate nodded, pulled up a chair, and sat down in front of Furhmann. His cold stare said, "Go on."

Furhmann seemed to be enjoying this. He was proud of the success of the operation.

"Despite an initial near disaster, it was executed beautifully. We knew bin Laden lived on the third-floor apartment of the compound. The plan was for Special Forces to surprise them, swoop in silently, fast-rope straight into bin Laden's third-floor bedroom before they knew the compound was under attack[2]. Once bin Laden was captured alive, using nonlethal tranquilizer darts, they were to switch to the standard ammunition. But, as the world now knows, the first helicopter hit a vacuum of air caused by the high walls of the compound. It crash-landed, and the element of surprise was lost. Instead of getting to bin Laden first, as planned, the SEALs had to improvise. They fought their way through the compound, building by building, room by room, killing soldiers and rounding up women and children. Each time they cleared a room, they dropped a glow stick in the doorway, informing the rest of the team that room had already been cleared. They eventually made their way to the concrete stairwell leading up to bin Laden's apartment.

Here, it gets interesting. Intelligence reports confirmed there were a total of six adult males in the compound. That is why they had wanted to get to bin Laden first—get him quietly first, by fast-roping into his bedroom. Once they secured bin Laden alive, they could switch to regular ammunition and fire indiscriminately at any remaining threats. By the time they reached the stairwell, they had already killed four adult males. So they knew two adult males were left, and one of them was bin Laden. The order went over the radios: 'Two adult males remaining. Switch to NLWs. Repeat, NLW.' This meant switch to nonlethal weapons. SEALs came up the concrete stairwell cautiously. Whoever was holed up with bin Laden knew Special Forces were coming. They knew they were the last line of defense for bin Laden. Plenty of time to get guns, grenades, and suicide vests. Talk about dangerous—coming up the stairwell toward the most-wanted man in the world into who knows what! It was a very dark night, and the SEALs had the benefit of night-vision goggles. In fact, the mission was planned for the darkest night of the lunar cycle, and minutes before the raid, CIA operatives cut electric power to the whole neighborhood. As the SEALs advanced up the concrete stairwell, a man peered over the half wall at the top of the stairs. The point man popped him with a knockout dart. It was Khalid, one of bin Laden's sons. As the team stepped over Khalid's body, an AK-47 lay next to him. And he had held the higher ground."

Nate interrupted by saying, "SEALs knowingly went up against AK-47s with tranquilizer darts? Stop. Tranquilizer darts are difficult to dose and can take several minutes to kick in. Several minutes in which Khalid could do a lot of damage with his AK-47."

Furhmann smiled and said, "You are correct. Tranquilizer darts contain an anesthetic. And the amount of time it takes to knock out the target is why I added a fast-acting paralytic agent to the darts."

Nate nodded. Dr. Furhmann enjoyed testing new concoctions on humans. Truth serums, paralytic agents—who cares? We wondered if human testing was done for this new concoction prior to the bin Laden raid.

Nate said, "And?"

"At the proper dose based on body weight—remember, we had a very good idea how much bin Laden weighed—the paralytic agent instantly incapacitates the subject. Paralyzes them. It still takes several minutes for the anesthetic to take full effect."

Nate said, "Tell me about the darts."

"Standard, except for the paralytic agent. Hypodermic needle with a barb near the tip—once imbedded in the skin, we wanted the whole dose to go in. Tails on the back stabilized the flight path. Weighted ball bearing at the back of the cylinder compressed the plunger and released the dose upon impact."

Nate nodded and said, "Back to the stairwell. One down, one to go?"

"Yes. Simple math. One adult male remaining in the compound and that had to be bin Laden! The point man on the SEAL team coming up the stairs whispered, 'Osama... Osama.' Remember, without night-vision goggles, it was pitch black. Bin Laden leaned out of the bedroom and peered down the stairs at the sound of his name. The point man nailed him, right in the side of the neck with a knockout dart. As bin Laden began to fall back in to his bedroom, the SEAL had the presence of mind to fire a few 5.56 rounds, over his head, missing him on purpose. Two of bin Laden's wives were in the bedroom. They heard the shots. His wives even heard and saw the standard rounds hit the ceiling of the bedroom above bin Laden, just as he toppled over. The near-simultaneous actual rounds fired into the bedroom would have made anyone standing there believe that bin Laden had been shot. Even if they heard the nonlethal dart, the nonsup-pressed knockout darts sounded similar to suppressed real rounds."

This was amazing. Laura and I stared wide-eyed at each other. Nate looked at Furhmann and said, "Okay, you have my attention." He looked at Furhmann, signaling him to continue.

"Two of bin Laden's wives would be our most reliable witnesses. They were in the bedroom with bin Laden and reported what they saw to the Pakistani authorities. And they saw their husband get shot! SEALs stormed the bedroom. Based on intelligence reports, we believed the wives would have suicide vests. Because of the helicopter crash and the time it took to clear the rest of the compound, the wives had plenty of time to put on vests. The first SEAL to enter the bedroom pushed the wives into a corner, shielding his SEAL brothers, and bin Laden, from the explosion."

I was amazed. For at least a few seconds, that first SEAL probably thought he was going to die. Yet he was willing to sacrifice himself for his brothers and for the mission.

Furhmann continued, "Several SEALs kept the wives pinned in the corner and verified they had no suicide vests. While they were doing this, other SEALs tended to bin Laden, checked his vitals. They put blood on his forehead and his chest. By then, the anesthetic had kicked in, and bin Laden was out cold. They were standing over bin Laden taking pictures as the wives were escorted out of the room. It was perfect. The SEALs let the wives get a glance of bin Laden on the way out. The wives told the Pakistani military, who had been helping to hide bin Laden, that he was indeed dead. Two reliable witnesses saw him get shot and then saw his bullet riddled bloody dead body on the floor!" Fuhrmann was giddy at retelling just how well the operation went. "Bin Laden's body was taken, officially to confirm his identity, to prove we got him. Remember, the SEALs had to get out. The United States did not have Pakistani permission for this incursion into their country, and Pakistan had been aiding and abetting bin Laden. Nonlethal darts were counted to ensure that none missed their intended target and were left behind, imbedded in walls or furniture. Next, bin Laden was cut superficially on his left leg, and blood was drained in the exact spot his wives saw him fall dead. His Pakistani friends could DNA test bin Laden's blood stain if they wanted. His blood, left on the floor where his wives saw him shot and killed!" Fuhrmann gave a devious smile as he continued, "His Pakistani friends bought it hook, line, and sinker! No one ever even thought that bin Laden might still be alive!"

Nate nodded. Everything Fuhrmann said sounded plausible. The operation was very close to how Nate would have planned it himself. And it was impressive how the SEALs had improvised after the first helicopter crashed. Some missions would have been aborted at that point.

Furhmann continued, still enjoying the retelling of it. It must have been tough to have an amazing story like that and not be able to share it with anyone. "One of the SEALs was a medic, and he had more than the usual load of lifesaving equipment on board the Blackhawk. The goal was to ensure bin Laden survived. As you know, nonlethal force is a tricky business. Sometimes, even protesters have been killed by so-called nonlethal weapons. And bin Laden is over seventy years old, frail, fragile, and weak. I was right there, when the helicopter with bin Laden landed back at the base in Afghanistan. By the time he was unloaded off the Blackhawk, he had an IV in his arm, and he was regaining consciousness."

Nate was impressed. "No glitches?" he asked.

"One minor one. They were only going to bring bin Laden back. But they had to also bring back his son Khalid, because he was hit with a nonlethal round. They could not leave behind any evidence of knockout darts. Like bin Laden,

Khalid is still in US custody. They have both been a treasure trove of actionable intelligence in the War on Terror. Al-Qaeda has since been decimated. In fact, you rarely hear of Al-Qaeda anymore—a tribute to the success of this mission, to capturing bin Laden alive. Bin Laden is gone. Of course ISIS is filling the void."

"And the pictures that were published? The pictures of a dead bin Laden?"

"That was the easy part, you probably can guess. General anesthesia. After he was unconscious, the makeup artists came in. I'm told they spent months rehearsing that, working on each other with various shades and textures. Snapping pictures. Then comparing the photos to actual cadavers. So the 'dead' photos the world saw were bin Laden."

Nate pulled out his cell phone and dialed Matt. When the call was answered, Nate said, "We have some garbage for you to pick up."

I couldn't hear what Matt said, but Nate smiled and said, "No, the living kind. And this garbage is quite valuable."

I noticed Dr. Fuhrmann breathe a sigh of relief. He was going to live, he surmised.

Nate gave Matt the address where we were and added, "I need the chief, face to face. Urgent." And then he hung up the phone.

Nate approached the doctor and demanded, "You said you knew about a terrorist attack. What is de Gaulle's interest in bin Laden? Was de Gaulle funding his terrorist network?"

"No, no, not at all. They never met. When I told de Gaulle that bin Laden was alive and in US custody, he offered me ten million dollars for proof. I gave him that digital video file. He said the same thing he had said about the president's blackmail video, 'Money baby!'"

I began to process this, running through my mind how de Gaulle could make money off of the video. Nate was doing the same as he said, "Sell it to an enemy of the United States? Sell it back to the United States? Highest bidder?"

"Nicolas discussed that with me, over cocktails. He decided those two options could get him killed. By people like you. So he devised a plan to make even more money, with less risk."

I interrupted, "Release the video anonymously on the Internet and profit from the resulting huge impact on world markets."

Fuhrmann nodded at me and explained, "De Gaulle is positioning himself and his bank, as we speak, for the major destabilizing effect the public release of the bin Laden video will have. Rioting in Muslim cities. United Nations condemnation of America. Spontaneous retaliatory terrorist attacks all over the world. World trade and tourism will plummet. Equities will tank. Oil prices will surge. The dollar will fall versus the Euro. US treasuries will see a flight-to-quality rally. There are countless ways to make money off of this, and Nicolas himself is still brainstorming. As soon as he and his bank are positioned properly, the video will be aired. It will go viral. No one will be able to trace anything to him. He will make a killing off these trades, and no one will ever suspect he had anything to do with the video."

I said, "I can see that. The media focus will be on the tapes themselves: bin Laden is alive in US custody! Who cares who and how the tapes became public?"

Nate nodded. "But you mentioned a terror plot. Is this it? News that bin Laden is alive?" Nate moved in close to Furhmann and spoke through gritted teeth. "Tell me about terrorist plots. Everything you know. You know what I am authorized to do if I believe a prisoner has information about a pending attack."

"This is all I know of!"

"No bombings or hijackings on US soil? No attacks on US embassies? Just the release of this video?"

"Yes, but think about it. The Muslim world will be outraged at the United States. This will have the effect of a real terrorist attack. In fact it will undoubtedly spawn countless spontaneous terrorist attacks—all over the world. Al-Qaeda has been weakened and their communications have been compromised. This news will be their communication, their call to arms! Many of these terror cells are disjointed. They share an ideology but have no cohesive organization or chain of command. Many cells are isolated. But this news will incite them to action. Even sleeper cells already in the United States will decide to launch their own uncoordinated attacks. They thought their beloved sheikh was dead. They were despondent. News that he is alive, even if in custody, will rally them."

Nate glanced at me. He had a grim expression. We were both beginning to grasp how calamitous the release could be. He glared at Furhmann. "How do we stop the release?"

"You cannot stop him. It's too late."

At that, Nate gagged Fuhrmann again with the rag and duct tape. This time he wrapped the duct tape covering his mouth around his head several times. Then he placed another piece of duct tape over his eyes.

Nate pulled a small external hard drive out of his gear bag. He examined the sides of Fuhrmann's tablet computer and fished out the right cord from his arsenal to connect the two devices. He initiated a data transfer and walked around the room pensively. When the transfer was complete, he returned the hard drive to his gear bag.

I was startled by the front door buzzer, even though we had been expecting the arrival of Matt and his team. We buzzed them in and opened the door to Fuhrmann's apartment.

Matt and several other agents entered. "Impressive," said Matt as he surveyed the bound-and-gagged Dr. Fuhrmann. He turned to Nate and said, "Chief is outside. Out the door, turn left, and go to the corner."

"He's already in Monte Carlo?" Nate was surprised.

"Came here as soon as you ID'd the doctor." Matt motioned to Fuhrmann.

It made sense. Fuhrmann was a huge priority for the US government because he was one of a few people who knew bin Laden was alive and in US custody. Now we understood why Matt had said the US seemed to have a disproportionate interest in Furhmann.

Nate walked over to Fuhrmann, ripped the tape off his eyes, and whispered, "I am no longer with the agency. I never could have hurt you. And, until you cracked, they had nothing on you except going AWOL."

Fuhrmann gasped and gagged and shook his body back and forth violently. His eyes got wide right before Nate pushed the duct tape back over them. He began fighting and straining against his restraints furiously.

One of the agents that arrived with Matt was right on cue with a syringe. He jabbed the needle in Fuhrmann's neck and held it there for a few seconds without injecting anything. Fuhrmann froze. The agent wanted Fuhrmann to know what was coming.

"Nighty night, Doc," he said, before pushing the plunger all the way down. Fuhrmann slumped over as they unbound him.

Chapter 41

Nate, Laura, and I exited Furhmann's apartment. We walked to the corner and found the CIA station chief in a black Mercedes limo with tinted windows. In Monaco, such a car fit right in and did not draw attention.

James Webster was sixty-seven years old and had been with the agency for almost forty years. An old warhorse, he was well liked by those he worked with. Relative to most former field operatives, James demonstrated uncanny diplomatic and political skills. He was the perfect candidate for station chief, able to balance the tender timidity of some US congressmen and intelligence committees on one hand with the sometimes rogue reputations of agents in the field on the other.

Nate served under James Webster for more than ten years. The two men enjoyed, and had earned, enormous mutual respect. Nate, Laura, and I settled in to the spacious back seat across from Chief Webster. Nate and James shared a robust, sincere handshake.

"Nate, we miss you around here. It's good to see you."

"I miss you too, but not everything about the agency." Nate smiled. He turned to me. "James, this is Christian

Roberts, the young man you have heard so much about, and his fiancé, Laura Baldwin."

James extended a smile and a warm handshake. "I hear wonderful things about you, Mr. Roberts. It is a real pleasure to meet you."

It was a little awkward to be called Mr. Roberts by a man as senior as the station chief. I said, "Thank you sir."

He turned to Laura, shook her hand, and said, "Pleasure to meet you," with a slight bow of his head.

Nate handed Dr. Fuhrmann's tablet computer to James and began by saying, "Icon on the desktop screen. 'Money.' De Gaulle and his cronies are blackmailing the president with a sex tape from ten years ago."

Webster squinted his eyes a bit, uncomprehending, as if to say, "Who cares about a ten-year-old sex tape?"

"It's a gay sex tape."

"Oh." Webster nodded at the gravity of this.

Nate added, "And the president can be seen smoking meth."

Webster shook his head from side to side with a disdainful look.

Nate said, "And the second one is even worse. Shows Osama bin Laden alive and well in US custody."

"Shit!"

"Yes, sir. Nicolas de Gaulle is, as we speak, amassing large speculative positions in global markets. Short the world's stock markets. Long US treasuries and oil. You get the picture. He intends to release the Osama video on the Internet. When it goes public, he will make a killing."

Nate opened the car door and began to get up.

James Webster looked surprised. "You just dump this on me and leave?"

"Yes, sir. We need to get back to our hotel and catch some sleep while you review this." He motioned to the tablet computer. "We will await further orders at the hotel, sir." Nate grinned.

Webster smiled and laughed. His voice was robust. "Welcome back Nate!"

"It's good to be back, sir."

On the way back to our hotel, I asked Nate why we were still involved in the mission. I understood why the CIA utilized us in Monte Carlo, other than the fact that Nate used to work with them. We were in the right place at the right time and had located Dr. Furhmann. The CIA did not have enough men on the ground in Monte Carlo, and by the time they arrived, we had already grabbed Furhmann.

But now, I was surprised that the CIA did not simply thank us and take over. Nate explained that the US government frequently used private contractors, including Strong and Associates. Strong and Associates is a civilian component of JSOC, the acronym for Joint Special Operations Command, which is itself a part of the US Special Operations Command (USSOCOM). JSOC consists of civilians as well as soldiers, sailors, airmen, marines. The idea behind JSOC, which was strengthened and given a broader mandate after 9/11, was to bring together men and women who possessed unique and specialized skills—the best of the best. In addition to military operations, JSOC units provide support to domestic law enforcement during high-profile, or high-risk, events such as the Olympics, the World Cup, political conventions, and presidential inaugurations.

I was glad we weren't excluded. I felt an obligation to Tom Minter to see this through to the end. And now, there was more at stake than justice for Tom.

The more I pondered the fact that Osama bin Laden was still alive, the more I realized just how devastating the release of this fact could be. Of course I despised everything Osama bin Laden stood for, and I was happy to learn that he was in US custody. But at the same time, I understood that he had a lot of followers and a lot of sympathizers. A lot of Muslims would become furious if they learned we had Osama bin Laden in custody and had lied about it. They would assume we were torturing him. America was supposed to be a place of law and order, a place where even the worst offenders had the benefit of due process. Radical Islamists would spontaneously rise up. There would be major social unrest across the globe. US embassies and outposts in the Middle East would come under attack. Israel would be attacked from both inside and outside its own borders. With no warning, Americans abroad would be in grave danger. Western journalists, tourists, and Christians in the Middle East and North Africa would be targeted. Radical Islamists in the United States might even use the news as an excuse to mount their own uncoordinated attacks similar to the Boston Marathon bombing and the San Bernardino massacre.

We had to stop de Gaulle. We had to prevent numerous terrorist attacks against innocents.

Chapter 42

Although it was difficult to sleep after all the excitement, Nate reminded us that we needed to. Soon enough, he assured, James Webster would be back in touch. The CIA was devising a plan with the full resources and backing of the US government. Nate offered us two more melatonin tablets, just like on the flight to Paris. Laura and I snuggled in close together and were asleep by 2:30 a.m.

At 7:00 a.m. there was a knock on the door of our two-bedroom hotel suite. I had made it to the bedroom door when I saw Nate open the front door. James Webster entered, still looking fresh and alert, in the same suit and tie as the previous night, along with three others—two men and a woman. Following them were two hotel waiters pushing two tables decked out with an assortment of breakfast foods, coffee, and orange juice.

James began by saying, "Good morning, gentlemen and Ms. Baldwin."

The hotel waiters left. Nate threw a robe on over his boxers and poured himself a glass of juice. I thought Nate might change clothes, or at least freshen up in the bathroom. When I saw him sit right down for business in his robe, I motioned to Laura. She nodded her understanding. We quickly threw on the same clothes from the night before and joined them.

James Webster wasted no time in getting down to business. "Nate, you know Susan, my attaché."

"Hello, Susan."

"Good morning, Nathan." She smiled. She was an attractive, well-dressed woman about forty years old. She spoke very clearly.

Introductions were made to the other two men in the room, also employees of the agency. Nate showed Laura and me to some chairs. When everyone was seated, James Webster said, "Mr. Roberts, Ms. Baldwin, we really appreciate the role you have played in helping us. We would not even be aware of this plot if it weren't for you. Thank you both."

Laura and I both nodded.

Webster added, "Although we greatly appreciate your help, Nate and I have to discuss some sensitive issues. Classified information. Would you mind stepping outside with these gentlemen for a few minutes?" He nodded toward the two agency employees nearby.

I looked at Nate pleading. *I can't sit this out! I want to finish this.*

Nate said, "James, as you know, Strong and Associates is a JSOC-approved contractor for the Unites States. We have worked with you many times." Nate gestured toward me and said, "Mr. Roberts here is now one of us, a member of Strong and Associates. You hire Strong and Associates, but we pick the individuals who work for us. So I believe Mr. Roberts should be authorized to sit in on this meeting, authorized to continue to participate on this mission."

Webster said, "I was not aware of that." He asked me, "Mr. Roberts, how long have you been with Strong and Associates?"

I hesitated. I couldn't lie to the station chief. Nate rescued me before I answered with, "About five seconds."

Webster nodded. "Oh. I understand." He looked a little skeptical.

Nate said, "The timing is irrelevant. You have never micromanaged what individual contractors we bring to a mission. We bring Mr. Roberts to this one."

Webster pondered this briefly. Then he nodded his approval and said, "Okay. Let's get started."

Nate said, "Laura, would you mind stepping outside with these gentlemen? Grab a cup of coffee maybe?"

Laura smiled politely, stood, and said, "Sure, no problem."

After Laura and the two agency men left the suite, the attaché said, "De Gaulle's yacht is scheduled to leave Monte Carlo tonight. As you know, the F1 race ends today. We have learned that a passage has been booked for *Cui Bono* in Port Said, for the Suez Canal. Based on past itineraries, it looks like de Gaulle is on his way to Singapore. He spends much of the year there. Societé Paribas has an office there."

Nate nodded. He was thinking, plotting.

The attaché continued. She spoke in a crisp, staccato tone. "Our intelligence indicates that all of his guests for the

Formula One Grand Prix, as well as the extra staff and crew he hired for the race, should disembark *Cui Bono* in Monte Carlo. De Gaulle is a curious man. Lavish parties, but he also likes his peace and solitude. We expect the yacht to have no guests and a skeleton crew, for de Gaulle's journey to Singapore."

Susan handed Nate a map. "The Suez Canal passes through Timsah Lake. We are gathering all of the necessary assets in the Egyptian town of Ismailia, on the banks of Timsah. Our best chance to board her will be in the canal, where she will be forced to travel slowly. We anticipate a covert nighttime operation, somewhere between Ismailia and the Red Sea. Our cover for the raid will be some small boats and tugs in Timsah Lake—boats common in that area, that won't raise the suspicion of de Gaulle's crew."

Nate nodded. I assumed from his silence that he liked the plan. If he disagreed, or had a better plan, he would speak up.

Webster added, "We have one chance, Nate. Once she hits the open water of the Gulf of Aden, she will pick up speed. We won't be able to catch her in our small boats, and even if we could, in the open sea, they would see us coming from a mile away."

"The canal then," said Nate. "Operation protocol?"

I wondered if this was Nate's way of asking if he was now authorized to use deadly force.

Webster replied, "De Gaulle and his B6 alliance have declared war on the United States of America. They are planning to release this Osama video, an inflammatory video that is, in and of itself, a terrorist attack. We have some of our best analysts drafting what-if scenarios, and frankly, they're scary as hell. We are already in the process of evacuating all nonessential diplomatic personnel and their families from two dozen countries as well as beefing up security at certain embassies and outposts." He took a breath as we absorbed this. "The president and congressional intelligence committees have been briefed. They all agree: as of one hour ago, de Gaulle and the other individual members of B6 are classified as an imminent danger to the safety and security of the United States."

We all knew what that meant. Webster continued, "We are authorized to utilize any and all means necessary, including deadly force, in defense of the United States of America against these blatant acts of aggression and purposeful attempts to destabilize the world. We are at war. Under threat of imminent attack. For your purposes," he said and looked at Nate, "there are no longer any limits."

This was much more unambiguous than I had expected. Nate had complained earlier about wishy-washy Washington bureaucrats, never willing to draw a clear red line. Sometimes they were intentionally vague, in order to avoid taking a stand or going out on a limb. Webster was refreshing. No cover-your-ass on the one hand and also on the other hand.

Susan said, "They have to be stopped, Nathan. Before Nicolas can release that video to the world."

Webster added, "Or humiliate the leader of the free world with that other video. That is not our priority though."

I said, "Imagine the impact of both videos going public at once."

James Webster nodded, as did the others. "Good point. A weakened, scandal-ridden president coupled with worldwide denunciations of America's covert actions. Unthinkable combination. We would be paralyzed, unable to respond to the attacks and the unrest."

The sex tape might even incite the jihadists more. In America, we are tolerant of gays. But Muslims throw gay people off buildings and stone them. If radical Muslims saw the president of the United States was gay, they might use that as an excuse, a further justification to attack innocent Americans.

Susan concluded by saying, "Nathan, if you think of anything you need, anything at all, we are preparing the staging area now. Just let me know. We will transport you, Mr. Roberts, and Ms. Baldwin to Ismailia on an agency jet as soon as you are ready."

Nate mused, "I have a suggestion for how to board her..." He walked over to Webster and whispered something. Webster did not reply, but a broad smile formed across his face. He loved working with Nate again.

Webster looked at Nate and said, "I'll see to it that the Spec Ops team is prepared for your scenario. I like it. I think they will too. Agents will transport you to the Nice Côte-d'Azur Airport as soon as you are ready."

Webster and Susan said good-bye and left. The other two agents dropped Laura back at the suite and told us that they would wait in front of the hotel, in an SUV.

When we were alone, just Nate, Laura and me, Nate explained the timeline to us. No rush right now, he assured. We would land in Ismailia later that day. *Cui Bono*, meanwhile, was about twelve hours away from leaving Monte Carlo and therefore at least thirty-six hours away from Port Said, all the way across the Mediterranean. Once there, the Suez Canal passage itself would take fifteen hours. At Nate's suggestion, we enjoyed the breakfast, which we hadn't even touched. Then we showered and changed. When we were all packed, we walked outside for the ride to the airport.

Chapter 43

The agency jet was a sight to behold. Whereas the charter flight we had taken from Paris to Nice was a small turboprop with cramped seating for four and a speed of 225 mph, the agency jet was a Challenger 604. It had a luxuriously appointed cabin with seating for twelve, and a cruising speed of 572 mph.

As usual, Nate slept on the flight to Ismailia. I tried, but I couldn't will myself back to sleep at 9:00 a.m. Monte Carlo time. I was amazed that, after Nate's years of operations work with the agency, he had trained his body to sleep on command, almost as if he flipped a switch somewhere in his body and was out like a light. He seemed to be able to store sleep the way a camel stores water, in anticipation of long stretches without any.

After landing in Ismailia, we were met planeside by an agency vehicle and whisked to the operation staging area, a warehouse on the shores of Timsah Lake. It was in an industrial area surrounded by run down shipyards no longer in use. The shipyards were scattered with old rusted out ship hulls. Laura, Nate, and I were greeted by Commander Davis, a lean, wiry man about fifty years old. He was in charge of the military's role in the operation.

Commander Davis had an aide take Laura to our temporary quarters. Then, he escorted Nate and me to the rear of the warehouse, closest to the water, where a series of tables had been set up. This area would serve as the operational command and control center. Detailed maps of the Suez Canal were spread out on a large center table. Soldiers seated at outer tables manned computers and communications equipment. A large LCD screen on the back wall showed a satellite view of the *Cui Bono*, still docked in Port Hercule.

Commander Davis explained, pointing to the maps on the table, "This is the route we expect her to take. You can see the estimated timeline here, based on her cruising speed." The commander then pointed up to the image on the LCD screen. "This is a live video feed from military satellites. The satellite cameras will remain locked on the yacht until our operation is complete. From the moment she enters Port Said," he told us, pointing back to the map spread out on the table, "two unmanned drones will circle high above, giving us more detailed real-time pictures and videos."

Commander Davis turned to a muscular man who appeared not much older than me, "Gentlemen, this is Chief Warrant Officer McCoy. He is responsible for the three SEAL platoons assigned to this mission."

Nate expressed surprise. "Three platoons?" A SEAL platoon consisted of sixteen men. This meant forty-eight SEALs were assigned to this mission!

"Yes, sir," answered Chief Warrant Officer McCoy.

Commander Davis explained, "This operation has just been elevated to the highest level of importance. In fact it has been elevated twice in the past eight hours. It seems the more the analysts in DC evaluate the possible impact of this threat, the more scared they become. As the what-if scenarios of global unrest and resulting death tolls get worse, they throw more resources at our disposal. The way this mission's priority has been elevated, I think they'll give us whatever we ask for. But we should be good with what they've committed. Platoons are en route here now. Our orders are to be prepared for anything. At four hundred forty feet in length, *Cui Bono* is as big as a cruise ship. We don't know what surprises she may hold, but we will be ready." He turned to McCoy.

McCoy continued the briefing. "Two platoons will engage in the initial assault. Platoon One will come alongside in Blackhawks, six hundred meters out on her port and starboard sides, snipers ready."

Nate asked, "If the water is calm and the air is still, sound carries a long way. Can you be sure De Gaulle's security guards won't hear the choppers?"

McCoy stated, "Yes, sir. These are specially modified Blackhawks with sound dampening rotors and tail mufflers. They won't hear us unless we are on top of them and rappelling down. The Blackhawks' skins use LO technology so the ship's radar will not pick them up." *LO* was military terminology for low observable, commonly known as stealth.

Nate nodded. He explained to me later that he didn't know the stealth Blackhawk helicopters existed. They were brand-new technology, and they would have made many of Nate's past missions less dangerous.

"The drones will be circling above the yacht from the moment she enters Port Said. Our team here," he said and motioned to the men manning the computers in the make-shift operation center, "will monitor and catalog the exact positions, rotations and habits of her security guards and lookouts. Before the Blackhawks pull astride, six hundred meters out, we will be dialed in on her guards. Sniper teams will wait until they have a simultaneous shot. Coordinated via radios, we will take them all out at once."

"Shooting from six hundred meters away?" I asked. And from a moving helicopter I thought!

McCoy said, "Six hundred meters is a long way, about six and a half football fields. But to SEAL snipers, it will be the equivalent of shooting fish in a barrel."

McCoy continued, "Nate, you will be standing by in one of the STABs. Because of the recently approved helicopter and sniper support, we've nixed the cover of slow tugboats and will be using fast STABs." This was the Navy term for Strike Team Assault Boat—very small, fast boats with low profiles.

McCoy politely turned to Laura and me. "The two of you will stay right here." He motioned to the screens. "You will be able to see everything in real time."

I said, "Wait—I thought I was going too."

Nate said to McCoy, "That was my understanding too."

McCoy said, "No civilians."

Nate said, "I'm a civilian."

McCoy nodded. "Yes but you are former agency, and your firm is a JSOC-approved independent contractor."

Although the United States government worked with outside consultants and specialized experts, they were selective. They did not like putting civilians, like me, at risk. But Nate knew how committed I was because of Minter's murder and the attempt on my own life.

Nate said, "Check with James Webster. He will confirm that Mr. Roberts is approved by JSOC and is critical to this mission. We needed to find out everything we can from de Gaulle, and none of us have Mr. Roberts's market and trading expertise. He needs to be present during the questioning of de Gaulle. He also has familiarity we don't. He is the only person to have been aboard de Gaulle's yacht. He was in de Gaulle's office!"

McCoy didn't respond immediately. He seemed to be considering this request.

Nate said, "Mr. Roberts pieced together the original illegal commodities trades, which led to de Gaulle in the first place. If not for Mr. Roberts, none of us would be here right now. We would never have known about this attack—never would have had a shot at preventing it."

McCoy nodded and said, "I will confirm, but if he is okay with Webster, he's okay with me. You understand what's involved in boarding the yacht while under way, right?"

Nate said, "Yes and I will take responsibility for him. No need to worry though. Look at him. He won't slow us down—Six foot four, two hundred thirty pounds. Four years of Division I lacrosse without an injury. And good instincts—he dodged the first attempt on his life."

McCoy put his hands up. "Okay, okay. He's JSOC approved, just like you."

My heart beat a little faster. I was about to go on the ultimate ride along—a ride along with Navy SEALs storming a megayacht. Too bad I didn't bring my GoPro camera.

McCoy continued the briefing. "As soon as the snipers in the Blackhawks hit their targets, we rush you in on the STABs. The SEALs will deploy grappling hooks to climb aboard. You will climb up midship, near de Gaulle's office and the master stateroom. Other teams will do the same fore and aft and on both sides of the ship. We will secure the bridge and any remaining crew, allowing you, and the men assigned to you, to get de Gaulle."

Nate asked, "You are taking measures to minimize casualties to noncombatants?"

"Yes, sir. Commander Davis passed on your idea to us. The men love it. They can't wait to pull it off. My men are confident, sir. They will minimize innocent crew casualties while removing suspicion from the United States for this operation."

Nate nodded. McCoy said, "The SEALs prefer to work in this manner, doing the difficult jobs covertly, without fanfare. I know some SEAL operations received a lot of media attention, but the overwhelming majority remain secret."

I didn't interrupt the briefing, but I didn't understand what they were planning. I would ask Nate later.

Commander Davis gave more detail. "The men have strict orders to not harm noncombatants—the ship's crew, mechanics, cooks, cabin stewards, and the like. The body-guards, on the other hand, pose a threat to us. They know what they signed up for; they chose to take these risks. The crew, not so much. The bridge personnel are potential non-combatant casualties. But, as long as they do as they are told, they will be okay."

Nate nodded.

Commander Davis added, "As you know, Nate's plan has us delaying *Cui Bono's* distress call until she is out of the canal, out in the Gulf of Aden. We will wait as long as possible to launch the assault. Let her get closer to open water. The noncombatants will be locked up somewhere inside the ship. If late enough at night, most of the crew will be sleeping at the time of the assault. And crew quarters are down below with no windows. They will not be able to reliably report the ship's position at the time the assault occurred. As a final safeguard, we will be jamming all cell phone signals in the ship's vicinity to eliminate the risk that a cook or a maid might call out an SOS before we want them to."

Nate looked at the map. "Have you settled upon a target location yet?"

"No, sir. Not yet. We estimate a late night attack, to catch them by surprise." He pointed to the map. "This time-line is estimated. We will update it based upon the ship's rate of speed across the Mediterranean and through the Suez Canal."

Nate nodded. "Initial planning was for a small, covert operation—one that did not include stealth helicopters?"

Commander Davis replied, "Yes, sir. But the mission keeps getting elevated, and every time it does they throw more men and equipment at our disposal. Now, they say pull out all the stops, helicopters, whatever is needed. Three SEAL platoons en route."

Nate continued, "So, originally, we had no choice but to storm her by small boats in Timsah Lake, before she got to Suez, while she was going slowly?"

Davis nodded.

Like the Panama Canal, the Suez Canal is not all narrow canals. It passes through some navigable bodies of water. The narrow canals cut through what used to be land, hopping from one lake to the next, and finally to the open sea. The Ismailia section of the Suez Canal connects Lake Manzala to Timsah Lake.

Nate said, "The Blackhawk helicopters change everything. We do not have to storm her in Timsah Lake where she is forced to travel slowly. Now we can board her while she cruises fast, anywhere we want."

Davis said, "Good point. Go on."

"We originally planned that the megayacht could evade our small boats and use defensive measures to prevent us from boarding, fire hoses, evasive maneuvering, even assault rifles. Any yacht traveling these waters is no doubt prepared to fend off pirates. But with the addition of the stealth helos, we can neutralize those deterrents."

Commander Davis nodded. "You're right. After upping their estimates of the damage from this attack, they added to the resources available for this mission but never bothered to reevaluate the entire mission in light of those additions."

Nate finished his proposal. "They can't evade the STABs when we have Blackhawks. Sharpshooters in the Blackhawks can eliminate any threats to the small boats' approach. They can even take out the bridge, if needed, to prevent evasive maneuvering. Bottom line, we can board her anywhere, at will. We don't have to hit them in the slow zone of Lake Timsah. We can wait until they clear Suez and pick up speed. The canal pilot will disembark in Suez, so we will have one less noncombatant to worry about."

Every ship transiting the Suez Canal brought aboard a harbor pilot who was responsible for navigating the vessel through the canal. These pilots were employees of the Suez Canal Authority, which owned and maintained the canal. They knew the deep and shallow parts of the canal, and were more familiar with the canal than the ship captains at navigating the crowded waterway. While on board, these pilots took over for the captains. They had complete responsibility and authority over the vessel, even outranking the ships' captains. For southbound ships, the harbor pilots boarded in Port Said and disembarked in Suez. Harbor pilots on northbound ships did the opposite.

Commander Davis nodded. "Better yet, out in open water, we don't have to worry about other ships witnessing any of this. Canals are crowded places. We want to get in and out before anyone can summon military or coast guard help." He traced his finger along the yacht's route and tapped a spot all the way out in the Gulf of Aden. "Why not wait all the way through the Red Sea, until she hits the Gulf of Aden? Or maybe even beyond there? That would work even better with your idea that the SEALs do not want credit for this mission."

What is Nate's idea? I thought.

Nate smiled. "Exactly. Look at this timeline." He pointed to the maps. "She should arrive in Port Said tomorrow at about three p.m. Fifteen-hour passage takes us to six or seven a.m. tomorrow—not a good time to launch a raid."

Everyone now nodded in understanding.

Nate continued, "South through the Red Sea, then east through the Gulf of Aden." Nate moved his finger along the map. "That should take her twenty-one hours, three a.m. Anytime between three and four a.m. would be ideal. Still dark, most of the crew deep in sleep."

Commander Davis processed this and then said, "I agree. I like it." He pointed to the map. "These areas near Somalia are where most pirate attacks occur. The crew will be on their toes. But once out in open water, they will be more relaxed, and more vulnerable. I will run this plan up the chain of command. The only objection I anticipate is that they expressed grave concern that the operation be conducted as soon as possible. The goal is to prevent a terrorist attack. They may not allow a delay of almost twenty-four hours."

I wasn't sure if Commander Davis knew Osama bin Laden was alive. My guess was, no. Best if as few people as possible were in on that. So without mentioning bin Laden, I said, "De Gaulle plans on rocking global markets with this terrorist attack. I do not believe he will do that while he is alone at sea. I think he will not set his plan in motion until he is situated back in his office in Singapore. He is too narcissistic—he will want to be surrounded by bank staff, to celebrate when all those risky trades start going his way."

Nate smiled and nodded at me as if to say, "Not bad, kiddo."

I asked, "I assume the CIA has the ability to check on the status of his trades, to reassure themselves of this? It will take the bank at least several days to accumulate the positions he plans to put on. Some of the markets they are trading in aren't liquid enough to move billions instantly."

Commander Davis gave a decisive nod. "Good point. I'll run it up the flag pole."

Commander Davis left, as did Chief Warrant Officer McCoy. Nate examined the maps himself for a few minutes, then walked outside to the wharf. I followed him. Nate paced the waterfront. He was deep in thought, rehearsing the mission in his mind. Satisfied with the preparations, he pointed to the north and said, "That is where she will be coming from."

An enlisted man brought us to Laura and gave us some food. Then he showed us to a small room that used to be an office in the warehouse. It was small and barren except for several military-issue bunk beds and a window-mounted air-conditioning unit that helped to drown out the surrounding noise.

As we ate, Nate filled me in more on Strong and Associates. He said, "Our clients include corporations and life insurance companies, and for them, we typically rescue kidnapped executives and tourists from garden variety thugs. But our biggest client is the United States government. They can call on us at a moment's notice and we can go in where they can't. They have to be careful sending US troops on operations into the sovereign territory of foreign countries. Such operations require the consent of both the foreign government and the US Congress. Many of these countries don't like us and won't help us. So it is much easier to hire private contractors for operations on foreign soil. If we succeed, everything is great. If we fail, the US does not have the public embarrassment of trying to explain the presence, or even the capturing of, US soldiers on foreign soil."

"Capturing?" I asked with raised eyebrows.

"Don't worry. Getting busted in Monaco would not have been the same as being captured in Venezuela. And the rest of our operation will be out at sea."

Nate climbed into an empty bunk and said, "Sleep while you can." It was very bright outside, too bright for me to sleep. I pulled some ratty old curtains closed as best as I could to at least block out some of the light.

I would have liked to fall asleep holding Laura, but the bunks were barely wide enough for one person. So I tucked Laura into one of the bottom bunks, and then I kneeled next to her bunk and leaned into the small space between her bunk and the upper bunk and gave her a hug.

With my knees on the hard floor, I held her for about five minutes. Whispering so as not to wake Nate, I smiled, held my face inches from hers, and said, "I love you. Good night."

She smiled back and caressed my cheek with her hand. After a bit she closed her eyes and let her hand drop away from my face, letting me know it was okay to go to bed myself. I took the bunk next to hers and settled in. I lay on my back and stared at the bunk above me. It was hard to believe how much had transpired in such a short time. A few days ago, I was settled into a normal routine in Chicago. Now, I was in a military bunk in a dirty old warehouse in an industrial area on the shores of Timsah Lake in Egypt.

When I closed my eyes, I found myself once again wanting to get back to Chicago, anxious to get my career back on track. Longing to make some real money in the pits. The challenges I had faced in the last few days seemed to confirm that I could succeed in the pits. I would make a good living. I still had a great career and a good life with Laura ahead of me.

I couldn't sleep. As I stared at the bunk above me, I couldn't stop thinking about the Navy SEAL who pushed bin Laden's wives into the corner, shielding his buddies from suicide vests. He was willing to sacrifice himself for his SEAL brothers, for the mission, for the intelligence that would be gained, and for the lives that would be saved. Against that, I was beginning to experience some self-doubt. Maybe I felt guilty. While I was focused on my career back home, US servicemen were performing selfless, heroic acts.

Chapter 44

The daytime sleep was difficult for me. It was designed to get our body clocks on schedule for the upcoming mission. The goal was to be awake and alert the next day at 2:00 to 4:00 a.m. Egypt time. After our nap, we met again with Commander Davis at 9:00 p.m. If the mission went as planned, it would be executed in about thirty hours.

Commander Davis opened with: "Mr. Roberts's idea to check the bank's trading has paid off. Covert checks of Societé Paribas's trading desks confirmed at least several more days are required to execute the volume of trades they have in the queue. The agency even tapped into e-mail accounts of the bank's trading personnel. They unearthed a detailed plan of accumulating large positions, but they seem to be taking it slow. E-mail exchanges express a strong desire to spread the trades out over multiple days so as to not spook the markets."

Davis paced back and forth with his hands clasped behind his back as he continued, "So the powers that be agree. We can wait to attack the yacht until four a.m., the day after tomorrow, or anytime sooner, if it suits our operational parameters." Davis pointed to a real-time chart plotter showing *Cui Bono's* GPS path and current location. "Our preliminary estimated timeline was pretty good." He pointed to Suez. "At her current speed, she will clear Suez at about six forty-five tomorrow morning. We have done some additional research on her past itineraries. She is capable of cruising at much faster speeds than most yachts of her size. She was a little slower navigating the canal due to congestion and wake limits imposed by the Suez Canal Authority. We anticipate her making up that time, and then some, through the Red Sea. Current projections have her entering the Gulf of Aden at two a.m. the day after tomorrow."

Nate examined the maps. "So what are you thinking? Wait until four a.m.?" He pointed to a spot just past the Gulf of Aden. "Right about here?"

"Yes. The timing is critical to catch the crew in their least prepared state. It also helps that she will be out in open water by four."

Cui Bono had to pass through waters off Somalia and Yemen, an area notorious for hijackings, kidnappings, and ransoms by pirates. While most attacks had been launched by Somali pirates, Yemen was also getting in on the game. The pirates operated from small boats that were limited in speed and range. Documented pirate attacks were clustered in the narrow waters of the Gulf of Aden, which is bordered by Somalia to the south and by Yemen to the north.

Once yachts made it around the northeast tip of Somalia and out in to the open sea, their crews could relax. Attacks farther out were very rare, and only the slowest cargo ships and private sail boats were at risk out that far. *Cui Bono* was much faster.

Nate nodded.

Davis added, "Chief Warrant Officer McCoy is positioning his men right here," he said, pointing to a location on
the map about fifty miles to the side of *Cui Bono's* anticipated
path. "His men will be deploying the STABs from a container ship owned by the United States, designed for these types
of deployments." He looked at Nate, and both men smiled.
Uncle Sam had extraordinary resources and equipment. The
container ship was a high-tech vessel with the appearance
of a container ship. It could swallow up several platoons of
Navy SEALs and then continue on innocuously. Just another
container ship headed for the canal.

"You and Mr. Roberts will be departing from here by
helicopter. The flight is about three hours, and we'd like you
in position, on the container ship, at least three hours before
the STABs launch. That puts us at an eight p.m. flight out of
here, about twenty-three hours from now. Questions?"

Nate answered, "No, sir. You and your men are doing a
great job. Thank you."

Nate arranged for some rappelling harnesses and gear so
that he could show me how we were going to board a moving yacht. I considered myself an intermediate rock climber.
It was one of the hobbies Laura and I enjoyed together. So
while I knew the basics, weekend climbs were relaxed, slow
speed affairs. I never anticipated boarding a moving yacht
in rough seas. It was helpful to familiarize myself with the
SEAL harness and belay/rappelling equipment. They had
a cool device I had never used, an Atlas Powered Ascender

(APA). Just squeeze the trigger, and the motorized device allowed you to run up the side of a mountain, building, or ship. These APAs were good for up to 350 pounds. A pulley system could magnify that capacity, but for this operation, we were interested in maximum speed. We rehearsed the climb multiple times, and I got comfortable running up and rappelling down the practice wall.

Nate reminded me that we should continue adjusting our body clocks for the upcoming mission. "We sleep from eight a.m. until three p.m. At three we exercise—just a light workout—and then eat a healthy breakfast and a lean, high-protein lunch at eight p.m., before we depart for the container ship."

Chapter 45

At seven p.m., one hour before our planned helicopter flight to the container ship, an officer arrived to take us to meet Commander Davis. An enlisted man was thoughtful enough to stop by a local newsstand where he picked up a selection of magazines and newspapers to help Laura pass the time.

It was time for Nate and me to go to our final briefing. I wrapped my arms around Laura and held her tight. I think she was stressed out about the whole situation. She didn't want to think about me storming a moving ship that was defended by armed guards. I understood. But I had to finish this, for Thomas Minter's sake, and also to get my career back on track. I kissed her good-bye and promised her it would all be over soon. My last words to her were: "I love you." And I said it more sincerely than I think I ever had in the past.

She said, "I know."

I smiled, gave her peck on the forehead, and left with Nate.

Nate and I had our final briefing with Commander Davis. All SEAL personnel were in place, *Cui Bono* was still on schedule. We boarded a Blackhawk helicopter and took off. I was not surprised when Nate fell asleep. But the excitement of riding in a Blackhawk helicopter, combined with anticipation for the upcoming mission, kept me wide awake.

Three hours later, the Blackhawk turned on landing lights as we approached an old, weathered-looking container ship. The helicopter settled in the middle of the vessel. In fact it landed right on the stacks and rows of containers. On approach, I estimated the containers must have been stacked at least ten high. So the helicopter perched itself almost ten stories above the water. Nate and I climbed out of the Blackhawk and were greeted by Chief Warrant Officer McCoy, who had flown out before us to prepare for the mission. He had to yell over the spinning blades of the helicopter. "Gentlemen, welcome aboard. This way, please."

We followed McCoy to a set of stairs recessed into the top of one of the containers. The Blackhawk turned off its landing lights and took off again. It had set down for about ten seconds. As we followed McCoy down the flight of stairs, a roof panel slid closed above us.

As the roof panel closed, McCoy pointed to it and said, "Entry and exit in this manner is only permitted under cover of darkness. Conceals the ship's true purpose from satellite pictures."

McCoy showed us to an elevator, which took us down what must have been at least ten floors. We emerged into a command and control center with every piece of state of the art communication equipment imaginable. It was a large, modern, clean room full of people and workstations, and it had a ceiling height of at least forty feet. It felt like a beautiful atrium on the main floor of the container ship. I was blown away. We were inside a large, open space inside the stacks and rows of containers. The vessel was a modern, high-tech fortress, with a façade designed to disguise it as an old, weathered container ship.

Chief Warrant Officer McCoy took us to the epicenter of the control room. It had a big, glass, tabletop electronic map in the center. McCoy went over the mission plan, in detail, one last time. Then he took us back to a different elevator. We rode down even farther into the huge ship and emerged in a large open bay that held the STABs, or Strike Team Assault Boats. Several dozen SEALs were in the bay, cleaning their guns, sharpening their knives, and getting their gear on. A few had earbuds and were listening to music on iPods. It reminded me of the pregame rituals we had on my lacrosse team at Duke.

Nate helped me get suited up with bulletproof body armor, a climbing harness, and an inflatable life jacket. He emphasized that all my gear would make me sink like a stone. But a regular life jacket was too bulky. The thin inflatable vest I wore was not bulky unless and until I pulled the cord to inflate the pouches, which rode up my front like suspenders, went over my shoulders, and then crossed my back before reconnecting to a strap around my waist. Nate repeated several times that in the chaos of storming the yacht, if I fell into the water, I needed to find and pull the cord that inflated the vest—or sink into oblivion. He emphasized that if it came to that, I would be dark, cold, disoriented, and possibly injured from the fall. I would be in total darkness and underwater. I wouldn't be able to breathe. I would be thrashed around in the water. My body, and my ears in particular, would sense that I was sinking fast. And in the midst of a natural instinct to panic, I would need to stay calm, find the inflate cord, and pull it.

No problem, I thought. *Stay calm. Panic is your enemy. Ice man.*

During final preparations, despite the fact that I practiced with the APA (Atlas Powered Ascender), Nate and the SEALs decided that the bulkiness and weight of the APA was something I would be better off without. It weighed about thirty pounds and was the size of a toaster oven. The SEALs would use APAs for their ascent, and then they would hoist me up. With all the body armor and gear I already did have, it was nice to shed the extra device.

When it was time, we were shown to a STAB and asked to sit down in the back. I knew enough about boats to know that the SEALs were being nice to us. The stern was the most stable place to be. The bow, in comparison, would rise and fall dramatically as the boat attacked the open ocean waves at high speed.

The STABs set out across the dark ocean at fifty miles per hour. After a few miles, I got in synch with the rise and fall of the boat through the waves. Watching others, I absorbed each impact with my legs rather than in a sitting position, which I learned could compress my vertebrae. I just hung on tight to the grab rails, and after a while I was used to it, even comfortable.

The STAB captain and copilot stood side by side at a center console, monitoring two screens—a chart-plotter GPS screen and a circular, rotating radar screen. The copilot held on to rail handles, while the captain held on to the steering wheel.

When the STABs approached within two miles of *Cui Bono's* path, they stopped. Although the boats were coated with radar-absorbing materials, and had very low profiles, two miles was a safe distance to ensure that we would not be spotted or picked up by the yacht's radar.

We sat still and waited in the open ocean, two miles to the side of *Cui Bono's* path. The plan was, after helicopter snipers took out the security personnel, we would rush in the final stretch in less than two minutes. Nate and I were aboard one of three assault boats lining up to the south of the yacht's easterly path. Three more assault boats were lining up to the north. So six STABs would storm *Cui Bono* simultaneously, three from each side. Our boat bobbed in the open ocean about a hundred yards away from the other two STABs on our side of the yacht's path. The men in our STAB did a final check on their gear, ensuring that nothing came loose on the wild ride across the ocean.

The captain of our STAB, who was wearing a radio headset, held up two fingers and alerted us. "Two minutes. Blackhawks incoming." The SEALs performed one final check, making sure grappling hooks, climbing ropes, and APAs were out and ready.

The assault boat captain said, "Blackhawks in position. Acquiring six targets."

Six people, I thought. *Six human beings. Six lives that were about to end. Maybe three on each side of the large yacht.* Although the guards standing watch on *Cui Bono* were well armed in the event of a pirate attack, by now they were probably relaxed and paying little attention.

The stealth Blackhawks flew silently over the ocean, one six hundred meters off the yacht's port side and one six hundred meters off her starboard side. Six SEAL snipers crowded together in the opening on the side of each Blackhawk. They huddled together in two dense rows, positioned on aerial platforms, their .300 Winchester Magnum sniper rifles resting on bipods to steady their aim. The Blackhawks were flying straight, maintaining a level altitude and the same constant rate of speed as the yacht. Good helicopter piloting made the snipers feel as if they were shooting at a stationary target from a fixed firing position.

The snipers in the helicopters would coordinate simultaneous shots. If they hit their targets, boarding would be easy. That is, easy in terms of pulling up alongside a massive yacht crushing through the ocean chop at thirty knots, getting close enough to launch ropes and climb up. Not easy, but at least with good snipers, we would not encounter resistance.

Nate smiled and said, "It's much easier to climb up a rope when people are not shooting down at you."

"Fire!" the STAB captain yelled as he heard the order over his radio for the simultaneous sniper shots. Before the word was all the way out of his mouth, he accelerated the STAB to full throttle. The force of the acceleration pushed me back until my arms were taut against my handholds. The speed leveled out at a rate much faster than the speed we had traveled at in getting to our waypoint—eighty mph.

I thought about Thomas Minter as our STAB flew across the ocean toward the megayacht, catching seconds of air every few moments. *Justice, Tom!*

Chapter 46

"Thirty seconds." Although the captain of the STAB was a few feet from me, I could barely hear him due to the wind. I could hear him through the headsets that we all had on. Pretty cool headsets. SEALs could communicate in the heat of battle much better than their enemies.

Another voice came over the headset: "Snipers confirm, no activity on decks. Repeat, no activity on decks." That was good news. Each sniper hit his mark, and there was no indication of any resistance. As our STAB flew up alongside the massive yacht and slowed, half the men prepared climbing ropes while the other half aimed assault rifles at the yacht and scanned for any movement. The SEALs with us placed a huge amount of trust in the snipers in the Blackhawks who were providing overwatch for the raid. Spotters in the helicopters were using night vision and infrared scopes to scan the yacht for any sign of movement. Any sign of armed resistance would hopefully be addressed by the snipers in the Blackhawks before we pulled alongside.

As planned, the STAB carrying Nate and I came alongside midship. As we got close to the huge yacht, the waves increased in size, and our STAB began to get tossed around.

Out in the open water, ocean waves were not bad. But in close to the yacht, the water became very turbulent. The big yacht was cruising fast, pushing a huge wall of water off her hull. As ocean waves hit that water wall, they increased in size the same way waves increase in size as they approach land. But at a beach, waves dissipate as they wash ashore. Here, the waves bounced straight back off the hull of *Cui Bono*. The closer the STAB got to the yacht, the more violently we bounced around, rising and falling as much as twenty feet. And we had to climb up in this.

One STAB was in front of us, closer to *Cui Bono's* bow, and the third was behind us, closer to her stern. SEALs in the STAB near the bow were already going up ropes, and the STAB on the stern was just pulling in behind us. I knew three more STABs were launching a similar assault on the portside of the yacht.

As our STAB turned in and slowed to match the speed of the yacht, the SEALs in our STAB fired a hook up the massive yacht, using a launcher that looked similar to an assault rifle, but it was pneumatic, powered by a refillable air canister. The launcher had a pouch on the barrel that held a neatly coiled rope. The equipment combination of the launcher and the APA was known as REBS, which stood for Rapid Entry and Boarding System.

The STAB behind us drew nearer. I looked in puzzlement. While the SEALs with Nate and me were decked out in modern uniforms and high-tech body armor, the men in the rear STAB were dressed in rags. I looked to the STAB near the bow of the yacht. The men in that STAB were also dressed in raggedy old clothes. Adidas sweatpants and dirty old T-shirts. No bulletproof vests! One of them even looked barefoot.

Their weapons looked different too. The SEALs with Nate and I had modern-looking Heckler and Koch 416 assault rifles. The ragtag bunch in the other two STABs held what looked like AK47s.

I looked at Nate, cocked my head toward the rear STAB, conveying, "What's up with that?" I asked out loud, "Are they SEALs?"

Nate looked back at the last STAB, smiled, and then looked back at me and said, "My big idea." As he said this, he smirked, hooked a carbineer to my harness, and then extended his arm out to the side of the STAB with a thumbs-up signal to SEALs from our STAB already aboard *Cui Bono*. I was yanked from the STAB and dangled in the air, ascending. Two SEALs on the yacht were rapidly hoisting me up. As I had been warned, I managed to put my feet out to cushion my initial impact with the hull of *Cui Bono* as I swung in. I would have hit the side of the big yacht very hard otherwise. The rest of the rapid rise up, I managed to touch my feet to the side of the yacht to keep from banging my body along.

The two SEALs grabbed me and hoisted my 230 pounds over the ships railing. With all my gear, I must have weighed about 270, yet they tossed me around as if I were a rag doll. As soon as I landed on deck, one of the SEALs put his face near mine and held a finger to his lips, indicating, "Quiet!" Then he dropped to a knee and motioned for me to get down and stay low. Our objective was to get de Gaulle. Other teams in other STABs were securing the bridge and the rest of the crew.

That's when it hit me: Other STAB teams were securing the bridge and the crew. And the SEALs in those other STABS looked like Somali or Yemeni pirates! Ragtag clothes and AK47s. I smiled to myself at what must have been Nate's idea for deception. It would also minimize casualties of noncombatants. No need to silence crew to keep the mission covert. Survivors would testify that they were attacked by a ragtag bunch of thugs, not US Navy SEALs.

The team securing the bridge would continue *Cui Bono's* course and speed. The whole operation had gone smoothly thus far. The sleeping crew members had not even been awakened by the quick and quiet assault force.

As soon as Nate was aboard, he took the lead. Two SEALs followed Nate, keeping me sandwiched between them. I felt safe, given the circumstances, between the two SEALs. Nate hopped a railing to a balcony off the master stateroom. The SEALs and I followed.

Chapter 47

While we were in Paris, Monte Carlo, Egypt, and the Gulf of Aden, politics were swirling back home. The president and the secretary of state had continued their well-orchestrated plan of not addressing the brewing scandal themselves. But the story would not go away. When the crescendo of news media demands for some sort of a direct statement from the White House peaked, Abigail Mason agreed to do a prerecorded television interview with a left-leaning journalist. Somebody had to say something, or their intentional silence might backfire.

In the prerecorded interview, Abigail Mason played the victim card. She came across as a female trying, against all odds, to make it in a man's world. She reiterated her frequent call-to-arms on the issue of pay inequality between men and women. She was battling on an uneven playing field, and she was targeted because she was a she.

Ms. Mason's hedge fund profit and Vince Fleming's suspicious suicide were all over the news. The media published pictures showing Fleming with Silvasconi and Hansen, making it clear that the White House might have had a role in the murder of the maid to frame Thompson. But direct accusations were weak and hedged. Still cowering from the inevitable lawsuits arising out of their irresponsible coverage of Jack Thompson, news lawyers decided allegations of the White House ordering the attack could not be broadcasted or printed until they were confirmed. This gave credence to the administration's view that the whole affair was much ado about nothing and would blow over. This was becoming a self-fulfilling prophecy as the liberal media gave it a pass.

During Abigail Mason's prerecorded interview with the fawning journalist, Ms. Mason said, "Look at the terrible ordeal Mr. Thompson has just been through! My heart goes out to Jack and his family. I feel his pain." She wiped away a tear.

Then she sat up straight and continued, "But we should all learn from Jack's experience. The wheels of justice in this great country may turn slower than we would like them to. But they turn. Our system works. I think, right now..." She paused to wipe a tear and compose herself. "And I think even Jack Thompson would agree with me on this: We need to be patient. We should not rush to judgment. Wait until all the facts are in."

Rather than ask pointed questions about the facts that already were in, the reporter changed tracks to the softball question of: "Tell me what these stories are like for you and your family, and for your daughter?"

Abigail shook her head and responded, "It's just so difficult." She sat up straighter. She wanted to appear human, not weak. "I feel like my family is the victim of a vast right-wing conspiracy."

The reporter nodded in sympathy.

The interview ended with Abigail Mason stoically saying, "Like poor Mr. Thompson, that terrible ordeal he endured! My husband and I knew…" She dabbed her eye with a tissue. "When we chose to enter public service, we knew we would become a target for wild accusations. But my husband and I have discussed this, even in light of these irresponsible accusations." She looked at the reporter and placed her hands on the reporter's hands. She regained her composure, looked to be in total control. No more tears. "I understand Mr. Thompson's decision to leave public service. It is a shame public servants face politically motivated attacks." She gritted her teeth. "But we will not allow this to deter us. We will continue our work for the good people of this great country. We will continue our work to create jobs, to improve education, and to make America a better place to live." By the time she delivered this last line, she was no longer emotional. She spoke with the resolve of, well, a leader. She appeared strong and decisive.

The scandal began to fade. The public seemed to rely on the notion that, if it were important, the liberal news media would let them know. Outside of that, they went about their lives.

The general public was also more skeptical of the appearance of things. They had just witnessed Jack Thompson, who they thought was guilty as hell, turn out to be innocent— framed! The general public was now more open than ever to the idea of a vast right-wing conspiracy.

While we were about to storm a yacht in the Gulf of Aden, back home it appeared that both the president and Abigail Mason might survive this latest scandal. Unless we obtained additional evidence.

Chapter 48

The four of us stood silently on the private balcony of the master stateroom. Nate checked the sliding glass door; it was unlocked! I guess there was not much need to lock a balcony door on a yacht at sea. Nate slid the glass door open and entered. The two SEALs and I followed. De Gaulle was still sleeping. Nate roused him and jerked him to his feet. The billionaire, head of the largest private bank in the world, looked rather pathetic in his pajamas. Nate pushed him toward his office, which was connected to the master stateroom.

As we entered de Gaulle's office, a bodyguard came from the other side. By the looks of him, we had just startled him awake. He was probably supposed to be guarding the office, which also served as an entrance to the master stateroom. He was armed, and he began to raise a gun in our direction. I think the guard was still dazed and a bit confused from napping. Or perhaps he hesitated because he was afraid to fire in the general direction of his boss, Mr. de Gaulle.

The SEALs did not hesitate. The closest one dispatched the guard with three suppressed shots—two to the chest and one to the head. Nate continued forward with de Gaulle past the fallen guard, as if nothing had happened, sending a clear message: "We mean business."

Nate released his grip on de Gaulle, pointed his Sig Sauer P226 at him with one hand and grabbed an office chair with the other. He wheeled the chair to de Gaulle and said, "Sit." De Gaulle complied.

"Let's discuss the videos: Osama bin Laden and the president of the United States."

De Gaulle raised his eyebrows in surprise. He realized he had just shown too much alarm. Recomposing himself, he tried to play it off. "What videos?"

"Osama bin Laden. The president of the United States." Nate raised his pistol and pointed it at de Gaulle's chest.

De Gaulle raised his hands so Nate could see his palms and mused to himself, "I guess it's over." He turned to Nate. "The fat lady is singing, so we can talk, right? How did you connect me? One sportsman to another, do tell."

Given the circumstances, I thought de Gaulle sounded composed, even arrogant.

Nate paused for a second and then replied, "Cui Bono."

"My yacht?" De Gaulle was puzzled.

"The yacht helped, because it is so ostentatious. But I mean the translation. Cui bono, Latin for 'who benefits?' All we did was follow the money. Everything leads to you, to your benefit."

De Gaulle cracked a half smile. He scanned the group of us and concluded, "Americans." He said this with disdain. Like he had a bad taste in his mouth just from saying it.

"Circumstantial, I think you call it. Your wonderful American courts will never find me guilty of anything. You cannot even extradite me. I have exceptional lawyers."

Cocky bastard, I thought.

"We have Dr. Fuhrmann," Nate replied.

"Not sure I know who that is." De Gaulle managed a wry, arrogant smirk. He was very confident.

"Don't be coy with me." There was anger in Nate's voice.

"I have no idea what you are talking about. You can take this up with my lawyers." De Gaulle started to stand up and walk away, showing remarkable chutzpa for someone who was a hostage. He scoffed at Nate. "Your wonderful American courts give me many rights."

A show of resolve then, Nate decided. He grabbed de Gaulle, slammed him back down in his seat, placed his pistol against de Gaulle's left knee, and pulled the trigger.

The shot, although muffled by a suppressor, reverberated through the room. Blood splattered. De Gaulle's body jumped, and he cried out in pain. I think I was as surprised as de Gaulle. De Gaulle looked at Nate in shock and disbelief. He had to be thinking, *Americans don't do this! They give criminals rights! Due process!*

Nate removed a restraint from his belt and cinched it tight around de Gaulle's thigh, just above his wounded knee, making a tourniquet. Nate looked de Gaulle in the eyes. "Maybe I'm not here to arrest you." He yanked de Gaulle's chair, wheeled him over to the other side of desk and said, "Scan your eye."

De Gaulle refused, or was in too much pain to comply. Nate grabbed him by the hair and shoved his face in front of the biometric reader. De Gaulle closed his eyes, refusing to cooperate.

Nate lifted de Gaulle up out of his chair and slammed him down hard, face first, on the desk. He pulled out a combat knife and forcefully grabbed de Gaulle's right hand. He held de Gaulle's hand on the desk and, quick as can be, sliced off his right index finger!

De Gaulle howled in pain and anguish. Nate picked him off the desk and slammed him back into the chair. It happened so fast that the clean, decisive cut probably did not hurt too much. But the shock of it was great.

Shock and awe, I thought. *Break him to extract the information needed.*

Nate took de Gaulle's severed finger, wiped off the blood from the tip, and pressed it against the fingerprint scanner. The computer beeped, and one of two red lights on the screen changed to green.

Nate looked at de Gaulle with a wicked, casual smile and said, "I can scan your retina the same way." He moved the knife toward de Gaulle's eye.

"Okay, okay!" he screamed. "You crazy son of a bitch! I'll do it!"

Nate grabbed him by the hair and held his head toward the biometric scanner again. This time de Gaulle opened his eyes and moved a bit to line it up. It beeped, and the second light turned green and the computer screen changed to "Welcome."

As the computer booted up, Nate looked at me, then back to de Gaulle. "Who killed Thomas Minter?"

This was not part of the mission plan. The mission was focused on stopping the release of the bin Laden video. But Nate knew Thomas Minter was the reason I was there. I appreciated it.

De Gaulle said, "I heard they caught the guys who did that. Saw it on the news." His cocky swagger was back. A bullet to the knee and a finger sliced off, and he was still arrogant!

Nate yelled, "Who gave the order?"

De Gaulle shrugged.

Nate picked him up out of the chair and threw him down, again, face first on the desk. Nate placed a knee on his back. Then he wrenched one of de Gaulle's hands out and spread it flat, palm down, on the desk. De Gaulle was positioned so that the left side of his face was pressed into the desk. His hand was held down inches from his face. Nate stuck the point of his combat knife into the desk right next to de Gaulle's thumb. Then he rocked the knife, bringing the blade down slowly, closer and closer to the thumb.

De Gaulle stared at his hand, inches from his face. His eyes got wide, and he squirmed and strained in vain to break loose. He tried to pull away but Nate was too strong. Nate shoved his knee harder into de Gaulle's back, forcing the wind out of him. De Gaulle was helplessly overpowered.

"I did it! I gave the order!" de Gaulle squealed.

"Why?" demanded Nate.

"He refused to play ball."

"Explain." Nate pushed a knee hard into his back, forcing him to gasp.

De Gaulle was out of breath and beginning to sweat. He said, "We asked him to prearrange, or cross, two simple trades through his firm. We thought he could be one of us."

"So you could funnel money to Abigail Mason?"

"Yes. But it is much more than one simple donation to the Masons. If it worked, we had a perfect new way to launder money. Large amounts of money. Millions per day! Laundered wherever and however we wanted. We needed a firm like Minter's to join us, to facilitate these transfers in the future." Nate let up a bit on the pressure. He knew de Gaulle was telling the truth.

"This particular trade—who was giving money to whom?" Nate bent down close to de Gaulle, clinched his teeth, and said, "Remember, sometimes I ask questions I already know the answer to, so I have a baseline."

De Gaulle pondered this for a few moments and then muttered, "Byson Foods. Abigail Mason."

"And Minter?" Nate said. It was a demand, not a question.

"Minter refused. No amount of money could buy him. He wouldn't even listen to the benefits our alliance could offer him. So we forced him to cross the trades. Then, we gave him one last chance to join us. We threatened to expose him for the illegal trades we forced him to do. We tried everything. He refused. He told us to go to hell! So he had to be eliminated."

To reward de Gaulle's temporary truthfulness, Nate lifted him off the desk and sat him in the chair. Nate sat on the desk in front of him.

De Gaulle settled down. He smiled. His arrogant swagger reemerged. "Everything you learn now can never be used against me. A warrantless search." He glanced at his knee and then raised his bloody hand. "A coerced confession. So I am happy to talk more. All inadmissible." He smirked as if he had just tricked Nate.

Nate ignored this and asked, "Was the president involved in Minter's murder?"

"Ha! That's laughable."

"You don't know this yet, but Silvasconi and Hansen are singing like canaries. They say this scandal goes all the way to the top. They say they were executing orders given by the president." Nate aimed the gun at de Gaulle's other knee.

De Gaulle pleaded, "The president is an idiot, okay? He is president almost by accident. No experience. Hope and change! Gimme a break." He paused and then added, "This is way beyond his pay grade."

"But Fleming? You're telling me an administration official was giving orders, and the president did not know about it?"

"There is a lot the president does not know. We turned Fleming. No, scratch that. We installed Fleming; he was already ours. Just like we installed the president."

"Then why are Silvasconi and Hansen fingering the president?" Nate demanded.

"Fleming took orders from us. We told Fleming to tell them that all orders came from the White House. We wanted them to think they were working for the president!"

Nate pressed him further. "Why? Why implicate the most powerful politician in the world—if you own him?" Nate had disbelief in his voice.

"To protect someone more important."

"More important that the president of the United States?!"

De Gaulle nodded.

"But why embroil him in a scandal? You control him through blackmail. Therefore he's on your team?"

"We are strategic, focused on the long war, not this or that petty battle. There is no evidence connecting the president to anything. If those idiots got caught, we knew their claims of a scandal going all the way to the White House would be dismissed. The president knows nothing. So, no risk there. Facing life sentences for murdering a maid, they will say anything. Convicted criminals with crazy conspiracy theories! No one will believe them."

Nate nodded. "But why risk it, if you own the president?"

De Gaulle looked at Nate as if we were a moron. "He is already near the end of his second term."

"Ahhh. So he is nearing the end of his useful life for you," Nate said this more as a realization than a question.

De Gaulle shook his head back and forth in disagreement. "No. He is still useful. Dangerous, but useful."

"Dangerous?" Nate grabbed the top of de Gaulle's ear with his left hand and sliced off the top portion of his ear.

De Gaulle squealed, "What the hell! I am telling you!"

Nate calmly said, "I don't like your attitude." He held the chunk of ear right in front of de Gaulle's face and said, "This is a reminder. Keep talking. How is the president dangerous?"

De Gaulle's eyes were wide with terror. "The president seems to think he can name his own successor. He's talking about throwing his support behind his plagiarizing bozo of a vice-president."

"And you have someone else in mind?"

"You give me too much credit. It is not for me to decide."

"Who?!"

"Someone who doesn't care if two thugs implicate the president. Someone who maybe even enjoys watching the lame duck get embroiled in a scandal. As you say, who benefits?"

"Who?" Nate demanded.

De Gaulle shook his head no. "Admissible or not, I cannot tell you. If I tell you that, I will be sentencing myself to death."

Nate moved his knife in close to de Gaulle's face and twisted it back and forth, letting the light glint off of it. "If you don't tell me right now, you sentence yourself to death."

De Gaulle looked surprised. He seemed to ponder this.

Nate pressed the point of the knife into the side of de Gaulle's nose and said, "You are smart enough to have figured out that I am not interested in the eventual outcome of a possible criminal trial for you." The razor sharp knife cut de Gaulle's nose. Not a deep cut, but enough for blood to drip down to de Gaulle's mouth.

He could feel the blood on his upper lip. Then he tasted it.

Nate leaned in with a crazy look in his eyes.

De Gaulle pleaded, "You have no idea who is controlling this. They will stop at nothing."

Nate said, "We can protect you."

"Like you protected Fleming?"

"You plan on releasing a video showing Osama bin Laden is still alive. We know the chaos that would create. The United States considers your plot an imminent terrorist attack. Therefore, you have been deemed an enemy of the United States. An enemy in the War on Terror." Nate paused as he let this sink in.

Then Nate looked him squarely in the eyes and said, "A candidate for extrajudicial action."

De Gaulle's eyes widened, and he looked at Nate in disbelief. Nate wasn't bluffing. No due process.

"So you see, you have already sentenced yourself to death. I am authorized to kill you." He stared at de Gaulle. "My orders for you are dead or alive." Nate caressed his 9 mm. "I think I will follow the orders that have been given to me. But I may follow those orders slowly. One knee at a time. One finger at a time." Nate aimed the gun at de Gaulle's other knee. "Unless you can help us."

De Gaulle pleaded, "Who benefits? Who benefits!" He was panicked. "Who benefits from framing Jack Thompson? Who benefits from the hedge fund trades! The next president of the United States!" de Gaulle was almost screaming.

"Abigail Mason? You take orders from Abigail Mason?"

"We all do. And you can't stop her." He looked down and shook his head slowly from side to side.

"She's the head of your alliance? I thought you had to be a billionaire to join your little group?"

"She has something better than money—power! And great political savvy. She's the president of our organization. Madam president. She is going to be the next president of the United States. Naked ambition, I think you Americans call it. She is very good at it."

Nate said, "I can stop her."

De Gaulle shook his head. "Nobody can stop her. Nobody is more determined! She was supposed to be president in 2008. Most of us cannot explain how the current president came out of nowhere, with no experience, and beat her in the primary. I have never seen her so mad! She had to wait eight more years. Eight more years for this dimwit! No one will get in her way this time. It's her turn! We even installed her as his secretary of state—the finishing touch on her presidential résumé. Don't you get it?! Can't you see the control she has?" De Gaulle paused for effect, then continued, "She hates the president, and he hates her. Yet he nevertheless still appointed her secretary of state! Oh, she will be the next president."

Nate demanded confirmation of Mason's role in B6. He asked, "Abigail Mason is orchestrating the blackmail of the president? She ordered Thomas Minter killed?"

"She controls everything. She is my boss." De Gaulle paused and then looked up at Nate. "Soon, she will be your boss too. Commander in chief."

"She's behind the Osama video being released?"

De Gaulle nodded. "Yes. Nothing happens without her orders."

"But you stand to benefit from the release of the bin Laden video—not her! All your trades to capitalize on the mayhem!"

"Au contraire." De Gaulle shook his head. "I may profit from it, but *she* benefits. She ordered this; it is her plan. All I am doing is following her orders and making a little money off it on the side."

"How does she benefit?" Nate was getting angry. Or at least making de Gaulle believe he was angry.

"The result will be chaos. Spontaneous terrorist attacks. Mass uprisings, perhaps even war. In difficult times, Americans don't like to change horses. And who offers more continuity during an international crisis then the current secretary of state?"

Nate and I both nodded.

"She might win anyway in 2016, but she is not taking chances—not after the 2008 election was stolen from her."

Satisfied, Nate turned to de Gaulle's computer and entered "Osama" in the search bar. He found the digital video file of bin Laden in US custody. Neither de Gaulle nor Furhmann had bothered to change the file name. Nate watched a portion of it, just to confirm.

In the same computer folder, Nate clicked on a video file named "Money" and located the video being used to blackmail the president of the United States. He let de Gaulle see which files he was opening. De Gaulle was surprised that this intruder had located the two most important files on his computer, by name.

Nate stared back at de Gaulle. "Is this video of the president how you installed her as secretary of state?"

De Gaulle was stunned. Nate moved in with the knife before de Gaulle nodded.

"How many copies of these videos exist?"

De Gaulle's eyes glanced up and left. He weakly said, "That's it."

"Bullshit!" Nate yelled. He was angry again. Or putting on a good show of it to scare de Gaulle.

He pressed his 9 mm P226 against de Gaulle's good knee. "Let's try a different question. Every time you lie to me, I pull the trigger."

De Gaulle closed his eyes, winced, and looked back at Nate.

"How many people have copies of these videos?"

De Gaulle looked him in the eye before answering this time. "Two. Just me, and Dr. Furhmann."

"Could anyone else have copies?"

"No. Only Dr. Furhmann. Remember, I got the Osama video from him. I trusted him alone with these."

Nate held the knife in front of de Gaulle's face again. "What about your associates? Your friends, influencing American politics?"

"No! No one else." He dropped his head and spoke in a defeated tone. He sensed Nate's skepticism and added to convince him, "It's too valuable! I would never let anyone else have a copy! They know about it. Most of my associates have seen the videos. But I keep them in my possession. For insurance, Furhmann has a backup. That's it."

"Jimmy Hughes?" demanded Nate. "Furhmann says that is who delivered the blackmail message to the president."

"Not a chance. We gave him the video on his way in to the White House and retrieved it when he left. I am not stupid. Such a video is no longer valuable to me if it gets out."

"Does Abigail Mason have a copy?" Nate demanded.

"No. She is always insulated. Would never go near such things. Would never leave an e-mail trail. She pulls the strings but keeps her hands clean all the time. This is why you will never stop her."

Nate was angry. "Who are your associates?"

De Gaulle hesitated. Nate pushed the gun into his kneecap. De Gaulle cried, "It's all right there." He looked at the computer screen. In a defeated tone, he said, "Meeting minutes of our group. Names. Everything."

Nate was shocked. "You kept all that?"

De Gaulle looked at Nate. "Americans are supposed to subpoena such things! Like IRS e-mails or secretary of state e-mails. We would never comply—we would carefully choose what information to turn over. You do not bust in with guns and shoot people!" He gestured to his knee, exasperated.

"So you have everything right here." Nate was almost talking to himself as he browsed through a folder called "Meeting Minutes." He said, "A record of all your activities. Amazing."

De Gaulle looked down. "Hubris, I guess. I was documenting our accomplishments." This was a surprisingly honest assessment.

"How many copies of the videos do you have, and where are they?" Nate's voice was forceful again.

"This computer, that's it. For safety, everything on this computer is backed up and synched to a secure cloud-based system." He motioned to the screen. "The eCloud icon."

"So that's it? This computer, and eCloud? Are there any copies anywhere else?"

"Besides Furhmann, no. No one else." De Gaulle whimpered.

Nate clenched his teeth. "One more chance. This computer, eCloud, and Furhmann? Are there any copies anywhere else?"

De Gaulle looked at Nate and swallowed hard. "No. That's it."

"Does anyone besides you have access to this computer or eCloud?"

"No."

"No IT employees with access?"

"No. Nobody! This is too valuable!"

Nate nodded and said, "I think you are telling the truth." He raised his Sig Sauer P226 and pulled the trigger. The bullet hit de Gaulle in the center of the forehead, and he fell back in his chair. Nate followed with a shot to the chest. Then Nate continued to examine de Gaulle's computer.

Nate did not have a choice in killing de Gaulle. Those were his orders: "Get as much Intel as you can, kill him, and get out." At first, this had perplexed me. What about due process, the right to a trial by a jury of your peers? Most Americans do not object to drone strikes against terrorists, and they do not get a trial. What is the difference between a drone strike and a human weapon like Nate, or a SEAL team? De Gaulle was a terrorist. He was about to launch an attack designed to destabilize the world. And he killed Thomas Minter. As far as I was concerned, justice had been served. I would sleep just fine.

As long as we obtained all copies of the bin Laden video and prevented its release, we would have thwarted a de facto terrorist attack. Further questioning of Furhmann and other members of B6 could assure this.

In comparison, the video being used to blackmail the president was less important, at least in terms of international affairs and global security. But if we obtained every last copy of that video too, all the better.

One key threat remained: Abigail Mason.

Chapter 49

We gathered up de Gaulle's computer and other evidence from his office and disembarked *Cui Bono* by rappelling back into the STABs. We rode the STABs back to the container ship, gathered in the ship's command center, and began sifting through the files. A terrorist attack had to be prevented, contained, and we had to be 100 percent sure. Copies of de Gaulle's hard drive were made so that multiple teams could tear into it simultaneously, including teams back in DC.

CIA analysts were focused on obtaining any and all copies of the bin Laden video, to prevent the release of it. After much analysis, the consensus was that the release of the bin Laden video would have spontaneous dire effects. As riots, attacks, and violence spread, the mayhem would spark even more brazen attacks. Analysts concluded that the ultimate result would be worse than 9/11 and truly global in scale.

Further interrogation of Furhmann verified that there were only three copies—one in Furhmann's safe, one on de Gaulle's hard drive, and the last copy on his cloud-based backup. The CIA computer experts still double- and triple-checked and then began a manhunt for the other members of B6. Overall, we were well on our way to not only stopping the terrorist attack, but to bringing the other members of B6 to justice.

Laura, Nate, and I forgot about the videos. I was focused on nailing the person responsible for killing Thomas Minter: Abigail Mason. Of course she didn't pull the trigger. And de Gaulle, serving as her lieutenant, executed the plans. But they were her plans. As secretary of state, Abigail Mason could not be taken out like de Gaulle. She was going to get due process, but I was determined that she would pay. She directed the killings of Thomas Minter, Vince Fleming, and God knows how many others. Although de Gaulle was doing the dirty work, she was the ultimate architect of the plan to release the bin Laden video. She was willing to launch a terrorist attack, willing to kill countless innocents, in order to shore up her presidential destiny.

The minutes from de Gaulle's computer files were very damning of Abigail Mason. There seemed to be no bounds to her personal ambition and no bounds to her arrogance. She believed the rules applied to everyone except her. She could do everything and anything as long as she stuck with her one core principle: advance her own career. That end justified any and all means. While the evidence we gathered was strong, we were confident that most of what we were finding would be corroborated by the other members of B6, once they were presented with indictments for their role in it.

The breadth and scope of the illegal activities of B6 were astounding—blackmail, bribes, political assassinations, and election rigging, on a global scale. But the most surprising find while sifting through de Gaulle's files was a new and different powerful force for corruption. The Mason Foundation.

The Mason Foundation was a well-known charitable foundation set up by Abigail Mason and her husband. On the surface, it provided funding for various noble causes including earthquake relief, vaccinations, and world hunger. But digging a little deeper revealed less than 10 percent of the foundation's money went to the various charitable causes. More than ninety percent went to salaries and travel of foundation staff.

Most charities are staffed by people who have made a career out of working at nonprofit organizations. The Mason Foundation's employees and consultants were a who's who list of career political operatives. In effect, the charitable foundation was a gigantic slush fund from which Bill and Abigail Mason lavished friends, political donors, and other cronies with other people's money. No-show jobs, one of the most blatant forms of political corruption.

And the other people the money came from were buying political influence. Some bought favors from Abigail in her capacity with the State Department. Others made down payments on access and influence due to the fact that Abigail Mason was likely to be the next president of the United States. Their donations to the foundation did not have to be hidden and were tax deductible. Unlike donations to politicians, there were no rules or limits on contributions.

De Gaulle served as a sort of middle man, because Abigail Mason was too smart to leave direct evidence of a quid pro quo. A typical donation, coordinated by de Gaulle, went like this: A Canadian billionaire gave twenty million dollars to the Mason Foundation. Abigail and Bill Mason took a trip to Columbia with an entourage—such entourages included influential businessmen. This particular trip to Columbia included the Canadian billionaire. The time in Columbia was spent in fancy luncheons at a lavish hotel where attendees, which included high-level officials from the Columbian government, ostensibly discussed issues like free trade. Lo and behold, shortly after the junket to Columbia, the Canadian billionaire was awarded logging rights to a large swath of Colombian rain forest. Thirty days after his twenty-million-dollar donation to the Mason Foundation.

De Gaulle's minutes documented that Jorge Moreno, the lawyer who helped negotiate the rain forest deal, was killed because he might get suspicious if he learned of the twenty million dollar donation. Jorge's wife and two sons, also murdered, were noted simply as, "Necessary collateral damage."

Another donation, one of the largest at fifty million, was made from a Russian investment bank. Oligarchs at the investment bank had close ties to Vladimir Putin. At the same time, the investment banking firm was seeking US government approval for one of its holding companies to sell a controlling stake in its Uranium mines to Rosatom, the state-owned Russian nuclear agency. The State Department, under Abigail Mason, approved the transaction—two months after the fifty-million-dollar donation to the Mason Foundation.

The deeper we dug, the more blatant the corruption. Road building contracts in Haiti, gold mining rights in Africa, oil drilling rights in Kazakhstan—all doled out to donors within weeks of major donations to the foundation. It was influence peddling for cash on a never-before-seen scale.

The ultimate irony was that the modus operandi of foreign businesses and even foreign governments' buying influence would have been against the law if done in reverse. The US Congress passed the Foreign Corrupt Practices Act (FCPA) making it unlawful for US businesses to make payments to foreign government officials to assist in obtaining or retaining business. The antibribery provisions of the FCPA are broad. They prohibit any attempt to make any payment, directly or indirectly, designed to influence a business deal or a foreign official. The FCPA goes so far as to prohibit donations by Americans to foreign charities if such donations may be used as a vehicle to conceal payments made to corruptly influence foreign officials.

Up to now, there had been the definitive appearance of numerous conflicts of interest for Abigail Mason through the Mason Foundation. But thus far, there was no smoking gun, no identifiable quid pro quo. Now, the information on de Gaulle's computer provided that—detailed quid pro quos arranged by the middlemen of B6.

When it was time to return to the United States, we shared our initial findings on the web of corruption and influence peddling with investigators and prepared for our trip home. Taking a page out of the Mason playbook, at my suggestion, we leaked details of the corruption at the Mason Foundation to reporters. The story blew up, and the news organizations began unearthing additional questionable donations and potential quid pro quos.

Due to our role in averting the terrorist attack, Nate, Laura, and I were flown back to Chicago on an agency Gulfstream G650. It was a large, comfortable private jet that cruised at Mach .9 and was commonly known as a G6.

On the way back to Chicago, we had one stop to make. Nate said I should wear my custom-tailored suit and Salvatore Ferragamo wingtips.

Chapter 50

Nate and I chatted with Richard Casey, the director of the CIA, in a comfortable waiting room just outside the Oval Office. Nate was relaxed, as usual. The situation was a bit surreal for me.

A secretary appeared. "The president will see you now." She opened a door and motioned with her hand for us to proceed.

As we entered the Oval Office, I heard a familiar voice. "Welcome, welcome!" The president was upbeat as he shook hands with Casey.

"Mr. President, Nathan Summers and Christian Roberts." Casey motioned to each of us as he said our names.

The president shook hands with Nate. "Richard tells me you are one of our finest. Thank you."

"Thank you, sir," Nate replied.

The president turned to me and extended a hand. "I am told you are an extraordinary young man. It is a pleasure to meet you."

I nodded, a bit awestruck.

"Please, please, come, sit down." The president led us to the sitting area.

I couldn't help but gawk at the famous presidential desk with the windows behind it. I walked past the Frederic Remington statue I had seen in so many Oval Office photographs.

After we were seated, the president said, "Richard tells me you have some good news." He turned to the director of the CIA and, pointing to the ceiling, added, "Private meeting, not recording."

The director nodded and said, "Yes, sir." He looked at Nate and me. "These men have bravely recovered the integrity of this office, sir." That was a bold statement. It got the president's attention. The director looked to Nate to explain.

Nate said, "First, sir, everything we accomplished was because of Mr. Roberts here. His efforts connected the murder of Thomas Minter to the folks who were blackmailing you. They tried to kill him too."

The president swallowed. As far as he knew, no one knew about the blackmail, or the video. His face dropped. He must have been thinking, *Had they seen the blackmail tape? Is the whole world going to find out? Or are they talking about some other failed plot?*

Nate sensed the president's discomfort and tried to put him at ease. "Mr. President, no one will ever see that video."

The president turned pale.

I knew Director Casey had told him that the meeting would reveal good news and that Nate and I were heroes, a word I wasn't comfortable with. The sex tape was probably the last thing the president thought was on the agenda today.

Casey said, "Mr. President, the people behind the black-mail plot have been neutralized."

The president cocked his head sideways and raised his eyebrows.

Mr. Casey understood the president's concern: *All of them? How can you be sure?*

The director shifted to a more positive tone. "Mr. President, let me first assure you, the video in question no longer exists. The agency has seen to that. No one will ever see it."

The president sighed, showed some relief. And some disbelief.

The director continued, "For your own peace of mind, that video was kept very private and secure by Nicolas de Gaulle. Multiple copies were never floating around. It was kept locked up tight because it was so valuable. That made it easier for us to contain. We are certain all copies were destroyed."

The president said, "So you know about Jimmy Hughes?"

"Yes. We know about every last one of them. De Gaulle documented these activities meticulously." Casey paused, looked at the president, and said, "Jimmy Hughes disappeared yesterday. He will never, ever be found." The director said this with a definitive certainty. "When I say the agency has eliminated this threat, I say that with complete confidence."

The president nodded and sat back. "Disappeared? He's a pretty high-profile guy to just disappear."

"He is a teamster," the Director shrugged.

The president managed a half smile and shook his head back and forth. The teamsters were famous for their ties to organized crime, and they had an illustrious history of gang-like battles for control. Jimmy Hughes's father had disappeared himself about twenty-five years prior, when he was president of the teamsters. The teamster president's disappearance would garner headlines, but all suspicion would fall on the teamsters' organization itself.

The president was still uncomfortable. "This sounds a bit like murder and cover-up—by my administration."

Mr. Casey interjected, "Quite the contrary. De Gaulle and Hughes and their fellow conspirators were engaged in multiple illegal terrorist activities. Their latest plot—the release of the bin Laden video—posed an imminent threat to the safety and security of the United States of America."

The president knew what this meant—no holds barred, complete elimination of the threat. No worries about trying to bring the perpetrators to justice in a courtroom. Under the new doctrine, supported by a famous and controversial memo from this administration, even American citizens could be targeted and killed in the War on Terror. The euphemism for the execution of American citizens without a trial was extrajudicial action.

Casey continued, "According to the letter of the law, de Gaulle's activities met the definition of terrorist activity. They intended to destabilize the United States—indeed, the free world—through their schemes, murders, and the release of classified bin Laden information. They funded terrorist organizations and murdered innocent Americans. They interfered with countless elections, and through threats and killings, they interfered with our legislative process. Putting aside the blackmail plot against you, we still have a mountain of evidence against them. We routinely stick a drone missile up a suspected terrorist's ass for a lot less."

The president absorbed this and nodded.

Casey added, "These bastards got what they deserved for terrorist activities. Period. Nothing to do with blackmailing you. I have already briefed congressional intelligence committees. Based on the murder of Americans and the intent to destabilize us through the release of the bin Laden video, the committees unanimously backed our actions. No mention whatsoever of any blackmail. Perhaps thirty years from now, redacted versions of these classified congressional intelligence reports might be released. Still, there will be no mention whatsoever of blackmail. We had plenty against these terrorists without that."

The president breathed a sigh of relief and found his voice. "Thank you."

"Yes, sir. You were not alone, by the way. They were blackmailing a number of senators, a few governors, and a member of your cabinet. This terrorist alliance was managed by Nicolas de Gaulle, the billionaire French banker. He ran the operations." Casey paused and looked at the president. "But he took orders from someone in your administration."

The president opened his eyes wide.

The director said, "This is all documented in de Gaulle's private computer which we recovered. Mr. President, your own secretary of state, Abigail Mason, orchestrated the black-mailing of you, the killing of Thomas Minter, and the setup of Jack Thompson. And that is just the tip of the iceberg. As you know, de Gaulle was poised to cash in on the release of the bin Laden video, but Abigail Mason was the mastermind orchestrating the release of it."

The president was shocked. "What? Why? I've had my disagreements with Abigail, but we are on the same team when it comes to bin Laden, aren't we?"

The director explained, "Abigail's presidential ambitions are, shall we say, robust. As you know, in times of war and geopolitical instability, the incumbent has a big advantage. As your second term winds down, war and global instability boost her chances in 2016 because she is the closest thing to a reelection of you. Voters like continuity at the highest level of government in challenging times."

The president shook his head in disgust.

Casey said, "You really pissed her off when you did so well in Iowa and New Hampshire. As far as she is concerned, you stole her presidency in 2008. You never paid your dues the way she has. I guess Karl was right—in 2008 America wasn't ready for a female president, but it was ready for the first African-American president. But Abigail couldn't wait eight more years. She wanted power sooner. She wanted to control you, through blackmail, until 2016. Now, she is taking no chances. She will eliminate the most viable Republican candidate and even cause global turmoil to solidify her own 2016 presidency."

The president nodded.

The director declared, "Back in 2008, when she gave up on her presidential campaign and threw her support behind you, she wasn't helping you. She was calculating, biding her time, helping herself. You became a stepping stone for a very patient and calculating woman."

The president shook his head in disbelief, or perhaps disappointment. He said, "I didn't have much say in some appointments, including hers. Not because of blackmail, but for the good of the party. It's an unwritten code that I have to appoint some Democrats with future presidential potential to high-level cabinet posts. Enhance their name recognition and future electability. Personal feelings aside, she legitimately fell into that category."

The president was beginning to sit up a little straighter. But a more unsettling feeling came over him. "De Gaulle documented everything you say? Enough to nail Mason? Put her in jail for a long time?"

Casey punted. "FBI and justice are responsible for that. We are helping them." He looked solemnly at the president. "Sir, we are all trying, but there may not be enough evidence to indict her."

The president's jaw dropped in stunned disbelief. He stared in silence at the Director of the CIA.

Casey said, "We are having a hard time finding any corroborating evidence. She has done a marvelous job of insulating herself, keeping operations compartmentalized."

The president became accusatory. "You know she did this, and you can't do anything about it? She conspired to release classified intelligence! Attempted to launch a terror-ist attack!"

"Mr. President, all the key players, all the links to her, are dead. Vince Fleming. Nicolas de Gaulle." He returned an accusatory shot back with: "You, sir, ordered the extrajudicial killing of de Gaulle. He was the linchpin to the whole opera-tion. He could have been forced to testify against her."

The president jumped to his feet in anger and put both hands on his head. He walked over to the fireplace in the Oval Office. "Are you telling me *we* took out the one key person who could have nailed Abigail?"

Casey nodded.

The president slowly regained his composure. He shook his head and muttered to himself, "Unbelievable. Unbelievable."

Casey said, "Sir?"

The president composed himself. He sat back down. His eyes went around the room, looking at each of us be-fore he spoke. When he did, his tone was quiet, subdued, and dead serious. "We gathered in the Situation Room after we got word from you," he said and motioned to Nate and me, "about de Gaulle's plan to release the bin Laden video. My vice-president, members of the national security team…" He paused and said, "And the secretary of state."

"Oh, shit!" Casey exclaimed.

The president nodded and continued, "We discussed the options. Abigail was the first to advocate killing de Gaulle. She wanted to hit his yacht with a drone missile."

We all shook our heads in amazement. I said, "That would have destroyed the evidence we did recover."

The president said, "We debated it. Others felt we should arrest him, that he deserved due process. Abigail made a convincing case that de Gaulle warranted an extrajudicial killing, based on the pending terrorist plot. She argued that, as long as de Gaulle was alive, he posed a threat; he could create instability by simply claiming that bin Laden is alive. Once others warmed to the idea, she withdrew from the conversation. We agreed on the plan you executed."

Nate said, "We could have captured him. She had us kill the last connection to her. Damn." He shook his head, part anger, part amazement, and part respect.

Casey said, "Investigators may be at a dead end."

We all sat in contemplative silence for several long moments.

Casey said, "If we can't nail her, one way to get back at her could be to undo the coerced actions."

The president looked at Casey inquisitively.

"Mr. President, I don't care if you like men or women. But I do care if you veto the Keystone pipeline, interfere with auto bankruptcies, bully Aerowing on the location of their factory, and sic the IRS on Americans with different political views—all because of blackmail or coercion."

The president was taken aback by this last barrage. He looked at Casey in surprise. While I was very respectful, almost in awe, at meeting with the president, the director seemed impatient and disdainful. At first, I thought he was disgusted by the sex tape itself. But now, I saw in his eyes anger over the fact that US policy had been corrupted and compromised.

Casey nodded and said, "It was all documented by de Gaulle. Every coerced presidential action. He was quite proud of his alliance's accomplishments."

The president was speechless.

Casey concluded, "The blackmail is gone. Perhaps it is not too late to right some wrongs? You can't undo some of those actions, but maybe some you can?"

The president nodded slowly. "So, I have a clean slate and about a year left in my term."

The president stood, signaling our meeting was over. He said, "Gentlemen, thank you for everything." He extended a hand, and I took it. He concluded, "Thank you for your service to our country." His handshake seemed warm and genuine.

More thank-yous and handshakes were exchanged. I followed Director Casey and Nate out of the Oval Office.

Chapter 51

The president sat alone in the Oval Office—a rare, quiet retrospective moment. First, he had used divisive rhetoric, class warfare, to get reelected. Then he had corrupted policy in order to avoid personal embarrassment.

Now he pondered, *Others risked their lives for me—for the integrity of the office of the presidency.*

The president removed his glasses and massaged his forehead. Maybe the office of the presidency, and America itself, was more important than one man's agenda or one woman's political ambitions?

I disagree with what you say, but I will defend to the death your right to say it. Could this quaint old principle of tolerance replace the current IRS targeting of Americans with different views? Had personal ambition gotten the better of him?

His presidency was coming to an end. *Others risked their lives.* He resolved that it was never too late to put America first.

Try telling that to Abigail Mason.

Chapter 52

Laura and I and the entire Strong and Associates crew sat in a private dining room at Gibsons Steakhouse. Nate proudly displayed an unlit cigar through a broad smile. The gathering was designed in part to debrief, but the mood was festive. A lot of energy had been exerted, both emotional and physical. It felt good to relax with friends like this.

While we were overseas, I was all over the news as a suspect in Thomas Minter's murder. The murder of the beloved Chicago icon had shaken the financial community. By the time we returned to Chicago, not only had I been exonerated but I was getting credit for solving his murder. I even became a bit of a local hero for surviving the ambush by Mr. Slick and for my role in catching the real killers.

Maco Commodities, determined to honor Thomas Minter's memory by carrying on and thriving, felt the best way to honor Tom was to reward my efforts. Maco offered me a position as a pit broker! And not just any deck—all the Maco bond orders!

The whole time we were abroad, I couldn't wait to get back to Chicago to resume my career. Now, I had my dream job—I would make millions per year! I had postponed taking the next step in my relationship with Laura for a career opportunity like this. A perfect happy ending, right?

With Laura's blessing, I turned down the Maco job offer and became the newest partner with Strong and Associates. All my priorities had been upside down: Laura, money, career and life goals, everything. I had a fresh start, a second chance. I was determined to help people and love Laura. I hope you can learn from my mistakes.

John Jr. tapped his wine glass with his fork, getting everyone's attention. "Mr. Roberts, I was going to give a toast, but I think that honor should fall to you, the newest partner of Strong and Associates."

Nate chomped his cigar and smiled so big I think I saw all his teeth. Emily, Louie, Isaac, and Bob raised their glasses and yelled, "Here, here," and "Speeeech!"

I patted Laura on her knee as I stood. I felt myself getting very emotional. *Hold it together, Christian.* As I stood I didn't know what I would say. "Thank you. All of you."

I looked around this room of very special people, and the words flowed naturally. "I thought I had life figured out, chasing a career, chasing money. But that was all empty and meaningless. A few days with you changed everything. What we did, in those few days, was more meaningful, more gratifying, and had a greater impact for good than anything I have ever done. Let's do that again."

The rest of Strong and Associates raised their glasses and heartily agreed. "Again! Woohoo! Let's do it again!"

Laura smiled her beautiful smile at me, and her eyes sparkled with pride and happiness. That was gratifying.

Postscript

Nicolas de Gaulle's yacht, *Cui Bono*, was stormed by Somali pirates just outside the Gulf of Aden. It was a brazen attack, farther from the Somalia coast than previous pirate attacks. By the time US naval patrol vessels reached the yacht, de Gaulle was dead, and the pirates had fled. The pirates tortured de Gaulle in an apparent attempt to get him to open a safe, shooting him in the knee and slicing off a finger before executing him. The pirates were never captured. De Gaulle's armed bodyguards were also killed in the attack, but other crew members were rescued unharmed.

Societé Paribas, the private French bank, as well as individual members of de Gaulle's alliance had accumulated large positions in various world markets designed to profit from the global turmoil caused by the release of the Osama bin Laden video. The video was never released, and the anticipated market impact never came. De Gaulle's cronies were forced to liquidate their positions at massive losses. Societé Paribas was brought to its knees by the risky trades. Faced with certain bankruptcy, Societé Paribas agreed to be acquired by a large American bank at a fire sale price. Numerous B6 members were tried and convicted for crimes, including conspiracy charges related to the murders of Thomas Minter and Maria Gonzalez as well as multiple attempts to blackmail various US politicians.

Dennis Faslowski, the CEO of Byson Foods was discovered to be a member of B6 through information retrieved from Nicolas de Gaulle's computer. Before he testified about his ties to Abigail Mason, Faslowski was found dead in the lake behind his summer home. The official cause of death was accidental drowning, although questions lingered. Faslowski had been an accomplished collegiate swimmer and was a frequent triathlon competitor. His partially eaten dinner was left in his kitchen, and his laptop computer and EPhone were never found.

A special prosecutor was appointed to investigate graft and influence peddling by Abigail Mason and the Mason Foundation. Mason furiously rejected all allegations, stonewalled, and refused to turn over e-mail communications. Her lawyers argued that because de Gaulle was dead, it was convenient that his so-called notes implicated Abigail. Investigators found corroborating evidence against other members of B6. But with Abigail Mason, they were having a hard time finding any corroborating evidence. A lot of *quid*, but no *quo*. Vince Fleming, Dennis Faslowski, and Nicolas de Gaulle might have testified against her, but their deaths insulated Mason. Other conspirators had no direct contact with Mason—their dealings were with lieutenants like de Gaulle and Fleming. Mason gained sympathy from voters who viewed the investigation as politically motivated. She continued to deride the vast right-wing conspiracy. The allegations faded. Despite countless conflicts of interest and piles of circumstantial evidence, she survived the scandals and became the Democratic nominee for president in 2016.

2016 voters were eager to elect the first female president. However, Abigail's long history of never-ending scandals created questions about her character, and the Republican challenger won a narrow victory.

The first African-American president slipped into a relaxed life earning $350,000 per speech. His memoir earned him another twenty million. All copies of the scandalous sex tape had in fact been destroyed, and the American public never learned that he had been blackmailed. His coerced actions were often cited by historians as blemishes on his ultimate legacy. Still, he earned a notable place in history as the first African-American president of the United States of America. He devoted more time to philanthropy, and his subsequent decades of charitable work eventually led to a Nobel Peace Prize.

As the newest partner of Strong and Associates, I received weapons and hand-to-hand combat training. Because Strong and Associates is a civilian contractor to the Joint Special Operations Command, my training included specialized instruction alongside America's Special Forces. With Strong and Associates, I had the privilege of participating in numerous assignments that helped countless innocents. We were often called into service by Uncle Sam. Other times, we were engaged by US corporations and families of kidnap victims. When you have time, I'd love to share some of these stories with you.

Acknowledgments

T hank you to my mom and dad. This book is not possible without both of you. Thank you also to all the money managers, bankers and politicians who provided inspiration for parts of this story. Especially the politicians.

Thank you to Lone Star Books. Throughout the editing process, a special thank you to Bob and Jane for your wisdom and experience. Thank you to Claudia Schweikert for your plot insights. Thank you also to Abigail Smith for your hard work and attention to detail during the final copyediting. The contributions of Bob, Jane, Claudia and Abigail were huge. I had the good sense to take most of their advice; the remaining shortcomings are mine.

Credits

1. *The Economist Magazine*, January 4, 2007, describing the death of Saddam Hussein.
2. While the fictional bin Laden raid described in this chapter is a product of my imagination, many thanks to former Navy SEAL Mark Owen and his excellent book, *No Easy Day*, from which I borrowed certain details about the actual bin Laden raid.
3. Back cover photo, Hunter Long Photography.

About the Author

James Force began his career with the best job ever—as a professional water skier for Sea World.

He graduated *cum laude* with a degree in Finance from Arizona State University. During his twenty-five year investment and finance career, he traded on the floor of the Chicago Board of Trade and worked with a large well-known hedge fund.

James lives in Austin Texas. He invites you to visit him at JamesForce.com.

48820090R00259

Made in the USA
Lexington, KY
16 January 2016